Bound by Belief

A Novel

AIA PUBLISHING

Raphael Aron

Author of *Cults: Too Good to be True*

Bound by Belief
Raphael Aron
Copyright © 2022
Published by AIA Publishing, Australia
ABN: 32736122056
http://www.aiapublishing.com

Paperback ISBN: 978-1-922329-41-7

Dedication

Dedicated to the survivors of cults and their loved ones whose courage and resilience are a reminder of the power and strength of the human spirit.

Introduction

A young woman deserts her children as she falls into the cruel clutches of a fundamentalist religious cult. A father is forced to make an application to the Family Court to prevent his wife, who belongs to a recently established doomsday cult, from bringing their children into the cult environment that has become his wife's 'second home'. A desperate father calls Child Protection Services for advice in relation to the disappearance of his fourteen-year-old son after he befriended the daughter of a self-declared messiah running a cult in regional New South Wales.

It is now over forty years since I began trying to understand and unravel the mystery of the phenomenon of cults and sects that appeared to operate across the globe. While some of those organisations that rose to prominence late in the twentieth century have now ceased their operations, practices of mind control and brainwashing, which are the hallmark of hundreds of these groups, still continue to this day.

Gone is the Symbionese Liberation Army famous for its abduction of Patty Hearst, the heiress of a publishing company in the US; gone are numerous cults including The Order of the Solar Temple, Waco, Heaven's Gate, Jonestown as well as other groups operating in Australia, perhaps the most famous being the Anne Hamilton cult, also known as The Family. In their place are radical fundamentalist churches, personal development groups, multi-level marketing organisations, new age gurus and self-proclaimed 'healers', directing their devotees to forms of extreme behaviour and the loss of personal freedom.

Families are torn apart and relationships terminated at the whims of a misguided megalomaniac or narcissistic guru. Cult devotees are robbed of valuable years of their lives, and then, even if they manage to leave, they struggle to repair the deep psychological and emotional trauma they suffered within the cult environs.

My experiences working with families both within the personal and the legal framework has taught me much about the human need to belong and the importance of family and community. These can be the strongest antidotes against the pernicious tentacles of groups that are ready to capitalise on human vulnerabilities. Even more than that, the cult phenomenon has exposed the frailty of the human mind and the fact that, under the right circumstances, few are immune from being drawn into these webs of control.

When I commenced this work, I often faced criticism for spending so much time and energy on a matter which, despite its gravity, affected a limited section of the population. When I established Cult Consulting Australia, I found myself having to answer to well-meaning critics who questioned the need for such an organisation.

Then came September 11, 2001, when the world was forced to confront the notion of radicalisation as the Twin Towers in New York were completely destroyed and other prominent landmarks targeted. Thousands of innocent people lost their lives. Not one of the terrorists who committed these unspeakable crimes had a criminal record; they were college educated. Suddenly, the notion of brainwashing and mind control took on a new relevance.

The COVID-19 pandemic also added fuel to the fire as cults capitalised on the uncertainty that gripped the world. Offering simple situations to complex situations as they often do, the cults offered a 'safe haven' to a frightened world caught up in an unprecedented crisis. For other cults, the pandemic was proof that the world was in fact coming to an end, further legitimising their misguided belief systems.

Bound by Belief is a collage of stories that highlight the risks and the challenges presented by the cult scene and reflect the nature of the work and its complexities. The stories are dramatic but so too is the real world of working in this field.

Raphael Aron

Acknowledgements

This book could not have been written without the input of numerous families as well as government and law enforcement agencies with whom I have worked and to whom I express my deep appreciation. To my publisher, Tahlia Newland and AIA Publishing, I express thanks and patience for the invaluable assistance in bringing the original manuscript to publication standard. To Megan Norris, author and journalist, who shares my passion for this subject, I thank her for the support and encouragement to publish this book.

A central story in this book features a powerful courtroom drama involving a young woman who had fallen under the influence of a Thai healer. My thanks to Kingsley Davis OAM, Robert Seifman, Barristers-at-Law, and Philip Henenberg, Solicitor, for their review of the manuscript and their astute comments.

To the many volunteers who have given their time and experience to assist in this work, I express deep appreciation for their dedication and perseverance. Their input has made a difference to so many lives. In particular, I would like to thank Matthew Klein, a former cult member himself, for his expertise and support over many decades.

I am indebted to the numerous media outlets that have provided a platform for me to offer commentary on the cult issue, so often misunderstood and misconstrued. I believe many lives have been saved through the dissemination of reliable information regarding the dangers posed by many of these groups.

To the many survivors of cults that are operating around the globe and with whom I have had the privilege of working, I express my deep appreciation for allowing me into their lives and helping to make a difference. Their courage and tenacity are an inspiration.

Above all, I thank my wife Shani for her assistance with this book. The challenging work would not be possible without her deep understanding of the nature of human vulnerability. Shani's belief in the need to preserve and nurture the universal drive for meaning and purpose in life has given me the strength and motivation to continue working in this field.

Raphael Aron

Prologue

Finally, after all the planning, Qantas flight QF434 taxied towards the tarmac at Sydney' International Airport. Michael cast a glance towards the passenger sitting beside him. The young, pale-faced man was reading his Bible. A dark-haired woman, Safiyya, sat on his right, flipping through the airline magazine.

Michael looked out the window. The ground raced away from beneath the aircraft. As the big bird took to the skies, he glanced at Safiyya and smiled. She returned the smile and seemed to relax. Michael sat back. 'Mission accomplished,' he mouthed to Safiyya.

The young man continued to read his Bible, though he appeared to be quite anxious. He turned to Safiyya and whispered into her ear, 'Safiyya, please can I hold your hand?'

1

Emma stared out the window and briefly wondered if she was doing the right thing. *Of course, you're doing the right thing. It's for Kira and God's Kingdom.* Helping Kira create God's Kingdom on Earth was the most noble thing she could do with her life, she reminded herself—more important than her father, more important than their relationship, more important than anything. Kira assigning her this mission was an honour, and she'd show her devotion by completing it perfectly.

The noisy old Holden spluttered along, shattering the tranquillity of the countryside, and eventually pulled up outside the police station. Emma got out of the car as planned, while the driver, a middle-aged man with a greying moustache and dark glasses, remained in the car. She didn't even know his name.

Emma wiped her sweaty palms on her jeans and took a deep breath to quell the rising tension. But it didn't curb the nauseous feeling that settled into the pit of her stomach as she contemplated the task ahead of her.

One dead tree jutted awkwardly from the cracked asphalt area in front of a plain concrete building in desperate need of a new coat of paint. Dwarfed by the mountains behind, it stood in stark contrast to the surrounding quaint cottages, bungalows and sheds that dotted the adjacent properties and their gardens.

Emma threw her scarf over her shoulder, walked to the station entrance and opened the front door. The room that greeted her was bare apart from one bench that looked as if it had been rescued from an old train station, a small desk and chair in one corner and, towards the back, a large counter covered with old, black linoleum tiles. A few posters hung unevenly on the wall behind the counter, and some well-used magazines lay on one end of the bench. As far as Emma could tell, nobody else was there. The room was quiet.

A policewoman dressed in blue appeared from a side door. 'Can I help you?'

Emma swallowed and looked away. She knew why she was there and why Kira needed her to do this, but that didn't mean she felt comfortable being there.

'I asked whether I could help you,' the policewoman said in a sterner and louder voice. Although probably only about fifty years old, the wrinkles around her eyes gave the appearance of someone older. She looked like she'd been born at the station and had never moved out. Certainly, her stoic look was in keeping with the stark surroundings.

'I'd like to make a statement,' Emma said. 'It's about my parents—actually, about my father. I want to report him. It's rather complicated.' She spoke in a low voice. 'No, no, it's not complicated; it was a long time ago, but I remember it very clearly.'

The policewomen stared at Emma. 'And why have you left this until now? Is there a reason why it's taken so long?'

Emma shrugged. 'I don't know. Please, I'd like to make a statement. Can I?'

'Well, yes, you can. But I'm on my own today, so you'll need to come back tomorrow.'

'No, I can't do that; I've come a long way. I live about thirty kilometres from here.'

'Oh.' The policewoman sighed, then appeared to relax. She even smiled for a moment. 'Okay. Your name, please.'

'Emma Carter, and I live at 65 Marks Street, Maleny.'

'I'm Fiona. Pleased to meet you.' She stretched out her hand, but Emma declined to take it. Fiona dropped her hand and continued, 'This is a country police station. We're not really set up to take statements. It might be easier for you to write down your story in an affidavit, and we'll take it from there.' She handed Emma a form. 'You can do that now, and here's a little guidebook about how to write an affidavit.'

Emma retreated to the desk in the front corner of the room. She sat down and flipped through the affidavit guidebook, then took out the form and started writing. Every so often she stopped and closed her eyes, trying to visualise the scenes about which she wrote. Truth, she remembered Kira saying, was what supported God's work. It took her about an hour to write the eleven-page declaration. She wrote slowly and methodically, stopping every few moments to review what she'd written. When satisfied that she'd completed the mission, she pulled out her mobile phone and dialled Kira. Once on the line, she read out the whole affidavit in a low voice, stopping every few moments to make corrections. Kira wasn't leaving anything to chance. At one point she asked Emma to repeat the same sentence three times before she let her continue.

'There, it's done,' Kira said eventually. 'How do you feel?'

Emma sighed. 'So relieved.' Finally, it was done. Though this was only part one of her mission.

'You've done well, dear,' Kira said. 'I'm very pleased.'

Emma smiled. Kira's praise warmed her heart. And Kira would be even more pleased when the money came in. It wasn't as if her dad needed it, and there wasn't a better use for it in all the world.

Fiona emerged from the side room. 'How's it going, Ms Carter?'

The officer's sudden appearance startled Emma. 'Oh, fine.' She looked away and put her mobile phone back in her purse.

'Well, when you've finished, you'll need to sign it in front of me. I'll be your witness.'

Emma nodded and took the completed form to Fiona. Her hand shook a little.

'Are you all right?' Fiona asked with a worried frown.

'Yes, I'm fine. Just a little tired today.'

Fiona pointed out that Emma would have to initial all the changes. 'It looks a little messy, but it'll be fine. Did you change your mind as you were writing?'

Emma shook her head.

Fiona witnessed her signature and took the form, then Emma walked out into the bright sunshine. She blinked and shielded her eyes. The man in the car waved his hand. Within seconds Emma was back in the car. After a few attempts to restart the vehicle and a few puffs of white smoke, the car sped off down the dusty gravel road.

2

Laura drove through the quiet Brisbane suburb of Kangaroo Point and parked her car outside the headquarters of CultAssist. She grabbed her bag, locked the car, and wandered past the neighbour's rambling Edwardian home behind which sat the mobile home that she and Matthew had converted into a work area when they'd started the grassroots organisation in 1991.

She paused and absorbed the view from the hilltop, as she did every day before entering what could be an emotionally charged workplace. Forest spread out before her, all the way to the Glass House mountains in the distance. On this balmy Monday morning, their jagged summits penetrated the thick white clouds hovering above them. The countryside had a mystical look, perhaps a reminder of what the world looked like before civilisation.

Laura took a deep breath and walked inside the converted mobile home. She loved her job despite the challenges. Working with families whose loved ones had been caught up in the cult scene was vitally important. And their successes usually outweighed their failures. They'd established links with various government institutions across Australia and were recognised now as a trusted media liaison, but their main battle was with ignorance. People in general simply didn't know enough about how cults operated to know how to recognise and avoid them. But Laura Fields, a slender, middle-aged woman with kind eyes, and her CultAssist team of several volunteers and one paid secretary, were working towards changing that.

'Good morning, Laura.' Margaret, the secretary, turned from the kitchen bench with a smile and handed Laura her morning cup of coffee.

Laura returned the smile and the greeting and gratefully took the cup. Margaret, a plump, grey-haired sixty-five-year-old, had the worst dress sense Laura had ever seen—today's bright-pink cardigan and green-floral dress a case in point—but the woman was all kindness and kept the team well organised. Her enthusiasm for life sometimes made fifty-year old Laura feel ancient, and today her clothes—black pants, white shirt and a relaxed black jacket—seemed positively dull in comparison.

Margaret grabbed a newspaper from her desk and waved it at Laura. 'That *Sydney Morning Herald* article came out this morning. You want to read it? Or should I summarise?'

'A summary will do.'

Margaret scanned the article while Laura took off her jacket, smoothed down her shoulder-length blonde hair and then settled into her desk to sip her coffee.

'It introduces the Sunananda Meditation Centre,' Margaret said, 'and says the leaders were jailed a year ago, but somehow the centre survived.'

'As they often do, unfortunately,' Laura put in.

Margaret indicated her agreement and then read part of the article aloud. 'It says that "a university graduate assumed the leadership of the group but has been recorded talking to his followers about self-immolation—death by burning—which sect members believe will herald their ultimate salvation. Supported by Brisbane group CultAssist, the parents of a number of members have gone public in an effort to have the organisation shut down altogether." Then it goes into the various stories.'

Laura nodded. 'Does it say anything about us?'

Margaret scanned the article until she found a relevant part. 'They say we're "a small grassroots group with an interest in the impact of cults and fringe religious groups on families" and that we've "gained a degree of prominence as a result of a number of major stories involving various bizarre cults and sects. They played a part several months ago when police found the bodies of two teenagers in a burned-out church. The metal wrist bands they wore heralded the end of the world, and CultAssist was able to identify their source. Following the fire, the leader of the church responsible fled and was believed to be living in Arkansas, USA, where the church has its international headquarters." That's basically it.'

'Well, I hope the article helps keep a few more people out of Sunananda's clutches,' Laura said.

'It all helps.' Margaret dropped the paper onto Matthew's vacant desk and asked, 'Email prep today?'

Laura nodded. Although CultAssist received several hundred calls each year, it had been relatively quiet over the couple of weeks since they'd dealt with the flurry of activity caused by the Sunananda Meditation Centre revelations. Laura needed such times to work on such things as fundraising initiatives, updating the email list, arranging talks to schools and community groups and running workshops for those recovering from cults.

Laura hadn't had any personal involvement in the cult scene, but the death of a close friend who'd had a mental breakdown after a long association with an eastern spiritual cult had deeply troubled her. The tragedy, which occurred when Laura was just nineteen years old, was an important factor in her decision to complete a degree in social work.

She'd met co-founder Matthew Fowler, a thirty-year-old father of two young children, when she'd been the Community Liaison Officer at the Brisbane City Council. He'd chaired a community meeting about the collapse of a fringe Christian church's multimillion-dollar property scam. As is common with cults, the pastor had convinced his followers of the insignificance of material possessions and had taken over the management of the cult-members' assets. Matthew's wife had been a member of that church and had lost over one million dollars' worth of property.

After researching other organisations working in the cult scene, Matthew and Laura travelled overseas to attend various conferences on the topic, and Laura completed a three-month exit-counselling training course in California.

The phone rang, jolting Laura from her memories.

'Just a minute, I'll transfer you to our director,' Margaret said to the caller. 'She'll be able to help you.'

Laura picked up her extension.

'Albert Carter here,' a harried voice said. 'I need to see you straight away. I have this number, but I have no idea where you're situated. And anyway, to whom am I speaking?'

'My name is Laura; I'm the director of CultAssist, and we're in Brisbane,' Laura replied. 'Could you please give me a brief outline of the problem?' Laura had been down this track before. An urgent call, an attempt to organise an appointment and then … nothing. 'Perhaps send me an email with some details? That way I can work out if we can help you or not.'

The phone went dead.

Laura sighed. 'He'll be back.'

The phone rang again a moment later. 'Look, sorry, Lauren, it's Albert Carter again. I'm a partner in the legal firm, Carter, Roache and Cain. You've probably heard of us.'

Laura frowned. 'Ah, um …'

'Anyway, I do need to talk to you urgently. My daughter, Emma, is in danger. She needs to be rescued. My wife and I are worried about her safety. You remember that story about the two guys burned to death? Well, I think my daughter is in danger of a similar fate. You said I should send you an email, but I can't do that; I just need to see you. And I assume you have police contacts because we'll need help to resolve this.'

Laura opened her mouth to reply, but Albert cut her off. 'We don't know much about cults, but we think Emma is involved in one. Something has happened to her—to her mind—and it's put me in a precarious position. You'll understand when we meet.'

Albert sounded distressed, but genuine. CultAssist received calls like this on a regular basis, and Laura needed to be cautious since the caller could be from a cult trying to pry into CultAssist's affairs or find out more about the organisation's methods of working with families.

'Okay,' she said, 'I'm flying to Sydney this afternoon, but I could meet you for an hour at ten thirty this morning. The address is on our website, CultAssist.org, and you'll also find a list of things you can bring with you. Please be on time. Better still, come a few minutes earlier because I need you to fill out a form.'

'Hmm. Could we make it later?'

'Not today. And then I won't be available until Wednesday.'

'Oh …'

'You told me your daughter's life is in danger,' Laura said, 'so let me ask you this, Albert; is your day's schedule more important than your daughter's life or are we on for ten thirty?'

Laura heard him sigh.

'I'll be there,' Albert said quietly after a brief pause. 'Thank you. Oh, and I'll bring my wife if she can make it.'

Laura sat back at her desk and stared out the window. 'Albert Carter. Hmm. I know that name from somewhere.'

'It's not an unusual name, though,' Margaret said. 'It could be from anywhere.'

Laura nodded. 'Can you do a quick criminal record search on him for me, please?' she asked.

'Sure, no worries.' She turned to her computer to start the process.

Laura looked at her list for today. Her schedule was suddenly full. She took the one-hour flight from Brisbane to Sydney once every few weeks, and today she was meeting a Lebanese couple whose son had become caught in a Christian fundamentalist group. Even during the quiet times, CultAssist received an average of ten calls a week from New South Wales. She had just enough time to see Albert Carter and make it to the airport in time for her flight. Hopefully!

3

Albert Carter had sounded to Laura like the sort of person who'd be punctual, and sure enough—and to her relief—he parked his silver Audi in enough time to arrive at her office door at 10.25 am. Laura watched through the window as he strode up to the building, carrying a briefcase. A tall man, with silvery grey hair, he wore a dark-navy suit, cream shirt and mushroom pink tie.

He took her hand in a tentative grasp. 'Albert Carter is my name. You must be Laura.'

'That's right. Pleased to meet you, Albert.' Laura noted that her new client looked younger up close than his grey hair suggested. She handed him a clipboard carrying a pen and the six-page form. 'Please take a seat and fill this out so we have all the necessary details.'

He sat and set to the task while Laura checked she had everything she needed for the Sydney trip. She'd have to leave as soon as she wrapped up the meeting with Albert.

'Finished,' he declared a few minutes later, holding up the clipboard.

Laura took the clipboard and walked around to her desk. A quick look over the information showed that, as was often the case with people who approached CultAssist for assistance, Albert had omitted certain questions, including personal references and his income. He'd written his business address rather than his home address.

'So, please tell me all about your daughter?' Laura asked.

Albert sat back in a relaxed pose and said, 'Emma is my daughter from my first marriage. Her mother, Natalie, died when Emma was only thirteen years old, so I raised Emma on my own, until she was eighteen, which was when I married Alison. Alison couldn't make it today, but she asked me to tell you that she fully supports me in anything I do regarding Emma.' He straightened up and moved forward slightly. 'We have a major problem, a potential disaster on our hands, and we desperately need your help. Our daughter's life is in danger.'

He opened his briefcase, pulled out a one-page, neatly written fax and handed it to Laura.

> *It's very simple, Mr Carter. You either deposit $500,000 into my teacher's bank account or I will expose the sexual abuse, you, Mr Carter, perpetrated on me as a child. I have already made a statement to the police. They will be questioning you within the next two weeks. I have also prepared a media release. Mr Carter, you should hang your head in shame as you continue to practice as a solicitor. Your participation in the local church as a choir master is also a matter for concern—how many stories have we heard about the abuse of choir boys or altar boys?*
>
> *I am sorry that Alison will be watching you go down in court. I am sorry that she will see you in handcuffs on the front page of the daily newspapers. But the wheels of justice are turning fast, and the law is about to catch up with you. It will be ugly. $500,000 will save your skin. The bank account*

*details have been faxed to your office. You are to act
without delay. Unless the funds are in the designated
account by Friday, I will pursue every option available
to me and my teacher.*
    Phitsamai (Emma)

'I assure you, Laura,' Albert said when she looked up at
him with a frown. 'I am guilty of no such thing. This is blatant
extortion, and not the kind of thing Emma would do were she
in her right mind.'

Laura read the fax again. Clearly Albert's concerns were
justified. It wasn't her place to make any determination on the
truth of Emma's accusations; her role was to consider whether
Emma was potentially the victim of cult mind control, and she
saw enough to warrant further investigation—extortion attempt
aside, asking for the money to be paid into her teacher's account
and referring to her father as 'Mr Carter'. When she finished
reading, she looked up at him and said, 'This sounds disturbing.'

He smiled, visibly relieved.

'Tell me more about Emma.'

Albert thought for a moment before speaking. 'She
completed school with exemplary results and then moved out of
home at eighteen. I think she just wanted to spread her wings.
It would also be fair to say that she didn't really get along with
Alison. It's not that they fought or argued all the time. They
just didn't see eye to eye; they weren't used to each other. Alison
came from a conservative background, a primary school teacher
and regular church-goer—she even sang in the choir. Emma
moved into some shared accommodation with my permission. I
paid for it, but that was fine.

'A year later she met Kira Thurin, a Thai woman who'd
settled in Australia some twenty years ago. Kira's a naturopath

and apparently a very good one. She also dabbles in acupuncture and reflexology. Emma became very fond of Kira, and we thought that was fine. Perhaps she saw the woman as some sort of mother figure, someone to make up for the absence of her own mother during her important teenage years.

'Anyway, it seems that Kira has gradually exerted more and more influence over Emma. We should've seen the writing on the wall when she suddenly deferred her university studies after only six months. She'd been accepted into Architecture—no small feat—then suddenly she announced she was deferring. And now this woman controls Emma. Totally. We're convinced Emma has lost the ability to think independently.'

Albert's manner as he spoke intrigued Laura. Though he was articulate, he appeared to lack emotion. There was something very clinical about his presentation. His body didn't move. He sounded more like a barrister arguing a case in court than a genuinely concerned parent. He was quite forthcoming in relation to Emma but said nothing about himself.

Laura wondered whether there was any significance to Alison's absence. Perhaps she would have put a different slant on the family history and Emma's personal situation.

Albert gave Laura further details of Emma's personality changes and her growing estrangement from him and his wife. He finished with, 'We need to get her out. Money is no object; whatever legal assistance you need is there. We'll do what's right for our daughter regardless of costs. Can you help us?'

'Take this booklet on cults and have a look through it.' Laura handed Albert the CultAssist information booklet for friends and family of cult members. 'And leave the fax with me. In fact, leave with me anything you think could assist in understanding Emma better.' She hoped she sounded reassuring.

Albert pulled out a pile of documents and a stack of photos.

'Here, take all of these, and if you need anything else, please tell us. I've written out a cheque for $5,000.00 to CultAssist. Please keep a record of all your expenses, and if we need to top up the account just call me.'

Laura had no time to dwell on her concerns, but she wasn't happy with Albert's approach to this. CultAssist wasn't a repair shop where you leave an appliance with a cash deposit while it's being fixed. Albert had discussed Emma's situation in detail and made a payment to CultAssist. Was he now waiting to have his daughter fixed and delivered back home?

Laura looked up and said, "That's very generous of you, Mr Carter, but that's not the way we operate. My PA, Margaret, will be happy to take you through our fees schedule for today, and once I've returned from Sydney and had the opportunity to review these documents, we can set up some appointments and take it from there. I'd like to meet Alison then as well."

He nodded. 'Okay. Do you have another minute?'

'Sure.'

Albert sighed, his features softening. He appeared more human, genuinely concerned now, as if he'd shed the mask of obscurity and was willing to bare his soul. 'How is it possible for a loving, beautiful young woman to be transformed into a cold extortionist?' he asked, his voice laced with pain. 'I'm no angel, Laura. I work hard and make a good living, but life for Emma hasn't been easy. When her mum died, I wondered how she'd cope. I thought Alison would be her new mum, but that didn't happen, even though Alison tried. It's like this Kira has adopted her, which wouldn't be so terrible if it was all benign. But this fax? That's another story. I just don't get it. Emma's smart and streetwise. She has everything a young woman could want. She's no dropout, no drug user. I don't think she's ever gambled. But her mind? I don't understand it.'

Laura took a deep breath and exhaled slowly. Was there a deeper message behind Albert's plea to understand Emma? It seemed that something didn't sit well with him. 'You aren't the first person to ask these questions,' she said, 'and you won't be the last. Mind control might be a controversial issue, but it's also a very complex and elusive concept. Some of our biggest critics are not even the cults themselves but the civil libertarians, the so-called upholders of democracy who would jump up and down if a kindergarten blocked the Ku Klux Klan from talking to little children. They just don't get it. One of our committee members used to be a member of a libertarian group. His son was lured into the Children of the Lord cult while backpacking in California. He hasn't seen his son for twenty years, and I assure you, he's no longer a civil libertarian.'

Albert frowned and shifted in his seat. He opened his mouth as if to say something, then closed it again. Laura waited, but he just stood, said, 'Thank you,' and left the office.

Laura looked out the window and evaluated what she knew of him as she watched him walk towards his car. Was he the kind of man who would do what his daughter had accused him of? He was a lawyer, but Laura supposed that didn't prove anything. Their criminal record research had come back clean, though— the cost of the one-hour service was worth it. Although somewhat detached from Emma, he seemed to be a decent enough person, and his account of Emma's life with Kira certainly did sound very culty. *We just need to get her out of there and then decide what to do.* If Emma stood by her abuse allegation after getting away from this Kira person, then Albert's innocence or otherwise would be tested in a court. Laura decided to proceed on the basis that Emma's statement was made up of a blatant set of lies.

Laura opened the folder and spread the contents on her desk. Albert had provided photos of Emma as a child playing in the sand at the local beach, her as a school debutante and at her graduation ceremony where she was delivering the valedictory speech. There were several pictures of Albert and Emma and some of Albert and Alison, but none of Emma and Alison. He'd also included a few photos of his home and his office.

The school reports showed that Emma had performed well at school—an A-grade student. Her Texts and Traditions teacher had written, *Although Emma does not appear to be very interested in religion or spirituality, she displays an admirable sense of tolerance to her peers and colleagues. She is a very personable and respectful young woman.*

Almost every teacher had something positive to say about her. Some were impressive:

It's a pleasure to teach Emma.

Emma is an inspiration for the rest of her class.

Emma's ability to succeed despite her difficult personal situation is inspiring.

Emma can look forward to a bright future.

Emma's work ethic stands as a shining example.

Laura photocopied the fax a couple of times and filed the copies in two different cabinets, then put the documents and photos together in a bundle.

A quick internet search of Emma and her teacher, Kira, came up blank. Nothing showed under Emma's spiritual name either, and Laura didn't know if Kira Thurin was a real name or a spiritual name that Emma's teacher had adopted. She sensed this was a genuine case, and if she still thought that after further research, then they'd have to attempt to remove Emma from her home—a risky plan, because they had to make sure that whatever they did couldn't be construed as kidnapping—an offence carrying a fourteen-year jail sentence.

'But who is Albert Carter?' Laura mused out loud. 'Why

does his name ring a bell? And why was he so uncomfortable when I talked about mind control?' She needed these questions answered. Until then, he was a bit of a wildcard.

Laura opened her filing cabinet and pulled out Helen's file, a case she'd taken in 1999 when Helen had contacted CultAssist about her nephew Anthony, who was involved in a cult. Anthony's father, Gary, was a policeman. Following a successful intervention during which time the young man left the cult, Gary told Laura that if he could be useful in the future, she shouldn't hesitate to call him. She'd pasted a note on the front of the file; just the name, Senior Sergeant Gary Wilkinson, and a phone number.

I hope this works, Laura thought to herself as she dialled.

Someone picked up the receiver. 'Gary Wilkinson. Hello.'

She breathed a sigh of relief. 'My name is Laura Fields, and I'm the director of an organisation called CultAssist. We've met before. I'm calling because we might require your assistance in relation to a matter involving a woman who has become ensnared in a cult. Her father thinks she's in great danger.'

Gary interjected, 'Of course I remember you. You don't need to go any further. But I can't speak with you on the phone. I work at the Kings Cross CIB and could meet you anytime today or tomorrow, but I won't be available after that until Thursday. Just give me a time and a place, and I'll try my best. I'm well familiar with how you saved Anthony's life. Our whole family owes you one.'

Laura smiled and checked her planner. 'Okay, great. I'm flying to Sydney early this afternoon for a meeting, but I need to be back here tomorrow morning. Can we meet at the airport at seven? My return flight leaves at nine.'

After a short pause, Gary agreed and they arranged to meet at a small bar in the food court at the domestic terminal.

4

Laura smiled as she strolled into the Coffee Café in Darlinghurst. The warm interior design and smiling staff brought back happy memories. Several years earlier, she'd had many meetings here when she'd worked successfully with a family whose daughter had become involved with the Orange People, an eastern mystical cult led by a very extravagant guru, Bhagwan Shree Rajneesh. Their group headquarters was at 108 Oxford Road, Darlinghurst, near the Sydney Central Business District, and members of the cult—called sannyasins—thought the address was heaven-sent because the malas they wore had 108 beads.

She ordered a coffee, then wove her way through the tables to the booth in the far corner where she'd arranged to meet Fadi and Nadia Haddad, Lebanese Christians, whose son, Amin, had been involved in the Church of Love and Faith since 1998. This fundamentalist Christian church believed in exorcisms as well as faith healing and had caused an outcry in late 2000 when a mother died following the birth of her child. She'd been bleeding internally but refused on religious grounds to have a scan or an ultrasound. By the time the Supreme Court ruled in favour of the hospital, she was extremely ill and had died as the tests were being administered.

Laura sighed. Just another of the many sad stories

surrounding such cults. She hoped they'd have a better outcome with Amin, but according to what Fadi had told her on the phone, he was wasting away from fasting three days every week. The aim of today's introductory meeting was to discuss the possibility of an intervention that could extricate Amin from the fundamentalist cult.

Laura had only had a few sips of coffee when a slightly built woman wearing a modest floral dress and carrying a basket entered with a taller, well-built man in suitcoat and trousers. Both had Middle Eastern features, and they looked around with worried expressions. Laura checked her watch—right on time. They had to be Fadi and Nadia. She gave them a wave, and they headed directly towards her, forgoing any food or drink order.

'Laura Fields?' the man said when he reached her.

Laura stood and extended her hand. 'That's right.'

He smiled and shook her hand. 'Pleased to meet you. I'm Fadi, and this is my wife, Nadia.'

Nadia smiled and dipped her head. 'I'm so very grateful you could meet with us. We're so worried about Amin.' She handed Laura the basket. 'A small mark of our appreciation.'

Touched by the gesture, Laura peeked inside to see an elaborate basket of Middle Eastern spices. She smiled and thanked Nadia as they sat.

Once settled, Laura asked them to tell her a little about themselves.

Fadi replied, 'Of course. We had a successful rug business in Lebanon, but we left it all behind in 1980 because of the civil unrest. It was becoming too dangerous there. Amin was just a baby, and we wanted him to grow up somewhere safe, somewhere with better opportunities. I didn't want to leave my mother, Halima, because she was getting older and her sight was failing even then, but Nadia felt that it was better to migrate when Amin was still young. She was right, of course.' He smiled at his wife, and she grinned back. 'Life was tough here at first, but I now have a small food-import business in the Western suburbs, and we're doing quite well.' Though he'd retained his Lebanese accent, his English was clear and fluent.

'I miss my family,' Nadia said. 'But we love Australia. All of us.' Though less fluent, Nadia's English was also clear.

Laura smiled. 'Yeah, it's not a bad place to live.' She handed them a booklet like the one she'd given Albert. 'In here you'll find a list of reading material and some web links for reliable information on cults and the challenges facing families whose loved ones are caught up in one. There are also general guidelines covering the kinds of interactions you might have with Amin.'

'Thank you,' Fadi said. He and his wife flicked through the booklet together, stopping to read some parts, then he placed it on the table and said, 'I appreciate this, but what we really want to know is how are we going to get Amin out of this cult.'

Nadia nodded, her eyes beseeching.

'We'll get to that,' Laura said, then she explained in detail what CultAssist did and then asked them to fill in a questionnaire. They bent their heads over the paper while Laura went to the counter to order coffee and cakes for them all.

On her return, she found Fadi filling in the form, but he deferred to Nadia when confronted with a difficult question. Once completed, Laura scanned the form while the couple nibbled their cakes in silence. 'That's excellent. Thank you,' she said when she'd checked that she had all the information she needed from them.

'So can you help?' Nadia asked.

Laura smiled. 'Well, we'll do what we can, but there's no guarantee that anything we decide to try will work. We make no promises. If there's any chance of getting Amin away from the church's influence, we'll have to find a way to remove him from the premises so we can work with him. There are several ways we could do this, but we work in a way that minimises negative fallout should the intervention not be successful. We don't use force, for instance, and his participation in an intervention must be totally voluntary.'

They both nodded, their hopeful gazes fixed on Laura.

'What do we have to do?' Fadi asked.

'You don't need to be present in the early part of the intervention, but we might call you later depending on how things progress.'

'What form will this intervention take?' Fadi asked.

'I'll look at the options and send you a detailed letter that covers the relevant points. After you've read that, you might think of other options that might be possible as well, and then we need to talk again to discuss these in greater depth.'

Fadi and Nadia beamed.

Laura talked about a number of interventions they'd done in the past. 'But each situation is different,' she said in conclusion, 'and we have to plan according to the person involved and the restrictions placed on them by the cult. We'll come up with something that has the best possible chance of success.'

'Thank you so much,' Fadi said. 'We've been to a few psychologists and family counselling agencies about this, but they didn't seem to believe us when we said Amin was in a cult. Some told us we shouldn't be trying to influence his path in life. They said he was an adult and even if his decisions didn't meet our approval, we needed to respect his choice.'

'We did that at first,' Nadia said, 'but now his health is suffering. If we do nothing and he becomes very ill or even …' Tears filled her eyes. She sniffed and wiped her sleeve across her cheeks.

Fadi took his wife's hand and looked at Laura. 'But you understand the danger, I think.'

Laura nodded.

Nadia managed a small smile. 'You give us hope. For the past few months, we've lived in fear that we'd never see our son again or that maybe he wouldn't survive. Now we're hopeful. May God bless you.'

Moved by Nadia's gentle nature and her faith in God, Laura took Nadia's hand. 'Thank you, Nadia.'

The meeting at the Coffee Café lasted just over two hours.

5

Laura arrived at the bar the same time as Gary, a handsome, well-built man in his fifties with a touch of grey hair at his temple. They ordered drinks and sat down at a small table facing the tarmac. The evening had turned cold and rainy; the lights of the planes landing and taking off were just a blur. Even the soundproof glass didn't block out the noise of the torrential rain beating down.

After greeting her with a smile and a handshake, Gary sat and delivered warm regards from Helen, then he repeated his family's appreciation for the work CultAssist had done for his son, Anthony. 'But let's get down to business,' he added with a smile.

Laura nodded and pulled some files from her briefcase.

'You look worried,' Gary said. 'It couldn't be that bad.'

Laura smiled. 'Right. So, a chap by the name of Albert Carter contacted us, saying his daughter's life was in danger. Her name's Emma and she tangled up with a Thai faith healer who appears to dominate and control her. Emma rarely leaves this woman's house. She's broken off all contact with her family, which, according to Carter, is totally out of character. I can't find any literature about this group, and there's no website. He wants to get her away from this woman.'

Gary frowned, sat back in his chair and looked straight at

Laura. 'You know I'm a senior sergeant. I need to be sure the girl is genuinely in danger before I can get involved. Parents tell you all sorts of garbage. They'll beat up their kids, the kids will run away, and then the parents say they're in a cult. Just do yourself and me a favour. Make sure this kid *is* in a cult, and let's be sure that her situation justifies our involvement. Let's not stuff around. I've done that too many times before.'

Laura nodded. Gary's business-like manner was no doubt a result of his being a seasoned policeman who'd dealt with some of Sydney's rougher and more testing cases. He'd been in the news several years earlier after he shot and killed an intruder who was about to attack a member of parliament. 'Of course,' she said. 'I understand. And I intend to look into it further, but Carter appears quite genuine, and I share his concerns. Take a look at this.' Laura gave Gary Emma's fax. 'He says the allegations are not only untrue but also that making such a claim is totally out of character for his daughter.'

Gary studied the fax for a few minutes. As well as the overall content, he seemed to look at each word and letter. 'Is this it?'

'What do you mean?'

'Well, for starters, there's no fax number or any information at the top of the page; there's no cover sheet either.' He paused briefly as if waiting for a response, and then continued, looking straight at Laura, 'But this is serious—dead serious. This woman means business. She says Emma's made a statement to police, but she doesn't say which station. If I knew, I could get the statement. Look, you know where she lives, right?'

Laura nodded.

'If it's a country police station, it'll be closed now, but I'll try a couple of stations tomorrow. I need to get the statement. That won't be easy, but leave that to me. Of course, if the letter is pure extortion, Albert could possibly have his daughter charged with extortion, but I'm not really sure if that will accomplish anything. I'd advise him to stay right away from any such idea. Either way, we've got a breather of a couple of weeks. That's about as long as it'll take for the cops to do their homework. They won't be calling—what's his name?'

'Albert Carter,' Laura said.

'Right. They won't be talking to Carter for a little while, although I tell you what, I wouldn't want to be in his shoes when they turn up at his home or his office. Does the guy work, have a job?'

'Does he ever. He's a senior partner in a very prestigious law firm.' Laura pulled out his business card.

Gary looked at it and smiled. 'So Kira knows who she's dealing with. Obviously, he has the cash. Not a good story.' Gary put the fax down and looked around the bar. The rain had eased off and the terminal seemed much quieter.

'So, I'm wondering,' Laura said, 'how do we get her out?'

Gary frowned. 'It looks like the only way we can help this woman is to physically get in there and get her out. That won't be easy. We need to do some serious surveillance. When is Emma there? When is her teacher there? We need to know the layout of the house and the property. What chances are there of other people observing our movements? And Laura, we don't kidnap people. We do lots of things, and there's a fine line between kidnapping and extraction, if you know what I mean.'

She grinned. 'Oh, I know. Believe me.'

'And there are limits to what I can do in my position. But I'll talk to a couple of ex-cops who should know what to do. What I need from you is a full written brief. I'll need a detailed map of the area where the young woman is living. Ideally, I'd like a floor plan of the house as well. We'll talk more later, but assuming you decide to go ahead, let's plan to have this happen by the end of this month. I need to prepare a plan and a budget. You'll have that within the next three days. Get that okayed by the family, and we can move ahead.'

'Sounds great.'

'Anything else you think is relevant?'

'Maybe it's not relevant, but I'll mention it anyway,' Laura replied. 'Carter seems a nice enough guy. A bit of a stiff upper lip, but he cares about Emma. He really does. But it's the mind-control issue. He just seems wary about it. I don't know why I'm saying this, but it's a bit odd. If I'm correct, he needs to learn about it and get his act together. Just thought I'd mention it.'

Gary smiled. 'Well, if this case is genuine and we do get her out, Albert will end up becoming one of the biggest defenders of the mind-control argument.' He paused for a moment. 'By the way, what do you know about him? Something tells me I've seen his name in connection to the cult issue, but I'm not sure.'

'Good question,' Laura said. 'I'm sure I've run into that name before too, and if you can do a check on him that would certainly be useful.'

'Sure, leave it with me. When you're ready to move on this, just message me. You've got my details.'

'Sure have.'

'Right then, I need to be on my way. I've got my work cut out and you've got yours.'

Laura didn't have a chance to respond. Gary stood and made his way around the table. After taking a couple of steps towards the door, he turned back and asked, 'It was Albert Carter, wasn't it?'

Laura nodded.

Within moments he'd disappeared into the crowd.

An hour later Laura was on a plane back to Brisbane. Days

like this made her glad that she only had her bonsai to look after. Though she loved animals, she wouldn't want some cat or dog waiting for her to come home and feed it.

She slept through most of the flight.

6

The next morning, Margaret plonked a plain-brown envelope on Laura's desk, then stood, one eyebrow raised, with an expectant look on her face. 'Registered post. Looks scary.'

Laura glanced up at her, then picked up the envelope, which was addressed to her at CultAssist. She turned it over. 'Hudson and Hudson Barristers and Solicitors.' She grimaced.

Margaret grabbed Laura's letter opener from her pen holder and handed it to her.

Laura took a deep breath, slid the knife along the top edge of the envelope and drew out a solicitor's letter. She read it while Margaret bounced on the balls of her feet in expectation of discovering the contents.

> *Dear Ms Fields,*
>
> *We act on behalf of our client, The Healing Mission.*
>
> *Our client is aware of the steps you have taken in denigrating The Healing Mission. As you would be aware, The Healing Mission is a division of its parent company, Divine Delicacies. The false and misleading information you continue to spread has affected Divine Delicacies and reduced its patronage and income.*
>
> *In addition, the comments you have made that*

have been publicised on your website are defamatory. Our client has downloaded the relevant pages, which we are continuing to review at this time.
Our client is in the process of instigating proceedings against CultAssist and its directors.
Yours faithfully
Hudson and Hudson Barristers and Solicitors

Laura groaned, handed the letter to Margaret, then leaned forward, placed one elbow on her desk and rested her forehead on the palm of her hand. Her heart felt leaden. Her day had just become a great deal more complicated.

The Healing Mission, a fundamentalist Christian organisation, ran several programs, including the Female Rehabilitation Centre of Our Holy Redeemer. CultAssist had successfully exited three women from this program. They kept an extensive file on the organisation and had been following their activities over the past year. Recently, Laura had started lobbying government bodies, seeking an enquiry into their activities.

And now this.

It never ceased to amaze Laura how organisations that claimed to help people could cause their members harm and not see it. Their beliefs completely obscured their ability to see what was in front of them—in this instance, women whose health had suffered under their 'care'.

The women who'd left the program had joined it because they had significant addiction issues or eating disorders. They claimed that apart from taking their Centrelink payments, the program did nothing to address their addiction. In fact, one of the three women said that at the time she left the program her eating disorder had worsened considerably. She entered hospital where doctors described her condition as critical.

Of course, the families of these women were deeply grateful to CultAssist for the work they were doing. Two of the women had agreed to be interviewed by the press, and a leading Australian newspaper had published a number of damning articles.

Margaret sighed and gave Laura back the letter. Laura picked up the phone, checked the card of important numbers she kept beside the phone and dialled.

'James?' Margaret whispered.

Laura nodded.

Margaret gave Laura a 'thumbs up' and returned to her own desk.

'James. It's Laura,' she said when he answered her call.

James Elder, a retired lawyer, was the president of CultAssist. He attended meetings, but otherwise they rarely saw him. His wife suffered from MS, and he spent most of his time with her and his two children.

After the usual greetings, Laura read him the contents of the letter.

'Good grief,' James said, sounding shaken.

'It's devastating,' Laura said. 'What do we do?'

'Don't worry. We can handle this,' he replied, but Laura wondered if he said this to reassure himself as much as her. 'I'll call an urgent committee meeting. You call Matthew; ask him to research The Healing Mission and leave no stone unturned. We need every detail about them.'

'They have a hierarchical structure,' Laura said. 'The rehab centre we've helped get a few women out of is run by The Healing Mission, and the mission is a subsidiary of Divine Delicacies, which is a big food-distribution company. I have no idea what the link is between them, other than the trading-company structure.'

As soon as she ended the conversation with James, Laura called Matthew. He said he'd get onto it straight away and promised Laura a report within the next few days.

Laura read the letter again, incensed at the brazenness of the organisation. She remembered Anne, the last person they'd helped exit from the cult. When she joined The Healing Mission at the age of nineteen, Anne had been a heavy marijuana smoker, and after leaving the cult, she'd said that the program had done nothing to address her addiction. Instead, they'd subjected her to a regime of three hours of prayers every morning and four hours of Bible study each evening. According to The Healing Mission, exorcism was the best way to rid the body of toxins left by the drugs.

Though CultAssist usually kept in contact with people they'd worked with, they hadn't heard from Anne since a few weeks after her departure from the cult. Her case worker couldn't get hold of Anne and found her sudden disappearance mystifying. According to her family, Anne was travelling and simply out of telephone range. Initially, her friends had received a few emails from her, but she hadn't said much about what she was doing or where she was living. Now even that contact had stopped.

Laura couldn't help wondering about the timing. Coincidence or not?

7

Today, as she watched Penny—her now seven-year-old prem baby—struggle to walk across the room, Rochelle felt every one of her thirty-four years. Penny was doing well, she reminded herself. Rochelle had to stay positive and keep her expectations realistic. At least the cerebral palsy was relatively mild—compared to some—and she'd had good support from the health system. It was just a pity that the love of her life, Graham, whom she married in 2012, a year before Penny's birth, hadn't coped at all well with the cerebral palsy diagnosis.

Despite the challenges, Rochelle had embraced her role as a mother with great enthusiasm, but Graham had never bonded with his daughter and had refused to seek assistance. He'd become depressed and, seeking answers to his plight, had started attending the Yoga and Body Mind Healing Centre. The centre was a branch of an organisation called Satykumari Purifying Spring, whose headquarters were an ashram in Puna, India.

At first, because his depression appeared to be lifting, Rochelle had been pleased with Graham's commitment to weekly attendance, but within a month of joining he was spending every weekend at the centre's community house doing a three-month course in The Healing Karma. Then when the course finished, Graham had told Rochelle that he planned to take some time off from work to travel to India to spend time at the Satykumari Purifying Spring. During all this, he'd become increasingly detached from his family, particularly Penny.

Rochelle blamed their separation squarely on the influence these people had exerted over her now-estranged husband. Something wasn't right, but she hadn't been able to get Graham to see it, and eventually, he'd moved out, citing her 'rigidity of mind' as an apparently unmovable obstacle between them. He'd changed—a fact that became more obvious each time she saw him.

She sighed and opened her laptop. After a glance at Penny—she'd taken out her playdough and now sat at her small table kneading it happily—Rochelle began to research the Indian organisation. She found their website, a glossy operation with glowing reports from happy members and wise-sounding quotes from the guru. On the surface it looked like a happy place, one of peace and healing, but Rochelle dug deeper. Some of the beliefs she uncovered shocked her, especially their ideas about medicine. And they had masses of rules. Members had to sign a document saying they wouldn't seek any form of medical assistance or intervention without the express consent of His Holiness Bakhavitda Krishnanada. The only way such consent could be granted was through a personal meeting with His Holiness, and the waiting time for appointments was around two years.

Warning bells rang in her mind. Clearly, this wasn't some benign local yoga group; this was a full-on cult. But how did one go about getting someone out of such an organisation? A bit more research brought her to the CultAssist website. She bookmarked it and made a note to email them.

Three weeks later, Graham asked Rochelle to have lunch with him. Hopeful that this meant he wanted to rekindle their waning relationship, Rochelle applied some makeup before she left home. She arrived at the little café on time, but before Graham, and took a table by the window. She'd not been people watching long before she saw him on his way. Had he lost weight? His clothes seemed less fitting than she remembered, and he wore casual clothes, not the usual business suit required by the prestigious IT company for which he worked. *Strange.* She looked him over and realised that he looked older than his thirty-nine years. His hair was even thinning on top. It seemed that the years since Penny's birth had weighed heavily on him.

He smiled when he saw her and gave her a peck on the cheek before he sat on the chair across from her. Once seated and they'd ordered, he placed his briefcase on the table, clicked it open and withdrew a stack of papers inside a plain manilla folder.

Rochelle glanced at it, then at her husband.

A dour and determined expression had replaced his smile. He took a deep breath. 'Honey, I've resigned from my job and booked a flight to India.'

'What!' Rochelle almost yelled. 'Why resign? You could just take time off. What are you going to do for money?'

Graham shook his head. 'Don't worry about that. There are more important things than money.' He smiled as if he had a secret to tell, and his eyes suddenly lit up with enthusiasm. 'Rochelle, Penny can be healed! Isn't that amazing? I just have to take her with me, and when I come back, we'll have a regular healthy little girl, but we need to get her a passport.' He handed her the folder. 'Here, please sign the papers. I'll pay the full cost of the visit. And Penny will be able to live a normal life.'

Rochelle's mouth hung open in surprise. 'You can't be serious,' she cried, searching his face. 'Do you think anyone, let alone a mother, would agree to that? Sorry, Graham, it's not happening. Penny doesn't leave Australia.'

His expression darkened, his mouth taking on a hard line.

'Are you saying I need to wait until His Holiness visits here?' he said, clearly irritated. 'That could take years, and Penny's getting older.'

Rochelle shook her head. 'I've looked into this guy and the things he believes, and I'm telling you now, Penny won't be seeing His Holiness'—she made air quotes for emphasis—'here, in India or anywhere else. Get that straight. And let's not fight about it. If anybody has a problem here, it's not Penny; it's you. From the moment she was born, you were the problem, not Penny. She's doing really well, and she's growing up quickly.' She paused, noting that Graham looked taken aback. Did he really believe she'd think this was a good idea? 'Frankly,' she continued, 'I don't know what you want from her.'

Graham opened his mouth, then shut it without saying anything. He stood up, mumbled a thank you for her meeting him, threw some cash on the table, then walked briskly out of the restaurant. Their meal hadn't even arrived yet.

Rochelle watched him with a sinking feeling. This was serious!

Her phone rang. She pulled it from her handbag and accepted the call.

'Ms Lightwood, it's Penny's aide. I'm calling from the school. Don't worry, everything's fine and Penny's having a good day. I just wondered why she has a photo of what appears to be an Indian religious leader on her lunch box. Her father dropped her off today, and we thought that was a little odd.'

Rochelle's free hand clenched into a fist. 'Thank you for calling. Let me look into this, and I'll get back to you shortly.' She raced out to the car park and across to where Graham stood by his car, talking on his mobile phone. She placed her fists on her hips, pressed her lips together and glared at him through narrowed eyes.

'Sorry, George, I have to go. We'll talk later.' Graham ended the call and faced her without expression.

'And who gave you the right to stick a photo of your guru, whatever you call him, on Penny's lunch box?' she hissed. 'Who, Graham? Who?'

He said nothing, just turned away, jumped into his car and drove off.

~

Rochelle thought her hands were remarkably steady as she picked up her home phone and dialled the number from the website. She took a deep breath, and when the line picked up, she said, 'Hi, my name's Rochelle Lightwood. Is this CultAssist?'

'Hi, Rochelle. I'm Margaret. How can I help you?'

8

On Friday, just a few days later, Rochelle arrived for a meeting at CultAssist at 2.00 pm. She'd had to convince Laura, the woman she was to meet, that the urgency was necessary because Laura already had a lot on her plate. And she'd had to fly from Sydney to Brisbane, but Laura had said these things were better discussed in person. Luckily, she'd landed some good house sales for her boss recently. Even so, she hoped it'd be worth it. But Rochelle had a really bad feeling about all this. Graham was far too enamoured with his Indian guru and his deluded ideas, and he really seemed to think the man could 'fix' Penny. She couldn't get Graham to see the flaw in the whole idea that Penny was broken and had to be fixed.

Her sister would pick Penny up from school today, and she'd assured Rochelle that the family would do everything possible to ensure that Penny was safe and protected from the influence of the Yoga Centre. She didn't know what she'd do without the support of her family.

Rochelle parked and stepped from the air-conditioned hire car into an unusually hot spring day. She hurried to the shaded porch of the CultAssist building and took a moment to look at the view and gather herself.

A plump, smiling older woman in a hideous dress opened the door. 'Hi, I'm Margaret. Come in before you roast to death!'

Rochelle returned the smile. Margaret might have a curious dress sense but she sure knew how to make someone feel welcome. A short while later, Rochelle sat—coffee in hand—in a soft chair across from Laura Fields. Her fine blonde hair had been expertly blow-dried into a neat bob, and her conservative business attire exuded professionalism. Rochelle self-consciously patted her wild, dark hair. A useless action. Her thick curls were about as far from Laura's smooth locks as you could get and resisted all attempts at taming.

Laura leafed through the school reports, medical records and gorgeous photos of Penny that Rochelle had given her, then summarised what she understood from their initial phone call and Rochelle's email before asking her to fill in the gaps. Since Rochelle was an articulate communicator, it didn't take long until Laura had a good picture of what was going on.

'I share your concern, Rochelle,' Laura said, 'but I need to ask what you're trying to achieve. Obviously, you don't want Penny anywhere near the Yoga Centre, and you certainly don't want her to travel to India, but what do you want to do about Graham's involvement?'

Rochelle nodded. 'Yeah, I don't want her to have anything to do with those people. She doesn't have a passport, but I've heard stories of cults getting people, in particular children, out of the country using false passports. As far as Graham's concerned, well, right now he's not my priority. Our marriage isn't sailing very smoothly anyway. We're living apart right now, but of course, I don't want him in that group either—after all, he's Penny's dad. But I'm not sure if I can do anything about that. I just don't want him to take Penny anywhere near that mob. He stuck a picture of his guru on her lunchbox! I mean, it's gone now, but how am I to know what he does during his time with her?'

Laura frowned. 'The bad news is that it looks like Graham's determined to involve his guru in Penny's life. It's misguided, but he really believes his guru can help her. The good news is that we have a Family Court system that is becoming increasingly aware of the danger of these cults.'

'So can I get a restraining order on him or something? Something to stop him taking her there, anything like that?' Rochelle asked.

'We can try, but successful applications regarding this kind of thing take time and can be expensive. You'd need to convince the judge that any affiliation with Graham's yoga group isn't in Penny's interests. You'd be asking for an order that prohibits him from doing anything that will expose Penny to the Yoga and Mind Body Healing Centre. Such orders can be quite substantial, though. You could, for example, request that Graham be restricted from bringing Penny into contact with any children whose families are involved in the Yoga Centre, and you can certainly request that she be not exposed to any of the guru's healing methods. These are achievable goals, and we've been successful in a number of similar cases in the past.'

'What if the judge doesn't believe me? He or she mightn't think cults are such a big issue. I mean, not everybody sees the world in the way you and I do.'

'That's true, they don't. Most people are unaware of the danger such groups can pose, and that's why we'd want the judge to commission an Expert Witness Report. Such a report would focus on the nature of the Yoga and Mind Body Healing Centre and its connection with the Satykumari Purifying Spring. Hopefully, the report's author would be able to interview former members of the group. The idea is to convince the judge that Penny must be protected at all costs from the influence of this group, because its influence won't contribute to her healthy development, especially since she has special needs due to the cerebral palsy. We might be able to help with the report, but you'll also need a good lawyer, someone with an interest in this area. We have people we can recommend. It's unconventional work, but on the importance scale it sits somewhere at the top.'

Rochelle exhaled forcefully through her mouth. It all sounded like so much work. All that convincing she'd need to do. *Lawyers, courts. Damn Graham.*

Laura looked at Rochelle as if she totally got it. 'It may sound like a long path,' she said, 'but you have a good chance of achieving your goals and restricting Graham from having undue influence over Penny. And we'll be here to support you and work with you and the lawyer. It's a very fluid situation, though; things could change quite dramatically before we know it, so if you do decide to make an application to the courts, we'll need to stress the urgency of the matter so it can be heard very soon. And we need to remain in touch.'

They ended the meeting with Rochelle promising to call as soon as she'd decided what she wanted to do—and what she could afford to do. Before she started the car, she called her sister to make sure Penny was well and settled.

'Don't worry, Rochelle,' her sister said. 'Relax. Penny's about to go to sleep. The doors are locked, and she's perfectly safe.'

'I just can't believe this,' Rochelle said to herself as she pulled the hire car out of the parking lot and headed back to the airport. A thought struck her, and she frowned. Had Graham slipped out of the country and travelled to India already? About a month ago, he'd said he was going to Melbourne on business, and he hadn't had Penny at all that week. She needed to figure it all out, needed to know what was going on. But lawyers were expensive, and though Rochelle's real estate job paid the bills and Graham did help support Penny, extra expenses wouldn't be easy to cover. Would her family help out if she got stuck? Could she bring herself to ask them?

'This totally sucks,' she muttered to herself.

9

Laura wasn't looking forward to Sunday. One day off just wasn't enough. She'd tried to spend her Saturday staring meditatively at the sluggish Brisbane River from the balcony of her townhouse, but the demands of her job had a way of creeping in, so she'd weeded her courtyard vegetable garden and planted some more lettuces, but still the worries surfaced. She'd even gone so far as to debrief to her bonsai trees. They were good at listening, but even if they did hold any wisdom on the matters that concerned her, they couldn't communicate it—at least not in words.

Margaret had given up trying to find her a boyfriend and now reckoned she should get another cat. But then Margaret had four of them, as well as countless grandchildren that spilled about her feet like puppies. Perhaps it was best she worked, since none of this would resolve itself while Laura took time to visit art galleries, go riding or lounge around the beach at Southbank.

As it was, she had to work when people could manage to get to her or she to them. Today, Sunday, Fadi and Nadia were flying in from Sydney for a half-day conference about their son Amin. Apparently, his health had deteriorated further in the two weeks since she'd seen them. Matthew would also present Laura and the board of CultAssist with a report about the legal threat from The Healing Mission and Divine Delicacies.

The weather was unusually mild. The sun shone, and the slight northerly breeze she felt when she got out of her car at the office made Laura feel a little better. Fadi and Nadia were due at 10.30 am, and the meeting would likely last until lunch, so Margaret was bringing sandwiches. They'd scheduled it so Amin's parents could stay overnight in Brisbane and see Michael the following day to follow up on their discussion with Laura.

The couple arrived on time.

'Any problems getting here?' Laura asked as they settled around the conference table.

'Not at all,' Nadia replied. 'Our business lives mean we spend a lot of time apart, and flying together gave us time to talk about the reasons why Amin might have become enmeshed in such a radical fundamentalist group.'

'That's great,' Laura said. 'What did you come up with?'

'Amin was just two years old when our family emigrated here from Lebanon. We'd heard many stories of children who'd left their homeland when they were older, in their teens and then found the adjustment to life in Australia very difficult, so we thought we'd avoid that. Well, that's what we thought, anyway.'

Fadi continued, 'But even during his teenage years, we felt something was wrong. We come from a very strong Christian background, and Amin felt something was missing. We still went to church regularly. We still prayed as we used to. But Amin really missed his grandmother, Halima, who remains in Lebanon. She's the matriarch of our family, and her home looked more like a church than a regular dwelling. It was beautiful.' Fadi shared a sad smile with his wife, then said, 'You know, we have hardly any contact with Amin since he joined this cult, but I'm sure he still thinks about his grandmother. It's really strange. She's the only person left in our family with whom we think he feels a link, something deep. It's quite amazing since he hasn't seen his grandmother since his childhood years."

'Is Halima your mother, Nadia?' Laura asked.

'No, she's my husband's mother,' Nadia said quietly. 'She's getting old and isn't so well. She's lost most of her sight and stays home much of the time. But she has a very large family, and every Sunday all her children and grandchildren visit her. She can't cook like she used to, but even now she manages to bake a few cakes. It's not the food we all love, you know. It's just being in her presence. Does that make sense?'

Laura smiled. 'Of course, it does. And I imagine Halima knows nothing about Amin's involvement in the Church of Love and Faith.'

Nadia looked at Laura with her piercing dark eyes. 'Laura, if my mother-in-law knew about this, she would die. We will never tell her. Better she goes to heaven when her time comes thinking that one day Amin will join her.'

Fadi sighed. 'Heaven or hell,' he said, 'I think Amin's days on earth are limited. Please Laura, help us, please.' Tears welled in his eyes, and Nadia patted his arm in sympathy.

Laura's heart ached at their pain. 'I'll do my best,' she said. 'But you need to be prepared for anything. What if we get him out of this cult, and he decides he doesn't want to know about any kind of religion? Will you be happy with that?'

Nadia and Fadi frowned.

'I've worked with many families,' Laura continued. 'Most have been happy when their child left the group, but some were extremely disappointed when he didn't return to his parents' or grandparents' faith. Do you want Amin back in his grandma's faith?' She looked from one to the other.

Amin's parents seemed taken aback at the unexpected question.

'I need you to think about this,' Laura went on. 'As far as I am concerned, he needs to get out of there. The Church of Love and Faith is bad news. Believe me. You know that. But we'll need to address this issue because it's so important. One young man I worked with was involved in an extreme Pentecostal organisation—exorcisms every time he had a bad thought, floggings and all that. We got him out. It was absolute hell for everyone, but we did it. But then the parents expected him to attend mass the following Sunday, and he refused. They had a huge fight, and eventually he went back to that cult. And— listen to this—he's still there.'

Margaret poked her head into the conference room and asked if she should bring in the sandwiches.

'Sure,' Laura replied. 'I'm starting to get peckish.'

Margaret said she'd brew some more coffee and be right back.

Fadi and Nadia exchanged a few quiet words, then Fadi said, 'No sandwiches or coffee for us at the moment, thanks, Laura. We'd like to take a short walk, if that's okay?'

'Sure, but don't take more than half an hour,' Laura said. 'There's a lot to do here.' And Laura hoped she might make it home while there was still some sunshine left to enjoy.

10

Margaret returned carrying a fresh pot of coffee, a plate of sandwiches and a wad of A4 paper tucked under her arm. 'It's Matthew report about The Healing Mission. He just dropped it in. Can you take it?'

Laura took the report, her chest tightening. 'I don't feel good about this, Margaret. Hang around while I skim through it, will you?'

'There's about fifty pages there, you know,' Margaret said as she set the sandwiches on the table and refilled Laura's mug. 'But I'll put my feet up.' She sat on one chair, pulled out another and rested her feet on it.

Laura glanced at her feet with a frown.

Margaret shrugged. 'It is Sunday. And don't worry, my old hippie feet will be off the chair before they return.'

Laura smiled. 'What would I do without you?'

'Suffer horribly, I expect.' Margaret took a sandwich and bit into it while Laura looked over the report.

Matthew had done a comprehensive job. He'd included the mission's history and various media reports, plus some annual reports and photographs for both The Healing Mission and Divine Delicacies as well as profiles of the people involved in both organisations.

A prominent newspaper article, published several years ago,

headed 'Solicitor Fights for Rights' caught Laura's eye:

> *A prominent lawyer and civil libertarian has continued his campaign to protect the rights of young people whose parents are concerned about the decisions their children have made to join fringe religious groups. Early this month, the lawyer, a board member of the Divine Delicacies food chain, issued a statement condemning various organisations for their anti-civil libertarian stance. He was particularly scathing about a small organisation called CultAssist operating in the Brisbane area.*

> *'This group believes in the now discredited notion of "thought reform", otherwise known as "mind control". The notion has been rejected in court case after court case, and it's time our government took action to monitor the activities of these so-called anti-cult organisations,' the lawyer said.*

> *The lawyer, Mr Albert Carter, is a senior partner in the firm Carter, Roache and Cain, which is based in the Brisbane CBD. Mr Carter is also a member of the Queensland Council of Civil Liberties.*

Laura felt the blood drain from her face. 'I think I'm going to be sick.'

Margaret leaped to her feet. 'Oh no, sweetheart. You'll be fine.' She grabbed a glass and poured Laura some water from the jug in the centre of the table. 'What is it? What did you read there?'

Laura took a deep breath and sipped slowly, thoughtfully.

'It appears that Albert Carter is trying to trap us. I expect there's no Emma, no police statement and no extortion attempt. Nothing.' She paused for a moment. 'Or maybe there is, and we're about to make a big mistake. First Gary, or his troops, get arrested. Then I'm charged with planning an act of kidnapping; CultAssist is sued, and who knows what else? No. He won't get what he wants. I'm not going to play his game. Fancy talking about the "now discredited notion of thought reform". Maybe we need to discredit him and his whole band of supporters. And I almost fell into this.' She handed the article to Margaret and waited while she read it.

'Hmm. So that's why his name seemed familiar,' she said as she handed it back.

'You know, Margaret, I had a strange feeling about Carter the whole time. I mean, he appeared genuine; he was certainly very polite, but when we talked about mind control, he seemed quite uncomfortable. I even told Gary about it. Well, now we have it, loud and clear.' Anger bubbled like a cauldron inside her. She pressed her lips together, shook her head in disbelieving fury, then grabbed the article and threw it on the floor in disgust.

Margaret remained quiet, apparently surprised at the force of Laura's outburst. They'd worked together for over five years, but she'd never seen Laura so upset.

Laura took a deep breath, exhaled and said, 'Strangely enough, if we hadn't received that outrageous letter from The Healing Mission, I wouldn't have had a clue what was really going on. At least I know. Now it's just something else we have to deal with. Well, they can take whatever action they want, and we'll respond with equal vengeance.'

'You tell 'em, girl,' Margaret said decisively.

'Could you please call an urgent board meeting for this week. Just talk to everyone and work out a time to suit as many people as possible. I might want Gary to make an appearance, but leave that to me for the moment. We'd have to fly him up, but that's fine. There's no two ways about it; this is serious.' She stood, breathing deeply.

Margaret nodded. 'I'll get right on it. If you're okay, that is.'

'I'll be fine. Thanks. And you might as well scan the article and include it in your mailout to the board members.' Laura scooped the offending piece of paper off the floor and handed it back to Margaret.

'Will do.' Margaret cast Laura one last concerned look, then left the room.

Laura followed her, walked out the door and sat on the steps in the sun. Fadi and Nadia were due back in the office any moment. She needed to calm down. If it had been possible, she would've found a reason to postpone the meeting, but Fadi and Nadia had travelled from Sydney to see her, and they still had to talk about how they might rescue Amin.

By the time the couple returned, Laura's heart rate was back to normal, and they entered the office together.

'We discussed it,' Fadi said, 'and whatever Amin decides about religion, we'll accept. We just want him away from this cult.'

'And with God's grace, he doesn't fall into another one,' Nadia added.

Laura nodded. 'Good.' Then she continued from where she'd left off before the break, 'We need a family history from you and a comprehensive personal profile on Amin. You're meeting with my co-worker Michael tomorrow, and he'll ask you things like, "Is Amin an emotional person? Is he a distant type? Would he be more responsive to a male or a female exit counsellor? What were his interests before he joined the church?" We need this information because it's extremely important that Amin can relate to his exit counsellor. If he doesn't feel comfortable with them, we have little chance of success.'

Nadia and Fadi listened intently as if every word was important to them.

'Michael is sensitive and patient, and I'm sure you'll feel comfortable with him. Once we have all the information, we'll go through this together and work out a specific plan. As far as we know at this stage, though, his church won't let him out of their compound. Whenever he goes out witnessing, people will be watching him. And we suspect that no matter who talks to him, he won't respond to an invitation to leave the church grounds. Their control is extremely tight.'

'Sorry to interrupt,' Nadia said cautiously, 'but it sounds rather hopeless.'

'No, not at all. We do have options, Nadia, but we need to consider them carefully. I'll give you a few examples—though they might not be relevant to Amin's situation. Cults like money, so we've managed to draw members away from their premises when they think there's money to be gained. For example, a parent writing a will and telling the cult he wants to discuss it with his son or daughter.'

Fadi nodded thoughtfully, and Nadia looked just a little less worried.

'In other situations,' Laura continued, 'cult members have been allowed to visit a sick relative. Negative publicity can follow if they don't grant permission, and cults don't like that. We've also sent volunteers undercover into the cult to form a bond with the cult member.' She shared some other options, and they discussed some of them at length. Laura finished by saying, 'Getting him out is only the initial step, though. There's a long way to go after that, and it will be hard work. And just to complicate the situation a little more, we can plan it all out—

we can even script it—but in the end, those plans may never eventuate. Things change; we're in a dynamic situation. We're used to that, but we've got to start somewhere.'

Fadi narrowed his eyes and straightened in his chair, his body suddenly rigid. 'I'm angry, very angry,' he said in a low voice. 'Here we are trying to find a way to talk to our own son, and we've got to walk on eggshells just to find a way to reach him. Who the hell do these people think they are? I'd shoot the lot of them if I could.'

'Fadi, calm down.' Nadia took his hand.

Fadi sighed heavily, then turned to Laura. 'You know if we could get Amin to my mother, she would knock the hell out of him. He'd be out of this *church* before he had a chance to say hello.'

'You may be right,' Laura said, 'but your mother doesn't live here, and Lebanon is a long way from Australia. What I need is for you to think about these options and any others that come to mind, then look at the practicalities involved. We'll meet again soon, and don't worry, things will start falling into place. I'm confident we can get there. If you want to discuss anything between now and the next meeting, please give me a call or write an email. It's important we stay in touch.'

By the time Fadi and Nadia left, Laura felt utterly exhausted. She watched them walk down the driveway and gave them an affectionate wave. They smiled back. For them it had been a good day. Laura had given them hope.

As she tidied up her desk, a stray and concerning thought flittered through her mind. *Does Amin really exist, or is he the creation of Albert Carter as well?*

11

Nadia and Fadi's story moved Michael even before he met them, probably because of the similarity between Amin's fate and Michael's own cult experience. He was the only one at CultAssist who'd been a cult victim himself. The involvement in a cult of people close to them had affected some of the other workers, but Michael had not only been involved in a Christian fundamentalist cult himself, he'd also almost lost his children to it.

When he met Nadia and Fadi at the CultAssist office the day after they'd spoken to Laura, he settled them in the lounge area, then apologised for the fact that the family assessment would take time and that he'd be asking a very long list of questions about Amin.

'That's fine,' Fadi said. 'Laura explained why it's all necessary. We'll do whatever it takes.'

Michael nodded, but before he could say anything, Nadia pulled a large, framed picture of Amin from her bag. Tears welled up in her eyes as she explained that he didn't look like this anymore. 'The last time we saw him, his eyes were sunken, his face was white and even his hair was thinner than usual. His clothes just hung on him. Even a slight wind would've blown him away.'

Fadi leaned forward, interrupting his wife. 'You know, we

came to this country to give Amin our best. We left everything behind, but we did it for him. And look where we are. We are cursed. Amin is cursed.'

Michael replied in a soft and sensitive tone. 'This is painful, horribly painful, I know. You can feel Amin slipping away, and I understand your concern that we may be running out of time. But Fadi, we need a plan; we need to know what we are doing. Where would we be if we tried and we failed? Within days, maybe on the same day, the cult would transfer him to another one of their centres, and you wouldn't see him again. He could even be sent overseas.'

Fadi took a deep breath and his expression calmed. 'I'm sorry, Michael. I'm just upset. We don't sleep; we don't eat; all we do is worry about Amin. Our lives have come to a complete standstill.'

'That's completely understandable, Fadi,' Michael replied, 'and we'll do our best to get Amin back to you as soon as possible. From looking at Laura's notes from yesterday, I sense that your mother may become the most important person in this picture.'

Fadi smiled. 'My mother *is* the most important person.'

'Shhh, Fadi.' Nadia motioned to him to be quiet and listen.

'If we can get Amin to Lebanon,' Michael said, 'we have a good chance of getting him out of the church and away from its influence. It would be a complicated mission, but I'd like you to think about it.'

Fadi's eyes lit up. 'You really think we could get him there? Seeing my mother would have a positive effect on him, I'm sure.'

Nadia frowned, sceptical. 'But if he won't even come home to us, how do you expect him to travel to Lebanon, ten thousand miles away?'

'Nadia.' Michael used his most soothing voice in an attempt to calm her down. 'I understand your concerns, but I believe we can overcome them. Leave this with me, and let me work on a few options. For now, let's get on with the questions.'

'Of course,' Nadia said. 'I don't want to be negative, but this is so painful.'

Michael nodded. 'I know, but please understand that we're in this together, and we need to work as a team.'

Fadi glanced at his wife, then back at Michael. 'We're ready.'

'Good.' Michael went through the questionnaire. He asked about Amin's schooling, his hobbies and his plans for the future. He talked about Amin's social life, his friends and his peers. At times, when she talked about the real Amin, the beloved son she missed, Nadia became tearful. But at other times, she laughed as she recalled some of the funnier moments of their lives together as a family. Fadi didn't contribute as much to the discussion, but when asked a question, he answered it.

The whole exercise took two hours, and Michael could see that they felt drained at the end of it, but they also expressed their deep gratitude to Michael for his efforts and encouragement.

After they concluded the session, Nadia looked at Michael and said, 'Please, Michael, may I ask you a question?'

'Sure.'

'We love Amin. He is such an intelligent, loving son. He's our only son, and he knows we're his only parents apart from God.' Nadia pointed her finger upwards. 'So why did this happen to him? Why did this happen to us? What did we do wrong to deserve the hell we're living and the fear that we may never see Amin again?' Nadia broke down, sobbing bitterly.

Fadi put his arm around his wife, but Michael could only bear witness in silence. His own emotions resonated with hers, but he wasn't sure whether those feelings were a reaction to her cry for help or if her pain had triggered a remembered emotional response to his own experiences. Either way, all he could do was sit and let them wash over him.

Eventually, Nadia composed herself. 'I'm sorry, Michael. I don't expect you to have the answers, but I feel you understand us, that you understand what it means for a family to be broken up by a cult, so I'm wondering, have you ever been involved in a cult? If you don't want to answer, that's fine. I understand.'

Michael poured himself a glass of water from the jug on the coffee table and took a sip before he replied. 'I don't normally talk about my own life, but I'll tell you. Yes, I was a member of a Christian fundamentalist cult for seven years. I left with my three children when I realised that those at the centre of the organisation didn't live by the principles they preached and that their practices were more about manipulation than a genuine path to God. But my wife, their mother, is still there. And I still wake up every day hoping and praying that she'll come home.'

'Oh dear,' Nadia said, her face a picture of compassion. 'I am so sorry.'

Michael shrugged. 'When it comes to cults, we never, ever, give up.'

12

Laura's mobile rang. Her eyes fluttered open. She rolled over, glanced at her bedside clock and groaned. Who called at 7.30 am on a Wednesday morning? Any morning, in fact! Usually, she'd be up by now, but she'd spent too much of last night thinking about Amin, Albert and Rochelle's Penny. She heaved herself upright and grabbed the phone, wondering what was in store for her today.

'Laura? It's Gary. Sorry for the early call, but I'm on a difficult assignment and won't be available later.'

Laura sighed as the weight of her responsibilities flooded back in. 'It's fine, Gary.' Her voice croaked with sleep. She cleared her throat and shook her head to clear her mind.

'Are you okay?' he asked.

'I'm fine. What's up?'

'Good news. I've got Emma's statement, and it's one of two things: either it's a litany of some of the cruellest abuse I've seen throughout my career or it's one huge set of lies. The police aren't sure how to deal with it. They, and I, have seen thousands of these statements. Literally thousands. The real ones are usually two or three pages, are relatively straightforward and they make sense, but Emma's statement is eleven pages long. That's a lot of pages, and it just makes you wonder. What's the best way to get you a copy?'

'Fax, please,' Laura said. 'As soon as possible.'

'Okay, but listen, I'm not meant to have this, at least not at this point in time. I managed to secure a few favours for favours to get it, but please keep it confidential. Carter should be able to get a copy of the statement. He doesn't need me for that.'

'Okay. I'll mark it sensitive and confidential. My team knows what that means.' Should she tell him what they'd found out about Albert Carter? No, she didn't want to go into it right now. 'I'll look it over as soon as I get it. But, Gary,' she added in a low voice, 'we need to talk soon about this case. We've had a major complication, and I'd prefer to talk to you about it face to face.'

'No worries; just tell me when's a good time for you, just not today. Happy to help you, Laura. Cheers.' He ended the call.

Laura climbed out of bed, opened the curtains and the sliding door, and walked onto her balcony. She smiled at the sunlight sparkling on the Brisbane River, then took a deep breath and stretched.

Her phone rang again.

She raced inside and accepted the call.

It was Gary again. 'I forgot something—a detail about the statement—but keep this between you and me. I spoke to the officer who was there when Emma wrote her statement. Apparently, after she'd finished writing it, Emma called someone from her mobile phone and read out the whole statement. I think she even made some changes while on the phone to the other person.'

'That rings alarm bells for me,' Laura said.

'Yeah, I reckon, and something else, someone drove her to the police station, waited outside for over an hour while she wrote it, and then drove her away. So, I don't think it's Emma's statement. It's more like someone coaxed her into writing it. I mean, altering parts while on the phone sounds almost like taking dictation. So, look, you don't need to convince me. Emma's in a cult, and someone's controlling her every move. Let's not kid ourselves.'

'Thanks, Gary, you're a legend. You'll fax it today?'

'Doing it now.'

'Great, I'll look at it as soon as I get to work.'

She ended the call, walked over to her oldest bonsai and said, 'Well, Mr Procumben, sir, the day is off to a racing start.'

Perhaps she should get a cat, she thought briefly. People talked to their cats all the time. Talking to plants, she suspected, wasn't quite so common. But what did it matter if no one heard you? And it wasn't as if she expected a reply!

When Laura arrived at the office, Margaret said, 'A really long fax came in from Gary, marked private and confidential, so I didn't look but …' She grinned and blinked her eyes, indicating she'd love to know what it was.

'Private and confidential, Margaret,' Laura said, 'and in this instance it really is on a need-to-know basis.'

Margaret shrugged. 'Ah well, there goes my attempt at procrastination for this morning. Coffee's made. Let me know if you need anything.' She walked to her desk and sat with a melodramatic sigh complete with back of the hand to her forehead.

Laura laughed. She grabbed the fax and wandered into her office while flicking through it. Eleven pages. She sat and skimmed through the document, and soon realised that Gary had been right when he'd said, 'This is either one litany of some of the cruellest abuse or one huge lie.'

Various statements caught her eye:

In 1985 my father repeatedly abused me. His legal practice was going through a difficult time. He would come home late at night and enter my bedroom and lie in my bed and abuse me. My mother was asleep at the time and completely unaware of his lewd behaviour. He would usually return to my parents' room before the morning.

Towards the end of the year, my mother had a mental breakdown. My guess is that he was abusing her as well. My mother ended up in a psychiatric hospital for over one month. My father took advantage of my mother's absence. On one occasion I found him hiding in the bathroom as I was showering. My father said he was looking for my mother's makeup to take to the hospital. When I screamed, he attacked me and attempted to rape me. I managed to escape and hid at the neighbour's house until my father went to work the next day.

And I write the above believing it to be true …

Laura studied the fax again. The writing was neat, but there must have been at least a dozen corrections on each page. Why didn't Emma simply rewrite the statement? A senior sergeant called Fiona had witnessed it—she couldn't make out the surname. But the fact that Emma's statement had been written and witnessed in a police station meant it was already being processed.

Laura leaned back in her chair, then got up and walked around. She opened the window a little wider and sat down again. 'What the hell do we do next? Oh God, how much more difficult can this be?'

The answer came quickly. Margaret buzzed Laura. 'Hi there,

phone call for you. It's Albert Carter. Wants to know when he can meet you. He says the situation is becoming urgent, and he's freaked out about his daughter.'

'Please tell him I've gone for the day, and I'll be busy all day tomorrow, but he can call on Friday afternoon.'

'Okay. Will do.'

Laura tried to catch her thoughts, but the phone buzzed again. 'Sorry, but he says it's urgent.'

'Then tell him to send me an email and say I'll see it in the next few hours. And, Marg? You don't need to be so nice to this guy. This whole story could be an elaborate farce designed to discredit us at the least and have us in prison at the worst.' She paused, 'Sorry, Marg, this has already been one heck of a day.'

13

Laura sat back on the couch and took another sip of coffee. That expresso machine had been a great investment, and Margaret used it like a pro. But every cup ended and left her back with her thoughts.

What was Albert Carter up to? Emma's case had all the hallmarks of a genuine cult entrapment, but the article that placed him as someone strongly against the idea of mind control meant she had to be cautious. She'd managed to put off thinking about it all day and hadn't opened Albert's email, but she couldn't put it off forever, and if Emma really was in trouble, then … and then there was that ugly letter from The Healing Mission and the risk to Rochelle's little girl.

Laura sighed. She understood all too well the pain caused by cults that isolated children from their parents. When she thought about Siddharth, her Indian lover, and the daughter he'd stolen from her, the pain was as fresh today as it had been then. She'd fallen in love while working as a community liaison officer in a small urban centre in India. They'd moved in together a few months before Anindita's birth, but the cultural differences between the Australian-born Laura and a young man brought up in the Indian hinterland were too great. He left her after two years, took their young daughter with him and never came back. Laura returned to Melbourne in 1978, and despite an extensive investigation and search, the police never located her former partner or their daughter. Rumours suggested that they'd died in the tsunami that ravaged the region in 1985, but that hadn't been confirmed. Although Laura vowed never to give up the fight to find her daughter, she'd resigned herself to the fact that this was more a dream than a possibility.

At least when Pierre—her second husband, a French national whom she married in 1979—returned to France to look after his ageing father, he left their two children, Dion and Dillon, with her. Laura was grateful for that. And their divorce in 1985 had been amicable. He visited Australia at least once a year, and the children spent their summer holidays with their father in Paris. The arrangement worked well for them all.

She'd not lost those children, and though they lived in Melbourne in the Trinity Residential College attached to Melbourne University, she spoke to them on the phone often and spent time with them whenever she flew to Melbourne.

But Anindita? Oh, that still hurt. Her first child, and she'd been so young. But now she had to stop thinking about it. She had enough on her plate without adding angst from the past.

Laura stood, walked outside and stood looking over the forest to the mountains in the distance. She took a deep breath of the fresh, warm air. The vastness of the view always inspired her and lifted her spirits, and the sun shining in a sparkling blue sky also helped ease her burden.

Laura heard a car drive up to the front of the building, and soon afterwards Matthew—wearing his signature blue jeans and t-shirt—joined her.

'Margaret said you were out here,' he said. 'I reckon it's a good place to debrief on a day like this.' He gestured to the bench in the shade of a tree.

Laura smiled and sat beside him.

'I'm sorry I haven't been around much,' he said, 'but I think I'm finally finished with the fallout from the Sunananda lot, and little Maria is pretty much better now. She goes back to school tomorrow.'

'That's good news.' He'd also been working on preparing a submission to the government on measures to regulate the personal development industry.

'Yeah. It is.' He brushed his thick hair back off his forehead and smiled at her. 'So fill me in. How are you managing? Wanna talk it through?'

Laura nodded. 'Yeah, well, it's pretty complicated, Matthew. I mean, we've got a guy, a top lawyer, trying to get his daughter out of a strange little group run by a naturopath, and now we find out he doesn't believe that mind control or thought reform is a real thing. So, he could be trying to close us down, trap us, you know. I mean that's sick, but …' Laura shook her head and stared at the horizon, then took a deep breath and exhaled forcefully through her mouth.

'But we know only too well what people are capable of when it comes to defending their beliefs,' Matthew finished for her.

'Yeah. He doesn't know what we know about him, though,' Laura continued. 'So we have an advantage there.'

Matthew nodded. 'But what if—'

'Exactly. What if Emma's in a real cult?'

'The evidence does point to her being a genuine victim of mind control.'

'Yes. And does it matter that her father's a nutter? Isn't his daughter the real issue? But then again, if she's not really under this woman's control, not really at risk of harm, and we go in to get her out, we're all stuffed.'

Matthew frowned and stared out to the mountains.

'And then, of course, we only found that out because The

Healing Mission is trying to sue us,' Laura continued in a tone of disbelief. 'And on top of that, we've got Fadi and Nadia wanting to save their son from starving himself to death. And he sounds like he's in a really bad way. They're a wonderful family facing a potentially terrible tragedy.' She sighed. 'I dunno.'

'It is a lot to juggle. But we'll work it out. We always do.'

She gave him a grateful smile. 'Yeah, but you know sometimes I wonder whether I should be doing this work. I mean, I've got a wonderful, dedicated team of people, and I seem to be good at what I do, but it's so hard sometimes. I wish I could open our files to the public and let them see that there *is* something called mind control. All the people we've saved … when you look at their stories, the fact that they were under mind control stares you in the face. Then you have this idiot called Carter who says mind control doesn't exist.'

Matthew nodded. 'Yeah, it's tough … I do understand the civil libertarians, but they tend to only see one side of the story. I've often thought that those against the idea of thought reform might think differently if one of their kids ended up in a cult and they were forced to deal with the same issues as all the parents who come to us.'

'Exactly,' Laura said. 'And that's happened now with this Carter guy, but it's just so complicated and, quite honestly, I'm struggling right now.'

Matthew slid closer and gave her a hug but Laura, on a roll now, didn't give him a chance to say anything.

'It's a great feeling when we're successful, when we get somebody out of one of these darned cults, but we don't always succeed, and for many families, we're literally their last hope. They've tried everything else—the counsellors, the therapists, the alternative do-gooders. And what about those who can't afford our fees? Our grants only go so far.'

Matthew sighed. As the person responsible for grant applications, he knew all too well the limitations on the number of clients they could help *pro bono*.

'Remember Julia?' Laura went on. 'That university student who got caught up in that Eastern doomsday cult. We worked for two years to try to save her. The police refused to be involved. The cult tried to sue me for I don't know what, and the media was critical of CultAssist, but we kept going. We were determined to save this woman. We almost had her out, and then I got that phone call at 3.00 am from Julia's mum.' Laura shook her head, remembering the tragedy. 'For three minutes all I could hear was her breathing deeply. And then she says, '"Julia's in intensive care. She was attacked by another cult member at their headquarters. She lost a lot of blood and is in a coma."' I sat next to her in ICU for three days. The cult members weren't allowed in, but they hung around the hospital. I took a break for a few hours, and when I returned, she was dead. Her mother had a breakdown and is only now beginning to get her life together.' Another sigh. 'Why did that girl have to die?'

They both remained quiet for a moment, then Matthew said, 'Laura, you do incredible work and our clients have such enormous expectations that the pressure is bound to feel overwhelming sometimes. But you are making a difference in people's lives. You're giving them back their lives, their freedom and their independence. That's a privilege and a gift.'

Laura nodded. 'Yeah. Sometimes I wonder what makes me tick. I do. I still often think about my beautiful Anindita, and she disappeared almost thirty years ago. Maybe I'm trying to save these people from cults because I couldn't save my own daughter. Maybe it's easier to search for them than to search for her. Sometimes I can almost feel her energy, and I think she must be alive, and other times I think it's her spirit I feel and so she must be dead. Maybe that's a reality I could never accept and why it's better not to know anything more than I do.' Laura wiped moisture from her eyes, and the fight in her drained away for a moment. She stared at the sky and watched a cloud turn into a whisp and disappear.

'Lots of maybes,' Matthew said. 'And we may never know the truth of any of it.'

Laura paused. 'You're right about that.' She sat up and looked at him, more focused now and somewhat less introspective. 'Thank you. Thank you for listening.'

Matthew smiled. 'No worries. You do the same for me when I need it, and we both know that talking things out helps put them in perspective.'

Laura nodded. 'It sure does.'

'Now, I suggest you take a break and have a nice relax on that lovely balcony of yours with a glass of wine and some cruisy music. Margaret and I can handle anything else that pops up today.'

'Yeah. I'll do that.'

He gave her a cheeky grin and raised an eyebrow. 'Just don't overdo the wine.'

She chuckled and biffed him lightly on his arm. He knew she never overindulged in alcohol. Coffee, however …? She'd have just one more cup before she left.

14

Despite considerable effort, Margaret had been unable to get the CultAssist board together for a special meeting. They had to address the threat by The Healing Mission and discuss the Albert Carter issue. As a rule, the board didn't discuss client-related matters, but on this occasion, the ramifications could have a severe impact on CultAssist, so Laura included both issues on the agenda. The earliest meeting Margaret could organise was two weeks away.

Meanwhile, as expected, Albert called again, seeking an urgent meeting. Laura suggested that they meet at 11.00 am on Saturday morning at the Café Q next to the Brisbane pier. She asked Matthew to come with her, and he agreed.

On Saturday morning, after some light work in the vege garden, she showered and donned a pencil skirt and corporate-style jacket, then drove to meet Matthew at 10.45 am so they could discuss their strategy before Albert arrived. They settled at a table right next to the large window facing the ocean.

'Not a bad place for a business meeting,' Matthew said as he stretched his denim-clad legs under the table.

Laura smiled at the sparkling ocean and the deep blue sky, clear all the way to the horizon. 'It helps my stress levels.'

Matthew chuckled, then got straight to business. 'I have to tell you, Laura, I'm very unhappy with Albert's involvement in Divine Delicacies, and his statement about mind control is seriously problematic. I'm quite prepared to dismiss him immediately if he can't change his tune. It's simply not worth the risk. And we can find him alternative assistance, so we'll not be leaving Emma high and dry.'

Laura shook her head. 'Except that we're the only organisation here that is really set up to deal with specifically this kind of thing.'

'True, but you don't have to personally rescue everyone, Laura.'

'Hmm.'

By the time Albert arrived—right on time and wearing cream trousers and a short-sleeved shirt—they had a rough plan worked out.

'I must apologise again on behalf of my wife,' Albert said after he greeted Laura and she'd introduced Matthew. 'She couldn't make it this morning.'

Matthew shot a questioning glance at Laura. She had a good idea what he might be thinking. Did Alison even know about the fax and Emma's threats?

'That fax is a big worry,' Albert said while Laura and Matthew sipped their coffees. 'I'm having nightmares about police turning up on my doorstep. I'm a lawyer; if this gets out, even though it's all lies, my career will be immediately and irreparably damaged. It's not only my profession and good name that will be ruined, it'll affect Alison as well. We've been married for a while, but this kind of thing was not part of the deal.'

Laura nodded. 'I understand your worry, Albert. Of course, your profession, your reputation and your marriage are important, but what about your daughter? You're not expressing any concern about her. She could be quite unsafe. You said she's a victim of mind control. Isn't that a reason to be concerned?'

Albert frowned. 'Well, I didn't use the term "mind control" exactly. To be precise, I said that she has lost the ability to think independently. That could've come about due to a whole lot of factors. What I do know is that we need to get her out, and we need to get her out fast.'

Matthew cleared his throat and said somewhat sternly, 'Mr Carter, let's get a few things clear. While we do sympathise with your plight, our concern is Emma. Based on what we know, we also feel that there is an element of urgency. For every day that Emma resides with Kira, she is regressing emotionally and psychologically. The fact is, Mr Carter, Emma is a victim of mind control, thought reform or brainwashing—call it what you like.'

Albert said nothing. Obviously uncomfortable, he looked around the room, avoiding eye contact with both Laura and Matthew.

'We need to talk about this, Albert,' Laura said. 'An issue has arisen that needs to be resolved here and now. I'm not going to mince my words. You're a board member of Divine Delicacies, a group connected with another organisation called The Healing Mission. You're on record for having condemned our organisation, and you've stated that the notion of mind control has been discredited. Therefore, Mr Carter, we have a problem.'

Albert's jaw dropped. 'But didn't you just say this is about Emma? What does it matter what I think and what I believe?'

Laura glanced at Matthew, fighting back a desire to roll her eyes. Clearly Albert, a lawyer through and through, wasn't going to go down without a fight. He was used to sifting through information and determining which pieces of evidence were relevant in court.

'So if your organisation really cares about Emma,' he continued, 'then please leave me out of it. My views are irrelevant. I want my daughter out of there, and time is not on our side.'

'Oh, we do care about Emma,' Matthew said. 'She is our primary concern, not you, your wife, your profession or your good name. We can and will, if necessary, refer you to another agency. We would provide them with support and be available to provide any assistance we can, but they aren't specifically set up to deal with cults and the mind control issue, and, naturally, there'll be a fee for their services. But we will not abandon Emma. In fact, we've already looked at a number of alternative options for you.' Matthew, being uncharacteristically assertive, looked directly at Carter.

Carter shifted in his seat. Perhaps he was sensing what it was like to be cross-examined in the witness box.

'But that won't be necessary if you're willing to work with us as a team,' Matthew continued. 'And a team requires a certain level of harmony and honesty. We need to be on the same page, so you'd need to resign from the board of Divine Delicacies. It's as simple as that. There are no ifs and buts about it. You'd need to commit yourself to our work together to the degree that you'll not rejoin their board or assist that organisation in any capacity for the next five years.'

Albert's eyes widened and his mouth opened, but he said nothing, just blinked several times, apparently at a loss for words. 'I think you're being quite unreasonable,' he said eventually. 'I had no idea there was a conflict between my role as a board member of a reputable company and my role as a loving parent.'

'Well then, Albert,' Matthew replied, 'you don't seem too well briefed on some of the goings on at Divine Delicacies. Do you know that The Healing Mission is threatening to sue CultAssist? I have no idea who provides Divine Delicacies with legal advice, but last week we received a registered letter that was nothing less than despicable. You check with the secretary of Divine Delicacies, and you'll see what I mean. He or she will certainly have a copy of the letter.'

Albert frowned. 'I'll do that right now.' He took out his

mobile phone.

'No, not now,' Matthew said. 'Please give yourself time to consider this matter seriously and let us know your intentions.'

Albert shrugged and laid his phone on the table. 'Okay, I'll consider your proposition, but I don't like it. Then again, if Emma is the real concern, and she certainly is, you're not giving me much room to move, are you?'

Matthew responded, 'No, we're not. But we're also being honest. You can approach another agency—as I said, we'll make the referral. But if CultAssist goes out of business, hundreds of people will lose a lifeline that could be the only way they can get back to leading normal lives. Because, Mr Carter, these people *are* victims of mind control.'

Albert leaned back in his chair, regarded Laura and Matthew for a moment, then nodded. 'I do understand where you're coming from. But it's more complex than you think. I can't go into it now, and nothing will happen on the weekend, but I will get back to you on Monday morning. I'll call you at nine. I also want to thank you for your support. This has been a difficult meeting, but it's been an important one. I suppose this had to come out, and now it has.'

His phone rang. He glanced at the screen, and said, 'Sorry, I have to get this. It's from my PA. She knows I'm meeting you and why, so it could be relevant.'

Matthew lifted his hands in a don't-mind-me gesture.

Albert answered the call, his frown deepening as he listened. 'Thanks, Jenny. I appreciate this.' He ended the call and looked from Matthew to Laura and back again, worry etched into his face. 'I was planning to go to the office after this,' he explained, 'but she said I might want to do a U-turn and go home or maybe drive up to my country property. There are two policemen waiting at the office to interview me.'

15

Ping. Laura checked her pager. Someone had left a message on her office phone. She glanced at the clock: 11.30 pm. Most people would probably leave anything business related until Monday, but in her job, things could deteriorate quickly and without regard for business hours. She called the office answer phone and listened to the message. It was Nadia, and she sounded distressed.

'Please, Laura or anybody, please call me urgently. I'm just … just … I need to talk to you. Please call as soon as you can.'

Laura sighed. Though tempted to call right now, she refrained. Whatever had happened, it was too late for her to do anything about it now. She had to get some sleep, and to do that, she had to put Nadia out of her mind.

Laura woke early the next morning and put on a load of washing, then dusted and vacuumed while she waited for a reasonable hour to phone Nadia.

Nadia answered right away. 'Oh, Laura. I … I …' She gave a little sob, then sniffed and cleared her throat. 'I can't … I don't … It's, it's Amin …'

'Take your time, Nadia,' Laura said. 'I'm not going anywhere.' Though bursting to know what had happened, Laura focused on calming Nadia down. Pressurising her in any way would only add to her distress.

'Thanks.' Laura heard her take several deep breaths, then she said, 'It's Amin. He's been fasting four days a week, and now he's in Bankstown Public Hospital with severe dehydration. He was there for three days last week as well, on an intravenous drip, but he discharged himself and returned to his church. Now he's back in again. I guess he went back to the fasting.' Another sob escaped her, followed by a pause in which Laura imagined her fighting back tears. 'He's literally wasting away!' she added in a voice rough with grief.

'Oh, Nadia, I'm so sorry to hear that,' Laura said, 'but tell me, how did you find out?'

'A nurse called us,' Nadia whispered. 'She must be Amin's guardian angel because she told us that if her superiors found out that she'd breached the hospital privacy laws, she could be dismissed immediately. She also said that if there was anything she could do to help Amin, she would, but she had to be really careful. I'm scared, Laura, scared that my darling son won't survive this.' Tears flowed freely then, and Laura could hear Fadi in the background trying to console her.

'Nadia, I have some questions for you,' Laura said gently. 'Can you manage?'

'His body must be so wasted and his heart so weak …' Nadia said between sniffles. 'How do these people get away with this? Can't they see he's sick?'

'You're not powerless, Nadia,' Laura said in an effort to console her. 'The nurse's offer could be key to getting Amin away from the cult. Can you tell me more about her?'

'Yes … yes, I can. She's a nonpracticing Muslim woman called Safiyya. Apparently, that's the name of one of Mohammad's wives, and she was a very saintly woman. Maybe that's why she offered to help. But the trouble is, Laura, she finishes her work at the hospital in a week, at least I think that's what she said. So,

I don't know how much help she can be.'

Laura, however, felt encouraged by Safiyya's interest in helping Amin. 'Nadia, listen to me. Please do one thing for me. Find out Safiyya's phone number. Tell her that a friend of Amin wants to call her. You'll need to act quickly, because the moment she leaves the hospital, it will be extremely difficult to find her. Don't mention my name or CultAssist. Can you do that, Nadia?'

'I'll try, but what do I do about Amin in the meantime?'

Laura sighed. The truth could be a bitch sometimes. 'Nothing, you can't do anything. But we do have a plan. Michael has been working on it since he met you for the family assessment. It's complex and will be difficult to execute, but it is possible. We'll work as quickly as we can, but we need to be careful. Safiyya may be able to assist us, but there will be risks. Please call the office on Monday to organise a time to meet. I realise you'll need to get to Brisbane once again, but please call. Margaret will look after you. Nadia, you need to think as positively as possible.'

'I'll try, and I'll go to the hospital as soon as visiting hours start.'

16

Nadia looked up at the huge chimney that arose from the middle of the Bankstown Public Hospital complex. The series of buildings filled a whole block near the suburb of Bankstown just outside the Sydney Central Business District. Some of the buildings were new, but most looked as if they had been built before World War II. She wondered whether the chimney was connected with some sort of crematorium.

Maybe that's where they burn all the body parts and the limbs they amputate.

She walked through the main doors into the imposing building and smiled at the coloured balloons celebrating seventy-five years of care that decorated the entrance. A few steps inside the hospital, she found a huge café area where families huddled together around tables. Several patients had drips attached to their bodies, accompanying them like loyal friends. A few wheelchairs jutted out of the long rows of tables. A beautiful little girl without hair caught her eye. She stared at Nadia for a moment, appearing fascinated by Nadia's dress, which stood out from the crowd of visitors dressed more casually.

Nadia headed towards the information desk and introduced herself as the mother of a former patient. 'I've brought a gift for one of the nurses.' She lifted the basket of spices and jams. 'She took special care of my son, and I'd like to thank her.'

The receptionist shook her head. 'Sorry, madam, I'd like to help you, but the privacy laws don't allow us to talk about patients or staff. If you know the name of the staff member who has assisted the patient, you can leave your gift here, and we'll pass it on. But we can't guarantee that he or she will receive it. This is a busy hospital with five hundred and forty-six staff members; just look around.'

'Of course,' Nadia said. 'I understand.' The woman was simply doing her duty. She looked around, wondering what to do now.

'Look, darl,' the woman said. 'Let me take your gift. Who is the staff member you'd like to thank?'

Nadia turned back. 'Her name is Safiyya. She looked after my son, Amin. She was wonderful. I've written her a small thank-you note as well.'

'Well, madam, perhaps you could leave a phone number. Maybe she'll call you, maybe not. I've got to be honest. I've never heard of Safiyya; but then again, I'm relatively new here.'

Nadia reached over the counter and clasped the lady's hand. 'Thank you ... thank you and may God bless you.'

The woman smiled, and Nadia left.

~

Three hours later, at exactly 8.00 pm, Nadia's mobile rang. 'It's Safiyya,' a quiet voice whispered. 'Thank you for the gift. You really didn't need to do it. How is Amin? Is he all right?'

Nadia's voice faltered, 'I don't know, Safiyya. We have no contact with him at all.'

'I thought as much,' Safiyya said. 'So you'll be pleased to know that he phoned me a couple of days ago and said he was fine.'

Nadia almost dropped the phone. 'Are you really in contact with him? God bless you. When do you finish up at Bankstown?'

'In a week; but why do you want to know?'

Nadia bit her lip, unsure what to say. 'I'd like to meet you then. Please, Safiyya.'

'Sure,' she replied, 'but please don't tell Amin.'

Nadia smiled to herself. 'If there's one thing you can be sure of, it's my undertaking not to tell Amin about our discussion. But Safiyya …' Nadia trailed off.

'What?'

'Please don't tell Amin that we are talking, okay?'

'Don't worry,' Safiyya said quietly, 'you have my promise. I think I'm getting the gist of this. I'll call you in a week, and here, take my phone number.'

Nadia scribbled down the number.

'I need to go; I'm being paged,' Safiyya said.

They ended the call, and Nadia collapsed into her chair, Safiyya's words echoing in her mind: *He phoned me a couple of days ago and said he was fine.*

17

Laura hadn't been at work long on Monday morning when the phone rang.

'CultAssist,' Margaret said, then after a pause, 'Yes, Mr Carter. She's flying to Sydney at eleven thirty this morning, but she could squeeze in a short meeting at nine thirty if you can make it ... Okay, we'll see you then.' She gave Laura a thumbs-up.

Albert arrived on time, dressed very casually. 'It's my golf day,' he said as he wandered in, 'but nothing is more important than Emma.'

Laura gestured him to the chair by her desk, and once settled, she asked, 'What have you decided?'

Albert looked directly at Laura. 'I've resigned from Divine Delicacies. Here's a copy of my letter of resignation.' He handed her an envelope. 'It was a very difficult decision, but you left me with no choice. Emma's safety and future is paramount and, quite honestly, I don't want to be referred to another agency. It's clear to me that you know what you're doing and that you have the connections needed to pull this off.'

'You've made the right decision,' Laura said. 'Now we can move forward, but just for interest's sake, Albert, what did you tell the other board members?'

'I said I had to resign for personal reasons, and I was surprised they didn't ask for more details. I expected to be grilled.'

'I expect that was a relief,' Laura said.

'Yes, and there's something else. Before I resigned, I cited the letter you received from them, and got them to shelve the matter indefinitely. The lawyer who wrote the letter is on Sabbatical leave for the next year, anyway, so don't expect to hear from him or the board. That's all I can tell you.'

Laura smiled, relieved. 'Thank you, Albert. I hope you appreciate where we're coming from. Many people depend on us, and we really don't have time to deal with that kind of thing.'

'I understand,' he said. 'So back to the drawing board now. What's the plan?'

'For the last week and a half, we've had two independent people—not CultAssist workers but experts in this area—conducting surveillance on Kira's property. What they're doing is perfectly legal, but it can be tricky at times. We now have a clear map of Kira's house as well as a schedule of Kira's and Emma's movements. Other people visit the house for Kira's meditation and movement programs.

'You need to leave the details up to us, but our plan is to remove Emma from the house, ideally when no one else is present. I prefer not to go into this now—we can do that later—but the principal objective is to take her to a location where our team will be able to work with her. It won't be easy, but it's a feasible plan.'

Albert nodded.

Laura continued, 'It looks like there'll only be a very small window of time when this'll be possible, so we need to be ready, and we're looking at the week after next to do it, either on Monday or Tuesday afternoon, which are the quietest times of the week there. I'll book a venue for the exit counselling for several days.'

Albert nodded. Laura thought he looked impressed, but

then he frowned and said, 'And what if it doesn't work?'

'What do you mean?' Laura asked. 'Which part doesn't work?'

'Oh, any part. The rescue, the transport to the secret location. I mean she could jump out of the car. And then once you get there, she may decide not to participate in any counselling.'

'Well, there are no guarantees, Albert. But we work in a manner that ensures that if we fail, we've not burned our bridges. That means we can always try something else later.'

'Hmm. Okay. Will my wife and I be informed about what's going on? I mean, will you brief us along the way?'

Laura took a deep breath. 'Look, Albert, I can understand your anxiety, but all I can say is that we'll do the best we can. If we get Emma out of the house, we'll let you know. But it's likely that you won't hear from us for a couple of days until we know how the counselling is going.'

'Do we need to be there?' Albert asked.

'I don't know yet. Certainly not at the beginning. It may be necessary to involve you later, but don't worry about that now.' Laura looked at her watch. It was already 10.30 am. 'We'll have to stop now. I have a plane to catch in an hour. Give me a call towards the end of the week, and we can continue this discussion.'

Albert smiled, appearing genuinely appreciative. As he stood, he thanked Laura, saying he'd be in touch.

Laura got up, scooped a folder from her desk and handed it to him. 'Take this; you might want to read it. It's a collection of professional articles about mind control.'

18

Laura and Michael stowed their bags in the overhead lockers, then took their seats for the flight to Sydney.

'Has Amin contacted his family since we last talked?' Michael asked once he'd buckled himself in.

Laura shook her head. 'No change. If Safiyya hadn't looked them up, they'd never had known he was in hospital.'

'So bringing him home for a family meeting isn't an option,' Michael said. 'I figured as much.'

'So what's this plan you've been working on?'

Michael explained his idea, and Laura listened without comment, nodding occasionally.

'Well, what do you think?' he asked when he'd finished.

'It's brilliant,' Laura replied, 'and nothing short of daring.'

'Yeah, I'm a bit nervous about what Amin's parents might feel about the idea, though.'

'It'll work if we can pull it off. I think they'll see that.'

Michael shrugged. 'We shall see.'

Laura glanced out the window, then turned back to Michael. 'And it is urgent. Nadia and Fadi know that another episode in intensive care could be the end of him. But we need to know how committed Safiyya is to helping.'

'Yeah, she's the lynchpin.'

Two hours' later, they walked into one of the conference rooms in a hotel in Redfern. Laura glanced at the clutter of old furniture that filled part of the room. It made it look more like a storage space, but the cosy arrangement of comfortable chairs around a small table at the other end meant the venue was suitable for their purposes. CultAssist had used this room many times before.

Nadia and Fadi arrived on time, and after greetings, Michael began the meeting. He regarded Nadia and Fadi with a quiet intensity, and said, 'As we discussed before, the most difficult aspect of this plan will be pulling Amin away from the influence of the group. He also needs to be away for a reasonable length of time so we can work with him, so I'm going to suggest a plan that may sound quite dramatic. CultAssist has never used a plan like this before, but I'm not sure if we have any other realistic options.' He looked from Nadia to Fadi, his eyes sparkling. 'And I'm pretty sure this will work.'

Nadia's brow creased with worry.

Fadi reached for her hand and held it gently. 'Just listen to what they have to say,' he whispered.

Michael kept his gaze on Fadi. 'It's clear that the only person outside this church who Amin respects is your mother. You told us about his love for his grandmother, and that's one aspect of our plan.'

Fadi frowned, looking puzzled, and glanced at Nadia, who moved restlessly in her seat.

'So I propose,' Michael continued, 'that we get Amin onto a plane to Lebanon, accompanied by two professional exit counsellors, who will sit with him. They'll have thirty-six hours in which to work on him. We'll organise a layover in Singapore or Bangkok, depending on the flight route, and we hope that by the time Amin arrives in Lebanon, his mind will be clearer.'

Fadi shook his head in disbelief. 'Not possible,' he said.

'Amin won't go. And anyway, there are too many risks. Is this your only idea? I don't mean to be disrespectful, but this sounds a little unrealistic.'

Nadia nodded, looking even more worried.

Michael forged on. 'Yes, there are a number of problems we'll need to overcome. We have to extract Amin from his environment, but if he'd like to see his grandmother, then that is possible. We'll also have to make sure he can be accompanied, so the seating arrangement on the aircraft will be vital. But arranging that is also possible.'

Nadia and Fadi glanced at each other, their brows furrowed.

'Safiyya is in contact with Amin,' Laura said. 'And her help will be crucial in getting Amin away from the group's influence. If she comes on board, I'm cautiously confident the plan will be successful.'

'Of course, we need to discuss all this with Safiyya,' Michael said, 'but I need your approval first.'

Nadia shook her head, a perplexed expression on her face. 'I really don't know what to say. In our wildest dreams we wouldn't have considered a plan like this, but do we have a choice?'

Fadi turned towards Nadia. 'But neither did we ever think our son would dump his family for a dangerous cult …'

Nadia gave him a sympathetic smile, then took a deep breath. 'So if this is the plan,' she said, 'is there anything we need to be doing?'

'Not a lot,' Michael replied. 'The next step is for Laura and me to meet Safiyya. You, Nadia, will need to call her and set up a meeting. All you need to say to Safiyya is that two friends of Amin would like to meet her. We'll give you an address and a time. Simply call me to confirm the meeting and it will go ahead. Very much will depend on the meeting. At this stage we have little knowledge of Safiyya's involvement with Amin. We have to be sure that we can trust her. We need to be extremely careful because we don't have many choices, and time is not on our side.'

'Do you have any questions?' Laura asked Nadia.

She shook her head, but Fadi spoke up. 'I have two questions. When do you want to implement this plan? And how much will it cost?'

'Much will depend on the meeting with Safiyya,' Laura said. 'As far as cost is concerned, it could be anything between ten thousand and fifteen thousand dollars, which will include air tickets, accommodation and all the other incidentals involved in helping Amin.'

Fadi nodded, apparently satisfied.

'Our son's freedom is worth any price,' Nadia said.

Laura smiled, acknowledging her wisdom. 'Michael and I are staying in Sydney for the next couple of days, so please try to set up the meeting with Safiyya as soon as possible. The preparation for this mission will take time, and the sooner we start, the better.'

'All right,' Fadi said. He glanced at his wife, and she nodded. He turned back to Michael. 'We approve the plan.'

Michael smiled and dipped his head in acknowledgment.

'I'll call Safiyya now,' Nadia said. 'We don't need to wait.' She stood, took a couple of steps away from the table and dialled her mobile.

No one at the table said a word. They heard the voicemail activate and Nadia say, 'It's Nadia, please call.'

She'd taken only one step back towards the table when her phone rang. 'Safiyya, my dear,' Nadia said after accepting the call, 'I hope I'm not disturbing you. I've been talking to two friends of Amin, and they'd like to meet you. I know I'm imposing on you, but is there any chance you could meet them? ... Yes?

Wonderful … When? Well, they're free today.' She glanced at Laura for confirmation.

Laura nodded. 'How about four thirty this afternoon?'

'At the Redfern Tavern,' Michael added. 'I'll give you the address.' He scrawled an address on a piece of paper and handed it to her while Nadia confirmed the time and place.

'It's a guy and a girl,' Nadia said. 'She'll be wearing a white top, and he's got bushy brown hair. … Okay, thank you. They'll be thrilled. … Yes. We'll stay in touch.'

Fadi looked at Nadia like a proud father watches his daughter. She certainly appeared to have everything under control. When she ended the call, he stood, gave her a hug and cried, his face buried in her hair. Michael and Laura looked away.

When Fadi had composed himself, they sat down again. 'What now?' he asked.

'Leave it to us,' Laura said. 'We'll meet with Safiyya this evening and then call you tomorrow to let you know how it went.'

They ended the meeting, and after Nadia and Fadi had left, Laura checked her phone. She turned it off silent and listened to the two messages that had come in. Margaret had called to say she'd organised the board meeting for the following Monday, and Annabel had left a message saying she needed to talk to Laura about Anne.

'Remember Anne Fletcher?' Laura said to Michael.

He nodded. 'The girl we got away from The Healing Mission?'

'Yeah. Her mum wants me to call. She has an update. And she lives in Sydney. How about I see if she can meet us at the tavern before we meet Safiyya? It won't take long.'

'Sure, we can squeeze her in,' Michael said. 'We just have to make sure she's out of there well before Safiyya's due. Let's move now. I want a coffee.'

'And cake.' Laura grinned.

19

Laura and Michael sat in the rear of the quaint little tavern at a small triangular table, just right for a meeting of three. A waiter asked them if they'd like drinks. Laura ordered a cappuccino, and Michael ordered a flat white, and they shared a slab of chocolate cake. Only one other table was occupied. Perfect.

They'd just received their drinks when Annabel walked into the tavern carrying a yellow polka-dot handbag and wearing a yellow top, purple pants and thick brown sheepskin boots. Laura waved to get her attention, and Annabel caught sight of her and strode towards them with a warm smile.

'It's so good to see you again,' she said as she took a seat at their table. 'Though I wish I had better news. But first …' She dug into her handbag, drew out a box of chocolates and handed them to Laura. 'For both of you. I can't tell you how much it means to me that you've made yourself available to talk with me.'

'We're pleased to help,' Michael said, and after establishing that she didn't want anything to drink, he asked, 'How's Anne doing?'

Tears welled up in Annabel's eyes, and she looked away. 'Anne's rejoined The Healing Mission. I don't even know where to begin. It's such a tragedy. She doesn't talk to me anymore, and she'd never talk to you again. She says you tried to kidnap her. I know it's not true, but apparently, she wants to go legal and even sue you. It's just terrible.' She paused and composed herself.

'Our family is devastated. I don't know if I told you, but I remarried. The marriage only lasted six months. It was a disaster. Anne couldn't stand Maurice, and that's also been part of the problem. She sort of lost faith in me. She became very critical. I'm just so glad you're here. Just seeing you makes me feel better.'

'Tell us what happened after she came home,' Laura asked gently.

Annabel took a deep breath. 'She had a few days of happiness and relief, but she'd been using all sorts of drugs there that people had smuggled inside, and within days, she was just sort of hanging out, aimlessly. I suppose she was going through some sort of withdrawal, but she wasn't well. She tried really hard, but she came home one night and said she couldn't handle life anymore.

'I put her into a proper rehab, and she did well for the first few days. But then she discharged herself and came home. And she wasn't in a good way. And then one day we were in the city doing some shopping, and she suddenly disappeared. I assume she saw someone from The Healing Mission who talked her into returning. I was beside myself and thought seriously about calling the police.'

Annabel sighed. 'Then that evening she called me. She was very subdued and sounded like she'd been crying. She said, "Mum, I need to tell you that I'm back at The Healing Mission, and I'll be here for a few days." Before I could talk to her, the phone went dead.' Annabel shook her head, pain etched on her face. 'It was awful, and that was three months ago. Since then I've received only one text message from her, saying she'll be home soon. I have messaged her so many times, but she doesn't respond. When I call the mission, they always say she's busy and doing well. If I become critical or raise my voice, they just hang up.'

She looked into Laura's eyes, and her voice took on a pleading tone. 'Is there anything we can do? Anything? I realise we can't go much further now, but I pray Anne will be okay. I just don't have a good feeling about her, and I feel so helpless.' Annabel sniffed back tears.

Laura swallowed, her heart breaking for another mother separated from her daughter against her will.

Michael leaned forward and said, 'We don't give up, Annabel, and you shouldn't give up either. If you have the time and the energy, let's regroup and revisit our options. Sometimes a second intervention is more difficult, sometimes not. One problem is that by now Anne will have become some sort of a hero, and she'll be lapping that up. The Healing Mission will assume that you'll try again to get her out, and they'll be holding onto her tightly.'

'What do you mean, "some sort of hero"?' Annabel asked.

'They'll make a big thing about her returning,' Michael explained. 'They'll hold her up as a shining example of someone who returned because she saw the importance of their teachings and community.'

Annabel's eyes narrowed. 'That's so devious.'

Michael nodded. 'It's a common cult tactic. They'll also make sure we're seen as an enemy of the truth.'

'I'll review the earlier files,' Laura said, 'and try to organise a meeting in the next week. There are still things we can do, and we'll work together. And here—' She reached into her bag, retrieved a small booklet and held it out. 'Margaret put this together. It's a selection of the best advice we have for parents in your situation.'

Annabel took it and managed a small smile of gratitude. 'Thanks, guys, you call me any time. If I need to travel to see you, just let me know. I'll be in touch in the next few days.' She stood, shouldered her garish bag and left.

Laura turned to Michael. 'I don't feel good about Anne.'

'Why?'

Laura shrugged. 'Instinct, I guess.'

Laura watched Annabel walk out. At the door, she bumped into an attractive young woman and dropped the booklet. The woman picked it up for her. Laura frowned. 'I hope that's not Safiyya.'

'What? Why?' Michael turned towards the door.

'She saw the booklet I gave Annabel.'

'The one with CultAssist written on the cover in large letters?' Michael said.

The young woman looked around, spotted them and walked towards them.

Laura groaned. 'I hope we haven't just blown our cover.'

20

'**S**he might not have seen Annabel with us,' Michael said as the woman they assumed was Safiyya picked her way through the tables towards them. 'Let's stick to the plan and play it safe until we know the extent of her connection with Amin.'

Laura could guess at one reason Amin would be interested in the woman. She was stunning—strong features on an olive-skinned face crowned with flowing black hair. Her modest but stylish clothes added to an overall striking presence.

The woman walked over to Laura and offered her hand. 'Hi, I'm Safiyya.'

Laura and Michael stood and shook her hand in turn. 'Welcome, Safiyya,' Laura said. 'I'm Laura, and this is my friend Michael.'

Once they'd settled and Safiyya had ordered a juice, Laura began. 'So we're friends of Amin, or perhaps we should say we used to be his friends. Since he joined this church of his, we don't see him. His mum, Nadia, is convinced he's in some sort of a cult. She said you met him at Bankstown Hospital and struck up a friendship with him. She even said you're still in contact.' Laura paused. 'Is it okay if we tell you all this?'

Safiyya spoke softly but clearly. 'That's correct. But I don't know if he is in a cult—in fact I don't know anything about cults—but he is very serious about his spirituality. I was on duty in intensive care when they brought him in, delirious, dehydrated and at significant risk. He was on a drip for several days and we recommended he stay longer, but he said his church needed him, so he discharged himself. Essentially, he had recovered, so there was nothing we could do to hold him in the hospital.'

The conversation paused while the waiter served Safiyya's drink.

'What about you and Amin?' Michael asked after Safiyya had taken a sip of her juice. 'I hope you don't mind me asking, but you said that you're still in contact with him.'

'No, that's fine.' Safiyya gave Michael a reassuring smile. 'You can ask me whatever you want.' She took another sip, and then said, 'Amin is an amazing person. His mum, bless her soul, thinks he has been brainwashed by this church, which she calls a cult. I don't know. I take things on their face value.' Laura glanced at Michael while Safiyya continued, 'We developed some sort of a connection. It's hard to describe, but I felt a certain respect for him and his commitment. I daresay his connection with me looked more like that of a guy wanting female company, and I don't think the church allows any contact between males and females. I made it very clear to him that I was happy to remain a friend but only after I finished up at Bankstown. I take great pride in my work and believe very strongly in professional boundaries. Now he calls me from time to time just to chat.'

'Can you call him?' Laura asked.

Safiyya shook her head. 'He says I can't call him because I'll disturb his studies. So I don't, but we do talk once, sometimes twice, a week.'

'Do you think he'd like you to join his church?'

Safiyya threw her head back and laughed. 'I think he'd be delighted for me to join his church, but I never will. I'm a Muslim, though I don't practice the faith. Amin's a Christian from a very strong Christian family, so what he's doing makes sense to him. I could never be part of his church.'

'Do you think his church is healthy for him?' Michael asked.

Safiyya frowned and looked from one to the other. 'Isn't that his business?'

'Only if he's not under some form of mind control,' Michael said.

She opened her mouth, paused for a moment, then said, 'Excuse me, I need to go to the ladies'.' She stood and headed towards the back of the room.

Michael and Laura stared at each other. Michael exhaled loudly. 'I'm not sure what to say, Laura. She isn't sure about him being in a cult, and I don't know if their relationship is something we can work with, anyway. Of course he likes her. Take one look at her.' He shook his head. 'I'm not comfortable with this.'

'Don't give up yet,' Laura said. 'We need to help her see that the church is why he's ending up in hospital nearly starved to death.'

'I don't know how far we'll get with that. The ladies' visit felt like a ploy to get away.'

'Maybe she just felt pressured. All we can do is see if we can bring her around to understanding what's really going on. Then we can see if she's prepared to help.'

'It seems like a long shot right now.' Michael glanced towards the restrooms. 'She might not even come back. Oh heck!'

'Let's order another drink,' Laura suggested.

The waiter had just left when Safiyya returned. 'Okay, guys,' she said as soon as she sat, 'can we cut to the chase? I know about CultAssist and your roles in it. It's all on the website, after all.'

'What?' Laura said at the same time as Michael said, 'How?'

Safiyya chuckled. 'Though you'd probably get a B grade for

acting, it wasn't that. I actually arrived early and saw you with that other woman. She looked so distraught, it made me curious, so I purposely bumped into her, hoping to see what you'd given her, and I did. I caught the name. I would have checked it out before coming over, but I noticed you'd seen me, so I figured I'd see what happened first.'

'So the ladies' visit was a ruse,' Michael said. 'I knew it.'

'Well, we're even now, don't you think?'

'Fair point. Sorry. It's just—'

'Wait,' Safiyya interrupted, 'there's more. It's not what I said before. I'm no friend of Amin. I mean, we do talk each week, and he tells me what he's doing, and I agree, he's in a cult, a dangerous cult. I know you're the experts, and I'm just a nurse trying to do the right thing, but I actually think it's heaps worse than you could imagine.'

Laura glanced at Michael, sharing both her relief and surprise.

'I don't think he'll survive,' Safiyya continued. 'From a medical position, one or two more admissions and he's gone. It's as simple as that. He was out of there before we had a chance to run a whole lot of tests, but the results wouldn't have been pretty. The only reason I'm staying in touch with him is because maybe I can help get him out of there. I risked my position as a nurse a few times while he was in emergency, which wasn't very wise. The truth is Amin is infatuated with me. I could tell you more, but treating him was a nightmare. Often I just wanted to hand him over to another staff member. Even now when he calls me, he says things that aren't right, and he has a photo of me in his phone, which freaks me out. I'm scared one of the cult leaders will find it. I'm scared for him, but for me too. He says the photo's hidden, but I'm not sure what he means by that. And he dreams about me. Oh God, I shudder to think. It's like I'm being abused, sort of violated.'

Laura realised that her mouth was hanging open. She shut it firmly, her gaze never leaving Safiyya, as the woman continued with her story.

'But I think about him as well. Stuck in that hellhole, deprived of female company, forever praying, studying or fasting. It's just awful. And you know what? He's actually a nice guy. He has a heart, a soft nature. I can see he's had a solid upbringing. And I know how devastated his mum is. She also sounds like a darling. Apparently, he has a grandmother he misses terribly. So he's still human, but I do wonder for how long?'

'Oh Safiyya,' Laura said, 'thank you so much for sharing all that. I can see it's a difficult situation for you too.'

'Yes, I'm sorry. I didn't mean to lead you on before, but I needed to feel comfortable with you guys before I could talk with you. That little break I took helped me gather my thoughts, but believe me, Amin needs help. And I'll do whatever I can to get him out of there. I need to work, to earn money, but if there's something I can do with you to get him out of that cult, I'll defer my employment. In the meantime, I'll stay in touch with him if that's what it takes.'

Laura felt so moved that tears pricked her eyes. 'You're an angel, and I can't thank you enough for being here and being willing to help. I'm inspired by what you've said and the way you portrayed Amin's situation. You've also pointed out the urgency.'

'We have a plan to get him away from the cult's influence,' Michael said, 'but it's very ambitious. We need to discuss it carefully and fully, and that will take time.'

'Okay. Just let me know when you want to go through it, and I'll be there,' Safiyya said quietly.

Michael smiled. 'How about this evening? Over dinner.'

Safiyya shrugged. 'Sure, I can do that. When and where?'

After Michael rang to check they had a table free, they agreed on Beaches' Dream in Bondi at 8.00 pm.

Safiyya left the tavern, leaving Laura feeling reinvigorated, her hope for Amin's rescue renewed, and Michael's grin indicated that he felt the same. But was it all too good to be true? Would Safiyya be willing to fly to Lebanon, and if so, would she be able to get Amin onto a plane? Even assuming it was possible, was it asking too much?

Michael's smile suddenly fled.

'What is it?' Laura asked, though she was pretty sure she knew.

He turned towards her. 'Is she really who she says she is? Is she being honest, or does she have some other agenda? Are we about to fall into a huge trap?'

Laura sighed. 'Sometimes you've just got to trust your instincts. I know we've done that before and we've been wrong, but I feel she's on the level. And if this falls through, what else have we got? Zilch. So let's move forward. We have little choice anyway.'

'Yeah, you're right.'

'I'll call Nadia to say we'll meet her tomorrow. By then we should know where we stand with Safiyya. Let's get out of here.'

21

Laura lay resting on her bed in her hotel room when Gary called. 'Our boys have been on the scene,' he told her, 'and we've got a good picture of Emma's movements, but they have reason to believe that Kira's about to take off to another location, and if that happens we'll have some problems, so I strongly suggest we move quickly. There is one significant issue, which, quite frankly, I didn't anticipate, and that's a wire fence around the entire property. I'd seen it on some of our photographs, but it didn't appear to cover the whole of the perimeter. I now see that it does. The only good news is that it's not that high. We can climb over it, but it'll still make getting Emma out difficult. If we're doing this, the best time to move will be Tuesday between 5.00 and 6.00 pm when there are very few other people, if any, in the house.'

'Okay,' Laura said. 'By the way, I'm in Sydney at the moment.'

'Great. Let's meet. Where are you this evening?'

'No good. We're in the middle of a major case, and it's moving well. We can't leave this midstream, but can we meet tomorrow morning?'

'Fine, but I'm on duty at 8.00 am, so it'll have to be at 7.00 am. Sorry it's so early.'

'No worries; we're both early risers anyway.'

'Great. How about King's Castle in Kings Cross? It's across

the road from the railway station. Funky little place. Don't know why they call it a castle.'

'You're on, and thanks a million,' Laura said. 'We'll be there.'

~

Laura looked around Beaches' Dream and smiled. Large windows displayed an expansive view of Bondi Beach, and the décor picked up the theme with a cream and pale-blue palette, shell-and-rope wall hangings and paintings of beach scenes. In the far corner of the large room, a pianist played background music on a grand piano, and a large fireplace crackled with warmth.

They took a table at the back of the restaurant and had just started perusing the menu when Safiyya joined them. She sat next to Laura, opposite Michael, looked around the restaurant and laughed. 'A little different from the Redfern Tavern. Nice!' Then she got straight down to business. 'I spoke to Amin an hour ago. He called to tell me that he'd written me a letter. He was very quiet; I could hardly hear him. He said that he wasn't allowed to send letters without them being approved by the church elders. But he couldn't show this letter to them because he was writing to a woman.'

Safiyya shook her head, apparently amazed at this letter-writing restriction, but that kind of behaviour was all too familiar to Laura and Michael.

Safiyya sighed. 'The cult stuff really freaks me out; I mean, he's not meant to be writing to anyone, let alone a woman, so he has to be careful not to get caught, but I am curious about the letter. He's sending it to a postbox at the hospital, but I can still access it.'

Michael nodded. 'Our plan for Amin is very ambitious. We've done lots of wild things in the past, but this is different.

We need to get him not just out of the church but also out of the country because we need time with him, time when we can be sure he can't go back, or to put it bluntly, escape. Were that to happen, we'd probably lose him for good. He'll be transferred to another location, possibly interstate or even overseas. It's happened before.'

A young waiter, probably a student, approached the table and asked Laura if anyone wanted a drink. Laura and Michael declined, happy with the water already on the table. Safiyya ordered a lemonade with ice.

Michael continued, 'Plan A is we book Amin onto a flight to Lebanon, where his grandmother lives. He won't be travelling alone. He'll be seated between two exit counsellors, who will have at least twenty-four hours to work with him. We'll probably organise a one-day layover in Bangkok or Hong Kong to further maximise our time with him.'

Safiyya's eyes widened. 'Sounds very gutsy. But how do you expect to get him out of his church?'

'It won't be easy,' Laura said, 'but we know that the one person he still loves is his grandmother. If he believed she was unwell, we think there's a chance he would want to see her. More importantly, we also know that she is a very wealthy woman. If the church knew that a significant inheritance may be coming their way, they would, hopefully, cooperate. That's the nuts and bolts of the plan. There's more to it, and we'll need to talk further about it.'

The waiter returned with Safiyya's lemonade. 'Are you ready to order?' he asked, looking from one to the other.

'Give us a couple of minutes,' Michael said.

The waiter retreated and the threesome scanned their menus, placing them down when they'd chosen their dishes.

After they'd placed their orders, Michael said, 'The main

obstacle will be our ability to communicate all this to Amin. We have no connection with him. His parents can't speak to him, and even if we get him onto a plane, we've got to make sure there are no last-minute seating changes. We don't want to find our counsellors sitting ten rows away from him, or even one row for that matter. The plan would fall apart very quickly.'

Safiyya sipped her drink, then sat back, crossed her legs and smiled. 'Is that where I come into it?'

'It is, but only if you're comfortable with the plan,' Laura said.

She nodded. 'That's Plan A. What's Plan B? Wait, I know … I travel with him. If I offer to fly to Lebanon with him, he won't say no. Is that it?'

Laura chuckled. 'You're spot on. But it's a big ask, so please don't feel obligated. But it won't be just you. I mean, Amin will think it's just you, but we'll have an exit counsellor by his side. We'll plan it out like a movie script.'

'It sounds like a movie already,' Safiyya quipped. 'Of course, I need to think this through, but I won't keep you hanging. In the meantime, there's a letter on its way that may shed some light on where Amin's at.'

'Will you let us see it?' Michael asked.

'Of course. And listen, guys, I'll give you an answer by the end of the week. There's heaps to think about, but I must admit that it sounds quite exciting.'

Their meals arrived, and while they ate, they relaxed and talked of other things, just getting to know each other.

'We've gotta get moving,' Michael said when they'd finished eating. 'Call us when you get the letter. We'll probably be back in Brisbane, but if we need to meet again, we will. And at some point, we've got to bring Fadi and Nadia into this. They know we're working hard, and they're aware of our general plan, of Plan A, but we'll need to let them know the details once we've sorted it all out.'

They stood and Laura gave a Safiyya a gentle hug. 'Thanks. We appreciate this, Safiyya.'

'Don't mention it. It's not often that I'm in a position to save a life like this. I'm used to working in hospitals, not in aeroplanes!'

As they left, the pianist played a melodious version of Gloria Gaynor's 'I Will Survive'. It seemed eerily relevant to Amin's situation.

'I've had it,' Laura said to Michael when they stepped outside into a cool spring evening. 'What a day.' She took a deep breath of the sea air. 'But you know what? We're on a winner. One day Amin will thank his lucky stars that he was admitted to Bankstown and that the nurse assigned to him was a young, attractive and idealistic woman called Safiyya.'

22

Laura dashed across the street through pouring rain, cursing her lack of an umbrella. She brushed herself off and entered King's Castle, an intimate café with rustic wood furniture and counter, and photos of famous customers all over the red-painted walls. Gary was already there, sitting in a booth facing the door, a coffee cup and a half-eaten plate of bacon and eggs before him. A manilla folder sat on the table beside the food. Laura ordered a sandwich, cappuccino, a croissant and joined him.

'Sounds like you're busy,' Gary said.

'Frantic is a better word,' Laura said. 'But we're doing some amazing work. It's hard, it's risky, and it's tricky. But it's good stuff. We're about to exit a cult member mid-flight between here and the Middle East. That has to be a first for any cult agency. Spent most of yesterday on it.'

'That does sound tricky,' Gary said between mouthfuls.

'I think it will happen, though. It's coming together nicely, but getting back to Emma, what do you think? Can we get her out?'

Gary shrugged. 'I don't know. I'm doubtful.' He pushed the folder towards her and finished his breakfast while Laura looked at the photos it contained. The wire fence around the property was quite visible. 'That front gate is kept locked.'

Laura grimaced, her heart sinking. 'Doesn't look good.'

Gary took a sip of his coffee, then said, 'The other option is to try to grab her when she's out of the house and away from the property, but the problem is that she appears to venture out very infrequently, so I still think the better choice is that we jump the fence and convince her to leave the property. Hopefully, the gate will open from the inside. We'll check that out. Otherwise, we climb over the fence, then while we're there, we can have someone pry open the gate so we can exit very quickly, but it's more complicated than I would like it to be.'

Laura frowned. Albert was expecting a clean result. Had she been too positive about the possibility of a successful mission? Regardless, there was no turning back now. They needed to try.

But Gary seemed undeterred, even by his own pessimistic assessment of the situation. 'Emma's definitely there late on Tuesday afternoons and usually on her own. I've got two guys ready to do the work. They walk in, explain that the police need to re-interview her regarding the statement, show her some sort of supporting document and lead her to the car without giving her time to think or ask questions.'

'Okay. That could work.'

A waitress delivered Laura's order, and she sipped her coffee while Gary continued, 'And your people need to be ready to receive her. Of course, once we get her out to you, she'll realise there are no police and no need to be re-interviewed, but I leave that with you to work out. It could be tough, but I'm sure you know your business.'

Laura nodded. That would mark the beginning of two to three days of intensive exit counselling 'That's fine. How's next Tuesday afternoon?'

'No problem. We shouldn't require more than ten minutes to do it, and hopefully we'll have sorted out the gate problem, but we should have Emma in our car within minutes of our team going in. As soon as she's in the car, one of my guys will text you, then we'll drive up, deliver her to you and we'll be gone. Make sure you find a reasonably isolated location. You don't have to worry about us. We'll get to you wherever you are.' Gary finished the last of his coffee with a big gulp.

'Sounds good.'

'What do you think your chances are of holding her?' he asked. 'I mean, if you make it through, and she walks away from Kira, you're fine, but if you don't succeed, and she gets away and returns to Kira, you won't be looking good if she decides to sue you. You could be facing a kidnapping charge and who knows what else?'

Laura put down her cup. Gary's question was one that passed through her mind every time CultAssist attempted an intervention. She didn't want to sound overconfident, but she knew what she was dealing with. And reassured by Gary's plan—he'd obviously spent a considerable amount of time on it—some optimism had returned to her assessment of the situation. Gary wouldn't be taking this on without a better-than-even chance of success. 'We'll be fine. We know the boundaries and the rules of the game. I think it's looking good.'

'Right. We'll do this, then.'

'We still have to discuss your fee,' she said.

He shook his head. 'There's no fee, Laura. As far as my guys are concerned, you can shout them a few drinks after it's all over. There aren't many people doing the work you're doing. The authorities are hopeless, and then you got the bloody civil libertarians who still believe it would've been wrong to deny Jim Jones freedom of belief and religion, and you know what happened there. Just keep up the good work.'

A few hours later, Laura and Michael boarded their flight back to Brisbane. They found their seats, and Laura leaned back, exhausted. She glanced at Michael. He already had his eyes closed. She'd managed to call Nadia to give her a brief update on their successful meeting with Safiyya. If Safiyya agreed to be involved, they'd meet the following week, probably on Friday or Saturday, either in Sydney or Brisbane, depending on Safiyya.

Once they were airborne and had taken a power nap, Laura reached into her shoulder bag and took out the photos of Kira's property. 'Look at this, Michael.'

He opened his eyes, took the folder and flipped through the photos.

'It's scary,' Laura said. 'The poor woman is basically a prisoner.'

Michael nodded. 'That's certainly what it looks like.'

'I must admit,' Laura said, 'I can't wait to meet Emma. I have heaps of questions about her story, and I think we're in for a very interesting time. Let's just hope we get her out of there.'

23

Rochelle looked around the waiting room—modern furniture, and a grey and white colour scheme. She picked up a leaflet from the coffee table.

We specialise in all matrimonial issues, including residency and visitation …

'He shouldn't be more than a few moments now,' the secretary said from behind her desk.

Rochelle nodded. She'd never needed a lawyer before. 'I don't know if I can do this,' she whispered to herself.

'Rochelle?'

She looked up. A man in his mid-thirties with shoulder-length, curly black hair stood in a doorway smiling at her. His pointy shoes and jeans made him seem like someone out of the '60s, a stark contrast to the conservative appearance of the other staff and secretaries who darted in and out of the offices adjoining the reception area.

'Yes, that's me.' She stood and shook the hand he offered.

'My name is Andrew Holden, and I'll be seeing you today. Please come in.'

She walked into a boardroom, and he closed the door behind her. A long mahogany table able to seat at least twenty people occupied most of the room, and at thirty-four stories up, the huge windows gave a magnificent view of the Sydney skyline. 'Any particular place where you'd like me to sit?' she asked, taking in her surroundings while trying to hide her anxiety.

'No, anywhere is fine,' Andrew replied. 'Thank you for the email and the documents you posted. I think I understand your predicament. I'm glad you're in touch with CultAssist. We've worked with them before.'

'Oh, that's good.' She thought Andrew was good as well. He had a softness about him and already looked concerned, as if he really wanted to help her. She relaxed, relieved that he had some familiarity with the cult scene.

'Now let me tell you a few basic facts about this kind of thing, and then I'd like to offer you some practical advice.'

'Okay.'

'The only way you're going to protect Penny from the influence of Graham's yoga school will be via an application to the Family Court. We'll need to demonstrate that any association with the yoga school will be detrimental to Penny's health and wellbeing. That's not an easy task, but it is doable. We'll probably have to ask the judge to commission an Expert Witness report to support your argument. Hopefully, CultAssist will assist in this regard.'

Rochelle stood, unable to sit still for a moment longer. She walked around the room, shaking her head. 'I can't deal with this, Andrew,' she said. 'It's too much.' She stared out the window and watched the mums and dads, office workers and shoppers go about their business thirty-four floors below. 'They don't have to deal with this, so why should I have it on my head?'

'I'm sorry,' he said. 'I can't answer that.'

She sighed. 'I know.' She drew another chair out from underneath the table and slumped onto the seat. 'How long will it take?'

'It can take months, especially if we need that report. But we can lodge an urgent application and hopefully have the matter heard within a few days. If all goes well, the judge will issue orders that will protect Penny.'

'Okay. What do I need to do?'

'Well, there's lots of paperwork that needs to be filled out. My assistant, Chloe, will call you in the next few days to brief you on all of this. But it won't be a problem, and we'll get this moving as quickly as possible.' He leaned forward, looked Rochelle in the eyes, and said, 'I've seen this too many times. You've got to be on your toes. Don't be surprised if he tries to get Penny away, even out of the country.'

'But she has no passport.'

He shook his head. 'Don't rely on that. Until we get those orders, you've got to keep an eye on him and Penny. Unfortunately, you can't deny him contact with her—that's his right—but you can try to stop Penny sleeping over. Take my mobile number. If there's anything you notice that makes you feel uneasy, call me. I mean that seriously. I'm not trying to scare you; I just want to warn you. Cults are powerful. They mess with your mind. Parents, loving parents, have done bizarre things believing it's in their children's interests.'

Rochelle knew he was just being honest. She tried to appear calm but she was shaking inside. 'Thank you, Andrew,' she said as he stood, signalling the end of their meeting. 'At last I feel we're getting somewhere. Please tell Chloe I'll be available whenever she wants to meet with me.'

She walked out of the building into a warm late-Friday afternoon. Graham would have picked up Penny from school by now, and in light of what Andrew had said, the thought of that didn't sit well with her. To top it off, she had to rush home and get changed for her mother's sixtieth birthday party, which was starting in an hour.

She parked on the road outside her apartment and, on her way inside, emptied the mailbox: just a magazine, a couple of bills and some junk mail—a letter from an Indian travel agency.

Once inside, she threw the mail on the entrance table next to the phone, then checked her watch. She had half an hour left to get ready, and her mother would expect a dress. She raced into her bedroom, in no mood for a family party, and after a quick shower, threw on the first dress she saw in the wardrobe. A quick brush of her hair later, she opened the bathroom cabinet and stared at her makeup, all neatly arranged on the shelves. Nah. She'd give it a miss. Comfortable shoes won out over pretty ones, and she didn't bother to change her handbag.

On her way to the door, she noticed the answering machine flashing. It hadn't been on when she'd walked in. It must've come in while she'd been in the shower. She pressed the 'play' button.

'This is a message for Ms Lightwood. Please call the Branson Clinic on Monday morning regarding an irregularity with the name on your Medicare card.' Rochelle frowned and listened to the message again. *Strange.* She called the clinic, but it was closed until Monday morning.

She pulled out Andrew's number and called him. 'Sorry to do this to you, but you said I could call. Can I share a message I just received a few moments ago?'

'Sure, go right ahead.'

She replayed the message for Andrew. He remained silent for a while, then said, 'Rochelle, I don't want you to panic, but I don't like this at all. What I'm about to say may be totally off the mark, but if I were you, I'd have someone at the airport checking departures for India over the next couple of days while Graham has Penny.'

'What?' In a flash Rochelle understood what novelists meant when they said someone's heart jumped into their throat. 'What do you mean?'

'Okay, here it is. And as I said, I might be completely wrong, but Graham might have had Penny's name changed by deed poll, then had some reason to process a Medicare claim. Medicare has recognised a discrepancy between her real name, Penny, and the new name, which is now on their system, and they've called you for clarification.'

Rochelle tried to digest the seriousness of her plight. 'She had a cult name. He could have changed it to that. Ugh. I'm so furious, I could kill him.'

'And it might be more than that,' Andrew added. 'He may have applied for a passport under her new name and may already have it. If that's the case, and I hope I'm completely wrong, he could be one step away from a trip to see his guru in India *with Penny*. And that would be bad news.'

'India? Yes. Oh my God. Hold on a second.' She reached for the mail. 'There's a letter here to Graham from an Indian travel agency offering cheap travel packages.'

'Oh dear. Another piece of unwelcome information, but I'm glad you noticed it. I just hope I'm on the wrong track.'

Rochelle was silent for a moment, 'Do I call the police?'

'You can try that, but don't assume you'll get anywhere. If he's carrying a valid passport, regardless of the means by which he procured it, their powers are limited.'

'What the hell do I do, then?' She had to do something. *Maybe go over to his place and strangle him right now!*

'Want my advice? Get a couple of people to the airport by tomorrow. All the flights to India depart in the morning. What have you got to lose? But be prepared to grab Penny if she's there. And if she's not there tomorrow, do the same on Sunday, and keep doing it until Graham brings her back, assuming he will.'

Her mobile phone rang. 'Hang on, Andrew, I have a call on my mobile. It might be Graham.'

But it was her sister. 'Where are you, Rochelle? We want to start Mum's party.' Rochelle pressed the button to end the call, but it rang again. 'Sorry about that,' she said. 'I'm coming down with something. I'll do my best to drop in, but please start without me.'

She ended the call and returned to the landline. 'Andrew, you still there?'

'Yes, Rochelle. Listen, don't take any chances. You might want to call CultAssist. They've seen this before. But if I were you, I'd have someone out there tomorrow. You'll probably want to be there too.'

'I'll be there,' she said in a voice iced with determination. 'Thank you so much. You're a life saver. I'll keep you posted.'

Rochelle ran into Penny's room and looked around. Her school backpack, the one with the little wheels underneath, wasn't in its usual place, causing another leap of her heart. She checked the drawers and wardrobe and found clothes missing. 'Argh!' She collapsed on Penny's bed and called Graham's mobile. No answer.

A growl emerged from deep in her throat. No one was going to take her little girl from her!

She raced outside, hopped into her car and drove, hands shaking. Within minutes she stood outside Graham's apartment, pounding on the door. 'Penny, Penny, let me in.'

No sound. Nobody was home. Rochelle returned to her car and realised she was hyperventilating. Her anxiety was working against her, and she needed to be as clear-minded as possible. If she wasn't careful, she might pass out. She took a deep breath and breathed out slowly, then again and again. Eventually, she calmed down, and the steely resolve returned.

CultAssist had a crisis line. Rochelle pulled out her phone and dialled.

To her surprise, Laura was on duty. 'Rochelle, what's wrong?'

'I'm so sorry, Laura; I know it's Friday night, but believe me I wouldn't be calling you if this wasn't an emergency.'

'Oh, darling,' Laura said, 'tell me all about it.'

Rochelle told Laura that she'd gone to a solicitor, Andrew Holden, who'd confirmed Laura's summary of her legal options. 'Andrew was great,' she said. 'He gave me his mobile phone number. I had no idea I'd be using it so soon, though. And that call from the clinic about the Medicare problem? You know, if I'd got out of that shower a minute earlier and had already left, I would've known nothing. It was that call that got me talking to Andrew.'

'Be thankful for small mercies, yes?' Laura said.

'Yeah, and that letter from the travel agency. If Graham had remembered to tell them his new address, I'd never have seen it. I'd thought nothing of it until Andrew's warning. But the missing backpack, Laura, and the clothes … I'd like to believe this is all one bad dream, but I have a very strange feeling about it all. I need someone to come with me to the airport, but I'm a bit out of my depth with all this. Can you help?'

'It certainly looks like Penny's at risk of being taken out of the country. Can you call back in an hour? I have resources in the office I'll need for this.'

24

Laura switched on the lights, turned on her computer and, while it booted, pulled a folder of airline schedules and brochures from the filing cabinet. She found the airline schedules for India and checked each airline. She'd just finished putting the pertinent information into an email to Keith when the phone rang.

'Hi, Rochelle,' Laura said. 'Don't worry, okay? I'm on this already. I have people in Sydney who can help you.'

'How many other people has this happened to?' Rochelle asked in a small, scared voice.

'Too many, but let's focus on this one. There's a Cathay flight out of Sydney at 10.20 am, a Qantas flight at 11.30 am and Air India sometimes has a flight leaving at 11.45. Since passengers on international flights are asked to arrive two hours earlier, we need to have Graham and Penny covered at the airport from about 8.00 am.'

'This is all too much. I can't believe it's happening.'

'It's hard, I know, but try to remain calm,' Laura said. 'We've handled this kind of thing before, and it just needs careful planning … and good timing.'

Rochelle groaned.

Laura ignored it. Laying out a plan was not only necessary, but it would also best help calm Rochelle's overwhelm. 'If

Graham is trying to get Penny out of the country, we'll need to stop him before he gets into the customs area,' she said. 'Once he and Penny are through those departure doors and into the immigration and passport-control area, they'll be out of sight and, for all intents and purposes, out of reach. But we'll grab Penny well before then.'

Rochelle took a huge noisy breath and exhaled loudly.

'Take a walk and breathe deep,' Laura continued. 'I need to speak to a couple of guys and see if they're available for covering Sydney airport in the morning. I realise we don't have much time, but I'll move as quickly as possible. I'll call you back when I have it all arranged.'

'Can I help at all?'

'Not at the moment. I'll make this as fast as possible.'

Laura ended the call, then picked up the phone and called Keith. She told him Rochelle's story and discovered he was available and willing to help. They covered a few details, then she called Rob and repeated the process, then scanned the photos of Penny and Graham that Rochelle had given her and emailed them to both men, along with Rochelle's address and contact details.

'I'll call Keith, and we'll sort out the details together,' he said after agreeing to help. 'Don't worry, Laura, we've got this. I'll call you back after we've talked.'

What a relief. Laura smiled as she replaced the receiver on its cradle. She had such a great team of volunteers. People whose lives had been impacted by cults understood what it was like and tended to be willing to help others.

She called Rochelle back.

'Oh, God, Laura, I'm going out of my mind here,' she said.

'It's okay,' Laura reassured her in her most soothing voice. 'I've spoken to two great guys who know Sydney airport well.

Their names are Keith and Rob, and they've done this kind of thing before. When it's all over, they'll probably tell you a few stories. Anyway, we have a plan. If Andrew's hunch is correct and Graham's trying to abduct Penny, you'll need to be there. They'll go through the plan in detail with you, and it's absolutely essential that you follow their instructions *and* that you keep calm. Although Keith and Rob will play the primary roles, you're an integral part of the plan. They're meeting right now to review their options for tomorrow morning, and one of them will phone you when they've got it sorted.'

'Oh thank God. No. Thank you, and them.'

Laura felt heat rising in her face. 'We usually take far more time to plan this sort of work. An eight-hour turnaround is highly unusual, but we can do it. We are doing it.'

'Sounds like a James Bond movie, but it's about my baby … I'll do anything. Just tell me what.' Rochelle sounded like she was trying to hold back tears.

Poor woman. Losing a daughter hit too close to home for Laura.

'I've emailed Keith and Rob the best photo of Graham and Penny, so they'll know who they're looking for. They'll tell you where you need to stand in the airport concourse. They're cool guys, and they'll be in control. I suggest you meet them at 7.00 am and drive to the airport together. Do you have any idea what Penny might be wearing?'

Silence.

Laura's heart went out to her. Rochelle was probably imagining her daughter being dragged through the airport. Laura had imagined that many times, starring her Indian lover and their two-year-old daughter.

'Oh sorry, Laura, you asked about Penny's clothes. The chances are she'll be wheeling her yellow backpack. That's the one missing from her room.'

'And talking about clothes,' Laura interjected, 'you need to wear dull colours, nothing that will make you stand out or attract attention.'

Rochelle reflected. 'The way I'm feeling, I think I should be wearing black, but I suppose that's hardly the issue right now.'

Laura frowned. 'Are you okay?'

'I am, Laura. Don't worry. I'm impressed by your support, but I'm also scared. I'm just an average mum with a very special little child. Never in my wildest dreams would I have imagined that my husband would join a cult and threaten to abduct our daughter. I wonder what she's doing right now. Do you think she knows what might be happening?'

Laura shook her head. 'Chances are she doesn't know. Graham will just take her to the airport. She may not even realise it's an airport. He might tell her it's a new train station or something. Experience tells me that he'll hope she won't realise it's an aeroplane until she's on it.'

'Oh God. My poor little girl.'

'Get a few hours' rest, Rochelle. Drink lots of water. You need to be as together as you can for this. But you'll be fine. And so will Penny. I'll have my phone on, and here's Keith's mobile number.' She gave him the number, then continued, 'He'll ring you to confirm, but be ready at 7.00 am. They'll pick you up and run through all the details again.'

'Okay, thanks. I will.'

Laura ended the call and slumped back in her chair. She hoped she'd sleep tonight. *Worrying won't help*, she reminded herself. *And Keith and Rob know what they're doing. It's not their first rodeo. Leave it to them.*

25

Emma screamed.

And woke herself up.

Another nightmare. Her father attacking her. Again.

But the only place he'd ever attacked her had been in that stupid statement she'd made to the police. A complete fiction. Not a word of it was true.

She'd hardly slept since her visit to the police station, and anxiety continuously gnawed at her. She'd lied. That was wrong, and she feared repercussions. Not from Kira, though. Kira had wanted her to do it, had convinced her it was for the greater good, a noble task—together they would create a new world, she'd said. And Emma had written it all following Kira's instructions. Up until that day, life with Kira had been good, fulfilling, and she'd counted herself lucky to be one of Kira's disciples.

But then the nightmares had started. Vivid scenes involving her parents. She dreamed about her mother, Natalie, even though Emma had only very vague memories of her. The worst one was seeing her father being arrested for the crimes she'd made up and her being hauled into court where she had to back up her statement in front of her father. The look of anguish and pain on his face as he was forced to take the stand shredded her heart into bloodied pieces—in the dream, literally.

The dreams terrified her, especially that one—it was all too possible—but she couldn't tell Kira. She felt terribly alone. She'd tried to convince herself that this was some sort of test; that at the end of the day she would come out a stronger person and a more loyal student, but it hadn't helped. It all seemed hollow somehow. Outwardly, everything appeared normal. She continued her intensive study sessions with Kira, did numerous chores around the home and tended the garden. But she couldn't get over the fact that, at Kira's request, she'd written and signed a statement that painted her father to be a criminal of the worst kind.

If the police accepted her evidence, he'd be jailed and it would be on her head. She recalled the agonising months of her mother's suffering as she succumbed to cancer and her teenage years when her father had brought her up single-handedly. She remembered her birthdays when he dressed up as a clown and tried to make her happy and how he'd taken her shopping only to buy the wrong clothes and the wrong sizes.

A tear trickled down her face. *I'm sorry, Dad. So sorry.*

The memory of the fateful day when she'd walked into the police station at Maleny haunted Emma. Kira hadn't even trusted her to get there on her own but had had her driven there by a man she'd never met. Why hadn't Kira simply written the statement and had Emma sign it with her name? It wouldn't have been the first time Kira used Emma's name for her own purposes.

It was only a matter of time until the police interviewed her father, and a couple of weeks had already passed since she'd visited the police station. She had to withdraw her statement as soon as possible.

She padded quietly to the window and looked down. The moonlight shone on the fence around the property. She'd asked Kira why it was fenced, and Kira had explained that she'd been attacked many years ago, and the police had advised her to increase her security. Emma wasn't sure she believed her anymore. Kira even looked different to Emma now. At first, she'd seemed soft and kind—a spiritual being with a special soul—but now Emma saw hard edges and a rigidity that didn't permit dissenting voices. Emma had been so sure of her once, but now, she just felt vulnerable and insecure.

She sighed. It was clear to her now. For the sake of her sanity, she had to get out of there. She had to abandon Kira and her supposedly 'idyllic lifestyle'. It didn't look idyllic now, not with that fence down there and Kira having manipulated her into doing a terrible thing. Emma had no idea how she could escape or where she'd go, but she'd made up her mind. She just needed to get her head together and find a way out.

Emma went back to bed, but she couldn't sleep. By morning, the need to leave Kira had become overwhelming. She couldn't even face Kira in the study group. Though she continued to take part, she was barely listening. She told Kira that she wasn't feeling well, but Kira didn't seem to care.

After study group, Emma went into the garden, supposedly to do her chores, but, actually, she just wanted to check out the fence around the property. Once again, the gate was locked. It seemed it always was.

While weeding the vegetable garden, Emma plotted her escape. It had to be a Tuesday, because every Tuesday afternoon, Kira left home for a few hours—supposedly running a course at a nearby community centre—and she returned around 6.00 pm. When Kira opened the gate to come in, Emma could race out. It'd be tough. She'd have to push past her, and Kira could try to stop her, but it was worth a try. She'd make a run for it and hope Kira wouldn't catch up.

26

A few minutes before seven on Saturday morning, Rochelle stood outside her apartment building in Randwick rocking from one foot to the other as she waited for Keith and Rob. A yawn overtook her, the result of only a few hours' sleep. She'd tried not to think about what might happen today, but the anxiety made her body restless. She re-tied her ponytail, then smoothed the skirt of her dark-grey, long-sleeved dress. She'd bought it for a job interview, worn it once, then stuffed it in the back of her closet because it was too boring, but it excelled at being forgettable—perfect for today.

She looked around. It was a lovely spring day, sunny, but not too hot. The street was surprisingly quiet, hardly a car and not a pedestrian in sight. Rochelle suddenly felt very alone. A nightmare she'd had last night flittered through her memory, reawakening the terror. She'd been at the airport, alone. Graham had Penny by the hand, and they were walking towards the departure area. Rochelle tried to run towards them, to grab her little girl, but she couldn't move. Her feet were rooted to the ground. She tried to shout, but no sound came out, just a strangled squawk. Helpless and with her heart sinking, she watched them walk through the door, and it slid closed behind them. Graham had whisked Penny away before her eyes, and she hadn't been able to do a thing about it. Would that be today's story, or would Penny be coming home with her? What was she doing now?

A blue station wagon drove up with two men inside. She glanced at her watch: 7.00 am exactly. It stopped beside her, and the driver, a big man—over six foot—got out. He had thick light-brown hair and wore dark-blue jeans and a maroon t-shirt with a multicoloured design on the front. She figured he was in his forties.

'Rochelle?' he asked.

She nodded. 'That's me.'

'I'm Keith. Let's go.'

He opened the back door, and as she slid inside, Rochelle noticed three small tattoos on his left arm. She relaxed into the seat, a wave of relief washing over her. It was actually happening. And she wouldn't be alone.

Keith got back into the passenger seat, and the man in the driver's seat turned around and smiled at her. 'Hi, I'm Rob. Pleased to meet you.' He was at least ten years older than Keith and wore a blue shirt, a more conservative look than his friend.

Rochelle managed a 'Hi' in return, but it came out as a tiny mouse-like squeak. She cleared her throat.

Rob nodded, then looked to the front, put the car into drive, and pulled away from the curb.

Keith turned to look at her. 'We'll go through it all when we get to the airport, but Laura has filled us in on all the details, so don't worry, we'll get through this together. Rob and I have done this kind of thing before. We know how to work as a team, and we rarely fail.'

'That was once only,' Rob interjected.

Rochelle nodded and gave a tentative smile. If they were trying to make her feel positive, it was working and they both seemed very relaxed, which also helped.

Keith turned back to the front, leaving Rochelle to her thoughts. She'd driven on this highway many times, the airport being the departure point for their family holidays—her, Graham and Penny. She shook her head. How things had changed. In her wildest dreams she would never have thought she'd be making this journey to protect her own daughter.

They parked the car in an industrial area near the airport, and Keith and Rob turned around to face Rochelle. Clearly, they knew Rochelle was about to embark on a daring plan. She took a deep calming breath.

Keith smiled and said, 'Would've been nicer if we could've met under different circumstances, but here we are. We've a job to do and we need to know exactly what we're doing.'

Rochelle blinked and nodded.

'For starters,' Keith continued, 'we need to get you into the airport without Graham seeing you. He doesn't know us, but if he sees you, we could have problems. He might take off with Penny, possibly panic and get a cab to who knows where. We don't need that.'

Rob pulled out a notepad. 'We've seen the photos you gave Laura. Anything else we should know about Penny and Graham?'

'Um. Okay. I'm not sure what information you have, so let me tell you what I think you need to know. Penny is seven years old, and she suffers from mild cerebral palsy, which means her walking is slightly impaired. But she's normal height for a seven-year-old. She has dark-brown, shoulder-length hair and will probably be wearing brown shorts and a yellowish top. My guess is she'll be pulling her yellow backpack. It's quite small and has wheels.'

Rochelle fell silent. She pictured Penny just as she had in her nightmare, and fear rose, laying siege to her tenuous calm. She took another deep breath and released it slowly. Now was not the time to express her distress. 'Graham's about 179 cm tall, a little chubby around the tummy, fair-skinned and has a receding hairline. Probably wearing summery clothes. He's a jeans and t-shirt person, if that helps. My guess is that he'll be holding Penny tight.'

Keith took out a large map of the international terminal and spread it in front of Rochelle. She managed to place it on her lap between her and the front seats.

'As soon as we arrive,' Keith said, 'you walk over to the gift stores behind the check-in and find a position obscured from the check-in area.' He pointed to both areas in turn as he spoke. Clearly, he knew the map well. 'We work on a simple rule: if you can't see the passengers, the passengers can't see you. We'll be hanging around that area, so that won't be a problem.

'Okay.' Rochelle felt faint as she grasped the enormity of the task before her.

'We won't be doing anything until after Graham and Penny have checked in and parted with their suitcases,' Keith continued. 'I don't need to be jumping over suitcases in order to grab Penny. Once they've left the check-in counter, we'll move ahead. My plan is to grab Penny and head towards the exit. At the same time, Rob will run into the gift store and accompany you back to the exit. You'll have to move quickly.'

'Obviously, Graham will react,' Rob said. 'He might try to grab Penny or wrestle with Keith. We don't know what he'll do, so we have to be fast.'

'Once I have Penny,' Keith said, 'Graham will need a crowbar to separate her from me; and I do know how to run. A white Commodore will be right outside in the emergency parking area waiting for us. We'll cue the car as soon as we see Graham and Penny walk in. It has a red streak on the passenger's side of the car, and the hazard lights will be flashing. You won't be able to miss it. Any questions?'

Rochelle chewed on her bottom lip, her eyes glued to the map. 'What happens if it doesn't work?'

'It will work,' Keith said. 'If Graham and Penny walk into the terminal, we'll walk out with her.'

With that last assurance from Keith, they all agreed to the plan and drove to the terminal. Keith and Rob dropped Rochelle off outside departures, and she walked into the huge terminal. She imagined Graham and Penny walking in together and remembered Laura saying that Penny might not even realise it was an airport. She'd certainly have no idea where she was going. But then again, maybe Andrew was wrong and this would all be a waste of time. Instinct told her otherwise, however.

Five minutes later, Rochelle stood in the back of the gift store. She couldn't see the check-in area, but she could see Keith and Rob standing together only several metres away. She couldn't believe they were so relaxed, but it gave her faith that they knew what they were doing. She suddenly felt a surge of strength. 'I can do this,' she said to herself.

She was just wondering how long they would have to wait, when Graham entered the terminal with a woman and two children and walked towards the check-in counter. Rochelle couldn't see whether the other child was a boy or a girl. *What if it's a girl and they grab the wrong child?*

There weren't many passengers around, and the group went straight to the head of the check-in line. Rochelle could see Penny clearly now. She wore her brown shorts and a green top and held the handle of her yellow backpack. Graham held her other hand. He spoke to the smartly dressed woman with him, but he looked at Penny every few moments. A young boy, about ten years old and presumably the woman's son, stood with them. The woman's clothes, suitcases and carry-ons screamed money.

Who was she? What was her relationship with Graham? Was she stealing her son away from a partner who had no idea about what was happening to his family?

Keith and Rob watched the group of four, but they didn't move, then the group walked to the check-in counter and out of Rochelle's line of sight.

About five minutes later, Graham and his entourage walked towards the customs area. Rochelle focused on Penny. She didn't seem upset, just walked slowly along pulling her little backpack while Graham held her hand. When they were no more than fifty metres from the doors to the customs departure area, Rochelle stepped forward, heart pounding, her eyes still on Penny.

Suddenly Keith ran forward and came up behind the group. Rochelle released the breath she didn't know she'd been holding. Graham glanced around just as Keith bent down and picked up Penny, breaking Graham's hold on her hand. Then Keith ran, clutching Penny to his chest as he sprinted through the terminal. Graham—out of shape as he was—had no chance of catching him. He just shouted after Keith, and when that did nothing, he looked around for help. The woman, wide-eyed and mouth agape, grabbed her son's hand and strode to the departures' gate without looking back. Her son did, but she yanked him after her.

An airline official stepped in front of Keith, trying to stop him, but Keith pushed him aside and raced on. Graham ran to a policeman who stood near the door to immigration and almost collided with Rob who was running towards the gift store. Rochelle joined Rob, and they tore down the concourse and out into the street, leaving Graham staring after them. By the time they reached the Commodore, Keith and Penny were sitting in the back seat, Penny in his arms, crying uncontrollably.

'See, here she is,' Keith said gently as Rochelle climbed in beside them.

'I'm here, baby. You're safe,' Rochelle held out her arms and Keith placed the sobbing little girl into her mother's embrace. Rochelle wrapped her arms around her daughter, held her tight and rocked her back and forth.

'Mummy,' she mumbled into Rochelle's chest.

Once Rob was in the passenger seat, the driver pulled out into the traffic and drove away from the terminal. But the drama was not over. Rochelle stroked Penny's hair and sang her favourite lullaby.

The car stopped suddenly.

Rochelle looked up. A police car blocked their exit, and a cop was checking the occupants of the car before them. Her heart sped up, thumping so hard she was surprised they couldn't all hear it.

'Damn, the cops have moved quickly on this one,' Keith muttered to Rob, 'but leave it with me. Open the windows,' he told the driver, then got out and approached the cop.

Penny stopped crying. She put her little arms around her mother and peered into her eyes. Rochelle felt tears threatening, but seeing her mother cry would upset Penny even more, so Rochelle held them back.

'Sir,' Keith said to the cop, 'my name's Keith Elmwood, and we know why you're here. We've got the little girl, Penny Lightwood, and her mother, Rochelle, with us. We're happy to meet you at the station. I think you might be more interested in interviewing the little girl's father than the occupants of our car. But we're happy to talk to you. I can give you all the names and any other details that may assist you. It looks like the father is booked on Cathay airways CX92. We have no idea whether he's boarded his flight or decided to go home, but you may want to take this picture of him. We believe he may be travelling under a false name.'

The police officer's eyebrows rose in surprise. He walked up to the car, peered into the backseat and saw Rochelle holding Penny. Rochelle opened her mouth, about to say something, but the cop raised his hand as if to say that wasn't necessary. 'You can take the woman and the little girl home, then come down to the station. If I need to talk to the mum, I'll contact her. But first, I'll need to see your licence and take your name and phone number.'

'No worries, Officer. We appreciate your understanding.'

The cop told the driver to move to the side of the road, then he motioned to his partner to remove the roadblock. After providing the cop with the required information, they drove on and soon pulled up beside the blue station wagon. The men got out, and after a brief conference, Rob took the driver's seat, and they headed home, Rochelle cradling Penny, who'd fallen asleep.

'Keith will drop by the police station to make a statement,' Rob said, glancing back at Rochelle with a smile. 'But I'll be parked outside your home for the rest of the day. It's just a safety precaution.'

After thanking him profusely, Rochelle carried Penny up the stairs into her apartment. She put Penny into bed and kissed her, then pulled the curtains and double-locked the doors. It was 11.30 am, four-and-a-half hours since Rochelle had met Keith and Rob.

She lay down on the floor next to Penny's bed and cried.

When she woke up, Rochelle called her lawyer. 'Hi, Andrew. I've got Penny back. I just want to thank you for all your help.'

'Back from?'

Rochelle realised she hadn't spoken to Andrew since Friday afternoon, so she explained what had happened.

'I know I predicted it,' he said when she'd finished her story, 'but it's upsetting that it actually did happen. You were lucky, you moved on it fast. It could so easily have gone the other way. But look, there are a number of things we need to do, and we need to do them fast. Can you be at my office at 8.00 am on Monday?'

'Sure, I'll be there.' Depending on how long it took, she might have to take some time off work, but that couldn't be helped. 'What do I do to keep Penny safe in the meantime? I feel sick in the stomach when I think he might try again.'

'Don't let her out of your sight, and I mean that literally. Tell anyone else caring for her the same thing. Before she goes to the bathroom, go in to make sure nobody's there. You can't take any risks. If there's any chance whatsoever that Graham has a key to your apartment, change the locks.'

'Right. Will do.'

Andrew ended the call, and Rochelle looked at her innocent little girl. She sat curled up on the sofa cooing to her favourite doll. This was all so unfair to her. 'Hey, sweetie,' Rochelle called, 'you want some ice-cream?'

Penny's eyes lit up with excitement; her face creased into a broad smile, and she nodded.

Rochelle's heart went all gooey.

27

On Monday morning, Rochelle arrived at Andrew's office a few minutes early, hoping they'd get it over with in enough time for her to get to work. Her boss was pretty cool, but she had a feeling she'd be asking for more time off before this was all over.

The receptionist led her into Andrew's office this time. He directed her to a soft chair in a little sitting area and sat in a matching chair on the other side of a small coffee table.

After greetings, Andrew said, 'Where's Penny now?'

'With my sister. I've left a message with the school saying that she won't be in for the next few days.'

'Good, so look, you need to take out an intervention order against Graham, even though we don't know whether he's in the country or has left on his own. We might be able to find out through immigration or the police, but that can be difficult because of the privacy laws. Either way, we still need to act.'

'Okay. But what's an intervention order actually do?'

'It will prevent Graham from coming within two hundred metres of your home as well as a number of other restrictions in relation to contact with you. We'll go down to the magistrates' court later and take care of it. They'll serve it on him straight away, and he'll have up to thirty days to appeal the order—assuming he is in the country. There's another element in this puzzle too.

Who was the woman with the little boy? You mentioned that Keith took some photos. Get a hold of them if you can and see if you recognise her. The police will certainly be interested in her.'

'Okay.' Rochelle felt somewhat deflated. She'd been on a high since getting Penny back, but the thought of all the legal stuff she still had to do punctured that balloon quick smart. *Damn you, Graham, for putting me through all this!*

'Graham could be charged with obtaining a travel document illegally,' Andrew continued, 'though there's nothing you need to do about that. It's difficult to know at this stage whether he has committed a crime. Changing her name by deed poll, if that's what he did, could've been part of an elaborate scheme to obtain a passport, and how he managed to change Penny's name legally is another question. But that's not your problem. Keith has made a statement to the police, so they can deal with it.'

Rochelle leaned forward. 'He had no right to take Penny out of the country without notifying me, though, right?'

'True, and that will work against him big time once we get to the Family Court, assuming you'll be filing for divorce. If you do, Graham's actions have increased your chances of getting an urgent hearing to protect Penny a hundredfold.'

'Right.' *Divorce.* Rochelle hadn't thought about that. Did she want to divorce him? She didn't know.

'You need to prepare a statement for the intervention order application. I'll introduce you to my assistant, Chloe. She'll help you with that, and then we'll get down to the magistrates' court.'

Rochelle blew out a breath. *There goes getting to work on time.*

'I also recommend you think about hiring a private investigator to find out whether Graham is still in the country. It would be very useful to know. I can recommend a number of companies for you.'

Rochelle bit her lip. Who was going to pay for this? Not

Graham, of course. The bugger. Anger rose up inside her.

'My only other comments at this stage concern Penny,' Andrew continued. 'She's been through a very traumatic time. The airport episode would have been very frightening for her, and it might be a good idea to get her some help. These sorts of events can leave scars. I'm no expert, though, so go to a children's services' clinic and discuss it with them.'

Rochelle nodded. *There goes a whole day.* She'd better call in sick.

'Let me introduce you to Chloe now.' Andrew stood, and Rochelle followed.

'Thank you again, Andrew. I came so close to losing Penny. It's been too awful to even think about.'

'Happy to help,' he said. 'Now let's get this paperwork done.'

28

Dear Safiyya,

God spoke to me last night. I had the most beautiful dream. I dreamed that you and I were in the Garden of Eden. God said that he had put us there to make a new world which is free of crime, of immorality and cruelty. We accepted the challenge and the world started anew.

And then I woke up and spent the whole day studying. I accepted another day of fasting and now I'm writing to you, Safiyya. Oh how I wish you could be part of the church. We met in the emergency ward, but that wasn't the reason we met. The real reason is so you can join our church.

If only you would have the courage to join like I did, then we could be together. I would no longer harbour the feelings and desire I have for you. We would be together spiritually as one. It would be like we were in the Garden of Eden again.

Safiyya, your beauty shines. You are the most special woman I've met. Apart from an occasional letter to my grandma, I write to no one but you. Let our spirits be together like one. How can I meet you again? I witness on Sunday morning at Dixon Park.

*Can you stand by the water fountain so I can see you
even for a moment?*
With all my love and God's blessings,
Amin

With letter in hand, Safiyya wandered outside to the refreshing space of her small balcony. She leaned on the railing in the far corner from where she could see the beach and stared into the blue expanse of the water. The letter unsettled her. Amin was too needy, too passionate about her, but she knew now that she would accompany him on a flight to Lebanon. Someone had to help him.

She sat down and read the letter again, then cast her mind back to that evening in the emergency ward at Bankstown Hospital.

A church elder had brought a young, dehydrated man into casualty, then filled out the forms and left.

'Didn't even bother to stay and find out what was wrong,' the duty nurse told her later.

A message on her pager had sent her to his room. 'Hello,' she said to him. 'I'm Safiyya, and I'll be your nurse tonight.'

Amin tried to look away. At the time she didn't realise that his church forbade him to look at a woman.

'Tell me about yourself, Amin.'

He didn't respond.

She took his blood pressure and found it very low, then she looked at his eyes and asked him to open his mouth. 'Amin,' she said, straightening up, 'we are going to put a drip into your arm. You are quite dehydrated, and this will make you feel better.'

He nodded and said softly, 'But no blood transfusions. I belong to God's church, and we are God's servants.'

The next time she visited Amin, he looked better. But when she asked to see his eyes, he took her hand and looked intently into her eyes. That made her uncomfortable and she pulled away, but Amin tried to draw her closer. Before she knew it, he had kissed her hand. She'd jerked away and raced from the room.

The sun came out from behind a cloud, and the sudden warmth and brightness brought Safiyya back to the present. She went to get her diary and a glass of lemonade—with ice. She liked to reflect when between jobs, and Amin provided plenty of fodder for examination.

She opened her diary and looked at an entry she'd made while working at Bankstown Hospital.

> *It isn't hard to see what's going on. Amin is falling in love with me, and I don't know what to do. I care about this patient, and I want to help him. Something is very wrong with him, but I'm not sure what. It seems that I'm the first human contact he's had since he joined this church of his. Maybe I need to be there for him; maybe I can help him.*
>
> *My mind and emotions are messing me around, and I'm scared to discuss Amin's infatuation for me with my supervisor. I'd have to hand him over to another nurse. But each visit, up to ten or twelve visits a day, is a challenge. I've become conscious of my dress, even the tone of my voice when I speak to him. My usual soft, nurturing manner isn't helping his infatuation with me, so I try to speak with a louder voice, but it isn't me. Even drawing the curtains around his bed has taken on a new significance. I think Amin believes we're in some sort of bridal chamber. It bordered on delusional.*

And another entry on the day Amin discharged himself.

> *Today was a day of mixed feelings. I'm relieved I still have my job even though I'm leaving soon. I'm glad Amin's out of my life, but he isn't out of my mind, and in a curious way not even out of my heart. In some strange way, my visits to his little cubicle did excite me. Despite the challenge, I did look forward to seeing Amin, and I missed him when he was gone. But that was then and now is now. Thank God I'm over it. It could have gotten very messy.*

'And that's how this all started,' Safiyya said to herself. 'And now I might be on a plane to Lebanon with him.' Safiyya closed her eyes. She could see her parents farewelling her in Iran. They had assured her that life would be better in Australia. She remembered how she could still feel her mother's hand on her face as she walked through the airport terminal, which was surrounded by soldiers. What would it be like to be in Lebanon? Would she be safe there?

She opened her eyes, but an image of Amin appeared in her mind. He looked so earnest and so innocent. That his admirable desire for a spiritual life had been taken advantage of made Safiyya uncharacteristically angry. 'I can't let this man down,' she whispered to herself.

Safiyya went back inside and called Laura. 'I'm on, Laura. I'll do it for Amin. Not sure whether I'll get him on the flight or whether I'll actually accompany him, but you can count on my involvement. I can't walk away from Amin—not after what I know and what I've seen. Let's talk later in the week.'

'Thank you so much, Safiyya; this is great news. It's really coming together now, and I'm pretty sure we can make it work. We have a great team, what with Fadi and Nadia as well.'

'Yes, they're lovely people.'

'Can you make it to Brisbane for our next meeting, or do you need to be in Sydney?' Laura asked. 'Of course, the family is paying for it all, which, by the way, leads me to something else. When we meet, we'll need to discuss payment for your time.'

Safiyya wanted to say that wasn't necessary, but she could see that she'd have to put off starting another job until this was over, and she did need to pay her rent. 'I'm between jobs at the moment, so I can come to Brisbane.'

'Great. Put it on your calendar for Saturday.'

29

'Safiyya's on the phone, Laura,' Margaret said early the next afternoon. 'She sounds agitated.'

Laura nodded and picked up the landline.

'First the good news,' Safiyya said. 'I've decided I'm happy to travel with Amin, but the bad news is that they're about to ship him out. Apparently, the church is opening a chapter somewhere in South America, in Guyana or something like that, and Amin's been chosen to work there. He called me last night.'

'Oh wow,' Laura said. 'That just happens to be the place where in 1978 Jim Jones murdered nine hundred and nine of his followers, including three hundred and four children. They say the followers committed suicide, but they didn't. They were brainwashed, which, as far as I'm concerned, means they were murdered, though technically they drank that infamous Kool-Aid laced with cyanide of their own free will. So that'll be Amin's new pad, ay?'

'Apparently so.'

'How much time do we have?' Laura asked.

'Maybe two weeks, but I wouldn't risk another day longer.'

'Okay,' Laura said. 'We're nearing the end of an important case. As soon as it is over, I'll get onto it. I'll call you, but we need to meet ASAP.'

She wandered over to Matthew's desk and gave him the news.

'Okay,' he said. 'I'll call Michael, bring him up to date and see if he can come down for a couple of hours. There's a lot of hackwork we need to be doing.'

'Sounds good.' Laura said. 'I'll confirm the meeting for Saturday. Emma should be stable by then—assuming we've got her out.'

~

Michael arrived at the office just after 4.30 pm and sat in the sitting area beside Matthew. He was glad to see that Laura had gone home already. She'd been looking pretty worn lately.

'Given today's development, it's time to address some of the fine print of the plan to fly Amin to Lebanon,' Matthew said. 'Safiyya has agreed to fly with Amin and an exit counsellor, so we have to organise the flights from Sydney to Lebanon with a connection in either Bangkok or Singapore. Laura and I both have our hands full with the Carter girl, whose extraction is planned for tonight, so can you do the flight research for us?'

'Sure, I'll get onto it tomorrow.' *So that's where Laura is, preparing to receive Emma.*

'Great. Don't forget it has to be a tight connection, which can be missed if the exit counsellor and Safiyya need more time with Amin.'

'Got it, and the airline needs to be one that allocates seats in advance.'

'Exactly. And the seats have to be on the side of the aircraft. No seats in the middle section where Amin would have contact with people other than Safiyya and the counsellor. He'll need them for support. Being stranded in a plane surrounded by strangers and left to his doubts won't help him at all. And the follow-on flight has to be one in which the three travellers can sit together. Their boarding passes out of Sydney will be scrapped once they 'miss' their connection in Asia, so they'll need to be re-seated on another flight, hopefully with an overnight stay between them.

'You'll also need to search for hotels that can be used when the party "misses" their connecting flight. They can't afford to be split up, sent by the airline to different hotels. I realise there's a lot of work here, but you've got a few days to pull it together before we meet with the team on Saturday. By then we'll have a better picture regarding the timing, but we need to be ready to book as soon as the dates are set.'

'Okay. Some questions. Does Amin have a passport? And is it in his real name or some sort of concocted spiritual name? I also need Safiyya's full name. And who's the exit counsellor for this mission?'

Matthew said nothing, just looked at Michael.

Michael laughed. 'I knew you didn't haul me into the office just to talk about our plan—which is actually my plan anyway.' He leaned over and gave Matthew an affectionate punch on his arm. 'So what you want to know is whether I'll take this on, whether I'll be the exit counsellor. I suppose I should feel honoured that you're asking me, but you've gotta give me a couple of days to think this through. I know I could do it, but should I?'

'That's fine, Michael. You know how I value your work and your approach to our clients. Of course, it's a big ask, but I'll leave it with you.'

'You'd like to know before Saturday though, right?'

Matthew nodded. 'Right.'

30

Emma hid in the bushes near the front gate, trying to keep her breathing deep and even. The small backpack on her back contained just some photos, her diary and a copy of the affidavit she'd written at the police station.

Kira had left around 1.00 pm, and she'd told Emma she'd be home by five and expected dinner to be ready. Kira didn't drive. She usually took a taxi, and every time a car came into view Emma's heart began to race. A taxi had already come by, but it hadn't stopped. She checked her watch; it was only a matter of minutes until Kira returned.

She wiped her sweaty hands on her skirt. Should she really leave? She felt she had to, but maybe it was selfish to choose helping her father over helping the whole world. Kira had often told her that a time would come when she'd have doubts. She'd said that Emma would need to push them away and remain focused on their mission—their mission to save the world. Was that teaching meant for now, when she was about to forsake her mentor, her guide, her teacher? Would her leaving damage humanity's chances for a better future?

A yellow taxi jolted her from her thoughts. It pulled up a few metres from the property and parked on the other side of the road. Emma rose into a crouch, ready to run, her heart racing. She watched Kira pay the driver, get out and walk across the road, carrying a small satchel and a box. She took out her noisy bunch of keys, and when she opened the gate, Emma made her move.

She sprinted through the gate, pushing Kira aside and ran down the road as the taxi sped off. Kira raced after her, calling her name, but Emma was faster. She glanced over her shoulder. The distance between them was growing, and Kira slowed to a walk. A few paces on, another quick look back showed that she'd stopped. The road curved, taking Emma out of Kira's view, and suddenly she felt utterly exhausted. Overwhelmed by the drama of her escape, she stumbled, then collapsed onto the side of the road, eyes closed. She stayed there for a few minutes, crumpled on the ground as trucks and cars whizzed by. If she opened her eyes, what would she see? The possibilities terrified her, so she kept them closed.

No. She couldn't give up. She couldn't go back. She had to get up and keep going. She staggered to her feet and walked on. A car came towards her, slowing. Why was it slowing? *Oh my God, she's sent someone to get me. They'll take me back. That's it; plan failed. I'm doomed.*

Emma crumpled back onto the ground, dazed, bruised, confused and scared.

The car stopped. A man walked over to Emma and laid his hand gently on her shoulder.

She blinked up at him. 'Okay, I'm sorry. I'm sorry. I should never have done it.'

'No, Emma,' the man said in a soft voice. 'I'm not with Kira. I'm here to help you. We were on our way to get you out of there, but you beat us to it.'

Emma's jaw dropped. She glanced around. No sign of Kira. 'Are you sure? Who are you? I've never seen you before.'

'Come,' the man beckoned. 'Get in the car. I promise you

everything will be okay.'

Emma frowned. If they weren't Kira's henchmen, who were they? 'I can't get into a car with someone I don't know.'

The man smiled. He had a kind face. 'Fair enough. My name's Hilton and the guy in the car is Andre. We're not taking you back to Kira; we're taking you somewhere safe. Your dad knows where, but we need to go now, before she sends someone after you.' He held out a hand, an offer to help her up.

Emma didn't believe him, but she had no strength left to argue. She grabbed his hand—what else could she do?—and he hauled her to her feet. She had a huge graze all the way down her leg; her face felt bruised, and the sole of her shoe had come half off, but with Hilton's help, she walked to the car. He opened the back door, and she climbed in and collapsed onto the back seat. Tears streamed from her eyes, and she trembled with fear. Her escape had gone horribly wrong, and Kira's punishment would be harsh.

But the car didn't turn around and go back to Kira's home. It kept driving. And driving. She heard one of the men talk to someone on a mobile phone, but she couldn't concentrate on the words. It didn't seem too long before the car pulled to a stop.

'This is your stop,' Hilton said. 'Wombat Flat.'

Emma sat up and looked outside. A middle-aged woman with a shoulder-length, blonde bob stood outside a dilapidated house surrounded by paddocks that seemed to stretch for miles. A few chickens strutted about in front of the house. Hilton helped her out of the car, and she stood in a daze, looking around in the hot sun. Parched fields on the other side of the road looked like they were crying out for a good soaking rain, and the road was quiet with hardly a car or truck in sight. Her surroundings were in stark contrast to the lush gardens and grand house she'd just left.

The woman walked up to her, smiled and said, 'Hello, Emma, I'm Laura. I'm here to help you. We all are.'

Emma swallowed and managed a nod.

Laura took Emma's hand and led her into the house. She noticed that it was cool and dim but didn't register anything else about it. The situation had become somewhat surreal. Had she really escaped Kira? Or was this her punishment?

A tall man with thick, brown hair and smiling eyes walked up and smiled at her. 'Hello, Emma, I'm Matthew.'

Emma just stared at him with wide eyes. Her mind had gone numb, and she thought her legs might buckle beneath her any minute.

~

Laura noted Emma's almost emaciated frame and drawn face. She didn't look like someone who'd always been thin. Her clothes appeared several sizes too big. She had bags under her eyes and avoided eye contact with anyone. After registering the graze on Emma's leg, Laura turned to Hilton and said, 'Did she fall after scaling the fence?'

At almost the same time, Matthew said. 'I'm guessing you couldn't get the gate open.'

Hilton shook his head. 'No, she was out of there before we got there. We found her running from Kira.'

Laura's eyebrows rose in surprise. Interventions rarely worked out exactly as planned, but the timing of Emma's escape and Hilton and Andre's arrival was far more dramatic than usual.

'At first, she thought we were Kira's henchmen sent to bring her back,' Hilton continued. He glanced at Emma, who stood, wavering slightly, her eyes glazed. 'She still might not be too sure. I think she needs to rest before you guys talk to her.'

Laura nodded. The poor girl looked quite traumatised. 'Come on, Emma; I'll show you to your room.' Laura took a couple of steps along the corridor and gestured to her to follow.

'We'll talk later,' Hilton said. 'Just look after this remarkable young woman.'

Laura glanced at Emma. Unfortunately, the girl didn't appear to have heard what Hilton said.

Emma followed Laura into her room and lay down on the bed without even a glance around. She closed her eyes, and Laura left to find something to treat her graze with. A few moments later, she returned with some antiseptic cream and a loose bandage. She gently bathed Emma's face and applied the cream to her leg, then placed an ice pack on the side of Emma's bruised face. Emma said nothing, but her expression softened, apparently soothed by Laura's care.

'There, all done,' Laura said when she'd finished. 'I'll leave you to get some rest. I'll be just down the hall if you need me.'

Emma mumbled her thanks, then pulled the quilt over her head and lay still. Laura left and eased the door closed behind her, but before it clicked shut, she heard Emma start to sob quietly.

31

Two hours later, Emma woke and looked around the room. Though old-fashioned, it appeared clean and tidy. The antiseptic cream Laura has used sat on the small bedside table, and a kettle, an assortment of tea and coffee, some biscuits and a small bowl of fruit occupied another table by the window. A cupboard stood against the wall at the end of the bed, and a chair by the table completed the arrangement. Emma got out of bed, wandered over and peeked inside the cupboard—just sheets, blankets and towels.

A door led to a bathroom. She stood in front of the mirror and looked at her swollen face—the result, she guessed, of collapsing onto the ground while still moving. Her leg felt tight and sore, but not as bad as it had before Laura applied the cream. Despite her close escape, she was out, away from Kira—a great relief—but what she was doing here? Laura and the men who'd brought her here seemed like kind, caring people, but how did they know her name? And how did they find her?

Someone knocked on her door. 'Are you awake?' It was Laura.

'Yeah. You can come in.'

Laura opened the door and walked in with a smile. 'Feeling better?'

Emma sat on the side of the bed. 'Well, yeah, but I'm confused about what's going on and how I ended up here. I mean, I was trying to escape from a woman called Kira Thurin. I'd planned it all out, and then out of nowhere, these two guys turned up. How did they know who I was, where I was and that I was going to escape?'

Laura sat on the chair. 'They knew who you were because your father contacted us and told us where you were. He wanted us to get you away from Kira because he felt you were in danger there. I'm guessing that we both worked out the same best time for you to escape, and we just happened to plan to rescue you on the same day you decided to make a run for it. It was a pretty bold move, actually. Congratulations.'

Emma grimaced. 'Except I'm not sure if I did the right thing.' She looked at Laura. 'My mind has been telling me for a while that Kira is bad for me, that she's controlled me in so many ways. But, somehow, I still feel for her. She took me in when I was at a real low. My mum died when I was thirteen, and Kira was like a mum. I still think she has a lot to offer me. Few people are as giving as she is.' She shook her head and trailed off, unsure. Should she even be telling this woman these things?

'It's okay, Emma. You don't have to be sure. We're here for a few days, so there'll be plenty of time to talk. As long as it takes to sort things out.'

Emma frowned. 'So you're what? Who's "we"?'

'We work for an organisation that helps people understand how they've been controlled by others, so they can make their own choices again.'

'You mean like domestic violence and battered wives' stuff?'

'Not exactly. It's more about people stuck in communities under the sway of the group leader.'

'Like Kira?'

'Yes. I'm not sure how much I should say right now, but I know quite a lot about you. For instance, that you made a police statement about your dad and then sent him a fax asking for money.'

Emma winced. 'Oh my God. How do you know all that?'

'Your dad came to us because he knew your statement was false, and we thought so too. It looked like someone convinced you to write this stuff just to get money.'

Well, she did. But Emma wasn't going to say that. Instead, she said, 'Kira needs the funds to help change the world, to save it from all the … the evil.' She stopped for a moment, suddenly unsure. She'd always considered Kira as one of the pure ones, but now … 'It *was* all false, though. What I wrote.' Emma felt tears threaten. Her mind was so fuzzy. She couldn't think straight. She sniffed back tears and scrubbed her hand across her eyes.

'Don't worry about anything right now,' Laura said kindly. 'How about you have a shower and then something to eat?'

She nodded. That did sound good. 'Can I see my dad?'

'Of course. We'll call him and let him know you're here, but I think we need to talk first.'

A sudden panic raced through Emma's veins. 'What if Kira finds me? She's a very smart woman and has some sort of ESP. I don't know what she'll do to me if she gets me back, but it won't be good.'

Laura shook her head. 'You'll be fine. Kira won't be coming anywhere near here, I assure you. Take a shower; we've got some clothes here for you. When you're ready, come to the dining room, and we'll eat a proper meal.'

'Okay.' The big fluffy towels had looked good.

Laura left, and Emma shut the door and ran the shower. She stripped off and peered at herself in the mirror. She hadn't realised how much weight she'd lost. She looked terrible. Apart from the bruise, her hair was dry, her acne was playing up, and she felt empty, vulnerable and scared. What was going to happen here with these people? She wondered what Kira was doing. Would she ever see her again? She turned the shower taps up high, so the noise washed away her words. 'Please forgive me, Kira. I don't mean to hurt you. I just couldn't stay any longer. I've always trusted you, so this time, please trust me. It was just something I had to do.'

The water washed away her tears.

32

Emma sat on an old couch on the veranda at the Wombat Flat homestead reflecting on the last four days. Matthew and Laura were inside—cleaning, she suspected—giving her some alone time before her father turned up. The few clothes Laura had given her were now in the little backpack sitting beside her, along with her diary, a few photos and the copy of her bogus statement. She'd spent a long time talking with Laura and Matthew, during which time she'd come to see just how much influence and control Kira had had over her. It hadn't been easy. The care and kindness Kira had shown Emma was difficult to reconcile with the conniving and manipulative behaviour behind the plan to extract money from her parents. Anger rose whenever she thought about that, and yet she also missed Kira's company and support.

The fax she'd sent to her father and the statement she'd lodged at the Maleny police station haunted her more with every passing day. First thing on Monday, she'd go and tell them it was a false statement written under duress. It must have caused her father and Alison so much suffering—and causing suffering was the direct opposite of Kira's mission! She'd felt so incredibly guilty at first, but Laura helped her to see that it wasn't really her fault. She'd been under Kira's control at the time. Kira had made her think it was the right thing to do; she'd turned Emma's desire to heal the world into a twisted way to get money. *Uggh.* She was lucky she'd got away before things got worse.

And she was glad now that she'd waited before seeing her dad. A few days ago, she hadn't been clear about any of this and wouldn't have known what to say. Now she looked forward to talking to him, and Alison—she kind of owed her a debt since she would've been the one supporting her dad through all this.

She looked at her watch. Her dad shouldn't be too far away now. Laura had phoned him, saying Emma wanted to go home, and he'd said he'd be there in an hour. He answered so fast, she figured he must have been virtually waiting by the phone. It was six months since she'd last seen him, and she couldn't wait to give him a hug and tell him how sorry she was.

A small dust cloud and the sound of Albert's Audi told Emma that her father was no more than a few hundred metres away. The reflection of the bright sun on the silver trim was almost blinding as he drove in the property, but Emma didn't care. She stood, whispered, 'Dad is here,' to herself and walked down the steps.

A solitary kangaroo skipped away from the dry grass in front of the veranda, and two kookaburras took flight from their perch. Even the animals and the birds seemed to appreciate Emma's need for her privacy.

Albert got out of the car. He looked different, and it wasn't just his casual clothes. She saw genuine warmth and sincerity in his smile of relief and joy. He opened his arms, and Emma stepped into his embrace, tears suddenly pouring from her eyes. She pulled away, suddenly self-conscious. He couldn't have missed her severe weight loss.

'Don't worry, darling,' he said. 'You'll be fine. I love you.'

Emma hugged him again, holding on tight. 'I'm so sorry, so

sorry,' she cried in his ear. 'I didn't mean to do any of this, and I'm so sad.'

He patted her back and then took her hand and led her to the veranda, where they sat on the worn couch together. His eyes were teary, and he seemed lost for words.

The feeling of intense love she had for her father stole her words as well, but it didn't matter, she was content just sitting with him, knowing she was free to be her own person again.

Laura interrupted the silence by poking her head out the door and asking if they wanted a drink.

Albert stood up and shook Laura's hand. 'Thank you, Laura, it's been a long journey, and we wouldn't be here without you.'

'Albert,' she said with a smile, 'you don't need to exclude yourself from the equation. You were the one who got the ball rolling, and your perseverance to save your daughter has been exemplary. Now about those drinks …'

Emma stood and grabbed her backpack. 'I just want to go home.'

Albert smiled. 'Sounds good to me.'

Laura walked with them to the car, and Emma suddenly found herself crying again. It was all too much. These kind people, and Kira … Kira not being at all what she'd thought she was. What was she going to do with her life now?

'Don't worry, darling,' Laura said as if she had some inkling of what Emma was going through. 'We'll be meeting again in the next few days, I promise you.'

Emma climbed in beside her dad, buckled in and, as he started the car and got under way, she rummaged through the small pocket of the backpack. She hadn't looked in there since she'd escaped. Now she found the picture of Kira, looked at it one last time and then tore it into small pieces. She opened the car window and cast the destroyed photo into the wilderness.

The pieces of paper shone in the sun as they floated down onto the parched road.

Tears ran silently down her cheeks.

Her father said nothing, just headed for home.

33

Safiyya, Nadia and Fadi took an early morning flight to Brisbane for the Wednesday 9.00 am meeting with Laura and Matthew. Though on the same flight, several rows separated their seats, but they shared a taxi to the CultAssist premises. Safiyya said little. It all seemed so unreal, as if she were a character in a spy movie.

Once the greetings were out of the way and Margaret had settled them all around the conference table with drinks and snacks, Matthew opened the meeting: 'After reviewing all the possibilities, Laura and I believe the best approach is the Lebanon trip. There's no point trying to work with Amin in Sydney because even if we can get him away from his church initially, he'd have no reason to stay away. And if a cult member in this kind of situation manages to contact their organisation— usually via a mobile phone—they can be pulled back in. The cult simply sends someone to pick them up. A failed intervention can push back any further opportunity to extricate the cult member by years, and, of course, we'd rather avoid that.'

'That sounds fair enough,' Safiyya said.

Fadi nodded, but he looked grave. Nadia just frowned.

Safiyya read out Amin's letter. When she finished, she looked up and noticed tears in Nadia's eyes.

'Why doesn't he just forget about Halima?' Nadia said in

a distressed voice. 'I don't want my mother-in-law touched by Amin's impure spirit. Halima is a pure soul; she has lived her entire life in purity and sanctity and is very close with God.' She turned to Safiyya, her face wreathed in sadness. 'Can you stop him from writing? I'm afraid that a letter from him will speed up her death. You have no idea how Amin's involvement in this so-called church will affect her.'

Safiyya's heart went out to Nadia. 'Perhaps I don't,' she said to her. 'Perhaps no one does, but the best chance we have of getting Amin out of this cult is through your mother-in-law. I might just be able to convince him to travel with me to see her. He's desperate for me to join the Church of Love and Faith— though I know it has nothing to do with faith or love, and I doubt Amin's capable of showing any genuine love right now. He claims to be following a spiritual path, but it's really all about himself. The thing is, though, I might be able to convince him that I'll join if Halima gives me her blessing, but of course, for that to happen, I'd need to travel to Lebanon to meet her.'

Nadia shook her head, and Safiyya saw disapproval in her eyes. 'Safiyya,' she said, 'you are young, and you are beautiful. But maybe you are naïve and also a little too innocent. My mother-in-law, may God protect her, will never give you her blessing to join Amin's church. And as much as we want Amin back—and we are desperate—I will never allow my mother-in-law to know about his new terrible beliefs. I cannot agree with this plan.'

Out of the corner of her eye, Safiyya noticed Laura glance at Matthew, but no one said a word. Safiyya moved closer to Nadia and took her hand. 'But she won't hear about Amin's church, because I don't really want to join that loveless church, so I don't really need or want her blessing. It's just a story we'll use to get Amin away from his church and onto a plane. If we can do that, then by the time Amin gets to Lebanon, he won't want to hear about that church again. He can then meet with your mother-in-law without mentioning it, and I'll just be a friend he's travelling with.'

Fadi broke out into a relieved grin. 'Marvellous. Absolutely marvellous.'

Nadia blinked and gave a tiny nod, but Safiyya wasn't sure that she fully understood even then. Nevertheless, she deferred to Fadi, sipped her water and said nothing more.

Laura spoke next: 'Safiyya's going to go to Dixon Park, just as Amin wants. She'll try to meet him for a moment, just long enough to give him a mobile phone and organise a time to call him. We've done something similar many times. She'll also ask him whether he'll accompany her to Lebanon to meet your mother-in-law in order to receive her blessing. We believe Amin will agree to travel.'

Safiyya felt her face heat and looked down at the table, hoping to hide her discomfort. Amin's feelings towards her obviously included physical attraction, and though she'd told Laura about Amin's behaviour towards her in the hospital, she didn't want to share that information with Fadi and Nadia. The situation was complicated enough.

'It is complex, Nadia,' Laura said, 'but we believe it is workable. We assume he has a passport.'

'Yes,' Fadi said. 'We have his passport.'

'Phew, that's good news,' Laura said. 'So Safiyya meets Amin at Dixon Park and convinces him to follow her. He leaves the witnessing group and travels to Sydney airport, where, together with an exit counsellor, they board a plane. Of course, Amin will have no idea about the exit counsellor. As far as he's concerned, he's travelling with Safiyya to see his grandmother.'

'What will Halima say when she meets Amin?' Nadia

whispered to Fadi.

He patted her hand and whispered back, 'Don't worry, my love, her sight is so bad she won't notice how thin he's become.'

'The good news is,' Matthew said, 'we've decided on the exit counsellor, and I'm sure you'll be happy because it's Michael. You really couldn't ask for a better person. He's also organising the tickets and seating, so if there's any last-minute changes needed, he can handle them relatively easily.'

Nadia's face lit up, her eyes suddenly sparkling with excitement. 'Oh yes, I was impressed with Michael, such a kind, sensitive soul.' She smiled tentatively. 'I am happy now, but we need to pray that it will work. Safiyya, you have such a beautiful name. I know we have different religious beliefs, but we can still pray, can't we?'

Safiyya nodded. She'd moved away from her religion many years ago and didn't pray anymore, but she wasn't going to disappoint Nadia. 'Of course, Nadia, I'll pray for you and Fadi. And I'll pray for Amin too.'

34

Safiyya stood behind an ice-cream trolley near the fountain, taking in the scene at Dixon Park. Only a few cars passed by on the road, but the perfect spring weather had brought many people out to stroll in the park, plus the joggers, some with strollers and a few early picnic-goers, who sat on blankets enjoying their breakfast. The Church of Love and Faith's witnessing table sat at the north end of the park near a small lake where a narrow footbridge spanned the water.

Other religious groups also peddled their wares. On the other side of the lake, God's Witnesses handed out leaflets proclaiming the end of the world, and thirty or so metres behind them members of the Ananada Meditation Centre performed a Sufi dance.

Safiyya wandered closer and stood near the witnessing table, but out of sight behind a garden of shrubs and trees. *What is this witnessing business, anyway?*

An elderly woman walked past the table, and one member of the Church of Love and Faith stepped up to her and said, 'Beautiful day. All God's creations—'

'God bless you,' the woman interrupted and continued on her way, never breaking her stride.

Another member accosted a woman who pushed a young boy in a wheelchair along the path. 'Would you like a booklet about God and happiness?' he asked.

The boy took the brochure and gave the man a gold coin.

'Thank you, you're so kind.'

Another member, a young man, approached a woman as she stepped off the footbridge. 'Hello, madam,' he said, 'you look a little stressed. Can I talk to you?'

The woman shook her head and avoided looking the young man in the face. 'No thanks, I don't believe in God.'

'Well, maybe that's why you're sad,' he replied.

The woman grimaced. 'Oh please, buzz off, will you? Why don't you guys get real jobs?' She strode on.

Safiyya could see Amin, but she wasn't sure if he could see her. He wore a crumpled white shirt and pants that hadn't been pressed for a long time, and his shoelaces trailed along the ground. He looked subdued and stopped fewer people than the other members of the church. Suddenly, he came over to her, holding out a brochure. His face looked gaunt; dark rings circled his eyes, and he hadn't shaved for a couple of days.

'Amin, how are you?' she asked softly.

He managed a half-hearted smile. 'Praise to God, Safiyya, praise to God.'

She smiled. 'Thank you for your letter. It was very beautiful—'

Amin interrupted. 'We cannot talk. I just wanted to see your face. The Lord shines from it.' He glanced over his shoulder at the other members of the group, but they were too busy to notice that he lingered with her.

Safiyya realised she had to work fast. She took out a mobile phone, a recent small model, and handed it to him. 'Here, Amin, call me whenever you can. My phone number is on the back. I have good news for you about me and the church.'

Amin's eyes widened.

'But you must be careful. Go now, before they see you

talking to me. I don't want you punished for it, and they could stop you from ever seeing me again.'

Amin nodded, slipped the phone into his jacket pocket and walked back to the group. No one seemed to have noticed his brief absence.

Must be God on our side. Safiyya laughed. *I'll tell Nadia the prayers are working.*

She walked further away, called Laura and told her what she'd achieved.

'Well done,' Laura said. 'I knew you could do it. I want to make the reservations for the trip to Lebanon for next Sunday. I don't think we can afford to wait any longer. Do you think you'll be ready by then?'

'I will. I'm not so sure about Amin, but so long as he's at the park, I can probably entice him away with a coy little eyelash flutter.'

Laura chuckled. 'Thank you, Safiyya. I'm so grateful that you're come on board for this.'

Safiyya ended her call and looked for Amin. He was back at the witnessing stand, a little more animated now, perhaps pleased he'd seen her. He touched his pocket as if to make sure the phone was still there, then glanced anxiously at the other church members. The Church of Love and Faith forbade the use of computers and mobile phones.

Safiyya walked past the witness stand on her way out of the park. A huge banner above it read The Church of Love and Faith Loves Families and Has Faith in You. A church member offered her a brochure. She declined, and the member said, 'May God bless your soul, and may you be successful in your mission today.'

Safiyya smiled to herself and kept walking. *Well, at least I have their blessing.*

35

Rochelle stared at the front page of the *Sydney Morning Herald* at the article titled 'Magnate's Wife Flees to India with Son'. She couldn't believe it.

> *Mrs Adele Kingston has reportedly fled to India, where she is living in an ashram with her son, Tyson. Mrs Kingston, who is the wife of Telco boss Ted Kingston, left Australia in September while her husband was overseas. Interpol has been called in to investigate the matter. A spokesperson for Interpol said that it does not comment on operational matters.*

Was she the woman with Graham? Rochelle peered at the picture of Adele Kingston attached to the article. It did look like her, but a couple of weeks had passed, and she'd only seen the woman briefly. She had to be sure.

She located Keith's phone number and gave him a call. 'Keith, this is Rochelle Lightwood. Remember me?'

'Sure, I don't think I'll ever forget your story. How's Penny doing. Missing her dad?'

'Oh, she's great.' Rochelle paused for a moment. 'Well, to be honest, the nightmare continues because I have no idea where Graham is. Penny doesn't talk about him. I've tried to explain what happened, but she's still confused. It'll take time, I guess, but I'm going to take her to see a counsellor. You know, I'll never be able to fully express my thanks for what you did for me.'

'It was our pleasure. We work on all sorts of assignments, but this was certainly a dramatic one.'

'I have something to ask you.'

'Sure, go ahead.'

'You took some photos of Graham and Penny at the airport. Any chance I can get copies?'

'No worries, Rochelle, I'll email them to you now.'

'Thanks a million, Keith.'

Rochelle went straight to her computer. The photos were exactly as she remembered it: Graham and Penny with a very well-dressed woman and her child, a little boy. She compared the photo with the picture in the *Sydney Morning Herald*. The woman was definitely Adele.

Rochelle felt for the boy's father, knew what he'd be going through. She could and should help him. She found the number for the *Sydney Morning Herald* and gave them a call.

The receptionist put her through to the reporter, Sue Daley.

'I'm sorry, I can't discuss details of the story since it's only unfolding now,' the reporter said tersely. 'And I'm really busy, so please, if you need to talk to me, send me an email.'

Rochelle rolled her eyes. *Typical.* But she had no intention of being fobbed off. 'What would you say if I told you that I saw Mrs Kingston and her son at the airport with my husband the day he tried to kidnap our child and take her to India with him? He didn't succeed because a friend of mine grabbed her and we got her away. But no one did that for Mrs Kingston's little boy. Last I saw of them, they were walking into the departures' area.'

Sue remained silent for a moment and then said, 'Sorry, could you please repeat that?'

'The day Adele Kingston and her son, Tyson, left for India, they were with my husband, Graham, and our daughter, Penny. I had reason to believe he might be trying to take her to India to see a guy called … just a minute …' Rochelle grabbed the brochure Graham had given her and read the name. 'Bakhavitda Krishnanada. Some friends and I managed to rescue Penny, but Adele Kingston and her little boy kept going. I have photos of them all at the airport.'

'Oh, right. Well, I apologise for my abruptness before.'

Ha! As you should!

'Could we meet so you can give me the details?'

'Sure.'

'In the meantime, how would you feel about emailing me the photos?'

She'd not be falling for that—the photos in the paper and Rochelle sidelined. 'I'd prefer to meet first.'

'Okay. How about this afternoon?'

They arranged a time and place to meet, then Rochelle called Andrew, her lawyer.

'Rochelle,' he said, 'I was just thinking about you. Have you seen the *Sydney Morning Herald* today? My bet is that the other person with Graham at the airport was Adele Kingston.'

'Yep, it was.' Rochelle told Andrew about the photos and the phone call with Sue Daley.

'Hmm. Very interesting.' Rochelle could just see Andrew leaning back in his chair. 'Listen, I suggest you don't talk to her until we discuss this further. You gotta know one thing about some of these journalists. They'll milk you for whatever information they can get. After that they won't want to know about you. It's sad but it's true. Sure, you should help her, but that's if she helps you. For example, Sue might very well know where Graham is, and we need to discuss how to extract that information from her. I'm free at lunchtime.'

'That works. I'm meeting the reporter at four.'

~

Rochelle had no experience with journalists or the media, but she imagined Sue would be a tough character, with an office oozing modern corporate elegance. When the receptionist showed her into the reporter's office, however, reality surprised her.

The mismatched desk and chairs looked like they'd come from different garage sales, and piles of newspapers and boxes of files were spread over the worn carpet. A black and white picture of two young girls walking on the beach holding hands hung on a wall marked from years of use. On top of that, Sue was tiny, with soft curls that matched her voice and manner. *But looks can be deceiving.*

Sue introduced herself, then gestured to two mid-century chairs set around a scratched coffee table. A vase of dried flowers and a small bowl filled with various sugar packets sat in the centre. 'So, Rochelle,' Sue said once they'd both sat down, 'it sounds like you've got quite a story of your own.'

Rochelle noted the recording device set up on the table between them, almost hidden by the flowers and the bowl. Rochelle looked Sue in the eye and raised her eyebrows. 'Are you going to ask me if I mind you recording this?'

'Oh.' Clearly, Sue hadn't expected that. She managed a smile. 'Sure. Is it okay?'

'Only if you give me a copy of the recording. I'll give it to my solicitor to check and give it back to you if he okays it.' She smiled inside. *Score one to Rochelle.*

'Right. Okay, I can do that. And I won't let anything go to press without your permission. And look, I'm sorry about our first conversation. I wasn't having a good day, but I am very keen to hear your story, especially the airport episode.'

Rochelle smiled. *And I'm keen to know what you know about all this.*

Sue pulled out a copy of the *Sydney Morning Herald.* 'Look, Rochelle, Ted Kingston is a big name, CEO of one of the nation's top companies, and constantly in the news. His wife, Adele, is a public socialite who appears in all the women's magazines and gossip columns. Now she abandons her wealth and fame for an unknown guru in a faraway ashram. Our readership and, for that matter, the public, will want to understand what drives people like Adele to give it all away—and for what?'

Rochelle nodded. 'Look, Sue, I'll be frank with you. I'm happy to tell my story and share it, but I won't do it for nothing.'

Sue's expression soured. She shook her head. 'We don't pay for talent, and we don't pay for stories. It would compromise our editorial standards.'

Rochelle shook her head. 'I don't want money, not a cent. I want information. I need to know where Graham is right now. That's what's important to me.'

'Ah, well, Graham hasn't been on our radar at all. There are thousands of people at that ashram, and our interest has just been on Adele Kingston and her little boy, Tyson. I understand you wanting us to help you in return for your story, but at the end of the day, it depends on where my editor wants to go with this. If he decides to send a crew to India to film the ashram, we might be able to find out what other people of interest are there. That's a big "if", though.'

'I get that.' Rochelle steeled her expression. 'I'm just a little person of no consequence.'

Sue winced. 'Not at all. It's just how the media works. We focus on names people know, but I'll do what I can for you.'

Rochelle sighed. 'Okay. Thanks.'

'By the way, do you know what the connection is between Graham and Adele? I mean, I realise this is a painful topic, but were they in a relationship?'

Rochelle paused before replying. Sue, no doubt, wanted a juicy titbit to feed the masses. Rochelle couldn't give her that, but she could use the question as an opportunity. 'Let's talk about this and everything else later,' she said. 'Can you find out about the filming in India?'

Sue frowned down at her recorder, then looked back up to meet Rochelle's gaze. 'Can you show me the photos?'

'I can, but I can't give you copies.' Rochelle found the photos on her phone and showed them to Sue, who studied them for a few moments. She lingered on the one of Graham and Penny together with Adele and Tyson.

'Have you noticed how both parents are pulling their children along?' Sue asked. 'It's almost as if they didn't want to go.'

'Sure,' Rochelle said, 'It was the first thing I noticed.'

Sue handed the phone back to Rochelle. 'Have the police seen these pictures?'

'I haven't shown them to them, but the person who took them may have.'

Sue narrowed her eyes, apparently—and correctly—suspecting that Rochelle had left out pertinent details. 'And would it be possible to obtain high resolution copies of these images?' she continued.

Rochelle looked directly at her. 'Let's leave it at this point. You have my number. Once you've worked it out, let me know how you plan to move forward on this. I'm not trying to be difficult, I'm just desperate. You might be desperate for a great story, but I'm far more desperate to protect my daughter, and knowing Graham's whereabouts is a huge part of that. If he is in India, which is what I believe, at least Penny is safe for the moment. But he could return at any time, and we could have a huge problem. I don't know if you've covered any other cult stories, but I've learned very quickly that there are no limits to the crimes such organisations will commit to keep their members on board and the money rolling in.'

Sue nodded. 'I know what you're saying. Let me tell you something. Have you got a couple of minutes?'

Rochelle shrugged. 'Sure, go right ahead.'

The journalist reached for her recorder and pressed the off button. 'I actually have a deep interest in your story, not just because I'm a journalist but because I think it's important to tell the world what cults really do to individuals and families.'

Rochelle sensed a genuineness in Sue's words. She leaned forward slightly, curious now.

'Do you remember when, in 1995, four members of the Aum Shinri Kyo cult released lethal sarin gas into four of the busiest trains in the Tokyo subway?'

Rochelle shook her head. Like many others, back then cults had had no bearing on her life, and if she'd seen the report in the media, she would've probably taken little notice of it.

Sue continued, 'Miraculously, only a small number of people were killed in the attack, but many were injured.' She stood, picked up a photo frame from her desk and handed it to Rochelle, then sat again. The photograph it contained showed two children—a boy around six years old and a girl of about ten. 'These are my beautiful children, Serena and Spencer, in 1995. At the time of the attack, they were with my ex-husband, Martin, who was in Japan on business. They'd never left Australia before, so it was a big treat for them.'

Rochelle frowned. *Is this going where I think it is?*

Sue took a deep breath. 'They were on the train when the cult members attacked. They struck just as the train pulled into the Shin-Ochanomizu station in central Tokyo.'

Rochelle's heart ached. This story could only get worse.

Sue sniffed. 'Today Serena is legally blind, and Spencer is battling a complex skin disease that isn't getting any better. I know not every cult is so cruel or callous, but I do know about cults, and every day I and my children live with the aftermath of what happened that fateful Monday morning in 1995 on the Chiyoda Line train in the Tokyo Metro.' Sue fixed her gaze on Rochelle's face. 'I promise you, I will do everything I can to help you.'

36

Safiyya was preparing for bed when her phone rang. She glanced at the clock on her bedside table: 11.20 pm. Who would call her so late, and on a Monday night? Only one way to find out. She answered the call.

A low voice said, 'Hi, it's Amin.'

Her heart skipped a beat. 'Where are you?' she whispered.

'I'm walking in the garden; it's dark. Don't worry, it's just the two of us. I'm fasting from tomorrow until Wednesday, but I'm okay. I was thinking about you the whole day.'

Safiyya took a deep breath, remembering what she'd planned to say. 'Amin, I had a dream I want to share with you. I dreamed that I decided to join the church.'

'Hallelujah!'

'Shhh, please don't raise your voice,' Safiyya said, worried that someone would hear him before she could finish. 'But in my dream you told me I needed your grandmother's blessing before I could join.'

'Hallelujah, praised be the Lord,' Amin said, this time softly.

'So we travelled to Lebanon together, and we met her. She was a very saintly woman, and she blessed us. It was a very powerful dream.'

'Wait, I need to go; someone's walking nearby.' The phone went dead.

Safiyya sighed. Had he been caught? Had they heard him shout? Would they find his phone and punish him? She shook her head, walked to her dressing table, and picked up her hairbrush. She'd just finished brushing her long, thick locks when her phone rang again.

'Sorry, Safiyya, it's Amin. God bless you and thank you for sharing your dream. I hope it'll come true. Wouldn't that be a miracle? But don't worry, I won't tell anyone about it. Maybe I'll call you on Wednesday after my fast is over.'

'That would be nice,' Safiyya said, 'but please be careful.' Safiyya smiled as she ended the call. *One step closer. This might actually work.*

She slipped into bed and tried to sleep, but too many questions and imaginings roamed through her mind. What it would be like to travel to Lebanon? Though born in Iran, she'd been very young when she'd migrated to Australia, and now the Middle East was far away and Lebanon just another country on a big map. But the thought of her mission sent excitement flooding her veins. She was ready to do this.

Safiyya decided that, as long as Laura and Michael agreed, she wouldn't tell Amin about the trip to Lebanon until the Sunday morning they planned to go. Hopefully, he'd be witnessing at Dixon Park as usual and she could get him into a car, which would go straight to the airport. It was all very risky, but she didn't want to give him time for second thoughts.

She reflected quietly. To think that when she met Amin in the emergency ward at Bankstown Hospital, she'd thought he was just another patient.

37

Laura got out of the shower and towelled off. She smiled at herself in the bathroom mirror. Safiyya's positivity when she'd called that morning had rubbed off, giving Laura confidence that their plan for exiting Amin from the Church of Love and Faith would work. She'd go to bed with a lighter heart tonight.

As she wandered into her bedroom, her phone pinged from its place beside her bed. She checked it and discovered an urgent text from Margaret, who'd been on emergency call duty. *Annabel wants you to call her. She's received some disturbing information.* Should she call tonight or wait until the morning? Laura sighed; neither option promised a good night's sleep.

'Oh, Laura,' Annabel said in answer to her call. 'Thanks for getting back to me. I got an anonymous call from a member of The Healing Mission. She says Anne is really sick. Apparently, she hasn't left her room for days. She couldn't tell me anything else, said outside calls were restricted and she'd be punished if they caught her. She said she'd try to call back in exactly twenty-four hours—if she can get access to a telephone. What can we do?'

Laura chewed her bottom lip. 'I don't know, offhand. The best thing for starters is probably to have a three-way conference call with Matthew.'

'Yes, please. As soon as possible.'

'Okay, I'll arrange it in the morning. I'll be in touch.'

The next morning, Laura and Matthew managed a quick chat before the conference call to review the options. They sat at the conference table, set up the call and put the phone on speaker.

Annabel began by repeating the brief conversation she'd had with the cult member. 'Clearly, Anne's deteriorating,' she said in conclusion. 'We have to do something urgently.'

Matthew glanced at Laura. She nodded. 'It certainly sounds that way,' he said.

'We have three options for you to consider,' Laura said. 'The first, which I recommend though the chances of success are limited, would be to call The Healing Mission and express your concern. You could make a lightly veiled threat that in the event of Anne being hurt or even hurting herself, you'll take the matter much further and, ultimately, they'll be held accountable.

'The difficulty, though, is that even if they take your call, they'll want to know how you knew she was sick, and if you mention an anonymous source, they may ground the whole group until that source owns up. They'd then punish that person and maybe Anne as well, and there'd be no chance of the promised follow-up call.'

'Another option,' Matthew said, 'would be for you to call them and threaten to approach the media. Anne's story is powerful, so I think there would be some media interest in it. It's possible, but unlikely, that The Healing Mission would rather get rid of Anne than have her as the source of bad publicity. Then again, they may decide that any publicity is good publicity. In which case, they'll try to use the media exposure to their advantage.'

'The third option,' Laura said, 'would involve planting someone in the mission. Over a period of time, the person would befriend Anne and plan how to get her away from the church.'

'You also have the option of calling the police or even an ambulance,' Matthew added. 'But the moment they see someone in uniform approaching them, they might ship Anne, and any other unwell members, out of their premises.'

All they heard in response was a deep sigh. Matthew and Laura glanced at each other.

Laura figured that the poor woman was probably overwhelmed. 'I realise this is painful and that you feel Anne's life is on the line, but we do need to look at your options.'

Annabel coughed and cleared her throat. 'I'm hearing you loud and clear. But what about Divine Delicacies? Can't they help? Aren't they a sort of parent company to The Healing Mission?'

'We'll look into that, Annabel,' Matthew said. 'And we'll do what we can from this end. We realise this is a serious situation. Please call back in the next day or two, and call straight away if the woman who called you last night contacts you again.'

Annabel thanked them and said she'd make a call to The Healing Mission the next morning to ask about Anne's health. She'd also consider the other options carefully.

Laura ended the call and turned to Matthew. 'How about we get in touch with Albert Carter since he was on the Divine Delicacies board? I'm really worried about Anne. In a situation like this, we can't afford to leave even one stone unturned.'

Matthew nodded. 'I was thinking the same thing. It might be a race against time.'

38

Matthew drove Safiyya to Dixon Park. Her luggage and a suitcase for Amin, which Nadia had packed, were in the trunk. Safiyya had Amin's passport and ticket and her own. Michael was travelling to the airport on his own.

'You okay?' Matthew asked as he pulled up.

Safiyya looked at his kind, smiling eyes. 'Yeah. I'm fine. We've been over it plenty of times.' And she'd decided she wasn't above flirting if necessary. Failure wasn't an option.

She left Matthew in the car and wandered through the park, barely registering the pleasant Sunday morning atmosphere, and took up the same position near the fountain. She saw Amin by the witnessing table, smiled in his direction and breathed a sigh of relief. Amin had probably seen her, but he gave no indication.

She waited, her heart beating rather too loudly. *Come on, come on, Amin. Come see me.*

Several minutes later, he walked towards her and, in a somewhat detached manner, said, 'Hello, Safiyya. God bless you.'

'Yes, Amin, I hope God will bless me, because if I receive his blessing through your grandmother, then I'll join the Church of Love and Faith. I don't doubt she has the power to give blessings.'

Amin's face lit up. 'Hallelujah, Safiyya.'

'But you must come with me now. I will join, but we must travel to see your grandmother first—you and I together. Come.'

She gestured and walked towards the car, where Matthew watched through binoculars. Amin walked beside her for a few metres, then stopped, looking confused.

Safiyya glanced back at the witnessing table. Everything appeared normal. No one had noticed Amin's absence. Yet. She placed her hand on Amin's shoulder, stared into his eyes and smiled. 'Can I take your hand, Amin?'

He frowned. His church strictly forbade all contact between unmarried men and women.

She batted her eyes. Just a little. 'Please. I would like that very much.' She took his hand, held it firmly and led him the rest of the way to the car.

Amin didn't resist. He looked at her with a love-sick smile.

Safiyya opened the car door, gently pushed Amin inside and climbed in after him. As soon as she shut the door, she heard the locks engage, and a moment later, they sped off. She looked back at the witnessing table. No one stood there, but about eight church members were spreading out in what appeared to be a search.

They were thirty minutes away from Sydney airport.

Amin frowned and turned to Safiyya, suspicion clouding his eyes. 'What are you doing? Who is this man? And where are you taking me?'

She smiled and took his hand again. 'Remember the dream I told you? It's coming true. We're going away together to see your grandmother, and then I'll join the church, and we'll be with God together.'

Amin listened, but her words didn't seem to move him. She shifted closer. 'Your grandmother's going to give us her blessing.'

'And who's he?' He jerked his head towards Matthew.

'That's my friend, Matthew. He's taking us to the airport so we can go see your grandmother together.'

Amin looked down at their hands, frowned and turned to stare out the window. Safiyya had no idea what was going through his mind, but she figured that for so long as he held her hand, things were still going well. She looked up and caught Matthew's gaze as he looked in the rear-vision mirror. He gave her a little smile and a supportive nod. She smiled back. Now they just had to get him onto the plane.

Matthew stopped the car outside international departures. Safiyya collected her small suitcase and Amin's travel bag, then took his hand again and led him towards the Qantas check-in desk. Amin looked around, his gaze flitting quickly over everything, and when she queued, he released her hand and paced up and down. Safiyya tried to calm him, but she could see his anxiety rising. Eventually, she reached the desk.

The agent looked at her computer, then at Amin and Safiyya and said, 'You have a third person in your party, yes? Three passengers who need to be seated together.'

Safiyya nodded. 'They should've checked in already.' Her heart raced. She hoped Amin hadn't heard.

'Correct,' the agent responded. 'Mr Michael Ballen in seat 54A. Mr Amin Haddad in 54B, and you, madam, in 54C. Here are your boarding passes. All okay?'

'Yes, thank you.' Safiyya breathed a sigh of relief. She turned to walk away, but the agent called her back.

'Excuse me, madam. Can I have a word with you?'

Safiyya edged back to the counter, keeping Amin in sight. He looked terribly lost and confused.

'I'm sorry I'm asking you this question,' the Qantas agent said, 'but is your partner fit to travel? Is he suffering from some disorder we need to know about?'

Safiyya fixed the woman with a smile. 'No, he's fine; just a little nervous about the long flight. There's nothing to worry about.' She couldn't wait to get away from the check-in area.

'My concern is that he appears extremely anxious. The airline has a responsibility to all the passengers, so we can't allow someone to board the flight if we have reason to suspect they're unfit to travel.'

Safiyya glanced back to check on Amin, but he'd disappeared—a nightmare realised. Out of the corner of her eye, she saw him running towards the exit. 'I need to go,' she said, hoping the agent hadn't seen Amin run. 'He'll be fine. I'll make sure of it.'

'Check just before you go,' the agent said. 'The flight crew has the final say on who boards the aircraft and who doesn't.'

'I understand. Thank you for your help and advice.' Safiyya found it difficult to be polite and walk rather than run away from the counter. She tried to appear relaxed and not as if she was chasing Amin, but as soon as she was out of the agent's sight, she ran towards the exit.

Amin was waiting in a long taxi queue. She walked up to him, pretending to be calm while her heart thundered against her ribs. 'Amin, please come with me, please come. God wants us to travel together. I've called the church, and they're happy for us to go see your grandmother. They're looking forward to me joining the church. And they thank you for it.' Safiyya didn't like to lie, but she'd come too far to not throw everything she had at this mission. She hoped he'd forgive her.

Amin just looked at her for a moment, then said, 'How long will we be away?'

'Just a few days. You do want to see your grandmother, don't you?'

He nodded slowly.

'Great. Come on.' She took a step and waited for him to follow. He didn't move. 'We can't see her if we miss the plane,

Amin.' She wanted to take his hand, but feared it might be too much, so she just smiled as confidently as she could manage while her palms sweated and her heart raced.

Amin finally seemed to relax. He managed a smile and joined her, and together they walked back into the terminal. Not taking any chances, Safiyya held onto his elbow and steered him straight for the departures' area.

A few metres from the sliding doors, Safiyya caught sight of three young men running towards them. Her heart beat even faster, and she hurried Amin through the doors.

'Amin, God loves you!' one of them shouted as the doors closed behind them.

Luckily, Amin didn't seem to have heard.

The doors slid open again as someone else entered, and in the space before they closed again, Safiyya heard a chorus of, 'Amin, God loves you!'

Too late, Safiyya thought with a smile. *Amin is safe.*

So long as they let him on the plane!

Though apparently calm now, Amin said nothing and remained subdued all the way through the departures' area. At one point he did smile at Safiyya, which she took as a good sign.

They sat down at the departure gate, and Safiyya spotted Michael on the other side of the room. He gave her a slight nod of recognition. Safiyya breathed easier. *Almost there.* She could still hear those voices crying, 'Amin, God loves you!' One minute later could have been too late.

She planned to walk with him if he became agitated or looked as if he might be having second thoughts, but her occasional comment about how she was really looking forward to meeting his grandmother kept him focused. At last, the boarding call came.

'Oh, Amin, I'm so excited,' Safiyya said as she stood. 'This really is my dream come true.' While they waited to show their boarding passes, she kept chatting about the dream and what a miracle it was that it had come to pass. The attendant checked Amin's pass against something on his clipboard, gave him an appraising glance for what seemed like a very long time, and then to Safiyya's immense relief, said, 'Enjoy your flight.'

Within minutes, they were settled in their seats inside the plane with Michael alongside Amin. After the usual safety talks, the plane taxied towards the runway. Amin took out a pocket Bible and began to read it, his lips moving quickly. He looked up for a moment and turned towards Safiyya. 'Please, Safiyya … can I hold your hand?'

39

When the aircraft reached its cruising altitude for the twelve-hour trip to Hong Kong, Michael knew it was time to start working with Amin. He was still reading the Bible, and every so often he closed his eyes as if dozing off. Michael had seen photos of Amin before he joined the Church of Love and Faith. He'd been a thin young man before, but now with his very pale skin and sunken eyes, he looked emaciated, tired and drawn.

Michael leaned over and looked at Amin's Bible. 'Good book?' he asked. 'Is it a novel?'

Amin kept his eyes on the book. 'It's the word of God: the absolute word of God as revealed to our Holy Saviour. Hallelujah.'

'Do you mind if I take a look?'

Amin pulled away slightly. 'Sorry, but I'm studying now, and if I take my eyes off the book, I may have evil thoughts.'

'Evil, huh. Like what?' Michael asked.

'Like thinking about women or doing things I shouldn't be doing.' Amin glanced at Safiyya.

She smiled.

'Oh. Right.' Michael sat back in his seat, pulled a magazine out of the seat pocket and began to read. Amin went back to his Bible. Michael yawned, discarded the magazine and closed his eyes. He might have appeared to be asleep, but he was wide awake and listening carefully.

'Amin,' Safiyya said quietly. 'Are you okay?'

'Yes, Safiyya, but I feel strange in the presence of the Lord. You shouldn't be sitting so close to me.'

'It's okay,' Safiyya said. 'I won't bite you, and I won't even touch you if you don't want me to. Are you excited about seeing your grandmother? I can't wait to see her.'

'The Lord will decide,' Amin said in a monotone. 'I only agreed to see her in order for you to join the church.'

'That's fine, Amin, I understand,' Safiyya murmured.

'Are you really going to join the church, Safiyya? You know that once you join, we'll never be able to talk to each other. I'll never be able to put my hand on yours. That's God's will.'

'Yes, you've told me that, Amin, but who said that's God's will? Where does God say that we can't talk or be friends?'

For a moment, Amin didn't reply, then he said, 'I don't question the Lord.'

'I'm sad that you think the Lord said this,' Safiyya said. 'Please, Amin, show me where the Lord says this. I don't think He actually says anything like it.'

Michael opened his eyes. Safiyya was doing well. *Impressive.*

Amin lifted the Bible and showed Safiyya the title embossed in gold: *The Bible of Love and Faith*, His Holiness Pastor Francisco Hollingsworth.

'So this pastor said it?'

'I … I suppose. But he says it's God's will, and I don't question the Lord.'

'And how does he know it's God's will?' Safiyya asked.

'Why, the Lord speaks to him, of course.'

Michael sat up. 'Hey, can I ask you a question? Who is Pastor Francisco Hollingsworth?'

'Oh, he's the Lord's messenger on earth. He gives us life and is the source of all life.'

Michael frowned. 'I thought God gave life and was the source of all life, not some pastor.'

Amin frowned but said nothing.

'Have you met this holy man?' Michael asked.

'Not yet.' Amin's hand hovered defensively over his book.

'Oh, so how did he gain the gift of holiness? I mean, was he ordained or blessed by another holy man?'

Amin shifted in his seat. He looked at Safiyya, but Safiyya turned towards Michael. 'Um, excuse me, sir, I didn't catch your name.'

'Michael's my name, and yours?'

'Safiyya.'

'Michael, I was talking to Amin before you dozed off. He belongs to a church called the Church of Love and Faith. You can look up all your questions on their website.'

Amin seemed to relax. 'Thank you, Safiyya,' he whispered.

'But I'm intrigued,' Michael said. 'This isn't the same Bible we all read, or at least I used to read. Who gave Pastor Francisco the right to change it?'

'I'm sure you can answer the question, Amin,' Safiyya said gently.

Amin swallowed, suddenly looking terribly lost. 'I can't, Safiyya; tell him to leave me alone.' He put his hands over his ears and stared at his Bible.

Question time was over.

Safiyya sat back in her seat. She looked tired. Michael wasn't surprised. It had been a long day for her. She closed her eyes and soon appeared to be dozing.

Michael returned to the magazine but kept an eye on Amin. He looked around the cabin, as if checking to see if anyone was watching, then nervously reached across Amin and put his hand into Safiyya's.

Is he expecting a bolt of lightning to hit him for his transgression?

When nothing happened, Amin relaxed back against the seat, closed his eyes and before long, his breathing deepened and his Bible fell from his grasp.

Michael picked up the Bible and opened it. On the inside cover, someone had written a list of dates under the heading The End Times: 1 September 1980, 31 October 1993, 12 June 2000, and 31 September 2105. Michael scribbled them down on the back of the duty-free magazine, stuffed it into the holder on the seat in front of him, and placed the Bible on Amin's seat tray.

When Amin woke up a couple of hours later, he yawned and looked around. When he met Michael's gaze, he dropped Safiyya's hand as if it was a hot poker.

'Say, Amin,' Michael asked casually, 'do you think the world is going to end?'

Amin's eyes widened. 'What do you mean? Of course, the world is coming to its end. It says in the Bible, "And behold, the end times are coming when salvation will fill the heavens and the earth."'

'Really? Where's that written?' Michael asked.

Amin flipped through his Bible. 'Oh, it's in several places. It's such a well-known prophesy.'

'And when do you think the world will end?'

'Oh, that's simple. His Holiness told us it'll end on 31 September 2025.'

Michael sat up. 'Hold on a minute, Amin, hasn't September got only thirty days?'

Amin thought for a moment. 'Yes, it has, but the Lord will add another day in order to destroy the world on that day.'

'Aha. You know, I remember reading about a prophesy from the Lord that suggested the world would end on September 1,

1980. What happened then?'

'I don't know what you're talking about. I told you the date.'

Michael pulled out the duty-free magazine and glanced at his scribble. 'Does the date 31 October 1993 mean anything to you?'

Amin looked away.

A voice came over the PA. 'This is your captain speaking. As we are about to land in Hong Kong, would all passengers please return to their seats and fasten their seat belts. Cabin crew, please prepare for landing.'

'May the Lord bless you, Michael. We're landing now.'

Michael looked at his watch. The plane was landing at Hong Kong airport thirty minutes ahead of schedule. *So we'll probably make the connection. Doesn't matter, I think we're doing well.*

Amin turned to Safiyya. 'I think we're halfway there. The Lord is with us. Can you feel His presence?'

She smiled. 'Of course, Amin. I can feel His presence just like you do.'

Amin and Safiyya disembarked and headed towards their new departure gate with Michael walking behind. He dialled Laura to give her an update. It was 4.00 am in Brisbane, but she'd be expecting his call.

40

Even though the plane had landed early in Hong Kong, they had little time for conversation before they boarded their connecting flight. Michael breathed a sigh of relief when he saw they'd been given the same seating configuration—as he'd requested—and Amin didn't appear suspicious about them being seated together again. Amin had little travel experience, and Michael figured he probably assumed that passengers retained the same seats throughout a flight regardless of plane changes.

When the plane took off, Amin got out his Bible again, but he left it closed. Though he touched it from time to time, he didn't read it.

'Hey, Amin,' Michael asked, 'can I have a look at your book?'

'It's not a book; it's the Lord's word.'

'Oh, I'm sorry; may I have a look at the Lord's word?'

Amin nodded and handed him the Bible.

Michael opened the book and studied the dates on the back of the front cover, making sure that Amin could see him.

Amin watched him with a frown. 'Thank you, Michael, my Bible, please?'

Before Michael returned the Bible, he said, 'Amin, what are all these dates?'

Amin looked away. 'I don't know, and you're disturbing me. Please respect the Lord's word.'

'Of course,' Michael said. 'It's just a bit strange, all these dates. Are they when the world was meant to end?'

Amin's frown deepened. He blinked several times and cleared his throat. 'The Lord can change his mind. Is He not almighty and all powerful?'

'Oh. Of course, Amin, you're so right.'

They all watched the sun setting, a stunning view from the air as the flaming golden ball descended below the curve of the horizon, leaving the sky in darkness. Safiyya peered through the window at the stars twinkling into view.

Amin took her hand again. 'You know, Safiyya, when night comes, the Lord spreads a blanket over the sun. He pokes little holes in the blanket, and they are the stars we see.'

Safiyya turned to him with a smile. 'That's so beautiful, Amin.'

Michael smiled. Amin was changing. He'd become more open and communicative, and he hadn't opened his Bible since flying out of Hong Kong. Michael wasn't sure that anything he'd said had made an impression, but just being away from the church for almost twenty-four hours would've helped.

The cabin crew turned off the lights. Though several people kept their eyes glued to their screens, most of the passengers dozed off. Safiyya looked like she was asleep, but Michael couldn't be sure she wasn't pretending. He set his seat back and turned on his side as if readying for sleep. Even though he closed his eyes, he could open them slightly to check on Amin.

After looking furtively around, Amin put his head on Safiyya's shoulder and his hand on her hair. It was the first time Amin had been so physically close with her—a good sign, since people were more open to changing their beliefs if it meant they could be close to the people to whom they were attracted. Amin stroked Safiyya's hair and touched her face, and soon he also dozed off.

Michael took Amin's Bible off his table and put it in his backpack, then he relaxed back against the seat and joined the others in sleep.

Two hours before landing in Beirut, the cabin crew served breakfast.

As soon as Amin had woken and orientated himself, Michael said, 'Hey, Amin, do you ever use the internet?'

He shook his head. 'Oh no, Michael, the internet is the tool of Satan. The web is one big pornography site.'

Michael's eyebrows rose. 'Oh, really? I just found an address for Pastor Francisco Hollingsworth on the web. All his lectures are available online.'

Amin blinked several times, clearly taken aback by this. 'Impossible. It must be someone impersonating him. Where did you find it?'

'Well, the story gets even messier. Apparently, Pastor Hollingsworth is all over the web, not just for his lectures but because of a series of newspaper reports that refer to his conviction for fraud and sexual molestation.'

'See, I told you the web is a tool for Satan,' Amin retorted. 'Someone is trying to give him a bad name.'

'Then they've gone to a lot of effort and pulled the wool over a lot of people's faces.'

'Satan is powerful,' Amin replied.

'Powerful enough to put photos and articles about the court case on reputable news sites?'

'I suppose,' Amin replied. He then focused on devouring his breakfast, but he didn't say his usual blessing before the meal. He seemed to remember afterwards and whispered a hurried prayer, but it was more like an afterthought than something he felt passionate about. When he'd finished, he smiled at Safiyya and said, 'Isn't it wonderful? We're about to see my grandmother, and then you'll join the church.'

'It is, but …' Her smile disappeared, and she sighed. 'It'll be the end of our friendship, won't it? Once I join the church, you'll never be able to touch me again, will you?'

Amin's eyes widened. He frowned, bit his bottom lip and shifted in his seat. Safiyya's words seemed to have hit home.

'But anyway,' she continued, 'we'll tell your grandma all about the church, about your special edition of the Bible, and about Pastor Francisco Hollingsworth. What do you think she'll say?'

Amin looked horrified. 'Oh no, Safiyya, please don't say anything to my grandmother. She's an old woman, and she's a little narrow-minded. I don't think she'd like it that I'm in a … a different church to hers. But I love her dearly. After the pastor, she's the most important person in my life.'

She took his hand. 'Leave that to me, Amin; whatever I say, I'll say very gently. You know I care about you.'

Amin pressed his lips together as if to stop himself from bursting into tears.

'It's okay,' she said softly. 'We'll be okay; you and I.'

Amin shook his head and said, so quietly that Michael had to strain to catch it, 'I'm not sure about that.'

She smiled. 'We'll find a way.'

Michael smiled. The woman was a natural at this. He hoped Amin would see that it had to be a way that involved never going back to his church.

They then chatted about ordinary things—favourite food, songs, art, movies, work history, people and so on. The conversation helped to reconnect Amin to the man he was before he joined the cult. He even admitted that he hadn't enjoyed many of his favourite things since joining up.

'Oh, Amin. That's a shame,' Safiyya said. She frowned

thoughtfully. 'I didn't think I'd have to give up listening to my favourite music.'

'We have hymns,' Amin said.

'Not exactly the same kind of thing, though, is it?' Michael said.

By the time the plane landed at Beirut International Airport, Amin hadn't asked for his Bible or even noticed it was missing. A sign that their intervention was proceeding well. Michael, Amin and Safiyya disembarked and moved smoothly through immigration, then made their way to the baggage claim area.

Michael walked slightly behind them, concerned that Amin might question why he was still with them. To Amin, Michael's presence on the flight was simply a coincidence. Surprisingly, however, Amin didn't appear concerned about Michael's obvious presence. But he would need a reason for them to travel together to Saida.

'So where are you guys off to now?' Michael asked.

'Saida,' Safiyya replied.

'That's great, I'm staying there at a hotel called Ghaziya. I have a hire car organised. You're welcome to share it. I'd like the company.'

'That'll be great,' Safiyya said. 'Thank you.'

To Michael's surprise, Amin smiled and nodded his agreement.

When Amin went to the bathroom, Safiyya and Michael had a quick conference.

'He's definitely wavering in his beliefs,' Michael whispered, 'but I don't think he's ready to hear the truth about why we've come.'

'I agree. I'll not say anything.'

'And, hey. You're really good at this. What you're saying is perfect.'

She smiled. 'Matthew coached me well.'

Within an hour after landing, they were in the hire car driving south down the coastal highway to the seaside resort of Saida. Michael drove and the others sat in the back. Safiyya and Michael occasionally engaged in some casual conversation about the flat landscape, the towns they passed through and the mostly rocky beaches, but Amin didn't say a word, and from time to time he closed his eyes. Michael asked Safiyya where they were staying.

'We're going to see Amin's grandmother,' Safiyya said, 'but we shouldn't assume we can stay there.'

'Why don't you check into the hotel I've booked? We can do some sightseeing together.'

Safiyya agreed, and Amin seemed happy to follow her lead.

At one point, when Michael checked in the rear-vision mirror, he had his arm around Safiyya. Michael smiled. Amin was a sweet guy. He really hoped they could break the hold the church had on him.

Thanks to a GPS device, they arrived at the pretty resort city of Saida forty-five minutes later.

Michael checked them into the two rooms he'd booked, then joined Safiyya and Amin in the lobby. 'Okay, we're all set. Amin and I'll share one room, and Safiyya has the other.'

Amin glanced at Safiyya and smiled shyly, his eyes twinkling.

Had he just thought of some other sleeping arrangement? Either way, it was the first time Michael had seen Amin smile—a good sign that he was becoming himself again.

They showered and dressed in clean clothes to refresh themselves after the long flight, then met back in the lobby.

Amin was keen to see his grandmother. 'She's a very wise woman,' he said. 'I listen to her. When you meet her, you should listen to her too.'

Michael said he'd like to meet this wise woman, and he was happy to drive them there. He suggested Amin call her to let her know they were coming. Amin didn't know that his parents had already told her what was going on. Nadia and Fadi had found it difficult to tell her about Amin's newfound religion, but they'd done it because they knew it was necessary if they were to get their son back.

~

Fifteen minutes later, Amin stood outside Halima's door while Safiyya and Michael watched from the car across the street. He looked at the old stone walls and up at the little balcony with its curly ironwork. He hadn't seen his grandmother for over ten years, and his heart raced with a mixture of nervousness and excitement. Besides Safiyya, she was the only person he'd communicated with since joining the church, and now he was about to be in her presence, he wasn't sure what he'd say. A man browsing the fruit piled in large baskets outside the greengrocer shop two doors down stared at him with narrowed eyes. Realising he probably looked strange just standing there, Amin took a deep breath and knocked.

The door opened slowly, just a crack, and a tiny old woman with snowy white hair tucked under a small pale-blue headscarf peered out at him. Amin didn't remember her being so small. Her head only came up to his shoulders. They gazed at each other for a moment, then her wrinkled face broke into a beaming smile, revealing quite a few gaps where teeth used to reside.

'Amin, Amin, my boy.' She opened the door fully, threw her arms around him, and cried with joy. 'My, how you've grown.'

Amin hugged her back and felt tears on his own cheeks.

She pulled back, still beaming her delight. 'What a fine

young man you are. So handsome.' She giggled, then gestured him inside and shut the door behind him.

He stepped into a cosy living room with white-rendered walls, sparsely but comfortably furnished and rich with traditional carpets, wall hangings in shades of gold and burgundy, and gilded icons of one or other saint, which filled almost every available bit of wall space. She served him tea and special Lebanese cakes while they sat on the sofa together, and Halima talked about herself and the family in Lebanon, often saying how grateful she was to God for every blessing. Amin felt humbled in her presence but also a little uncomfortable. He could never share his secret about his new church with her. She was as passionate about God as he was and as dedicated to her church.

Was there really only one way to God? And only one man who knew that way, as the pastor said? His grandmother might be stuck in the old ways but, given the almost-heavenly light of love that shone from her being, those ways had clearly brought her very close to God.

When Amin commented on the icons, impressed and inspired by their beauty, Halima reached out, took his hands and looked into his eyes. 'My boy, beware of the soothsayers; those who claim to represent the truth but represent only themselves. Beware of the pastors who change our holy Bible, for they do it for themselves and not for God. No man or woman has the authority to change God's words. And beware the prophets who claim that their truth is the only truth. Anyone can claim to hold the truth, but those who truly hold it need not claim anything.'

Amin couldn't respond; he found himself trembling with fear. Her words cut too close to his situation. He remembered what Michael had said about the court case and imagined the pastor with his hands on Safiyya. The image made him feel sick.

His grandmother peered up at him, and he suspected that

even with her limited sight, she didn't miss much. 'Amin, my boy, I have had dreams about you, and they have not been good dreams. I have prayed for you, and my prayers have been difficult. But I will never leave you, and you will never leave me.'

She knows. Oh God. She knows! Amin burst into tears. His grandmother wrapped her arms around him, and he held her tight. And it felt right. Comforting. Nothing sinful about him touching this woman. Her love was pure. He felt that. Knew that. And it poured into him from her embrace. How could the pastor ban all physical contact between the sexes in his followers and yet be convicted of sexual molestation?

He remembered Grandmother's words. *No man or woman has the authority to change God's words.* And Michael had asked, *Who gave Pastor Francisco the right to change it?* No one, he guessed reluctantly. And somewhere deep inside, his grandmother's last words rang true: *Anyone can claim to hold the truth, but those who hold it need not claim anything.*

A spike of anger laced with the bitter flavour of betrayal shot through him.

He finally drew out of his grandmother's embrace and wiped his arm across his cheeks to dry his tears, but he said nothing. His mind was all jumbled up. He felt so confused. His world was tumbling upside down. Why had he left? He should go back. They'd tell him it was all lies and everything would be all right again. He glanced at the door, but knew it was impossible. He was on the other side of the world.

'How did you get here, my boy?' Halima asked quietly.

He swung his gaze back to her. 'My friend Safiyya travelled with me. She said that if you bless her, she'll join—' He stopped in the middle of his sentence, his heart sinking at the thought. He'd enjoyed this time with Safiyya and didn't want it to end.

And no one had smitten him down. He'd see her if she joined the church, but only on the other side of the hall. He'd never get to touch her soft hair again. He couldn't believe he was thinking like that. Had Satan got a hold of him already? He swallowed and pulled his attention back to the present, where his grandmother watched him as if waiting for more. 'And … and I met a clever man called Michael on the flight here. He drove me here. They're both waiting outside.'

'Then invite them in. I am sure they are good people.'

Amin composed himself and walked outside. Michael and Safiyya stood beside the car, chatting and people watching. He walked over to Safiyya and hugged her and found he didn't want to let go. He held her tight and cried again. 'I'm so sorry; I'm so confused,' he sobbed into her hair.

'Don't worry, Amin,' she said kindly. 'Just relax. We've got all the time in the world. Are we able to meet your grandmother?'

'Sure,' Amin pulled back with a smile. He wiped away his tears and led them inside.

When they walked in, Halima stood and held out her hand. 'Sit down, my children. It is a pleasure to meet you.' She peered at Safiyya and Michael, straining to see them.

'It's an honour for us to meet you,' Michael replied.

They talked and ate together, but it grew late and Amin felt tired. He even caught Safiyya stifling a yawn. Halima suggested they go back to their hotel and visit again tomorrow, and they all readily agreed.

No one spoke on the short drive back. Only the sound of the GPS broke the silence. Even Amin's mind was quiet, as though he didn't want think in case it shook the ground of his being even more than the events of the last couple of days. Back at the hotel, they all agreed to get an early night and walked together to their rooms.

They said goodnight at Safiyya's door. He wanted to kiss her—just on the cheek—but he couldn't quite give himself permission, so he just smiled and gave her a quick hug before walking on to his own room. A hug was radical enough. But oh, it felt so good. So right. Michael followed a few steps behind him.

41

The next morning, Michael left Amin sleeping and wandered downstairs to use the hotel phone to call Laura.

'Mission accomplished,' he said enthusiastically. 'Everything went like clockwork. Safiyya is a natural at this, and Halima was amazing at drawing him out and showing him the depth of life he could have outside his church—without ever mentioning his church, of course. And last night over dinner he actually sounded normal. And he hugged Safiyya. Twice.'

'What a relief. I'm so pleased.'

'I'll email you a diary of what happened since leaving Melbourne. You should call Nadia and Fadi and let them know.'

'I will. What's Amin doing now?'

'He's sleeping. Don't worry, we've made sure there's no phone in the hotel room. He doesn't have a mobile phone either.'

Michael ended the call and almost bumped into Safiyya, who was on her way back from a run. They rode up in the elevator together.

'Great work yesterday,' Michael said, 'but we can't take any chances. One of us needs to be with Amin all the time. He seems to have made a break from the church's control, but even with successful interventions, in the first few days it's still easy for something to draw him back into their influence. Anything, even the sight of a cross or a person who reminds him of one of the church members, could trigger a flashback to his time there.'

'Yeah, Matthew explained all that,' Safiyya said. 'When are we going to tell him the truth?'

'Not just yet. But leave it to me. I'll wait until I think he's ready to hear it.'

The elevator stopped and they wandered slowly down the hallway, talking as they went.

'After he knows why I'm here, Amin might ask you some serious questions,' Michael continued. 'Like, are you his friend or just an exit counsellor? Or are you actually a nurse or did his parents send you into the hospital to extricate him from the church?'

'Yeah. The second one is easy, but I'll have to think about my answer to the first one.'

'Now that he's away from the direct influence of that church, our task is essentially to treat him like a normal person, get him to do normal things, and gently help him to examine whether or not those church beliefs were actually healthy for him.'

'Speaking of healthy,' Safiyya said, 'his body's wasted, and so far he's eaten whatever he can get his hands on. He has to replenish it with a healthy diet.'

'Exactly, and I'm sure you can handle that, what with being a nurse and all.' He grinned.

They stopped outside Safiyya's door.

'The next few days will be difficult for him,' Michael continued while she found her key. 'He'll start to wonder how he became involved in the church in the first place, and without the constant bombardment of church doctrine, he'll need to take stock of his own values and redraw a roadmap for the future. He's also going to need to explore his feelings about you and come to understand why he's so attracted to you.'

Safiyya grimaced, clearly uncomfortable with Amin's

infatuation.

'Don't worry,' Michael said. 'The same rules apply as with anyone: you set whatever boundaries you feel comfortable with.'

She nodded. 'Thank you, Michael.'

'Let's meet downstairs for brunch in an hour.'

'Sounds great.'

When Amin awoke about fifteen minutes later, he gave Michael a friendly greeting. No sign of the cult member mentality at play.

'I've arranged for us to have brunch downstairs on the veranda with Safiyya,' Michael said. 'How does that sound?'

Amin nodded. 'I like it, but could we go for a run first, or a walk if you'd prefer. I've missed my early morning runs.'

'Sure,' Michael said, 'I enjoy a good jog along the beach.' That Amin had recognised that something had been missing from his life was a very good sign.

They ran for fifteen minutes along the expansive white-sand beach, then Amin suggested they take a rest. 'I didn't exercise while in the church,' he said by way of explanation, 'so I'm a bit out of shape.'

They sat together on an outcrop of rocks, watching the water lap gently at the beach. The sun was shining, but it wasn't particularly hot. Michael said nothing, allowing Amin to take the lead should he want to talk.

After asking if Michael slept well and receiving an affirmative answer, Amin said, 'I slept well, but I feel a bit strange ...'

'Any idea why?' Michael asked.

Amin sighed. 'Yeah. I dreamed I ran away from you guys and went back to the church. They gave me a rapturous welcome and said I'd neutralised the voice of Satan.'

Michael frowned. Was he slipping back into his cult mindset? He needed to take the conversation elsewhere. 'Well, it was just a dream, Amin. Right now, we need to go meet Safiyya for brunch and decide what to do today. What would you like to do? Go back to your grandmother? I'd love to see her again.'

Amin shook his head. 'No. I mean, yes; yes, I would like to see her again, but right now I need to talk because my mind is in a spin. I keep thinking about what my grandmother said about false prophets and everything you talked about on the plane. It seemed like you were telling me that the Church of Love and Faith isn't a real church, that it's some sort of a cult. But I don't see how that can be, because most of the people there were really good people. There were a few I never trusted, but … all in all … I just don't know. Are you trying to tell me I've been brainwashed or something?'

'Mind controlled is the term I'd use, Amin.'

Amin frowned. 'How does that work?'

Michael explained the concept and found Amin genuinely interested and willing to re-evaluate his experience in light of the idea. Michael went on to talk about the difference between a religious group and a cult, and after an initial resistance, Amin was able to recognise how some of the markers of a cult related to aspects of his life in the Church of Love and Faith: the intensity and rigidity of the routines with no space for self-reflection that wasn't strictly directed by the church, the constant repetitive chanting, the weakening of his resistance through fasting, the control over every aspect of his life, the oft-repeated slogans, the upholding of devotion to the pastor as the pinnacle of one's spiritual path, the demonisation of those outside the church, the public humiliation if one transgressed, and so on.

'How do you know all this stuff?' Amin asked.

'I'm a cult exit counsellor.'

'Wow.'

Telling him about the purpose of their journey and Michael's role in it came easily after that.

At first, Amin seemed a little peeved, saying that he didn't like being lied to.

'It wasn't all lies, Amin,' Michael explained. 'Safiyya did want to meet your grandmother. I did too. Your parents made her sound like the trip was worth it just to see her—and I wasn't disappointed on that score. She's a pleasure to be around—as are both you and Safiyya. The subterfuge was only to get you away from the church long enough so you could start to examine their beliefs, to allow you to become aware of aspects of the church that you wouldn't have noticed while under their influence.'

Amin nodded. 'I guess I am seeing them in a different light now. But it's not all bad. I have some good friends there.'

Michael nodded. He knew that if Amin stayed out of the cult, he'd never see his so-called friends again. They'd no doubt say he'd gone to Satan or some variation on the theme. He'd be written off, seen as the enemy and soon forgotten. Anyone who kept fond memories of him would likely be chastised for it. 'Well, we're here for a few more days,' Michael said, 'so we'll have plenty of time to chat. Anything you want to discuss, I'm up for it.'

'Is Safiyya a counsellor as well?' Amin asked.

'No, she's a nurse. Just what she said she is. A nurse who saw a patient who she felt needed more care than he was getting.'

'Does she really care about me, or was that all a ruse?'

'Of course, she cares. She cares enough to contact your mother to let her know you were in hospital, and she cares enough to travel to the other side of the world with you. But more than that, you'll have to ask her.'

Amin grimaced as if the thought of talking about feelings was somewhat daunting.

'My advice, man to man,' Michael said, 'is to trust

your instincts.'

By the time they made it to brunch, Safiyya had already ordered. Amin apologised for being late and explained that he'd had a really good talk with Michael, and he now knew why he'd travelled with them.

Safiyya sighed with relief. 'I'm glad it's all out in the open, Amin,' she said with a smile.

Michael felt the same, but he knew there'd soon be some sticky questions coming her way.

42

Margaret ushered Albert into the conference room, then left, closing the door behind her.

Laura greeted Albert and, while he took a seat across the table from her and Matthew, she thanked him for coming, then asked, 'How's Emma?'

'All in all, she's great, Laura,' Albert replied with a smile. 'She has her moments, and Alison and I try to leave her alone and respect her privacy; something perhaps we never really did properly before. Of course, we still worry about her. I mean the privacy thing is a balancing game; we want to be there for her too. I'm sure you know what I mean. Do you think she'll be okay?'

'Of course we do,' Laura replied. 'Although you need to understand that this will take time. Some cult experts believe that former members take as much time to recover from their experience as the time they spent in the cult. Emma was there for well over two years.'

Albert's eyebrows rose in surprise, then he frowned. 'What about overseas trips? Alison and I planned to go skiing at Aspen in a couple of months.'

'That should be fine,' Laura said, 'but we should talk again closer to the day. Emma's attending counselling here every week, and that gives us a sense of how she's progressing. It's very important that continues.'

Albert nodded. 'Of course, I understand that. Has anything come up that I need to know about?'

'That's a good question,' Matthew said, 'and though I can't discuss details, I can talk about the broad issues we've discussed before. She needs to reconnect with you and her extended family, and with old friends, if she wants to. She'll likely question her spirituality and wonder where to go from here. Typically, people who emerge from cults either explore other forms of spirituality or religious practice or they move right out of that scene.'

'I think I'd prefer the latter,' Albert said with a smile. 'I'd hate for her to fall right into another cult.'

'And that can happen,' Laura put in, 'but our cult-recovery counselling will give her the tools she needs to avoid it.'

'It sounds like Emma has a lot of work to do.'

Matthew nodded. 'And she needs to come to understand what happened to her, that Kira stole her independence, and she lost her free choice, and that's going to be hard to deal with. But we'll provide her with the information she needs to understand that any person can be a victim of mind control and it is possible to recover and move forward. But it's tough. She needs to learn how to trust again, how to be vulnerable, but in a safe environment.'

'And how to recognise the difference between a safe and unsafe community,' Laura said.

'If she knew that before, she wouldn't have got trapped there in the first place,' Albert pointed out.

Laura nodded. 'Which is why it's important that how to identify a cult needs to be common knowledge.'

'And while we're talking about ifs,' Matthew said, 'if she hadn't got out of there, you probably would've been hauled into court at some point. Not to make light of that, but the real tragedy would've been the loss of Emma's future and all her dreams. A few months, perhaps a year longer, would have been devastating for her. We know how depressed she was and how desperately unhappy she was becoming. And, Albert, I'm sure you know as well as I do that desperate people do desperate things.'

'And Alison and I are eternally grateful for what you did and are still doing. I understand now that without counselling, she could be back with Kira at this moment. So thank you for the opportunity to talk. Perhaps we can do this every so often. And, yes, I'll talk to you shortly before we depart for overseas.'

Albert made a move to stand, but Matthew said, 'Hold on a moment, Albert, I need to ask you something. I know Divine Delicacies is a bit of a raw topic and you're no longer involved, but we could use your help with something related to them.'

Albert sat back, a curious expression on his face. 'Okay. Go on.'

'What's the connection between Divine Delicacies and The Healing Mission. Are they both sort of divine entities?'

Albert shook his head. 'Not at all. Their connection is just a coincidence, really. Divine Delicacies used to be a small cottage business selling all sorts of sweets, but it grew fast. When the owner put the business up for sale, some colleagues and I saw its potential for growth and decided to make an offer to purchase it. This was over twenty years ago, and the asking price was quite high, but we decided to go for it. We found a guy, some sort of venture capitalist, to give us the funds to purchase it. He was an interesting guy, Chuck, a sort of spiritual fellow, who said his money came from heaven. But we checked him out and he was quite solid.

'There was one problem, though. Chuck invested in only one state at a time, and he'd already invested in a project in New South Wales, so he couldn't invest in another one. That project was The Healing Mission, so we decided that Divine Delicacies would purchase an interest in The Healing Mission. Does that make sense?'

Matthew nodded. 'Yeah, I get it. So here's the story we hope you can help us with, but we need your absolute confidentiality before we can share it. We're dealing with a life and death situation here.'

'Done.' Albert leaned forward slightly.

'There's a member of The Healing Mission we need to get out,' Matthew said, 'a young woman with severe depression who is possibly suicidal and isn't getting the care she needs. We're wondering if, due to your earlier involvement in Divine Delicacies, you could help us find someone who could facilitate her removal.'

Albert frowned thoughtfully. 'I don't know. Divine Delicacies and The Healing Mission see very little of each other. The relationship is purely historical, really. But I'll see what I can do.'

'Thank you, Albert. Your Emma managed to get out of the hell she was living in. And we always felt sure that she'd make it, but we don't have the same confidence for this young woman. And time isn't on our side.'

'I understand. I won't and can't ignore your plea. I've been in the same place where this young woman's parents must be now. I'll do my homework and get back to you. And yes, I'll keep this all totally confidential. You can always trust a lawyer.' Albert laughed.

43

Early on Monday morning, Rochelle sat in the waiting room in the Interpol headquarters in Sydney, amazed at the hive of police activity taking place behind the building's rather bland façade. Probably because Penny was safe—at least until Graham returned from India. If he ever did. She felt stronger, clear in her determination to keep Penny away from that unholy man. And she was becoming used to meeting all kinds of people.

Just after 8.00 am, Raymond Lester, a tall, well-built man with a shaved head, called her into an equally bland interview room and seated her at a small table. A laptop and a manilla folder sat open on the table where he sat across from her. The edges of a few photos peeked out from beneath a typewritten sheet.

'Ms Lightwood, thank you for coming in so quickly,' he said.

'Rochelle, please,' she responded quietly.

'Okay, Rochelle, you know why you're here. Interpol is aware of your husband's attempt to abduct your daughter, Penny, and travel with her to India, and we know his plan is linked to the disappearance of Mrs Adele Kingston and her son, Tyson. Graham, Penny and the Kingstons were all booked on the same flight. In fact, Adele's credit card paid for Graham and Penny's flight. The media is onto the story. We would have preferred they stay out of it, but that's life.'

Rochelle's jaw dropped. *The Kingston woman paid for Graham and Penny's fares!* Anger burned through her in a flash, but she controlled herself enough to say, 'Obviously they planned this together. I'm embarrassed to have to ask this, but … have you any idea what kind of relationship Graham had with Adele?'

Raymond shook his head. 'Fair question, but we don't have that information right now. While I understand the pain you're feeling—'

Rochelle interrupted, glaring at him. 'No, you have no idea. How could anybody know how it feels to have your husband attempt to abduct your own daughter?'

Raymond grimaced. 'Yes, I'm sorry, Rochelle.' He paused for a long moment. 'Perhaps I should have put it differently. We're not looking at Graham and Adele's relationship, rather, we're looking at a range of offences they may be guilty of; for instance, how he changed your daughter's name by deed poll and got a passport for her. Then there's the issue of extradition. We do have an extradition treaty with India, but if we go down that track, it can be an expensive and protracted process. And that's assuming both adults and Tyson are in India. They could be anywhere by now. What we do know is that Graham, Adele and Tyson did go through immigration and boarded the flight that day.'

At least I know he's out of the country now—or was.

'And we have no record of Graham re-entering Australia with the passport he used to exit,' Raymond continued. 'But he could have come in on someone else's passport, and Adele may have done the same. We don't know that, but our hunch is that they're still there. We are also working on the assumption that Tyson is with his mother.'

'I doubt Graham would want to come back,' Rochelle said. 'He was so keen to meet his guru.'

'Right. And apart from the legal issues, we are very concerned about Tyson's wellbeing. He's very close to his father and has been living a very different lifestyle from what he'll face living in an ashram in India. The embassy in India has been informed of all this, and they're trying to locate Graham, Adele and Tyson, but that could take time. If they've joined the cult led by …' he glanced at his notes, 'His Holiness Bakhavitda Krishnanada, it will be difficult to find them because the man has thousands of followers and a large ashram.'

Rochelle nodded and leaned forward. 'How can I help?'

'Well, we have the statement Keith made after your successful rescue of Penny. And may I congratulate you on this fine piece of work. A minute later and you could have lost her. But I need you to give me as much information as you can about Graham's involvement with His Holiness and his connection with Adele. We have ten people working on this, and we won't stop until we locate them.'

'Okay. Frankly, I know as little as you about his connection with Adele, but I guess he would have met her at his yoga classes—the ones run by the cult. But there's something else I want to run by you. Yesterday I spoke with a journalist, Sue Daley, from the *Sydney Morning Herald*. She wanted to talk to me, but my solicitor says I should clarify what they can do for me in return for an interview or any other information.'

'That's correct, Rochelle. This is a huge story. Ted Kingston is a big name, sitting on a twelve-million-dollar annual salary, and Adele is one of Australia's best-known socialites. The *Sydney Morning Herald* is probably already syndicating the story to other media groups. It was on CNN and NBC in the States this morning, and that's just the beginning.'

He glanced at his laptop. 'Well, there you are, Rochelle. An email's just come through saying there're a dozen reporters with film crews at Ted's office building.' He looked back at her. 'The chances are that the *Herald* will send a team of journalists to India. That has nothing to do with us, of course, but they may be able to crack this quicker than we can. Interpol is heavily regulated—all sorts of rules and red tape regarding infiltration into groups, be they cults or anything else—but the media has pretty much a free rein.'

'So I should work with them?'

'I think you should find out first what they intend to do and how their investigation might assist you in finding Graham, and only then agree to be interviewed. Believe me, they need you as much as you need them.'

'Okay. Thanks. I'll think about all this and get back to you if I come up with anything that might help.'

'Excellent. And one more thing, Rochelle. Ted Kingston is desperate to meet you. I have no problems with the meeting if you don't.'

'Sure, that's fine. Just let me know when.'

'Okay. Thanks. I appreciate your help.' He handed her a card. 'Take my mobile number and call at any time.'

Rochelle stood and grabbed her handbag, preparing to leave.

Raymond glanced around the room, then at her. 'Ah, Rochelle, could you sit down for just one more moment?'

She shrugged. 'Sure.'

'Look, I've dealt with every possible scenario you could imagine, and I've had my own personal challenges, but this is dramatically different, and I want to understand why people do these kinds of things. I mean, this guru guy is a real fraud, so why did Graham hook up with him? And what about Adele? A mother, a highly respected member of society, a devoted—or at least so we thought—wife to Ted. A woman who has it all. And she decides to become a fugitive. She abandons her husband, effectively kidnaps her son and stuffs up her life forever, not to mention her son's. How will living in an ashram and sitting in front of this self-indulgent, corrupt spiritual master who refers to himself as His Holiness affect him?' Raymond rubbed the back of his neck, looking perplexed. 'You strike me as a caring wife and a loving mother, so what's his problem; what's his issue? I don't get it.'

Rochelle thought for a moment. Now wasn't the time to talk about Penny's premature birth and her developmental problems. 'Frankly, Raymond, I don't understand it either, and, believe me, I've asked myself the same questions.'

~

A phone message awaited Rochelle when she returned home after work. 'Hi, Rochelle, it's Sue from the *Sydney Morning Herald*. I thought I should tell you we're going ahead with the story. Please call me when you have a moment.'

Well, that's encouraging.

She made sure Penny was settled with a snack and a TV show, then called Sue.

'We're on, Rochelle,' Sue said. 'A team of two journalists and two cameramen fly out to India in two weeks. Judging by the feedback from the article we ran last week about Ted Kingston, this is a huge story.'

'Great. Will they look for Graham as well as the Kingstons?'

'I'll make it clear that if they find one of them, they'll probably find the other, so they'll be looking for them both.'

'Great. That's what I need.'

'And Interpol has agreed to talk to us,' Sue continued, 'which is great, and a bit of a coup. Our relationship with them is often messy. We both tend to want information from the other without revealing our own. But we've offered to give them anything useful. I have a feeling Ted Kingston's on their case, and he has enormous clout both here and overseas. I don't know him personally, but he has made it patently clear in every interview that he'll not stop his campaign to get Adele and Tyson back, not until they're home.'

Nice he wants them both back! Rochelle wasn't sure she could be bothered with Graham. Her feelings of ambivalence towards him grew stronger by the day, but all she said was, 'I'm meeting with Ted tomorrow afternoon. The cops told me he'd requested a meeting, so I'm going.'

'Great. Don't forget you can call me any time.'

'Okay. Thanks.'

~

Rochelle stared at the clock on her nightstand again: 3 am, tired, but still awake. *Ugh.* The knowledge that she'd almost lost Penny still haunted her, and now Interpol was involved, and the media spotlight was turning her way, not something she felt comfortable with. And then there were Sue's children, damaged by that attack in Japan. She couldn't get it all out of her mind. It was all too much.

Raymond intrigued her too. He seemed to understand her pain to some degree, and she wondered about the personal challenges he'd mentioned.

She got up, grabbed her laptop and googled Raymond Lester. She didn't have to search far:

> *Following a successful career in journalism, Raymond Lester joined Interpol, rising quickly in its ranks. His decision to leave journalism and join the force was a result of the abduction of his only child in*

*the summer of 1989. Seven-year-old Madeline Lester
has never been found and neither has her body, and
to date no one has been charged with her abduction.*

'Oh, my God!' Rochelle's eyes became so watery, she couldn't read the screen. But she didn't want to read more anyway. She shut down the laptop.

44

Annabel agreed to the undercover option for getting Anne out of The Healing Mission, and a woman called Caroline, who'd done this kind of thing before, had volunteered. She'd presented herself at The Healing Mission's front desk in Sydney as a homeless woman with an eating disorder and a fondness for drugs.

Caroline would do her best to blend into the community at The Healing Mission. She'd attempt to talk to Anne and establish a rapport with her. But she'd be careful since any overt attempt to bond with Anne would raise suspicion. Only after she'd established a bond with Anne could Caroline plan how to coax Anne out of The Healing Mission environs. One idea was that she could try to convince Anne to spend time with some of her friends on the two days they had off each month.

For Annabel, it all seemed to be taking too long.

She'd called various government authorities as well as the mental health board, seeking their assistance, but it was a frustrating task. Invariably, the responses referred to Anne's age and the fact that Annabel had no jurisdiction over her. Others requested more information regarding the person who made the call alerting her to Anne's condition. As soon as Annabel said the call was anonymous, the trail went dry.

She'd also called The Healing Mission, but they told her their privacy laws prevented the staff from releasing any information about the members. The woman Annabel spoke to tried to assure her Anne was being well looked after, and she told her that if she had any concerns, she should put it in writing. She also said that they'd look into the matter, 'although it could take some time'.

Annabel sighed and lay back against the soft cushions on her sofa. She wished she could do more. It felt as if an avalanche was poised to descend on her and there wasn't a single thing she could do to get out of its path.

The phone on the side table rang. She stood and picked up the receiver. 'Annabel Rogers speaking.'

'Listen, I won't be able to do this another time,' a voice whispered—the anonymous caller again—'but you need to get your daughter out of here fast. This place isn't for her. It's evil. I'm only here now because of Anne. I promise you the moment she leaves, I'm out of here.'

Annabel's heart raced, swinging between joy to hear from the caller again and despair at her words. 'I don't know what to call you,' she said to the woman at the other end of the phone.

'I'd rather not say,' the woman replied.

'Okay, then I'll call you Angel, because that's what you are to me. Could you please look out for someone called Caroline? She's there to help you get Anne out.'

'Okay, yes. I'll try to find her.'

'Thank you. Now tell me, Angel, what is wrong with Anne?'

For a moment Angel said nothing, then she sighed and said, 'Anne is deeply depressed. She doesn't talk; she hardly ventures outside her room. And she's getting worse.'

The words felt like a slash to Annabel's heart. 'What're the staff doing?' she managed.

'Nothing,' Angel replied. 'Absolutely nothing. I mean they're praying. Last week we had a special "Pray for Anne" meeting, but it didn't help and I wasn't surprised.'

Annabel suddenly felt dizzy and nauseous. She dropped the phone and collapsed on the floor, her back against the sofa.

'Hello, hello?' Angel called, then silence.

By the time Annabel recovered, Angel had gone.

'Oh my God,' Annabel groaned. 'What now? Help me, God. Please help me.'

~

Caroline knew she feigned her eating disorder well. The clothes she'd chosen and the defeated way she carried herself supported her ruse that she was homeless and at risk. She often walked out of the dining room during mealtime and headed towards the bathrooms, then returned looking sad with her head down.

For the first few days, she hadn't seen Anne. She'd seen photos of her, of course, but her picture didn't match any of the twenty or so members of The Healing Mission community that lived in the old convent—a dark, brooding building with a high ceiling and narrow windows with dark, sheer curtains that filtered the light and kept out the sunshine. It did have a lovely little chapel, though.

A whole week passed before Caroline spotted Anne sitting quietly in the den staring at the log fire with a blank look on her face. The woman looked so thin and pale that Caroline feared she was near death. Her straight, fine hair fell lankly around her face, and her white dress—it looked like a nightgown—hung off her emaciated frame. She wore no shoes or socks, despite the cold floor.

Caroline sat down on the other side of the room. She'd take her chance to get close to Anne as soon as the two gossiping older members had left the room.

She picked up a book called *The Eating Disorder Bible*. A self-published book of some two hundred pages, it contained a number of crude pictures and looked very amateurish, but judging by the state of the book, it had been read many times. The prologue was titled 'Only the Lord Heals.' And another chapter boasted the title 'Vomiting and Exorcism'.

Caroline looked up. Only a few members remained in the room, but they'd soon be called to prayers. Now was the time. But just before Caroline stood to head over, Anne got up and walked unsteadily down the corridor that led to the seniors' rooms.

Damn. New folk like Caroline weren't supposed to go down there. Could she risk following? Maybe just to find out which was Anne's room. She stood and took a few steps towards the corridor, then stopped. Anne was returning, accompanied by another member.

Is that Angel? Caroline had managed to call Anne's mother to let her know she was in place, and Annabel had told her the name she'd given the mysterious caller. The woman accompanying Anne was probably Angel, but Caroline needed to be sure, and she couldn't wait for another opportunity to present itself. It was time to make her move.

She walked up to the pair and gave the woman a friendly smile. 'Excuse me, I've been here for only a few days. I'm trying to get to know the other members of this wonderful community. Is there a woman here by the name of Angel?'

The woman's eyes widened, and she looked intently at Caroline.

'I'm Caroline.'

Their eyes met, and the woman smiled, apparently relieved. She moved towards Caroline and held out her hands. 'Yes, I'm Angel, and would you like to meet Anne?'

'Sure.' Caroline turned to Anne. 'Hello, Anne, pleased to

meet you.'

Anne didn't respond. She didn't even look at Caroline. She just turned to Angel and whispered, 'Can we go back to our room?'

'Of course.'

Caroline watched them go, then sat back down with a leaden heart. *This isn't going to be easy.* How was she going to break through Anne's indifference?

Angel returned just as the gong rang for prayers and met Caroline before she left the den. 'Meet me at the end of the south corridor,' she whispered. 'Follow me, but make sure you're at least twenty steps behind. Once you reach the garden, walk straight. I'll be sitting by the lake in the shadows. Okay?'

Caroline nodded. 'I'll be there.' Apart from this being her first big break in her mission, she'd grab any chance to miss a prayer session. All that nonsense about demons being the cause of all their illnesses was enough to make any logical person sick.

45

Rochelle looked up at the glittering skyscraper in central Sydney. Telco Headquarters occupied fourteen floors of this modern monstrosity. It seemed bizarre that she should have any business there, let alone an appointment with the boss himself. She walked into the foyer, feeling out of her depth in this high-rise corporate world. Thank goodness, her sister was always happy to look after Penny, so she could do things like this because her stupid husband went and got himself caught up with an Indian guru and his followers.

The woman at the desk gave her a priority pass and a man in a security uniform escorted her upstairs. She stepped from the lift into a huge executive area with stunning views of Sydney harbour, the bridge and the opera house, and then she followed her escort into a waiting room for Ted's office. He left her looking at the pictures that covered the walls. She found a large photo of Ted, Adele and Tyson, another of Tyson as well as an oil painting of Ted sitting at his desk. It was all rather ostentatious and overwhelming. Maybe that was why Adele swapped the pomp and grandeur for the Indian outback and life in an ashram.

The contrast between Ted's office and Rochelle's home couldn't have been more striking. But not because of the opulence of Ted's office and the modesty of Rochelle's home, but because the photos showed the differences between her relationship with Graham and Ted's relationship with Adele. Ted continued to proudly display the family photos whereas Rochelle had removed every picture of Graham, including those of him with Penny.

The door to Kingston's office opened, and a man of average height with a receding hairline and smartly dressed in a distinctly European suit stepped into the doorway. 'Good afternoon, Rochelle, if I may call you by your first name. My name is Ted Kingston. Please come in.'

Rochelle smiled and walked into a huge office. She tried not to look around too much and chose to sit on a small couch near the big windows. His smile and manner as he offered her refreshments seemed friendly, not the kind of multinational corporation CEO she'd expected.

'Thank you for coming,' he said once he'd arranged for afternoon tea. 'I never thought this kind of thing would happen to me. I haven't slept for the past three weeks. I fear for Adele and even more for my child.'

Rochelle cast her mind to the fateful day at the airport. The image of Graham and Penny with Adele and Tyson seemed fixed in her mind as if time had frozen it at that moment. She could see Graham pulling Penny and Adele tugging at Tyson. And then Keith running forward and plucking Penny from her father's grasp and Adele and Tyson continuing to walk towards the departure gates.

'Oh, Ted, I'm so sorry,' she said. 'I keep wondering if there was anything else I could have done, like grab Tyson as well, but we didn't know who they were or what their story was …'

'Of course, you didn't know. How could you? I'm just glad you saved Penny. I'm not so confident about our chances of getting Tyson back, though. This guru's ashram isn't just a few buildings bunched together in the Indian countryside. It's more like a small city.' Ted laid an aerial map of India's Puna region on the coffee table and sat beside her on the couch. 'I've had our people fly over the ashram and take photos. Take a look at this.'

The photographer had zoomed in over an assembly area where the guru sat on a golden throne on a huge stage. It looked like two or three thousand disciples gathered in the open area before him. 'Somewhere among this crowd are my wife and son. And my guess is that Graham is there too. How the heck are we going to get them out?' He shook his head and closed his eyes for a moment, clearly trying to maintain his composure, then he picked up a remote control and switched on a video screen set in the wall. 'Watch this.' A video played, showing the guru talking and gesturing into the air. Then suddenly everybody was prostrating. A moment later, they appeared to be dancing in a wild swirl.

Rochelle screwed up her face. It was worse than she'd imagined.

'What the hell is going on there?' Ted said. 'I mean, I've read about cults and these weird religions, but my wife is a fine, upstanding woman. I don't think you'd ever find a woman as devoted as she is to our son. We love each other, always have, and our family has always been our priority. Only a week before she disappeared, we were enjoying a skiing trip, just the three of us. And believe me, I'd give away my job, my position and my wealth in order to have them both back.'

He fell silent and Rochelle had no idea what to say.

'She was a country girl from the Victorian bush,' he continued after a moment, 'and her parents ran a yoga and meditation centre, so maybe there's some link there. But they weren't in a cult. They're as devastated at this as I am. Or maybe the loss of her best friend set her off somehow,' he mused. 'We were all in a light plane crash a few years ago. Adele was badly injured, took months to heal, lots of physiotherapy, but Candice didn't survive. I tried to be there for her while she was healing, but …' He gestured around his office. 'I suppose she did become a little more introspective after the crash, but … I don't know. I'm at a loss here.'

'Well, there is a big difference between a simple country upbringing and the one I figure she's been living with you,' Rochelle ventured. 'So … there is that.'

Ted looked at her as if he'd suddenly remembered she was there. 'I'm sorry, Rochelle. I'm just so furious. I want to understand, but I don't get it. Are you saying she might not have enjoyed the great life we lead? Rochelle, am I missing something?'

Rochelle remained quiet while she thought about how to respond. 'I can't answer that, Ted, though I wish I could. My story is different. After Penny was born, Graham became depressed and I'm not sure if he has ever gotten over it. Penny was premature, and she suffers from mild cerebral palsy. Her first few months were a battle; we really didn't know if she'd make it. Graham started asking questions about life, about suffering and about God. I think this cult gave him simple answers that appealed to him. He was so desperate to see Penny better that he believed His Holiness could actually heal her. I think he swallowed the cult's bizarre belief system so fully that he lost touch with reality.' She sighed. 'It was his disappointment with Penny's health that changed him, though, so maybe Adele's friend's death did something similar for her. Made her question. Made her look for answers to spiritual questions.'

Ted smiled. 'That's very insightful, Rochelle. Thank you. You might have a point there.'

Rochelle told him about Sue and the news team, saying that she'd agreed to look for Graham as well as Adele and Tyson. She also shared her conversation with Raymond at Interpol.

'I don't want Adele charged,' Ted said, 'but I'll do whatever I can to get her and Tyson back to Australia, and I want to offer you my support and my resources as well. If you need anything, just call me. You won't need to ask twice. Somehow, we've become connected through a terrible disaster. I take this extremely seriously, and you can count on my loyalty.'

Rochelle also shared how CultAssist had arranged Penny's rescue and suggested that he contact Laura. He agreed to do it immediately. 'Perhaps we could meet with her together.'

'Well sure, but they're in Brisbane.'

'That's no problem, you can fly with me in my jet.'

'Uh. Right. Sure. No problem.'

With that, Ted reached down and took Rochelle's hand, drawing her to her feet. 'I'm scared and I'm worried. Your being here has given me enormous support. I can't thank you enough.' His voice broke and moisture filled his eyes.

So the man isn't without a heart.

Rochelle called Laura as soon as she'd left the building.

46

Dear Ted,

I have no idea whether you expected to hear from me, but even though I now live thousands of miles away from you, not a day goes by when I don't think about you.

Not in my wildest dreams did I ever think I would find myself living in a dusty ashram outside an Indian village. Never did I imagine my life without you. The thought of our family splitting up was not an option at any time until now.

And walking through the international terminal at Sydney airport with our Tyson by my side was the product of the most painful decision I have ever made. But Ted, I couldn't continue, and I know that if I had told you about my plan, you would've stopped me. You had every means available to ensure that I didn't depart from Australian soil.

I couldn't continue to live the lie that I was living; a life of plenty in a material sense and a life of emptiness in every other sense. I could no longer contemplate our beloved Tyson being brought up in a sterile world of commercial success and materialistic indulgence.

For weeks, maybe months, I debated with myself

what to do. I knew that I couldn't continue to live this lifestyle. The trips, the parties, the restaurants, the cars, the hotels, the private jets, the clothes and everything that accompanies this lifestyle, I had to give up.

My heart began to bleed, but I couldn't share my pain. Yes, you provided for me; we cared for each other, and we loved each other. But the need for meaning, perhaps some spirituality, was growing larger, and I was falling apart quickly. And when Tyson started speaking disparagingly about his friends who didn't live in a two-hundred-square metre home or have a fancy car, the alarm bells went off. I suddenly realised that I was on the wrong track and we, Tyson and I, had to get out.

But where to? And then almost as if God heard my cries, I saw an advertisement about the Satykumari Purifying Spring in India. I made some enquiries; I met a fellow here by the name of Graham Lightwood who told me he was travelling to the same ashram. We travelled together. He, like myself, was taking his child to a better place.

And Ted, now I have found the truth and seen the light. I drink from the knowledge of one of this world's most holy men. I bask in his glory, and I delight in his presence. Yes, I still think about you, but I know I can never return.

Tyson will grow up in a pure environment. Instead of playing with his Nintendo games, he will practice yoga. Instead of surfing the Internet, he'll be able to practice meditation.

But I want to say to you that if you do really

love me and you want me back as your partner, you need to come here and live this lifestyle. Crazy? It is, but only until you taste the ashram's energy, see His Holiness's light and drink from his sweet nectar.

I am fulfilled and I have found what I am looking for. I intend to educate Tyson in this truthful space. I hope, like me, that he will be inducted into His Holiness's pure way of life.

And I still wait for you in hope.
With all my deep love,
Adele

47

Rochelle followed Ted up the stairs to his sleek private jet. Even though she still had Penny and wasn't entirely sure she cared if Graham came back or not, she felt she had a stake in how this drama unfolded. Ted clearly valued her support and, knowing what it felt like to be in his situation, she wanted to help in any way she could. So here she was, about to board an executive jet.

She stepped through the door into an expansive lounge area with mahogany fittings that screamed opulence. Her eyes widened and her mouth actually fell open, like a fish out of water, which was exactly how she felt. She quickly shut her mouth and, following the smiling instructions of the flight attendant, sat in a wide, soft leather chair. Ted, the only other passenger in the twelve-seater plane, sat in the next chair and buckled himself in.

It all felt unreal, as if she were on a movie set. Never in her wildest dreams had she thought she'd experience such affluence. But then never would she have guessed that one day Graham would be living in an Indian ashram. He'd never believed in God, used to make fun of church-goers and had said that Penny would never go to a religious school. And yet he'd tried to take her off to a fanatical eastern cult run by one of the most charismatic gurus in India. And as a result, Rochelle was about to be thrust into the media spotlight. It was just her luck that Graham's co-

conspirator was one of Sydney's best-known socialites, married to one of Australia's top corporate executives. She sighed, daunted by the mere thought of the exposure and publicity.

The executive jet took to the skies, and as soon as they'd levelled out, the hostess offered drinks. Rochelle noted the labels on the booze—expensive stuff—and though tempted, she asked only for water. It was, after all, only lunchtime. Despite the relatively short flight time to Brisbane, the attendant served a full—and very delicious —meal. It couldn't be further from the crowded discomfort of economy class travel, and to Rochelle, it felt all wrong. *This just isn't me.*

When not eating, drinking or engaging Rochelle in brief conversation about the food, weather or her comfort, Ted spent the time reading some kind of file.

Rochelle cast her mind back to her early fun-filled days with Graham when his goodness and kindness had moved her. He'd do anything for someone else in need. Their wedding had been a fairy-tale event and their marriage seen as a match made in heaven. Rochelle stared out the window, hiding silent tears as she reflected on their present state. Penny was fatherless, Graham caught up in some make-believe world, and Rochelle was petrified about what might happen next. She wiped her eyes and glanced at Ted. He'd abandoned the folder, reclined his seat and was reading a book called *Cults: Too Good to be True.*

Spot on!

She hoped Penny was okay. It was hard being away from her. Even though they were quite sure Graham wasn't in the country, she'd carefully briefed her sister on the long list of security measures she needed to observe.

An hour after take-off, the jet landed in a special section of Brisbane airport. A chauffeur met them and drove them to the CultAssist office in a fancy silver car with tinted windows.

The contrast between Ted's grand office and CultAssist's modest converted mobile-home headquarters couldn't have been more obvious. But then you wouldn't want an organisation like CultAssist spending the limited funds they had on fancy premises.

Even so, Ted appeared very comfortable in the small, cluttered office. He thanked Laura for her willingness to make the time to see them, and once Margaret—resplendent in a bold red-and-green floral dress—had them settled around the small conference table, he said, 'Rochelle has told me all about you and the incredible work you do. I have no idea whether you can help us, but we are here to ask for your advice and direction.'

'Yes,' Laura said, 'Rochelle has already filled me in on the details. My understanding is that Graham travelled to India on his own without Penny after we managed to snatch her at the airport. Your situation is even graver with Adele and Tyson no longer in Australia. I assume they're living at the ashram on the outskirts of Puna?'

'Yes,' Ted said, 'I received a letter from her that confirmed it, and I'll do everything in my power to get my wife and son back. But, Laura, I have no idea of my chances of success. Interpol is looking at the possibility of extraditing Adele with Tyson, but it's not going to be easy, and they can only do it if Adele is charged with kidnapping. And the thought of Adele being charged doesn't appeal to me. My other option is for them to leave Adele there while we try to get Tyson back, but I have no idea if that would be possible.'

Laura looked at Rochelle. 'Have you made any progress in your thinking about Graham?'

Rochelle shook her head. 'I honestly don't know what to do about him. Because he didn't actually manage to kidnap Penny, I assume that the only offences the police could charge him with are passport related, and I'm told you don't extradite someone for those types of offences, so that's not on the cards. But I still want to know where he is and if he's well. He's suffered from severe depression in the past, and that could be happening again—it would explain a lot. And mostly I need to be sure that he doesn't pose a risk to Penny. Even if he remains out of the country, I'm scared he could do something like find another cult member to abduct her.' She sighed.

Laura nodded. 'Sue Daley from the *Sydney Morning Herald* has been in touch with me, so the big question is how do we all work together, you two, Interpol, the media and our organisation? If we can organise something, that'll be great, but either way, we need to work out how to find your loved ones. A warrant for arrest is useless if we don't know where they are, and of course, Ted, it makes perfect sense that you don't want to see Adele charged.'

Ted pulled out the letter from Adele he'd read to Rochelle in the car and gave it to Laura.

~

Laura took the piece of paper and glanced at it. A letter. From Adele. She looked up at Ted. He appeared to be biting back tears.

'Read it,' he said in a broken voice. 'I want to know what you think. Why she did this.'

She nodded, and Rochelle and Ted remained silent while she read.

When she'd finished, she looked at Ted and said, 'The way she describes her inner conflict is moving and clear. I could argue that she had a good point. She was torn between her love for you and a deep desire to preserve your family unit and at the same time a yearning to understand herself and find a way to give Tyson what she sees as a more real and meaningful life away from the materialism and superficialities that appeared to surround him at home and in the circles in which you mixed.'

Ted opened his mouth as if to protest but closed it without a word.

Laura continued, 'The tragedy is that, in seeking answers, she fell into a cult that has entrapped her and brainwashed her. Adele's ability to make rational decisions has been compromised; she has developed an unhealthy dependence on His Holiness, and let me tell you, Ted, he isn't very holy. We can talk about that another time, but I'd be concerned about any well-presented, attractive and wealthy woman getting too close to him. And Tyson is going along for the ride. He may even be enjoying it.'

Ted shook his head miserably.

The poor man looked quite broken, but he had to know the truth, so Laura continued. 'Don't think for a moment that His Holiness isn't aware of who Adele is, her background and her wealth. That's the way these people operate. It stinks, but it's how it is.' She handed the letter back to Ted. 'We need to get them out of there, and we need to do it soon.'

'So it's entirely my fault,' Ted said quietly.

Laura shook her head. 'Ted, I'm not even going to go there. I'm sure there are lessons to be learned from this for all of us, but let's not get into the blame game. We need to think proactively and move ahead.'

'Thank you, Laura. I just hope this won't be the last I ever hear from her.'

'I hope so too,' Laura said.

Rochelle patted his hand.

'Now,' Laura continued, 'I've done some research on His Holiness Bakhavitda Krishnanada and the Satykumari Purifying Spring. It seems that most observers, including a number of former followers, believe it's little different from the other hundreds of cults operating in India. There've been widespread allegations of brainwashing at these ashrams but attempts to have them closed down have come to nothing because government authorities can't distinguish between destructive organisations and other, more benign, groups. Spirituality and the quest for nirvana are, after all, interwoven in the fabric of Indian life and culture.

'But late last year, a young American tourist who'd become involved with the ashram wrote a number of newspaper articles revealing a far more sinister side to His Holiness's ashram. The story goes that Lionel Campbell, a former US Marines officer, became curious about the group when he came across some of His Holiness's followers while on leave from an assignment in New Delhi. He visited the ashram frequently over a period of several months, and according to various websites, actually lived there for several months in 1997.' Laura glanced at her notes, and Ted leaned forward, clearly keen to hear more.

'During that time,' Laura continued, 'Lionel struck up a close friendship with a woman in His Holiness's inner circle, and they continued communicating even after he left New Delhi. Based on what she told him, Lionel claimed that His Holiness was preparing for an assault on the Indian establishment. Apparently, only a select number of trusted followers were aware of the plan, one involving chemical weapons being used against various government officials and institutions.'

'But why?' Rochelle asked.

'That's just the thing,' Laura replied, 'there didn't appear to be any clear objective or goal. Anyway, government officials dismissed his claims, saying they'd investigated the ashram. Lionel argued that the officials had been bribed with huge sums of money, and His Holiness issued a number of public statements denouncing the negative press reports.'

'How does this help us?' Ted asked.

Laura smiled. 'I managed to find an email address for Lionel, and I've sent him a brief email explaining the situation and asked him if he'd be willing to have a conference call with the three of us. I also sent scans of a couple of media articles on Adele and Tyson's disappearance.'

Ted nodded approvingly. 'Good work.'

'We try all avenues,' Laura replied, 'because you never know which one might help.'

'Have you heard back?' Rochelle asked.

Laura shook her head. 'No, but you'll be the first to know when I do.' *If I do.*

48

Lionel did get back to Laura, though he took a few days to respond. She assumed that he would've spent some of that time checking out CultAssist and Ted. She doubted he'd find anything on the internet about Rochelle—yet. He was keen to talk, and Laura arranged the conference call for Wednesday at 9.00 am.

Once they'd all gained access to the call and made the appropriate introductions, Lionel talked about his involvement in the ashram and his deep concerns about His Holiness's plans of an assault on the Indian government. 'You need to understand that my information about His Holiness's plans is accurate,' he said. 'I can document every claim I've made, and I believe he'll implement his plans within the next three months.'

'Could this affect my family?' Ted asked.

Laura heard Lionel sigh. 'Unfortunately, Ted, given her wealth, it's likely that Adele has been accepted into the inner circle. No doubt they'll have praised her as being special, highly evolved and on a fast track to enlightenment, someone worthy of His Holiness's personal attention—not all of it benign, given her attractiveness.'

'Bastard,' Ted muttered under his breath.

'If that's true,' Lionel continued, 'she'll be spending most of her time with His Holiness and his inner circle, and she'll probably be aware of everything I'm saying, because they'll be planning the execution of a highly risky and dangerous plan. This is serious stuff. But there is some good news, if you can really call it good. My guess is that Tyson won't be with her for much of the time. He's probably been placed with one of the lowliest followers. It's common practice.'

'Why is that good news?' Ted asked.

'Well, if you have plans to snatch him away from the cult, it will make it easier.'

'Okay, but if you're right, the next thing we know my wife will be implicated in a major terrorist act. I just can't see that happening.'

'With respect, Ted,' Lionel said, 'this is not a theory, it's a fact. I'll let you in on one more aspect of this story. My contact is His Holiness's twenty-three-year-old daughter, Gita. She's an illegitimate child born after an affair he had with one of his devotees, though His Holiness's story is that he picked her off the streets after having looked into her soul and seen that she was born to be his successor. What a load of trash!

'Gita's a good woman, and she's desperate to get out of there, but she's afraid that if she leaves, she'll lose any ability she might have to convince him not to go ahead with his plan to attack the Indian government. But His Holiness is extremely disturbed and dangerous, and frankly I'm scared about what might happen. He could emulate the Aum Shinri Kyo and execute a nerve gas attack on the Indian hierarchy. He could do a Jim Jones and you'll have five thousand dead followers in an instant.'

Rochelle groaned, and Laura remembered her saying that the reporter's children had been injured in the Aum Shinri Kyo attack in Tokyo.

'What's so disturbing,' Lionel continued, 'is that he appears to have two personalities. There's the gentle, seemingly spiritual side to him. He welcomes his followers and appears to care about them. But then there's the paranoid, wild side of him when he shouts, screams and orders people around. And he coerces women into his bed with promises of tantric sex, a spiritual experience that will fast-track them to enlightenment. And by the way, he talks to his followers about the evil of alcohol, but you should see him when he's drunk!'

'What makes you think my wife is part of what's-his-name's inner circle?' Ted asked. 'Sorry guys, I just find it hard to use the term "His Holiness" for this charlatan.'

'I can't be sure, but I can find out. His Holiness or whatever we want to call him picks his inner circle very carefully. Adele's fame as well as her wealth and beauty qualify her for all of His Holiness's graces. Let's leave it at that.'

Laura waited for Ted to reply, but he remained silent, probably stunned by what he was hearing. 'Ted, are you there?' she asked gently.

'Yes, Laura, but let me tell you something. I've been through some pretty tough stuff in my time. I won't bore you with details, but I run one of this country's largest and most successful companies. I regard myself as a reasonably capable person. I can deal with challenges, big challenges. But with this, this bloody "Holiness" guy, the loss of my wife, the abduction of my child … no, this is too much. I have no idea where we go from here. And that's not to say I don't appreciate your input, Lionel; I certainly do. And you, Laura; where would I be without you? Rochelle, you're a very special person and a great support, and you have your own problems to deal with. But what the heck do we do now?' Ted's voice rose until he was shouting, then he paused long enough to sound relatively calm when he said, 'By the way, where are you, Lionel?'

'Right now, I'm in my apartment in downtown Los Angeles.'

'Are you married? Sorry for asking.'

'No, Ted, but I'm engaged. Gloria and I intend to marry at the end of next year. Right now, she's working for CNN in Africa. She's a great woman.'

'Okay. The reason I'm asking is because I'd like to see you in Australia, if you're willing to do me a favour and come over. I'll cover all expenses and remunerate you. Just let me know when you can fly, and I'll take care of the rest.'

Lionel said he could rearrange his work to free up a couple of weeks and that he'd always wanted to visit Australia, so he was happy to accept Ted's offer. Laura ended the call, saying they'd meet again when Lionel was in Australia.

An hour later, Ted called Laura and told her that Lionel was flying out of LAX International airport in forty-eight hours. They arranged to meet in Sydney early the following week. Laura was impressed. The man sure knew how to get things done!

49

Annabel stared into the flickering flames in the fireplace. It was a cold night for November, but not that cold, not really. Her chill was one of the heart, and it went bone deep. She'd heard from Caroline, but she hadn't got very far. She'd found Anne but hadn't been able to get to her because her room was in an area that was out of bounds for new members. She'd worked out how she could get her out without having to go through the main doors, but Anne had to want to leave. And that was the problem. Angel had found Caroline and told her she was working on that. Anne knew she was unwell, but she still thought her best chance of healing was at The Healing Mission. She was firmly in the grip of their dogma.

And all Annabel could do was wait. And pray to a God she no longer believed in.

Tap, tap.

Was that someone knocking? She put on a shawl and walked down the narrow passageway towards the front door.

'Please let me in; please let me in,' a soft voice pleaded.

Annabel opened the door. Her heart lifted instantly, misery gone. Anne stood shivering before her, wearing just a nightgown and an oversized sweater, her face almost expressionless. Overwhelmed with a mixture of joy at her arrival and sadness at her state, Annabel folded her daughter into her arms and held her, warming Anne's cold body against her. Anne didn't return the hug, just stood there unresponsive, then mumbled, 'Can I come in?' against her mother's shoulder.

'Darling, of course you can come in.' Annabel took her daughter's hand, led her inside and sat her before the fire, then she brought her a cup of tea, which Anne gulped down. 'Do you want to talk to me, my darling?' Annabel asked, tears welling up in her eyes.

'No, not now,' Anne said. 'I just want to sleep. We'll talk in the morning.' She stood and walked to her room.

Annabel sat in her favourite chair and stared at the bright embers at the base of the fire. *She's home. Oh my God. She's really home.* But relief warred with a burning question she couldn't answer. Will she stay? And why wasn't Caroline with her? She'd expected her to bring Anne home. She couldn't ring Caroline in case she blew her cover, so she'd have to wait to hear from her. Or did her cover not matter now? Annabel was warring with herself trying to decide whether to phone or not, when her phone rang. She rushed to answer it.

'Annabel, this is Caroline,' a voice whispered. 'They've kicked her out. They saw how sick she was and told her to leave. I hope she makes it home. She's not wearing much. I'm leaving tomorrow, and I'll call you once I'm out. I hope she makes it home.'

'She's here already,' Annabel whispered. 'She arrived about thirty minutes ago.'

'Oh, wow, that's great news. I'm so relieved … Whoops, I have to go now, someone's coming.' The call ended.

Annabel peeked into Anne's bedroom. She was already fast asleep.

With tears in her eyes, Annabel went into the spare room, dragged the single mattress from the bed and quietly pulled it into Anne's room. She simply couldn't leave her daughter alone. Not in that state. She grabbed the doona, threw it on the mattress and climbed beneath it, not bothering to change. She turned off the hall light and tried to sleep.

Those bastards, she thought through her tears. *They gave her hope, promised her the world, then when she became too ill for them to handle, they kicked her out like a piece of dead meat.* Annabel pulled the doona over her face to muffle her sobs.

50

Emma peeked through the window at the person who'd knocked on the front door. A policeman stood there. Had someone had an accident? She raced to the door and flung it open.

'Emma Carter?' he asked.

'Yes.'

He held out an envelope. 'You've been served.'

Emma frowned and took the envelope.

'Have a nice day, miss,' the policeman said as he turned and walked away.

'Wait. There must be some mistake …' she called after him.

He glanced back over his shoulder. 'No. No mistake, miss.'

Emma stared at the envelope. Yes. It bore her name and address. She walked back inside, shut the door and tore the envelope open.

'Oh my God,' she whispered as she read the contents.

Emma's hands shook as she dialled her father. He was a lawyer; he'd know what to do.

'I'm sorry, but he's in a conference right now,' his secretary said.

'Please, tell him it's urgent. It's Emma, his daughter.'

'Just a moment.'

Emma scanned the document again as she waited. She didn't really understand it, but she got the main point. She felt sick. It was all too much. Tears welled in her eyes, and no matter how hard she tried, she couldn't make them stop.

Her dad finally answered. 'Emma, love, what is it?'

'I, oh, Dad, I …'

'Now now, honey, take a moment and start from the beginning.'

Emma took a deep breath and managed to compose herself enough to say, 'I've just been served with a summons.'

'What?' he sounded shocked. 'What kind of summons? Is Kira back on the scene?'

'No, Dad, it's from the courts.'

'What? Why? Oh. What's it say?'

'It's something to do with making a false statement, and there is a date when I have to show up at the Brisbane Magistrates' Court.'

'Oh. Right.' He'd put on his lets-get-down-to-serious-business voice. 'Have you talked to the police after leaving Kira?'

'I went to the police station where I made that statement and asked them to withdraw it. I said it was false and that someone had forced me to make it.' The tears returned, and Emma sobbed into the phone.

Albert paused, seemingly lost for words, then he said, 'Okay, darling, just relax. We'll talk about it tonight after I get home. Don't worry; your dad's a good lawyer. We'll look after you.'

When her father returned home that afternoon, Emma was sitting at the outdoor setting on the patio scanning the employment section of the *Brisbane Herald* for jobs. She heard his car draw up, wandered inside a few minutes later, and heard him and her stepmother talking in the dining room. She could tell her father was trying to be quiet, but he was too upset to keep it down. Emma stood just outside the door and listened.

'Damn it,' her father said. 'Just when I thought the nightmare was behind me, she gets a summons. I don't get it. Couldn't they see what a mess she was? Don't they understand what's going on, what's happened to her? And obviously this is going to court. Making a false statement is no picnic.'

Emma stuffed her fist in her mouth to stifle a sob.

'Darling,' Alison said, 'we'll get through this one as well. You're a top lawyer; the whole legal field is open to you. Right now, let's concentrate on the function this evening at CultAssist. It's Emma's night; we can't afford to spoil it. There'll be time for the summons later.'

Emma checked her watch. They were due at CultAssist in an hour for drinks and nibbles.

'I guess her defence will have to be that wretched mind-control argument,' her father continued. 'Remember Patty Hearst and the Symbionese Liberation Army back in 1974? The famous defence argument in relation to the crimes Patty committed under the watch of the SLA was that "she didn't do what she wanted to do, but what she had to do." I've no idea how that washes in the Australian court system, but the US court dismissed Hearst's defence. How can I get up on the stand to support that? How can I not when it's my daughter, and I know it wasn't her, not really? Do I really need this, do I?'

'I'm sorry, Dad,' Emma said as she walked in.

He opened his arms and gave her a hug. 'It's okay, honey, it wasn't your fault. I know that. We'll just have to convince the court, that's all.'

'You should ring Laura,' Alison said. 'It's probably best she knows before we get there.'

Her father put the phone on speaker so Emma and Alison could listen in.

After he'd explained the situation and Laura had expressed her disappointment and frustration, she said, 'This isn't the first time a former cult member has retracted a statement. But for us, it's the first time one has been charged with making a false statement. It's not good, but dealing with this has to be better than a trial over the allegations Emma made.'

'True.'

'Are you still coming for drinks?' Laura asked.

'We'll all be there. But listen, I've made contact with someone at Divine Delicacies, and he said there is someone there who he feels—'

'It's okay, Albert,' Laura interjected, 'the girl in question has left The Healing Mission and returned home.'

'Oh, that's wonderful. Her parents must be so relieved.'

'Her mother, yes. She's very happy to have her home.'

'As are we with Emma. Thanks for everything you've done and for your continuing support. It means a lot to us,' her father murmured before hanging up.

'So what do I do about this summons?' Emma asked. She'd been trying not to think about it all day.

Her dad shook his head. 'Let's not go into it now. We've got an event to attend, then tomorrow I'll make some enquiries, and once I know a bit more about what's involved, we'll go from there. Don't worry. We'll overcome this together.'

Emma nodded.

'Let's get ready,' Alison said. 'We need to get a move on.'

An hour later they arrived at the CultAssist office. Emma felt a little nervous. Even though she'd kept in contact with her counsellors since the intervention, this was the first time she'd met them in a social setting. The conference room table had quite a spread on it—lots of finger food and a few drinks— and Margaret, wearing a garish multicoloured, hippie-style dress that only she could pull off, bustled around, making sure that everyone had something in their hand.

Emma was nibbling some delicious concoction when the hubbub of conversation died down and she heard her father's voice say he wanted to say a few words. *Oh my God, he's making a speech.* She wandered into the main room and stood next to Alison.

'On behalf of Alison, and my beloved daughter Emma and myself,' her dad said, 'I want to thank you. A few weeks ago, none of us could have imagined that we'd be here tonight with you. It's been a very intense journey over a short period of time.' He took a couple of steps to where Emma stood and put his arm around her. 'And, my darling, welcome home. I know there's still a way to go, but we're here to support you. I've learned a few hard truths during the last few weeks and the onus is on me to start adjusting my priorities. If that means reducing my workload, so be it. If that means spending more time with you as you begin this new phase of your life, then so be it. Emma, I love you.'

Emma sniffed but couldn't contain her tears. She held her dad's hand tight and looked at the small gathering all looking at her with kind smiles. 'I want to say thank you as well. I wasn't the only one Kira got her hooks into, and I think about those who are still there every day. Sometimes, I don't sleep at night because I wonder if they'll escape what I now see is a bleak future.' She turned to her father. 'Dad, if not for your and Alison's support, we wouldn't be standing here as a family. I don't think I'll ever be able to repay you for fighting for me.' She looked around at the CultAssist team.

'And Laura, and everyone else at CultAssist, you're the angels that restored my freedom and independence. I can't find the words to express the depth of my appreciation for everything you've done.' Laura's cheeks were wet with tears. Emma reached out to her, and they hugged, both crying happy tears.

51

The moment Laura walked into the office on Friday morning, the phone rang. As usual, Margaret had arrived before her, and she grabbed the phone.

'CultAssist. How may I help you?'

Laura dumped her handbag by her desk.

'Just a moment, I'll put you through.' Margaret waved to Laura.

Laura nodded and picked up the phone. Ten minutes later, with a mixture of relief and trepidation, she was calling a therapist in Sydney and arranging for an urgent psychiatric assessment and counselling for both Anne and Annabel. The big question was whether Anne would be willing to talk to anyone. Laura sighed. All they could do was try.

When Laura told Matthew what Annabel had said about Anne's depleted and unresponsive state, he said, 'It sounds like Annabel needs to get her sectioned and into a psychiatric hospital.'

'My thoughts exactly,' Laura said. 'But that's not going to be easy. Even if she can get Anne out of the house and into a psychiatrist's office, and even if the psychiatrist agrees with our assessment, apparently finding a bed in a psychiatric hospital isn't easy right now.'

'She's out of the cult,' Matthew said, 'but not out of danger.'

Laura nodded. She still had a bad feeling about Anne.

'Caroline's planning to visit regularly, so hopefully she can get through to Anne and get her to see the psychiatrist.'

'That's probably the best we can hope for at this stage.'

'At least she'll get properly fed at home,' he said with a cheerfulness that sounded somewhat forced.

'Assuming she'll eat,' Laura added. Sometimes she wished there was some kind of cult-recovery pill that could speed up the recovery process for cases like this where health issues couldn't wait for engrained beliefs to change enough for them to accept treatment. *Yeah, in your dreams!*

~

The next Tuesday morning, Laura took a morning flight to Sydney to meet Lionel, Ted and Rochelle for lunch in Darling Harbour. The taxi driver dropped her off as close as he could, and she walked through the park and found Rochelle at the bottom of the stairs that led up to their meeting place. They walked into a large, upmarket restaurant and found Ted sitting with another man at a table by the huge windows overlooking the harbour.

'Ritzy,' Rochelle said as she looked around at the white starched tablecloths, roses in the centre and gleaming silverware. 'But then, this is Ted, isn't it?'

Laura chuckled.

Both men stood as they walked over. Lionel, a tall, athletic young man, had the bearing and short hair Laura expected from an ex-Marine. His t-shirt and black jeans contrasted with Ted's business suit, but the men seemed relaxed in each other's company.

After introductions, they placed their drink orders, and then Laura said, 'Welcome to Australia, Lionel. I hope you've adjusted to our time zone.'

He smiled. 'I have, but, wow, you guys live a long way from anywhere. I've never flown over so much ocean. I'm glad to be here, though. I just hope I can help. I really feel for you. Ending up with His Holiness is not a good place to be, believe me.'

'Oh, I do,' Ted said.

A waitress delivered their drinks, and Laura asked, 'What work are you involved these days, Lionel?'

'After leaving India, I established a mentoring program for wayward teenagers' he replied. 'I've managed to get enough private funding to have what I hope is a positive effect on a few people's lives.'

'I think he's being modest,' Ted said. 'He's quite possibly a saint.'

Ted lowered his eyes dismissively. Laura smiled, and Rochelle chuckled.

'He's told me,' Ted continued, 'that he's on board with us all the way. We're going to get them out.' He turned to Lionel. 'Tell them what you told me.'

'Sure, let's get right to it. I managed to contact Gita, and she confirmed that Adele is part of the inner circle already. Tyson lives with a local family on the outskirts of the ashram, so it won't be that difficult to grab him. They've assigned some sort of a guard to protect him, but if it's only one person, we shouldn't have too much of a problem.'

'That's the good news,' Ted said with a smile.

'Adele's a different story, though,' Lionel continued. 'Gita has no idea how she'd react if she finds out we've got Tyson before she's out of the ashram.' He looked at Ted. 'I didn't mention this before, but she doesn't think Adele is particularly stable at the moment.'

Ted frowned. 'Are you saying they're giving her drugs? I've

read that some of these cults do.'

Lionel shook his head. 'Not necessarily, but you don't need to be on drugs there. The whole atmosphere is like a drug. It gives you a high. His Holiness has a magnetic personality and many of his followers pick up on his craziness. It seems that Adele is right there with them.'

'So we'll need two people for this operation,' Laura said, 'or two teams—one to remove Tyson and the other to remove Adele.' Laura drew a notebook from her handbag and made some notes.

'How did you meet Gita?' Rochelle asked. 'I assume she's in the inner circle, so …'

'I have my Marines' background to thank for that. His Holiness is paranoid, and when I was there, he decided the Indian government was out to get him. All a load of rubbish, but he asked me to head up a security team. At the time I thought that was an incredible privilege, so I agreed.

'We had to do some crazy things, like checking all the flour in the kitchen. One guard had to stand by the clothesline twenty-four seven to make sure no one sprinkled anthrax on His Holiness's clothes. It was ridiculous, and Gita wasn't comfortable with all these guards running around checking food and staring at her clothes on the washing line, so we started chatting and just hit it off.'

'And now?' Laura asked.

'After leaving, I had little contact with her at first, but then she called and told me about His Holiness's plans to attack the government. She was beside herself, but she managed to smuggle out some documents and have them faxed to me. I checked them out, and then approached various government officials. Suffice it to say, I didn't get much of a hearing.'

Lionel took a sip of his iced water. 'But I might be in a

better position to do something now. According to Gita, as of last week, His Holiness's plans are becoming more extreme. She's copied a whole lot of documents and is trying to get them to me, including maps of the targets and the details of a stockpile of chemical weapons. If I can get them, we can get the Indian police involved.'

'This is all great,' Ted said, 'but how does it help us?'

'Well, if we can get the police in there, we'll be in a good position to pull Adele out. We can take advantage of the chaos. And if they arrest His Holiness, that'll make it easier to get Gita out as well. She desperate to leave, and I want to help her. It'll take some precision planning, but it's coming together in my head. I'm prepared to try and pull Adele and Gita out, but we'll need someone else for Tyson, and, Ted, that may need to be you.'

Ted nodded. 'Sure, no problem.'

'What about the news crew?' Rochelle asked.

Lionel shook his head. 'They're just there to get footage, and we don't want them anywhere near us when we go in. Their presence would blow the whole thing.'

'And I don't want my family issues all over the news any more than it already is,' Ted said.

'Yeah,' Lionel said. 'It's important we say nothing to the media about our plans, not just for those reasons but also because His Holiness has a media watch officer checking for any mention of him in the media.'

'Wow,' Rochelle said. 'Is that paranoia or egomania?'

Lionel grinned. 'Both.'

'The plan,' Ted said, urging Lionel to continue.

'Right. Now, if the police arrive at the ashram and try to arrest His Holiness, all hell will break loose. It's impossible to predict what his followers will do. They could rally behind him and march to the city watch-house where he'd be held. They could run for their lives. There could be real pandemonium, and some people might get hurt or even die. Not that it's any comfort, but I think His Holiness's followers' days are numbered. I don't think mass suicide is off the cards.'

Rochelle gasped, and Ted banged his fist on the table in anger, then jerked his hand away, looking mortified at his loss of control. Laura just frowned. She knew it took only a word from the guru for someone's dream of salvation to turn sour, or even deadly.

Lionel looked at them each in turn, his expression serious and determined. 'Don't think I'm not doing my own soul searching. It's me who's going to be pulling the plug on His Holiness. But I'm convinced it'll save lives—government officials, possibly commuters. Who knows? But I'll also be partly responsible for what happens in the aftermath at the ashram.'

'What about Graham?' Rochelle asked in a small voice.

Lionel shrugged. 'I don't know because we have no idea where he is.'

Rochelle nodded. 'Can Gita find out?'

'I've asked her to see if she can find out where he's staying, but the place is huge, and she can't do anything that will cause suspicion. She'll do her best, though, and I'm prepared to see if we can find him before pulling the trigger, but right now there are at least five thousand followers camping out at the ashram, so we need to be prepared for … well, you know …'

Failure. Laura didn't doubt that everyone else also filled in the missing word.

'At least as far as Graham is concerned,' Lionel added with a shrug.

Rochelle buried her face in her arms, and Ted put his arm around her. Laura stared at her notebook. No one said a word. The meeting took on an eerie feeling; four people sitting at a

Sydney restaurant were about to decide the fate of some five thousand people in a rundown ashram in India.

Rochelle lifted her head. Her eyes were dry. 'I'm not sure what to say about Graham. I hope you find him, and I hope you get him out of there, for his sake. He deserves a better life than that, but …' She looked out the window and said nothing more.

Lionel frowned, perplexed. He glanced at Laura for help. She gave what she hoped he recognised as a 'softly-softly' gesture.

He looked even more puzzled.

Laura shrugged. Mime wasn't a talent she'd ever had.

Lionel took a deep breath. 'But what, Rochelle? I'm hearing you, but I need to know whether you want us to get Graham out of there. It won't be easy, but we can try if you want it. It's your call.'

Rochelle turned back and looked him in the eye. 'Okay, let me say this. I do want Graham out, and yes, please do whatever you can. But I'm not sure if I want him back. I can't see him just walking back into my life.'

'Okay,' Lionel said. 'We'll do our best to find him and get him out. I hope to get onto Gita on Thursday to get more information, and then if it's okay with you, Laura, Ted and I'll sit down and start nutting out the practicalities. Then we can all get together again and go over the details.'

'Sounds fine to me, Lionel. You seem to have it well in hand.' Laura was happy to let someone else take the lead for a change, and there was no substitute for having been inside a cult compound when it came to working out how to get someone out.

~

While in Sydney, Laura called on Nadia. Fadi was at work, but Laura finally got to meet Amin, a darkly handsome young man with deep eyes and a proud bearing like his father. He'd been back nearly three weeks now and had been receiving intensive counselling. Michael had spent a lot of time with him, flying from Brisbane to Sydney every weekend, and Nadia whispered that genuine romance seemed to be blooming between her son and Safiyya. He still had a lot of exit counselling to do before their relationship could become more, but Nadia was sure it would come because Safiyya kept calling.

She also visited Annabel and Anne but left with mixed feelings. Having her back home was a great relief, but the girl was seriously underweight, emotionally unresponsive and refused to leave the house to see the psychiatrist Laura had arranged—or for any other reason. Laura had also talked to Caroline, and they agreed that her continued contact was important, but Laura had no idea where that story would go from here.

On her return flight to Brisbane, Laura felt the satisfaction of a job well done with Amin along with trepidation about the proposed extraction in India, and a sense of foreboding over Anne that she didn't seem able to shake. *Ah well*, she reminded herself, *it's all part of the job.*

~

Ted joined Lionel for his call to Gita. They sat on the balcony of his Point Piper home in Sydney overlooking the harbour, sipping drinks and watching the light change from afternoon to early evening. Ted had spared no expense in making sure that Lionel got to enjoy all that Sydney had to offer. He'd opened his house to the ex-marine, and Lionel had impressed him with his integrity, intelligence and empathy. They'd become fast friends, and Ted felt blessed to have found him.

Lionel had explained that he could only call Gita at certain times—times when her father and his minders were most likely elsewhere engaged—and even then, he never knew whether she would be able to answer. This time, however, she answered. Ted thought the sweet Indian voice sounded alarmed.

'I don't know how long I can stay here,' she whispered. 'It's dangerous. It's not just His Holiness's plans, which are disturbing enough, but the whole ashram is becoming one big fraud. It used to be a kind of beautiful dream; now it's one big nightmare. If anyone finds out I've leaked this information, they could quite literally lynch me, but I've just sent a whole folder of documents Fedex Express to the address you gave me in Sydney. They're proof that His Holiness intends to send over one thousand envelopes containing anthrax to the offices of every Indian member of parliament and release sarin gas in the main hall of parliament. It's a horrific plan, and they've laid it out with the precision of a military exercise.'

'Good grief. That's horrible. We have to stop it,' Lionel said.

'Exactly. I'm so angry with him, but I worry about him too. I hope and pray he'll get the treatment he needs, but I can't stay silent about this, not with all that's at stake.'

Ted paced up and down the balcony while Lionel reassured Gita and told her to leave it with him to get the message through to the authorities. His drink suddenly tasted liked vinegar, and the nibbles seemed to turn to ash in his mouth. He couldn't believe what Adele had got herself caught up in. Did she know? How could she stay there if she did? The only way to get those answers was to get her out, and luckily for all of them, Lionel appeared to have the skills and ideas to pull it off, and hopefully save the Indian parliament as well.

52

The documents arrived on Monday morning, just a few days later, and the day after that, Ted flew Lionel, Rochelle and himself to Brisbane for a follow-up meeting with Laura.

Together, they poured over the documents. There were detailed maps of the parliamentary compound, and Google map printouts of every parliamentary office around the country. Thirty-two pages contained instructions laid out to the finest detail. The letters to the parliamentarians' offices had to be sent in different-sized and styled envelopes with different stamps and sent from at least fifty different post offices.

One document suggested two different dates for the operation, either Friday, 12 December 2003, just over a month away, or roughly a month later on Thursday, 14 January 2004.

Lionel appeared quite calm, approaching their mission in an almost military manner. 'I propose the following, and I make no secret of the fact that this will be a risky mission,' he told them. 'We let the Indian authorities know that we have important information relevant to national security and in return we need their cooperation. We inform them of His Holiness's plans. How we do that is something that will require further work, and Ted, I may be leaning on you for this. I assume your business and corporate connections in Asia will be useful in establishing the best means of communication with the government.'

Ted nodded. Telco was involved in several joint ventures in Asia. The company was also negotiating an optic fibre contract with a company part-owned by the Indian government.

Lionel continued, 'I'm quite sure that if presented with accurate information as well as back-up proof, the Indian government will act. My guess is that they'll carry out an extensive raid on the ashram. We'll ask the police to give us the date they plan to move, a few hours' warning and to conduct the raid at dusk or after dark. This is because Tyson will be at home with the family he lives with and His Holiness will be giving his evening lecture, so Adele will be more accessible. Apparently, she doesn't attend the evening program.'

Ted and Laura nodded. She seemed as impressed with Lionel as he was. A real professional, he showed no emotion as he described the plan in detail, but he appeared totally committed to its success. 'As they approach the ashram, and there will be carloads of them, I will go into His Holiness's quarters and grab Adele. You, Ted, will head for the small dwelling on the perimeter of the ashram and take Tyson. Of course, we will do our best to locate Graham. I've already spoken to Gita about Graham, and she's going to try to find him and work out where he's likely to be.'

He paused for a sip of Margaret's steaming coffee. 'We then regroup at the gates of the ashram, where I'll have a car, and we'll head straight to the airport. By that time, the police will be all over the ashram. I don't know what will happen then.'

Ted hoped Lionel wasn't being overconfident. 'Why do you think Adele will be such an easy take?'

'Leave it to me,' he replied with a wry smile. 'She'll know very quickly that she either comes with me or she'll be carted away by the police. I know that in these situations loyalty to a guru can lead people to make strange decisions, but I'm banking on the fact that, although she's become part of the ashram and appears to eat from His Holiness's hand, there is still some of the old Adele in her, or at least I hope so.'

After they'd polished off the pastries Margaret had supplied, Lionel suggested a timetable working on the first of the two days His Holiness had chosen for his attack. He asked Ted to explore the options for contacting the relevant officials in the Indian government. If they moved fast, the Indian police would have the information and the evidence in a couple of weeks at the latest, giving them time to plan their raid for the first week of December. Lionel and Ted would travel to India at the end of the month and be outside the ashram in the afternoon several hours before the police arrived on the day of the raid.

'The whole operation should take no more than twenty minutes,' he said. 'And if we're successful, we'll be at the airport an hour after the raid.'

53

Annabel looked up from her knitting. Her heart truly felt as if it were breaking. Anne sat on the sofa with a book on her lap, but she wasn't reading it. She'd been out of The Healing Mission for three weeks, but she wasn't getting better. She barely spoke, spent much of her time in her room, and on sunny days she sat outside and stared blankly at the trees.

Anne had refused to leave the house to see a psychiatrist. Annabel had finally found a woman willing to make a house call. The woman called the nearest psychiatric hospital to inquire about their services and possibility of Anne being admitted but there were no beds available. The hospital told her to keep her eyes on Anne, and they'd call her if a space became available. She hadn't heard back.

No one had called from The Healing Mission, not a single soul. Anne had vanished from their community, and apparently they were content with that. Caroline had visited once a week, but Anne had only managed very brief conversations with her. The woman Annabel had called Angel had left the cult and visited once to make sure Anne was all right before she left the city to return to her country home.

'I know you want to put me into a psychiatric hospital,' Anne said suddenly, 'but I won't go. I never want to live in an institution again.'

'Oh sweetie, I understand that,' Annabel said, 'but the doctors will help you to get well.'

Anne shook her head. 'I don't trust them. The Healing Mission said they'd heal me, but they just took away my soul.'

Annabel joined her daughter on the sofa and gave her a hug. Anne's thin arms wrapped around Annabel for a moment, but the action was robotic, as if she only did it because she felt it was expected.

Annabel couldn't bear it anymore. She stood, walked outside and screamed out her frustration. 'What right did those bastards have to take my daughter away?' she yelled, shattering the night's silence. Dogs barked, and a feral cat darted across the yard. She closed her eyes, took several calming breaths, then returned to the living room.

Anne looked up at her. 'Mummy, I love you. I do love you, but I need to sleep,' she said weakly, then she stood.

Annabel kissed Anne on her forehead. 'I love you too, my darling.'

Anne managed just a hint of a smile before making her way to her room.

It was the first time Annabel had seen anything remotely like a smile since Anne had returned home. She wanted to see it as a good sign, but it highlighted how far away Anne was from normality. Annabel picked up the phone and called Laura. 'Sorry to call you so late, but I'm at my wits' end. I need to talk to someone. The hospitals are all full, the psychiatrists booked up for months ahead, and Anne won't leave the house anyway.'

'Oh dear, Annabel. I'm so sorry it's not working out. Look, it's a bit late for me now, but I'll call you first thing tomorrow morning, and we'll have a long chat.'

Annabel ended the call and plonked onto the sofa. *Maybe The Healing Mission didn't do this. Maybe she was always sick?* A few minutes later, she headed to bed.

~

Annabel woke in the middle of the night. Something didn't feel right. She turned on the bedside lamp. The clock read 3.05 am. She got up, wrapped a dressing gown around her, then checked Anne's room, but her daughter wasn't there. Her heart started racing and her breathing quickened in fear. She searched every room in the house, but Anne wasn't inside. She ran onto the back veranda and grabbed the old torch from its place on the little table by the door.

'Anne?' she called.

No answer. Annabel turned on the torch, but the dim beam did little to illuminate the darkness. She tiptoed around the backyard, calling softly. Still no answer. Every so often the clouds shifted and the moon shone brightly, but mostly the yard remained dark. She stopped, called again, then listened. No answer, just a creaking sound coming from the huge oak tree at the very end of her garden. Annabel walked over, her heart pounding in terror. The moon emerged from the clouds and illuminated a devastating scene.

Annabel gasped, and a terrible keening sound emerged from her throat. Anne hung lifelessly from the tree, eyes closed, legs and arms dangling, swinging almost rhythmically in the night wind. One of her slippers lay on the ground, the other still clung to her foot. She wore the same gown she'd worn every night since leaving The Healing Mission, and she'd used her white bedsheet to strangle herself.

Annabel pulled herself together and approached her daughter's limp body. She touched her skin. It was cold. She was too late. She looked up at the noose Anne had fashioned in the sheet, tight now around her daughter's neck. She brought the ladder from the garden shed and lifted Anne's emaciated body onto it so she could loosen the knot and lower her to the ground, then she raised her arms to the sky and, looking up, said, 'Here, God, she's yours now. You know why she has returned to heaven, and I know her suffering is over. Dear God, I ask You, please give me the strength to survive this.'

She took off her dressing gown and covered Anne's face, then pulled a few small branches off the tree, picked up a bunch of dried leaves and covered her body. She stayed with Anne until the light of dawn heralded a new day.

Annabel walked slowly back to her house. The log fire was still burning. She threw another chunk of wood onto the fire, then picked up the phone and dialled Laura. 'Sorry, darling, to call you so early, but you're the only person in the world I can talk to right now. Anne is dead. She hung herself a few hours ago. I don't know what to do.' Annabel burst into tears.

'Oh my God,' Laura said. 'I'm so sorry. I'll call Caroline right away and take the first plane I can get a seat on. Someone will be there soon. I promise you.'

54

Laura looked at her clock. 7.00 am. She felt sick. How did Anne hang herself? *Is she hanging suspended from a staircase, or maybe from a tree?* And what could she do to help Annabel? *Poor tortured soul.*

She pulled the quilt over her head. A flood of powerful and confronting images flashed through her mind: Annabel walking into CultAssist for the first time, Anne's tortured face following her first rescue from The Healing Mission, Annabel walking up to the table at the Redfern Tavern and Anne's emaciated frame and vacant expression when she saw her last in Sydney.

Laura sighed. She had a job to do. She sat up and called Caroline. 'Anne is dead. She hung herself a few hours ago. Annabel is beside herself with grief.'

There was silence. 'Oh no. That's terrible. I'll go over as soon as I'm dressed.'

Laura told her she'd see her later, then phoned and secured a seat on a plane leaving in seventy minutes. She had to get moving. After whipping on whatever clothes she could find and gulping down a cup of coffee, Laura drove straight to the airport. Just before boarding the plane, she called Matthew, told him the news and asked for advice.

The flight should have given her time to think, but Laura's mind was a blank slate of shock. She couldn't imagine what it must be like for Annabel. All Laura could do, she decided, was be there for her and do whatever seemed appropriate at the time.

I'm not trained for this!

When Laura got out of the taxi, Annabel's front door was open. She found Annabel sitting on the couch with Caroline holding her hand. A tea pot and cups sat on the coffee table. Annabel's eyes were bloodshot and teary, but she appeared calm.

She stood, and Laura gave her a hug. 'Have you called an ambulance?' Laura whispered.

Annabel pulled out of the embrace. 'I wanted to wait until you got here,' she explained. 'It's peaceful right now. They'll ask questions and the police will come, and it'll be … mayhem, I expect. I'm sorry to have called you so early in the morning. Thank you for coming. I didn't expect that.'

Laura held her hand. 'It's the least I can do.'

'Do you want to see Anne?'

Laura nodded.

'I've taken her back into her room. Come with me.'

Laura followed her, relieved that she didn't have to see Anne hanging.

Anne lay on the bed as if she were asleep, but unnaturally still, no rising and falling of her chest. A burning scented candle and a bunch of fresh flowers sat on the bedside table. Annabel sat on a chair by the bed and Caroline and Laura stood beside her. An eerie silence filled the room along with a sense of calm and stillness.

'Before she went to sleep last night,' Annabel said, 'she told me she loved me, twice. I kissed her goodnight, and she looked at me. She didn't normally do that, and it made me uneasy. I guess that's why I woke up. And when I saw she wasn't in her bed, I searched the house and then the garden. She'd hung herself from the oak tree at the end of the garden.'

Laura pressed her lips together to stifle a sob. She swallowed. 'Did she leave a note?'

'No, nothing that I can see.'

'Okay,' Laura said. 'Look, we'll get out of your way now so you can spend these last moments with Anne. I'll call the ambulance and the police.'

Annabel nodded and sniffed back tears. 'Thank you.'

Caroline and Laura laid their hands on the blanket, stayed for a moment, then left the room.

Laura phoned the ambulance and police while Caroline made tea, and the authorities arrived half an hour later. Laura spoke to the two officers on the veranda. 'It's a suicide,' she said. 'She hung herself from the big oak tree at the end of the garden.' Laura pointed to the back of the house. 'Her mother got her down and took her to her bedroom. That's where she is now. If I can be of any help to your investigation, here's my number.' She handed him a card. 'I work at CultAssist; we're in Brisbane, but I can help you with Anne's history.'

'And the connection?' the policeman asked.

'Oh,' Laura said, 'the deceased woman was involved in a very suspect organisation that claims it can heal people.'

'It wouldn't be The Healing Mission, by any chance?' the officer asked.

'Yes, that's it,' Laura replied.

The officer shook his head and sighed. 'Why the hell can't the authorities close it down? Or do we have to wait for yet another tragedy?'

Annabel appeared in the doorway, tears now streaming down her face. Laura went back to her, her heart aching painfully. Annabel wrapped her arms around Laura, and they both cried. Behind them, the ambulance officers took a stretcher from the back of the ambulance, and the police officers walked towards the oak tree.

Laura led Annabel back to the sofa and poured her another cup of tea. Caroline was in the kitchen preparing some food. She rushed in suddenly, a piece of paper in her hand.

'She did leave a note,' Caroline said breathlessly. 'It was by the toaster.'

They waited in silence while Annabel read the note. By the time she'd finished, she was heaving great sobs. She handed the note to Laura.

My beloved Mum,

This will be my last letter to you, and I write each word with another tear. My time is up, there is no way out, no path on which to continue, and we will not see each other again in this world, but I will await you at another time and in another place. Not one which is filled with hatred and pain, but a place replete with peace and harmony. Mum, I can't do this anymore. I can't continue to cause you the pain and the uncertainty of not knowing if I will be here tomorrow or not. You deserve better and you deserve some closure so you can live again.

Since the time I came back home, I was not alive and you know that. The Healing Mission was my last hope. Maybe if I wouldn't have gone back after you rescued me, life would have been different, but I did go back. Yes, they made me feel good at first, but then it was back to the same routine: the floggings, the abuse, the control. My life has been one of pain. You know that I never recovered from Dad's death.

I have not stopped missing him, and there has not been a day when I didn't cry for him. And even now I think of how he played with me, how he held me, how we laughed together. He was my dad, and he is still my dad. Why was he taken away so early in my life? Other people have their dads for so many years. I didn't. Will I now see him again? I just don't know.

And there are other things that have hurt me and pained me. I don't know why, but my vision of life on Earth was never fulfilled. I would open the newspaper or watch the news and see another war, another murder, another rape. And it went on and on. I cried and cried, but what did that achieve? Please, Mum, close down The Healing Mission. All of us are damaged people, our wounds are deep and our pain so strong. We need genuine love, real love. If there is a God out there, I can assure you that He hasn't been near The Healing Mission. They wouldn't recognise him, and He wouldn't want to be there. God didn't want us to become mindless Bible bashers and pathetic puppets of a cruel and selfish cult.

But, Mum, you did everything you could. Whatever goodness I experienced in my life has been yours. I only hope that I have given you back some of what you gave me. My heart is heavy, and the tears are flowing. Please forgive me, please forgive me, please forgive me. I will always love you. I will always love you. Just trust me now. Please. Love and kisses and one more hug. Goodbye for now. — Anne

55

Ted reclined in his plush lounge suite and looked around his lavish townhouse. It felt bare, cold. Life had stopped at his Point Piper home after Tyson had disappeared. At first Ted had entered his room each evening and whispered, 'Good night, Tyson. Mummy and Daddy love you.' But now he found that too painful and didn't set foot in the room. He had tried, but something held him back.

Sleeping had been difficult. He often woke during the night and the quietness of the house overcame him. At least he had Lionel here now. Not that he was any substitute, but he gave Ted hope, and that was precious indeed.

To think that he and Adele had wanted to have another child, had looked forward to Tyson having a little playmate. But now his one child was lost, perhaps never to be seen again. Would the pain in his chest ever go away?

Few people at his workplace would be aware of his pain. A highly focused and energetic person, he hid it well. But inside himself, work now lacked meaning. The opulent office, the loyal staff, the media coverage and the multimillion-dollar salary meant little to him. Sometimes he shut his office door and stared at the walls, looking at the family photos and thinking about the fate that had befallen him. He tried not to feel sorry for himself, but that was becoming difficult.

He still couldn't grasp the cult issue. Adele didn't take drugs; she wasn't a hippie, and she wasn't a particularly spiritual person. She'd always enjoyed high fashion, although inwardly she was a very private person. 'I just don't get it. It doesn't make sense.'

He got up and poured himself a scotch. It was a little early, but to hell with it. Lionel was out somewhere enjoying Sydney while they waited to hear back from India.

Ted returned to the couch, took a sip of his drink, and reflected on their marriage, how they met each other and how their love towards each other grew. 'No, it's not the marriage,' he muttered to himself. 'It's not Tyson. I don't know what it is, but if you'd have asked me whether my darling wife could join a cult, I would have said never. Never.'

Now he was about to be transformed from one of the nation's top CEOs into a cult buster. Ted would be waiting outside a sprawling, ramshackle and dusty ashram in the middle of India ready to retrieve his son. At the same time, the fate of his wife would be in the hands of a young, former US Marine.

He thought about Rochelle and her seemingly hopeless situation. *Would she ever find Graham?* And what made Laura tick? Why did she do this work? It must be heart-breaking when they failed to get someone out, or when they did but the cult just continued, luring more people in. After all this was over, he'd see what he could do to assist CultAssist. But right now, the pain was becoming intolerable.

For the first time in many years, Ted realised, he wasn't in control of his own life. He felt vulnerable in a way he never had before. And he wasn't used to dealing with limitations.

Ted stood, walked to the window overlooking the bay and said, 'Well, it's all going to change. Adele and Tyson, I'm coming to get you.'

56

Emma always hated Monday mornings, but this had to be the worst one ever. She stood, feeling slightly nauseous, outside the Brisbane Magistrates' Court—a modern, twelve-story building in the heart of the city's CBD—with Alison while her father parked the car. Vehicles raced along the major thoroughfares on each side. Across one street, the dome of the Supreme Court towered above the more-than-one-hundred-year-old building. On the other side of the road sat the far-more-modern building housing the County Court.

Emma's case was due to start at 10.00 am in Courtroom 4. She'd spent the previous weekend with her solicitor, Glen Taylor, a senior lawyer in the firm Nissen and Humble—the guy who did the prep work—and the barrister James Keller QC—the guy who'd represent her in court. Her father told her that James had a reputation of being a hard-hitting, no-nonsense advocate. He'd sat in on all the conferences, and—though they were both still reeling from the suicide of one of their clients the previous week—Laura and Matthew had joined the family and the legal team on Sunday as they prepared for the big day ahead. The whole thing—planning, discussions and questions—was already overwhelming, and sometimes she'd had to walk out and be on her own.

Though making a false statement carried a possible jail

sentence, her father had said there was no way she'd go to jail. 'On the other hand,' he'd mused to himself at one point, 'if she was sentenced to a term of imprisonment, I wonder if they'd deduct the days she spent locked up with Kira as time served.'

Emma hadn't known whether to laugh or cry at that. The whole thing seemed horribly unfair. She'd put up with so much when she lived with Kira, and now she had to defend herself when all she'd wanted to do was correct the police records. She shouldn't have to pay a price for honesty.

Her dad turned up and led them to the courtroom, a large modern room with wooden panels on parts of the walls, a raised dais for the magistrate and his sidekicks, long desks for the lawyers and room for an audience at the back. The clerk seated her in the place for the defendant on the first row of desks. James sat on her left with Glen next to him, and her dad sat on her right as her support. Alison sat directly behind them.

'Silence. All stand,' the clerk boomed.

Everyone shuffled to their feet, and the magistrate entered—a well-groomed, middle-aged man with bushy black hair. Once he'd seated himself, the clerk told everyone to be seated.

The prosecutor was Mr Ian Sinclair SC, a tall, confident and distinguished-looking man. He stood, looked at the magistrate, cleared his throat, and said, 'On twenty-sixth August 2002, Ms Emma Carter willingly gave and signed a statement alleging that her father had molested her over an extended period of time. On the same day, she sent a fax to her father's office demanding a payment of five hundred thousand dollars in return for her willingness to remain silent about the abuse.

'Some weeks later, Emma returned to the Maleny police station, acknowledged she had made a false statement and requested that it be withdrawn. My reading of the relevant section of law leads me to the indisputable conclusion that she has committed a serious act of making a false statement.'

Emma gulped, feeling suddenly like a criminal. *Kira's the one who should be on trial!* Albert gave her a reassuring look.

'It comes as little surprise,' Mr Sinclair continued, 'that the defence will argue that Ms Carter was not acting independently but that she was under the influence of what has been loosely termed 'mind control'. Why wouldn't they say this? After all, Mr Carter appears to have extensive contact with an organisation called CultAssist, which, quite incredulously, actually believes that this mind-control defence is an adequate argument to have Ms Carter discharged.

'Your Honour, wouldn't it be wonderful if every defendant in this country could attach his criminal activity to this notion of mind control, which has been discredited by numerous experts in the field of psychology and sociology? The prisons would be empty, and many could close down. The fellow who robbed the bank could say he was controlled by the guy who devised the plan. The drug mule could argue that he was controlled by the big dealer. It would be all so easy.

'But, Your Honour, such arguments are absolutely fallacious. That's not to say that clever barristers haven't tried to attach their clients' crimes onto the mind-control theory. But take a look at the history of such actions. You will recall the celebrated US case of Patty Hearst. A young woman, the heiress of a huge publishing company, is kidnapped by the Symbionese Liberation Army in 1973. She's held captive in a tiny closet. Eventually, she is released and participates in the SLA's criminal activities. She is arrested. Her defence attorney uses the mind-control argument: What Patty did is not what she wanted to do but what she had to do. Your Honour, the judge found her guilty, and she was sent to prison.

'And what about the case of Lee Boyd Malvo in Washington?

Malvo was charged with murder following a random shooting spree. His defence argued that he was unduly influenced by his mentor, a much older man by the name of John Allen Muhammad. Your Honour, once again the defence argument was thrown out the window. Indeed, in that case, the famous Robert Lifton, the so-called guru of mind-control theory, sided with the prosecution, saying that despite some mitigating factors, "there remains the issue of responsibility".

'I propose to call Ms Lorraine Underwood as a witness. Ms Underwood has had a long association with Ms Thurin and has completed her course in natural medicine.

'Emma Carter needs to face up to her crime and bear the consequences of her activity. She needs to recognise that the statement she wrote could have potentially destroyed her father's practice, his good name and future. These are not insignificant consequences. She wrote that statement and indeed she did so in good faith. She signed the statement believing it was true; the document was witnessed by a senior member of the Queensland Police Force. She knew exactly what she was doing. Your Honour, it will be submitted that in now conceding that the document was false, she be convicted of the criminal act of making a false statement and be sentenced accordingly.'

Emma grimaced. He'd made his point and, though apparently what happened in the US wasn't always relevant here, the magistrate seemed far too receptive to the prosecutor's submission.

'I call Mrs Lorraine Underwood.'

Emma knew about Lorraine Underwood. Shortly after Kira arrived on the scene peddling her natural medicines, Lorraine's sister, Sasha, sought help from Kira for a skin condition. Kira's treatment was a disaster, Sasha ended up in hospital and they advised her to take legal action against Kira to recover her medical costs. When Kira found out about this, she offered

Lorraine a heap of money if she could keep Sasha quiet about the botched treatment. Emma didn't doubt that Kira had told Lorraine what to say today.

Lorraine, a thin woman with cropped brown hair and sharp cheekbones, walked in with her head held high, a determined look on her face.

After she was sworn in, Sinclair looked at his notes and asked, 'Ms Underwood, when did you first meet Ms Thurin?'

'Some time in 1995. I was unemployed and figured her course might provide me with a work opportunity later on. Many of Kira's students have become successful practitioners.'

Emma rolled her eyes. None of Kira's so-called graduates had set up a practice or even worked with another practitioner. She looked at James, but he appeared unperturbed by Lorraine's evidence.

'So what happened then, Ms Underwood?'

'I did the course. It was great, and I graduated at the end of 1997.'

'And how would you describe Kira?'

'Kira's a very special woman. She cares about her students and doesn't ever try to influence them. She's very respectful of other people's opinions. I can't remember one time when she tried to tell me what to do or how to behave.'

Emma's jaw dropped. She glared at Lorraine, but the woman wouldn't meet her gaze. *What a liar!*

'Thank you, Ms Underwood.'

James stood to do his cross-examination. 'Ms Underwood, has Ms Thurin ever paid you any money for work you've done for her?'

Lorraine blinked, apparently stunned by the question. She glanced at Sinclair, who was busy writing. 'No, I've never worked for Kira.'

'Well, perhaps I'll put my question differently. Has Ms Thurin ever paid you any money?'

Lorraine's eyes widened. She blinked and cleared her throat, then pulled a tissue from her pocket and wiped her forehead. 'I … I don't recall.' Sinclair was still writing, but Emma could see his frown. *Good.*

'Ms Underwood,' James continued, 'you said you graduated from Ms Thurin's course in 1997. I would imagine you would have a certificate to prove this.'

'Yes, I'm sure I do have one.'

James lifted a piece of paper. 'I have here a list of the graduates of 1997. I even have a photo of the class sitting with Ms Thurin. Your name does not appear on the list, and your face, as far as I can see, does not appear on the photo, unless of course you've changed your appearance altogether.'

Lorraine took a sip from the glass of water in the witness box, then wiped her brow again but said nothing. Sinclair stopped writing and stared at her.

Emma smiled. Though he showed no expression, Sinclair would know his case was sinking fast. His witness had just proved herself unreliable.

James didn't bother to wait for Lorraine to try to answer his question about the graduation. 'No further questions.' He sat down and gave Emma a small nod of encouragement.

The clerk rose. 'The court is adjourned and will resume at 10.00 am tomorrow. All stand.'

57

When they returned to court the next day, James started the proceedings. A tall, rugged-featured man, he stood straight, shoulders back, cutting an impressive figure in his suit and tie. For a moment his eyes scanned the court. He gave Emma a small smile, which helped calm her fluttering stomach.

'It's difficult to know why the defendant Emma Carter is even in this court today,' he began. 'Emma is the daughter of two respected members of our community, Mr Albert Carter and his first wife, Natalie Carter, who passed away when Emma was thirteen years old. On all accounts Emma had a normal upbringing. Her father did everything possible to ensure that she would not be disadvantaged by the tragic passing of her mother.'

He went on to talk about her excellent school reports, being on the student council, giving the valedictory speech and the principle's glowing comment about her in the school journal, then her enrolling in Architecture at the University of Brisbane and moving out of home into shared accommodation. He then filled them in on what happened once she met Kira.

'Shortly after, she met a fifty-year-old Thai woman, Kira Thurin, and her relationship with her parents began to sour. Kira was a naturopath who had migrated to Australia from Thailand in 1980. The following year, Ms Thurin set up a small school for young women wishing to study natural medicine.

At any time up to twenty-five students undertook the course, which involved ten hours of study each week. It appears that Kira took a particular liking to Emma, and eventually Emma left her shared accommodation and moved into Kira's home. My understanding is that of all Kira's students, Emma was the only one to move in with her.

'Around that time, Emma also stopped seeing her friends and took a spiritual name, which she insisted people use. This shocked her parents. Contact with her family became irregular and eventually stopped altogether. It was clear to all who had been close to Emma that Kira was exerting a significant degree of influence over Emma. In fact, it would be fair to say that Kira was in full control of Emma's life. Her parents felt that they had lost their daughter.'

He then told the court about her statement to the police, the fax to her father, his contacting CultAssist and Emma returning home.

'Following her reunion with her parents, Emma returned to the Maleny police station and withdrew her statement, claiming it was false and written under great duress from Kira. As a result of Emma's brave attempt to correct the police statement, she was charged with making a false statement for which she faces this court today.

'Understandably, this whole episode has not only almost destroyed Emma but has also had a most adverse effect on her family. The fax she sent to her father, Mr Carter, who is here in court today, came as a great shock to him. It was impossible for Mr Carter to comprehend what had happened to his daughter. The fax was provocative and accusatory. Mr Carter instructs me that it was based on lies and deception.

'It is my submission that at the time of making the statement incriminating her father, Emma Carter was under the influence of mind control. She was unable to think independently. She was unable to make decisions. Her mind was entirely under the influence of Kira Thurin. Making a false statement involves a willing and conscious act to write a false statement. I put to you that Emma's mind was so controlled by Kira that she lacked the capacity to make a free and truthful statement. She cannot therefore be convicted of making a false statement.

'I propose to call a number of witnesses. Laura Fields is the director of an organisation called CultAssist. They have an understanding of cults and the manner in which mind control works. Their insights are central to this case. I also propose to call Mr Albert Carter. I have no doubt whatsoever that the evidence of these witnesses will be enough to convince Your Honour that this charge should be dismissed.' James looked at the magistrate. 'I wish to call Laura Fields.'

Laura stood from where she sat behind Emma and walked to the witness box in the front of the room. After being sworn in, she gave her name, address and role at CultAssist. 'Our task is to assist families whose loved ones have become entangled in what is commonly referred to as the cult scene. We also conduct research into cults and fringe religious groups. We work with the media and have assisted the police and other statutory authorities regarding cult issues.'

James asked how long she'd known the Carter family, and then, 'Why did Mr Carter approach your organisation?'

'Well, Mr Carter was extremely concerned by the personality change his daughter, Emma, appeared to have undergone as a result of her connection with Ms Kira Thurin. He told me that until her involvement with Ms Thurin, Emma was a warm and affectionate daughter. Within several months of her association with Ms Thurin, Emma had disassociated herself from her extended family, adopted a new spiritual name and completely severed her ties with her father and his wife Alison.'

'And what did you conclude had happened to Emma?' Mr Keller queried.

'It was my professional assessment that Emma had become a victim of mind control. She was under Ms Thurin's spell. It appeared that she had lost the power of independent thought. This was the only way that her behaviour could be understood.'

'Thank you, Ms Fields.'

James sat, and Sinclair rose and said, 'Ms Fields, I am instructed that Emma left home at the age of seventeen and that a year later she took up residence with Ms Thurin. She was extremely happy with Ms Thurin. Six months after she moved in with Ms Thurin, she wrote her father, Mr Albert Carter, a letter expressing great satisfaction with her new lifestyle. I tender that letter as Exhibit P1.' He handed the letter to the clerk, who handed it over to the magistrate.

Emma bit her lip. This wasn't unexpected, but Emma couldn't relate anymore to the person who had sent that letter. She'd been so sucked in.

'Is it not quite common for a young woman to temporarily cease contact with her family, her loved ones?' Sinclair continued, looking at Laura. 'I suggest that a fair share of people in this age group do exactly the same. They yearn for time out and the opportunity to reassess their direction in life. Are you familiar with such behaviour?'

'Yes, I am, Mr Sinclair,' Laura replied. 'In fact, I did exactly the same thing. But I didn't change my name to a Thai name, I didn't break off contact with all my friends, I didn't defer my university studies and I stayed in contact with my family. Emma's behaviour following her meeting Kira was not normal. It is not normal for a young woman from a caring, loving home to suddenly land a fax on her father's desk in an attempt to extort money from her father.'

Sinclair raised his voice. 'Instead of allowing this evidence to be tested, Mr Carter, a lawyer himself, engaged your organisation to abduct Ms Carter with the intention of subjecting her to several days of intense brainwashing during which she would conveniently change her mind and let her father off the hook. Was not that the intention of Mr Carter, Ms Fields? The fact that Emma eventually left of her own accord does not detract from the plan you had devised. I put it to you that the very fact she left of her own accord demonstrates that she was in full control of her life.'

Laura shook her head. 'I absolutely deny these outrageous allegations, and the best evidence to refute them will come from Emma herself.'

Sinclair continued, 'I suggest that Ms Carter wrote the statement of her own volition. She knew exactly what she was doing. She was not brainwashed; her mind was not controlled by Kira. Her decision, regardless of the circumstances that led her to change her mind and withdraw the statement, constitutes making a false statement. Incidentally, how much did Mr Carter pay CultAssist for its services, Ms Fields?'

'I believe the total bill was twelve thousand, five hundred dollars. All our fees are based on a fee schedule. Our accounts are audited; we are a registered Public Benevolent Institution and pride ourselves in our accountability and transparency.'

'No further questions, Ms Fields.'

The clerk rose. 'The court will resume at 2.00 pm. All stand.'

Emma couldn't wait to get out of there.

58

In the break, Emma's team met in a nearby coffee shop. Laura and Matthew made a few calls before joining them.

'Don't worry, Emma,' James said as they sat down, 'we're doing fine. We're only at the beginning of this. But we've got to make a few decisions. Ian is being tough, but that's his manner and you shouldn't feel intimidated by it. Magistrates are used to it, so it doesn't really help.'

Emma nodded and tried to smile, but all she wanted was for this to be over.

'Laura, you were great,' James said. 'You kept your cool and answered the questions. And you did well by challenging Sinclair, even though he didn't think so. We've got three options now. I could call you again since you know the mind-control theory, and I'm sure the magistrate would be interested to explore this further. Or I could refer to a number of cases where the courts have upheld the mind-control argument and, believe me, there are many. Sinclair made a huge mistake by mentioning Robert Lifton. Yes, he talks about responsibility, but he is, as Ian said, the guru—excuse the pun—of mind control. If there's one authority who believes in mind control, it's Robert Lifton.

'There is a third option, though it may be an uncomfortable one.' He looked at Emma's father. 'I put you, Albert, in the witness box. Your evidence will be powerful, and I think it'll clinch this for us. The choice is yours, but I'm comfortable with calling you.'

Albert looked at Emma. 'What do you want, Emma?'

Emma shrugged. 'I don't know, but I trust you. You're a lawyer. I'm just a sucker who got conned into a cult, made a horrible statement and dragged you all into a courtroom. I'm so ashamed.' She bit back tears.

'Emma,' Laura said, looking intently at Emma. 'That's not what this is about. And you know that. You're a real gem; this wasn't your fault. How many times do I need to tell you this?' She gave her hand a squeeze. Emma nodded, but tears leaked out anyway.

'James, you can call me,' her father said, sounding confident. 'I'll handle this; I need to do this for my daughter, and I will.'

'No problems, Albert, I know you can do it.'

Albert hugged Emma, and they both cried softly.

~

Back in the courtroom, James called Emma's dad to the stand. After the usual preliminaries, he reaffirmed Emma breaking with her family, then James asked, 'What did you think happened to your daughter?'

'To be quite honest, I had no idea. It felt like something was wrong, but I couldn't work out what it was. Alison and I just hoped that she'd call or write. It got to the point where I thought every time the phone rang it must be her, but it wasn't. Once we knew she'd changed her name and refused any address by her real name, we knew we were in serious trouble.'

'What did you do, Mr Carter?'

'A close friend who worked in the media referred me to an organisation called CultAssist. The staff there were sure that my daughter was under the influence of mind control. I wasn't sure. I mean, I knew something was seriously wrong, but I couldn't place it. To be honest I had originally been a critic of the whole idea of mind control.'

'And what do you believe now?'

'Mr Keller, I'm a father. I believe you are a father too. I did all the research I could on mind control. I looked up numerous cases, I read a heap of books and psychiatric journals, you name it. I was amazed at the amount of information on this whole issue. There were academic reviews on the mind-control phenomena. Social scientists had studied Jonestown, Waco, The Order of the Solar Temple, Heaven's Gate and Beslan—there have been so many tragedies. It really astounded me. It appeared that the phenomenon of mind control did actually exist. How else was it possible for any person, my daughter included, to act in a way that was so obviously against her nature, unless she was controlled by another person?

'Two months ago, following Emma's escape from Kira's incarceration, she revealed to the counsellors what her teacher had taught her, and she conceded that she believed all of it. I saw my daughter just after she'd escaped from Kira's clutches. She'd lost weight, had an extremely pale complexion, was confused and cried easily and bitterly. Your Honour, I watched my beloved wife die. I was with her until her last moment. But as tragic as that event was, there was something natural about it. But there was nothing natural about Emma after she escaped from Kira. I could hardly recognise her, and it was the most heart-wrenching experience I've ever had.'

The courtroom was deathly still and quiet, all eyes riveted on Emma's dad. Emma's heart swelled with love and pride.

'But over the next few weeks,' he continued, 'as the exit counsellors worked with her, her confusion dissipated and she slowly regained her composure. She was, once again, able to look me in the eye. Your Honour, my daughter had returned home.'

Albert paused for a moment as if overcome by emotion. Sinclair looked away. The magistrate watched patiently.

James said, 'Please continue, Mr Carter.'

Albert nodded and straightened. 'Your Honour, we welcomed our daughter back into our home. The next morning, Emma went back to the Maleny police station to withdraw her statement. It was her way of saying, "It's over; I've woken up." It was her way of bringing closure to a traumatic event that no one should ever have to experience.'

'Thank you, Mr Carter.' James looked around the court.

Emma took a deep breath as Sinclair began his cross-examination. 'Mr Carter, you wrote an article that was published in the *Tamworth Tribune* in July 1998. The article refers to a statement purportedly made by you referring to the "now discredited notion of mind control and thought reform." Are you aware of this article and your statement?'

'Your Honour, I made the statement several years ago. I have no idea why it was reported only last year. During the past few years there has been considerable research into the phenomena of mind control and thought reform.'

'Mr Carter,' Sinclair continued, 'the article suggests that you are highly critical of the CultAssist organisation—the very organisation you engaged to assist your daughter. Are you able to explain this puzzling U-turn in your opinion of CultAssist?'

'As I've already explained, the last few years have shed new light on these issues as well as CultAssist's work. They deserve credit for saving our daughter's life.'

'Well, Mr Carter, my understanding is that you were, at least until recently, a board member of the food chain, Divine Delicacies.'

'This is correct, Your Honour.'

'Is it also correct that Divine Delicacies is the parent company of an organisation known as The Healing Mission, which in turn controls The Women's Rehabilitation of Our Holy Redeemer? Are you aware of the recent negative publicity surrounding The Healing Mission, including allegations that it practices mind control?'

'I recently resigned from the board of Divine Delicacies and do not intend to rejoin their board in the future.'

Sinclair asked him about the timing of his resignation and involvement with CultAssist, and then said, 'Mr Carter, was your resignation something you felt was necessary or were there any forces urging you to resign? I remind you that you are under oath.'

'The staff of CultAssist suggested that there would be an inconsistency between my involvement with Divine Delicacies and my efforts to extricate my daughter from a cult. I chose to resign.'

'And Mr Carter, now that your daughter is no longer involved with Ms Thurin, would it be presumptuous for me to suggest that you are free to join the board of Divine Delicacies?'

'My commitment to cease involvement in Divine Delicacies was for five years. But I assure you, I have no intention of ever joining them again.'

'Thank you, Mr Carter.'

The magistrate looked at his watch, then glanced at the clerk, who then adjourned the court until the next morning.

Emma chewed her lip. Her dad looked worried, and she felt tension in the air as they trooped into the lobby.

59

Emma, her dad, Alison, Matthew and Laura gathered around James. 'There's only one way forward,' he said. 'We'll win this. Don't worry about Sinclair. He's good at what he does, but he's run out of ammunition. He's concocted a story that, to be fair to him, makes some sense. But only *some* sense. The solution is simple.' He turned to Emma, patted her shoulder and gave her a reassuring smile. 'I'm putting you on the stand. You'll get us over the line. We'll talk tonight, but that's the strategy. Won't be easy, but we'll get there. It'll all be over by lunchtime tomorrow.'

Her dad looked at her and the stress on his face eased. 'I know that you can do it, Emma.'

She swallowed and managed a small smile. 'I can, Dad, and I will do it. As they say, tomorrow is my day in court.'

Laura looked at Emma. 'We have a few things we need to do. You'll be conferring with James later, and if you need us, we'll be there. But do yourself a favour, take a break. Go for a walk, get some sunshine and try to clear your mind.'

'Funny that. That's what Kira used to say.' *But then, that's how she got me in, wasn't it? Some of what she said was genuine wisdom. I just made the mistake of thinking that because some of it was, all of it was.*

The next morning, Emma found herself back in the courtroom, looking confident—she hoped—in the smart navy suit she'd bought for job interviews.

James called her to the witness box. The court went quiet. The students observing the proceedings put down their folders, and her dad angled forward in anticipation. No way could Emma swear on a Bible. She wanted nothing to do with religion or spirituality ever again, so she chose to make an affirmation instead.

She answered the preliminary questions in a loud, clear voice, hopefully projecting a clarity of mind that she'd so recently fought to regain. James asked her how she met Kira and, after Emma told them about joining the course, she said, 'Kira showed an intense interest in maybe two or three of us. On the last day, she spent two hours with one of the guys and about three hours with me. I felt privileged. Kira was an unbelievable communicator, and at the time I felt that she spoke to my heart.

'I don't really know why, but I started questioning why God took my mum away so early in my life. I suppose I was going through a tough time, and Kira seemed to have the answers to many of my questions. She invited me to stay with her for a weekend and asked if I'd be interested in doing some work for her. I needed the money, so I agreed. I felt honoured to be working for her and slowly started seeing her differently. I can't describe the feeling. I suppose I could say I began to love her deeply. Not in a romantic sense, but spiritually. Eventually, she invited me to move in with her.'

The magistrate listened intently. Ian Sinclair wrote furiously, and James sat relaxed in his chair.

'So you felt that Kira was some sort of a guru to you?' James asked.

'Objection,' Sinclair retorted.

'Disallowed,' the magistrate said.

Emma answered the question. 'Yes. The connection was very powerful. What was bizarre was that eventually Kira stopped running courses apart from the odd weekend at her home. She spent a lot of time talking to me about how the world desperately needed us to create a new kingdom, God's Kingdom, one without suffering, and how she saw that I had special qualities that would help bring that about. I was flattered, I suppose, so I bought into it. Everyone likes to feel special. Anyway, in June, Kira told me to drop out of my course in architecture so I could focus on preparing myself to do God's work, and so I did. By the end of the year, I'd stopped talking to my dad.'

'Ms Carter, you're an intelligent woman; you have excelled academically. What do you think happened? How did you become so involved with and so dependent on this woman? After all, it is because of that relationship that you are here today. It led you to the Maleny police station where you wrote your statement and then the fax to your father's office. Please, can you assist the court in understanding what happened.'

Emma paused and composed herself. Sinclair stopped writing. No one moved or spoke. She cleared her throat and looked straight at the magistrate, who leaned forward to hear every word. 'It was the twenty-fifth of August 2002, a mild day for late winter. I was in Kira's garden. The sun was setting. She came over to me—oh, by the way, my name was no longer Emma. Kira had changed it to Phitsamai—it's a Thai name that means Adorable Woman—and I wasn't allowed to use the name Emma anymore.'

Emma's mind wandered back to that time and place. She heard Kira's voice as if she were standing behind her. 'Phitsamai,' Kira said softly. 'It's time that we built the kingdom you and I have been talking about for months. God's Kingdom on Earth.

You and I will lead the transformation as the end times approach.'

Emma shook the image from her mind and relayed Kira's words to the court. 'She held my hands, looked deep into my eyes and said, "Money is the tool of Satan, but we fight Satan with Satan. We need half a million dollars for the new kingdom, and you are to find the funds. Your father is wealthy, and he abused you when you were a child. You will let him know that unless he provides these funds, you will expose him publicly."

'Your Honour, even though my father had never abused me, I agreed to fulfil the mission she laid out for me without asking a single question. In line with Kira's teachings, I thought helping to build God's Kingdom was the most important thing I could do with my life, and I would've done anything she asked to help bring it about.

'The next morning, after my meditation, Kira told me what I should say in my statement. She said that truth was what supported God's work and so every word I wrote would be true. And then a man I'd never met before drove me to the Maleny police station. Before I signed it, I read every word to Kira over the phone to make sure it was what she wanted, and I made alterations to the statement when she asked me to. I wanted her to be proud of me. The man then took me back to her.'

Emma stood, raised her voice in determination and spoke not just to the magistrate but to all in court. 'In the past few days, you've heard the issue of mind control mentioned several times. I've never studied it formally, but during the past few weeks I've done a fair bit of reading, and Your Honour, I can say without a doubt that I was the victim of mind control. There is no other way to explain how I could change from someone who knew right from wrong to someone who felt the only right thing to do was whatever Kira told me to do.

'How else can you explain my descent from a life based

on true morals and ethics to the point where I was prepared to blackmail my own father? I was able to escape because I somehow regained some sense of myself, and I had CultAssist on my side, but many more people remain ensnared in similar situations with little or no chance of escaping.

'Your Honour, I have no idea what happened to Kira. She was once a wonderful woman and many people drank from the wisdom I first saw in her, but she became reclusive, her personality changed and her behaviour became extreme. I followed her on that path because I'd become part of her reality. Apparently, Jim Jones was also a good man and so was David Koresh. But as their paranoia and fears grew, so did the sentiments of the people who'd put their faith in them. Their fate became the fate of their followers, and all are dead today.'

Emma took a deep breath. She'd planned what to say. She could do it. 'When any human being puts all his or her faith into one person, they risk the danger of following that person into oblivion. Their moral compass can become confused, and they can lose their grip on reality. Your Honour, if Kira Thurin had told me to murder my father while I was under her control, I would have committed that crime out of my love and respect for her and my belief in her teachings.' There, she'd said it. The terrible, terrible truth. She sat down, buried her head in her hands and cried. She didn't hear what was said next, but the court cleared of people. Apparently, Sinclair wasn't going to cross-examine her. That was a relief at least.

She was vaguely aware of someone walking over to her. She looked up and saw her dad smiling at her. 'James said you just got us over the line. Even Sinclair knows that. He had nothing to say. Emma, it's all over.'

Emma sniffed and swallowed back more tears. 'Please, Dad.' She looked into her father's eyes. 'Just, please … I need to be alone now.' She rested her head on one hand and said nothing more. He kissed her gently and the sound of his footsteps receded as he left the court.

So that's it. It's over? No, it can't be. Kira Thurin, a manipulative con woman? No, she isn't, not really. But that's virtually what Emma had just said, and under oath. *Damn it!* Sure, she did the wrong thing with the statement and the fax and all that, but did that make her bad, bad, bad? What about all the good times? Laura had told Emma a hundred times not to be swept away by Kira's kindness. *Easy for her to say.* Kira was the one who'd given Emma confidence. If not for Kira, there was no way she could've got up in court just now to talk the way she had. No way at all.

Emma stopped crying, got up and walked around the empty courtroom. She stared at the magistrate's bench, knowing that very shortly he would deliver his judgement. She put aside her confusion and composed herself.

'Kira,' she said aloud. 'Thank you for all the good you did for me. I'll carry with me fond memories of your care and concern, and I'll remember the laughter and good times. But something went wrong, and that's why I'm here today. You took advantage of me; you tried to pull me into your world of deceit. And today I've risen above that and defended myself. It's all over now, the good and the bad. Let this be a lesson for you, because I've already learned my lesson. I've already paid a huge price, as has my family.'

60

When court resumed, Sinclair stood up, looked around the court and said to the magistrate, 'Your Honour, the guilt or otherwise of Ms Emma Carter rests on one fundamental issue: the contentious, unproven and elusive notion of mind control.

'Throughout this trial, neither Ms Carter's counsel nor the witnesses who gave evidence have been able to substantiate the mind-control theory. Their attempts to clear Ms Carter from the crime of making a false statement have been misguided, based on a theory which has been thrown out in case after case around the world.'

That doesn't make it any less real, Emma thought.

'It is clear beyond any reasonable doubt that Ms Carter knew that she was giving a false statement. She spent over an hour writing the statement of her own accord. She was not accompanied by any other person. She was clearly not under any duress. The officer at the Maleny police station did not pressure her at any time during the period she was there.

'We have heard the testimony of Ms Laura Fields, a loyal devotee of the mind-control issue, a woman who runs an organisation called CultAssist and who was paid no less than twelve thousand five hundred dollars to be able to find the means by which to ensure that any charges against Mr Carter would never see the light of day. Is it any surprise that Ms Fields would have a vested interest in arguing that Ms Carter was not acting independently and of her own volition when making the statement?

'Ms Lorraine Underwood's experiences with Ms Thurin have painted a very clear picture of a woman who is respectful of the rights of every individual. In her words, Kira never told Lorraine what to do.

'Mr Keller thought that calling Mr Albert Carter would strengthen Ms Carter's case. Your Honour, I submit that Mr Carter himself rejects the notion of mind control. His somewhat miraculous about-face on this issue was nothing more than an attempt to solicit the support of CultAssist, an organisation he condemned several years earlier. I further submit that Mr Carter's resignation from Divine Delicacies was merely a ploy to have CultAssist support his self-protecting view that his daughter was a victim of mind control. He could then argue that the highly incriminating statement made by his daughter was false to get him off the hook.'

But that is certainly not true.

'Let us not forget that Emma Carter approached the police to withdraw her statement only after she had been in CultAssist's care for several days. It may be somewhat presumptuous for me to suggest that it was CultAssist that convinced this young, vulnerable woman that she was a victim of mind control. But it would be equally presumptuous to assume that this was not the case.'

Except that I was in no state to go anywhere when I first got out!

'Your Honour, in conclusion, I submit that Emma Carter made the statement to the police knowing it was completely false. The idea that she genuinely thought her statement to be true and that she was under the illusory influence of mind control is a preposterous theory. The issue is Emma Carter's decision to make a sworn statement, which was false. She has committed an act of making a false statement and should be sentenced accordingly.'

Emma guessed that she'd have Buckley's chance of him accepting that she'd believed so fervently in the importance of building God's Kingdom that her desire to help in this noble cause had overridden her sense of right and wrong and even, to some extent, her awareness of what was real and what wasn't. At the time, helping Kira to achieve the new kingdom on Earth in any way she could had seemed the right thing to do, so much more important than anything mundane, like truth or her father. Emma sighed. Kira may not have had a gun to her head, but she'd convinced Emma that something wrong was the right thing to do.

Sinclair sat, and James stood to give his closing remarks. He glanced at Emma and gave her the tiniest of nods. *At least he gets it.*

'It is difficult to stand here today without being moved by the seriousness of this matter,' he said. 'It is even more difficult not to feel extreme sympathy for Ms Emma Carter, whose life was almost ruined by the overbearing and intrusive influence of Ms Kira Thurin.

'The evidence tended to the court on Ms Carter's behalf clearly indicates that Ms Carter was a victim of a serial and protracted effort on the part of her teacher and mentor, Ms Kira Thurin, to draw her into a deceitful plan to extort money from her parents. This evidence, together with the evidence provided by Ms Carter, leaves no doubt whatsoever that mind control was the active ingredient that almost brought about the downfall of the entire Carter family.

'I note that Mr Sinclair chose not to cross-examine Ms Carter. I would submit that his silence speaks volumes about the veracity and truth of her claim. And I found it incredible that Ms Lorraine Underwood's evidence was the best that Mr Sinclair could find to support the view that Ms Thurin is a virtuous and honourable woman. If as many people did graduate from Ms Thurin's school as Ms Underwood suggested, I would've thought there would've been a line of people ready to give evidence to support Ms Thurin's credentials and credibility. Instead, we have evidence from a woman who has yet to prove that she even undertook a course with Ms Thurin.

'But after all this, the evidence of Ms Carter has shown beyond any reasonable doubt what in fact happened to her; how a young woman was reduced from an A-grade student in architecture with a promising future to a dependent, needy and aimless woman who had lost her bearings, her dignity and her independent sense of purpose. Even physically she had almost been destroyed as her father described when he saw for the first time after six months.

'No evidence has been tended that suggests Ms Carter suffered from a mental illness or an eating disorder. No evidence has been tended to explain her physical regression as well as the psychological and emotional instability with which she presented after she managed to escape from Ms Thurin.

'The prosecution argues that the very fact that Ms Carter was able to plan her escape from Ms Thurin suggests a level of mental competence, which would appear to conflict with the mind-control theory. That argument denies the well-documented research that refers to the fact that cult members retain at least some of their pre-cult personality even while under the influence of mind control.

'I put to you that it was this feature of Ms Carter's personality that enabled her to finally make the break from Ms Thurin as her mind and body screamed to her to get out of the hell she was living in.'

A hell masquerading as heaven in the making, Emma thought bitterly.

'And it was only after she had received the professional help from CultAssist that Ms Carter realised how she had been duped by Ms Thurin. It was also clear that at the time of Ms Carter writing the statement at the Maleny police station, she genuinely believed its contents to be true.

'Your Honour, the facts and the evidence speak for themselves in clearing Ms Carter from the crime that has been alleged by the prosecution. Your Honour, all the evidence points clearly and undeniably to the fact that Ms Carter is not guilty of making a false statement.'

The clerk rose. 'The court is adjourned and will resume at 10.00 am tomorrow. All stand.'

61

The magistrate looked around the court. He glanced at Emma's father, then put on his glasses and looked at his notes. Emma's fate rested with this man's decision, and Laura had explained the significance of his decision in terms of what they called the mind-control defence.

The magistrate spoke with grace and humility and surprised Emma in delivering his judgement with compassion and understanding. 'The matter that was heard in this court over the last three days has deeply troubled me,' he said. 'The issues raised in this trial have touched some of the basic aspects of the human condition and the function of society. As human beings, we distinguish ourselves from other forms of life because we have free choice. The constitutions of most democratic systems have enshrined the notion of free choice as a precious aspect of society today. As such, any systems, be they totalitarian or undemocratic, that challenge the notion of free choice must be confronted.' The magistrate looked directly at Emma. Her father and James flanked her, and Laura, Matthew and Alison sat behind them.

'The case before me has centred on this very issue and primarily Ms Carter's intention at the time. The prosecution has argued that the defendant was in full control of her mind when she made the statement accusing her father of a serious crime. The prosecution submits that having now withdrawn the statement, she stands guilty of making a false statement.'

'The defence contends that at the time Ms Carter made the decision to sign the affidavit, she was not in control of her life and that she lacked the capacity to make an autonomous decision. As a result, the defence argues that the statement was not a genuine expression of Ms Carter's free mind. Accordingly, the withdrawal of her statement does not retrospectively mean that Ms Carter committed an act of making a false statement.'

James nodded in silent agreement.

'Despite the various arguments presented in this court in regard to the mind-control issue—and I am certainly no expert on this issue—it was Ms Carter's evidence that has struck a chord, I believe not only with me, but also with everybody who heard her yesterday.

'In relation to Mr Carter, I find the manner in which he has viewed the mind-control issue as well as his resignation from the board of Divine Delicacies irrelevant. Equally irrelevant to this matter are the reasons why Mr Carter chose to seek the assistance of the CultAssist organisation. This court has no jurisdiction in regard to Mr Carter's behaviour or parenting of his daughter. Were a complaint against Mr Carter, or for that matter anybody else, lodged with the relevant authority, the matter would be dealt with within the appropriate jurisdiction.

'I am satisfied that Ms Carter did not make her affidavit willingly or of her own accord. The fact that she then withdrew the statement needs to be looked at in this light. I dismiss the charges.' The magistrate gathered his papers and stood. The court stood with him.

Emma looked at her father with a smile. He leaned over and kissed her, and Emma hugged him for a long moment. For Emma, this matter wasn't only about justice; the magistrate's verdict was the final step in the battle to reclaim her personal freedom.

Sinclair looked like a defeated man as he bent down to collect his papers.

James smiled at Emma and turned to Laura. 'This verdict isn't just a victory for Emma and CultAssist; the ramifications are far broader in terms of the mind-control issue. A court of law has ruled that individuals can be programmed to relinquish their free choice and independent thought. The court has demonstrated that what Emma did wasn't what she wanted to do, but what she felt she had to do. That's a powerful message.'

'Let's get out of here,' Emma said.

62

Rochelle groaned and rolled over. Again. She opened one eye and peered at her little bedside clock: 2.30 am. *Ugh.* She'd been tossing and turning for a good couple of hours, but how could she sleep when the operation to find Adele and Tyson was underway at the ashram.

Lionel and Ted had photos of Graham as well as an album she'd put together with pictures of Penny and her father. But somehow Rochelle knew Graham wouldn't be coming home. Even if they found him, he'd probably refuse to leave. Stubborn and pig-headed were highly appropriate adjectives for the father of her daughter. Even if he'd decided his journey to the ashram had been a big mistake, he wouldn't admit it or concede any error in judgement.

Rochelle got out of bed, sat in the lounge room and stared through the patio doors into the black night. She wanted to telephone Lionel and see what was happening, but he'd told her not to, told her he'd be in touch when he had something to report.

Rochelle sighed. She had to admit, finally, that she didn't really want Graham back again. She still cared for him, but something had changed, not when he left for India. No, it had changed after Penny was born.

Rochelle recalled how ecstatic she'd been when she'd found

out she was pregnant. Graham had been even more excited. Until then he'd travelled regularly for work, with many nights spent in hotels and motels. But when Rochelle told him the good news, he reduced his workload and spent far more time at home with her.

He'd delighted in feeling her tummy grow and had a counter on his desk that marked down the days until the anticipated birth date. He read books about the birth process, attended prenatal education groups and accompanied Rochelle on every visit to her obstetrician. She'd been thrilled with his participation, and they felt closer than ever before.

When her waters broke at twenty-six weeks and she went into early labour, Rochelle knew the implications of such a premature birth. Graham became anxious and tried to hold her, but she pushed him away, too preoccupied with trying to cope with a quick and painful labour.

Penny was born just thirty minutes after the ambulance had rushed her to the hospital. Graham missed the birth. He was talking to his mother on the phone when a nurse emerged from the ward and told him he was 'the proud dad of a beautiful little girl'.

Graham had rushed into the ward and kissed Rochelle, who was extremely distressed. The nurse had cut the umbilical cord, an honour Graham had always thought was rightfully his, and was already placing Penny in an incubator. Graham looked around with a blank look on his face. Gone was the idyllic image of the baby on her mother's breast after birth. The nurse tried to explain to Graham why Penny was in an incubator, but he didn't understand and wasn't really listening. He left and sat alone on a chair in the waiting room.

That was when everything started, or rather when everything stopped. Within days, the doctors called a meeting and explained that Penny's premature birth could cause her significant developmental problems. Several weeks later, they said she was displaying symptoms consistent with cerebral palsy. Graham fell apart. Rochelle knew there'd be challenging times ahead, but she didn't realise that Graham would be a large part of that challenge.

Rochelle visited Penny at least three times a day, but Graham visited her only every other day and just for a few minutes. They went in together but barely spoke.

Rochelle had bonded quickly with Penny. She'd held her whenever she could and talked and sang to her. As the trauma of the birth retreated, Rochelle felt the excitement of being a new mother, regardless of the challenges that lay ahead.

One day she told Graham that she wouldn't want Penny to be anyone else but who she was. He'd looked at her as if she were crazy. He cut down his work hours, stopped playing golf, rarely returned his friends' phone calls, often cried and admitted that he felt disconnected from Penny. Depression held him in its grip.

She realised that his intentions to have her healed, although misguided, were good. But he'd never welcomed Penny, nor bonded with her. He hadn't been able to accept her for who she was, and he needed her to change before he could accept her and love her.

For Rochelle, that was simply unconscionable.

Laura had told her that regardless of the outcome of the Indian mission, she'd be prepared to work with her in trying to find Graham and extricate him from the ashram. But Rochelle knew now she wouldn't accept the offer. She wasn't prepared to expose Penny to a man who didn't love her for who she was.

The time would come when Penny would want to know more about her father, and maybe Graham would want some contact with his daughter, but Rochelle would face these issues later. Now was not the time.

She tiptoed into Penny's room. She was fast asleep, oblivious of the drama unfolding at the ashram in India. Rochelle sat on the floor next to her bed and gently touched her daughter's face. She tried to hold back her tears, but it was all too much for her.

She still couldn't believe that Graham had joined a cult, that he had surrendered his mind and soul to a man he barely knew but now called God. He'd turned his back on his wife and daughter and stopped communicating with his extended family. Rochelle accepted now that she could never take him back, and Penny would grow up without her father. Between her tears she wished him well, but she hoped he wouldn't return. Although she couldn't help feel a little guilty, she was at peace with her decision.

A notepad sat on the floor next to Penny's bed. Rochelle picked it up and wrote one final letter to Graham.

63

Dear Graham,

I can't let the night pass without writing to you. Although this is not a love letter like the many I wrote to you during our marriage, I still write as someone who cares for you and feels for you. And, of course, you are the dad of our beautiful daughter, Penny.

As I write, some wonderful people are at the ashram looking for you. They're also trying to rescue Adele Kingston and her little boy Tyson. I have no idea whether they'll manage it, but I pray for all of them and most importantly for you, Graham.

It is not easy for me to admit to you that the love I once had for you is no longer there. It's even more difficult for me to describe how our relationship has unravelled since the time I was rushed to hospital for Penny's birth. But since that time, which I'll never forget, I've seen a different side of you.

I've never been religious. I'm not even sure what that means. But I'm a spiritual person. I've always believed in a Higher Power. Call it that or call it God; it doesn't matter. From the moment Penny was born I knew she'd entered this world at the time when the world was ready to welcome her; not a minute earlier and not a minute later. Why she was born with what the doctors call a disability, I don't know. But I embrace her, and I love her. I always will.

You wanted Penny to be born on your terms; you wanted her to fit your expectations. That didn't happen, and you rejected her. I remember the times you visited her and stared out the window in the ICU ward, wondering, as you once put it, 'why everything went wrong'. Graham, nothing went wrong. Nothing at all. But that's what you believed, and you still do.

And then you found this guru, and you decided that he could 'fix' Penny and turn her into the little girl you really wanted.

You thought I was crazy when you said I wanted Penny just the way she was.

I learned to love Penny's smile even though at times it was awkward. I held her little hands as she took her first steps several months after most babies begin to walk. I was so proud of her. I thought her smile could light up the world.

But Graham, you looked the other way and you left Penny and me alone.

As Penny's new life began, I knew that huge challenges lay ahead, but that didn't worry me. I felt she deserved a companion and thought about having another child. But I dared not mention that to you. I knew I couldn't endure another pregnancy and birth with you as the father.

When you stuck the picture of your guru to Penny's lunchbox and changed her name, you tried to take Penny out of God's hands and put her into the care of a corrupt and false guru. You thought this guru would take away the pain and suffering. Well, Graham, did he do any of that?

No. Instead, you've lost me as your partner, your friend and your lover. And you've lost the most special little person in the whole world, because whatever connection you may one day have with Penny, you'll not be there to watch her at crèche or at school; you won't be there to watch her run and swim, even if she doesn't win the race or out-perform her classmates.

Because Graham, life is not about winning, and it's not about being perfect the way you define perfection. It's not about shifting responsibility to a guru; it's about taking responsibility. Life is about accepting reality, thanking God every day for who we are and recognising His blessings. But you've surrendered your entire being to a guru at enormous cost to yourself.

At the same time, I hold no grudges and bear no malice. I pray that you grow and find genuine peace of mind. I hope that one day you'll find time to reflect upon our marriage and the blessing of our daughter. I still pray that you'll one day have a relationship with Penny, that you'll see her beauty and embrace her for who she is.

Although I will still try to be there to support you, I know that I can never be with you again. Those times are over, and nothing will bring them back.

I pray they'll find you tonight, but I'm not waiting

for you. I pray that you turn your back on your guru, but please do not return to me. It's up to you to find true meaning in your life and a way to face the future.

Thank you for the good times we've had. I wish you only good for the future.

Rochelle

64

Ted sat in a small hire car near the ashram's big metal gates, the only road entrance through the high concrete wall. Though the sun was setting, the temperature must have been at least one hundred degrees Fahrenheit, and that was on top of high humidity and a strong northerly wind. He glanced at his watch, then back at the gates just as Lionel wandered out, casual as you like, looking like all the other Western devotees. That's why he was the one looking for Graham. He'd been inside before. Knew where to look, where a newbie like Graham might hang out before the evening talk. But no one accompanied him out.

Lionel opened the driver's door and slid inside.

'Any luck?' Ted asked.

Lionel shook his head. 'Nothing. There're too many people and too many places he could be. People are heading in for the meeting now, so I hung around one of the entrances for a bit, but we're talking thousands of people and several access points. I'll keep an eye out for him when we go in, but the focus now is on our main objectives.'

Adele and Tyson.

Ted drummed his fingers on his thighs.

'Relax, Ted,' Lionel said. 'We've been through the scripts and checked the maps enough times. You know the plan. And the police are the best distraction we could have. It'll be fine.

So long as you're back here twenty minutes after entering the ashram, we'll be out of here before the all hell breaks loose.'

Ted nodded. But he couldn't stop the fluttering inside. How could Lionel be so calm? *Years in the Marines, probably.* Adele and Tyson were nearby. He felt like calling out to them, wanted to run in and grab them both, but he had to follow the plan. Sweat stuck his shirt to his back and anxiety tightened his chest.

Lionel's phone pinged. A text had come in. He checked it. 'They're on their way.'

Ted turned and looked out the back window. A convoy of at least six police cars wound slowly down the hills behind them.

'Okay,' Lionel said. 'Let's go.'

They sprang out of the car and strode through the gates. Lionel walked briskly towards His Holiness's quarters on the hill, and Ted headed right along the flat land on the ashram's perimeter. Though most of the inhabitants would be at the gathering, a few people wandered about, mostly with children in hand. The place was little more than a shanty town of dust, tiny huts and occasional clumps of trees. He glanced at the higher ground covered with lush gardens and shady trees. One of the large concrete structures with deep balconies and ornate window casings would be His Holiness's quarters. Ted marvelled at the stark difference in the level of accommodation. Wasn't that enough of a hint that something wasn't right here?

He stopped, frowning. The road split in two, and it wasn't clear which was the main route—the one he was supposed to take. He didn't remember anything like this on the map. One of the paths probably showed up as just a tiny line, and he'd missed it. The map sat in his pocket, but he didn't want to draw it out because the few people around all seemed to be looking his way—wondering, no doubt, why he'd stopped. Anyone who should be here would surely know their way around. Ted nodded, smiled at a man who stared suspiciously at him, and walked on, taking the road that appeared to follow the outer edge of the ashram. But it soon curved around to the left and narrowed to a track. He was just about to retrace his steps when he saw that his route joined a vehicle-width road a few houses on. He quickened his pace and turned right along the roadway, looking for the well that should be here—somewhere. The house where Tyson was staying was just past that. Only he couldn't see a well. The place was like a rabbit warren—not that he'd ever been in one, but … Past caring if anyone challenged his right to be there, he ducked into an alleyway and pulled out his map. It took him far too long to find his bearings. They didn't want to be here if the police engaged the guru's security forces—and Lionel thought it unlikely they'd give him up without a fight. But it looked like he was on the right path again. The house should be just a little bit further along.

He stuffed the map back in his pocket, not waiting to fold it properly, and, mindful of the ticking clock, began to jog. He'd fixed in his mind the photograph of the house he sought: a small, two-bedroom, fibre-cement hut; a clothesline in the front of an untidy yard, and two small chimneys. But the huts all looked alike. He passed the well—glad to have confirmation he was in the right place—and slowed down, scanning the shanties. Was that it? Or that? No. They only had one chimney. And that didn't have a clothesline. Yes. There it was. He raced through the yard, threw open the door and yelled for his son. 'Tyson!'

An Indian woman in her forties stepped forward and tried to block his entrance, and a young man appeared brandishing a long piece of bamboo.

Ted pushed the woman aside, ignored the man and walked in. 'You have my son.'

Tyson, wearing pyjamas, cowered in the back of the dim

room, eyes wide and frightened. The man stepped in front of him, holding his stick like he might know how to use it. Did this guy know aikido? Too bad; he hadn't come this far to be put off by a stick.

'You have no right to my son!' Ted said. 'Hand him over.'

The man stepped forward, stick held before him as if he planned to push Ted out the door.

Tyson peered around the man. 'Daddy?'

'Hi, son.'

Tyson's face broke into a huge smile, and at that moment, Ted knew why people said their heart burst with joy. He grinned back, and before he had time to say anything, his son ducked around the man with the stick and ran to his father.

Ted scooped him up, hugged him to his chest, spun around and ran towards the door.

The woman stood in the doorway, arms out. 'His mother is here,' she said in heavily accented English. 'You cannot take him.'

But Ted didn't stop. He turned his shoulder towards her and barrelled past as if on a rugby field, pushing her aside. The woman fell, and Ted took off, back towards the gate. They shouted for him to stop. People stared as he passed, but no one moved to stop him. Ted sprinted as if his life depended on it.

Perhaps it did.

Feet pounded the dusty earth behind him—the man and woman following.

'Help!' the woman yelled. 'Someone stop them.'

A man stepped forward, arms out.

Ted dodged him, thankful for his years of rugby playing, and more feet thundered after him.

Just past the well, he saw a swarm of police heading down the road towards them, guns drawn. Both he and his pursuers stopped. Ted swallowed, then took a deep breath and walked towards them.

'Daddy? What's going on? What's happening?'

'Hang tight, kid. We're going home.'

One of the police stepped forward.

'He's kidnapping the boy!' someone yelled from behind him.

The policeman's eyes narrowed, and he scanned Ted from head to toe and back again.

'He's my son,' Ted said, trying to sound cool and confident, though his heart pummelled his chest from the inside. 'They were the ones that kidnapped him.'

Tyson wrapped his arms more tightly around his father's neck.

'What's your name?' the policeman said.

'Ted Kingston. This is my son, Tyson.'

'Ah, Kingston. Yes. Continue.' The policeman waved him past.

Ted breathed again. Lionel had prepped the police well— and greased a few palms.

One glance behind him confirmed that his pursuers had given up.

Ted raced through the gates, threw open the car's back door and slid inside. Heart still racing. He sat in the car, holding Tyson, who stared at him in disbelief. Ted stroked his son's face, trying to hold back tears.

'Where have you been, Daddy? I missed you so much.'

What to say? Adele or His Holiness would've spun some sort of a story that Tyson no doubt believed. He went with, 'I've missed you too, but we're going home soon. Mum's coming too.'

Tyson smiled and leaned into his father's chest.

The police set up a roadblock at the entrance. Ted frowned. Lionel was supposed to be out before that happened. A voice shouted over a loudhailer, but he couldn't hear if it was even in English, then gunshots rang out, making him jump. He tried to contain his emotions and expectations. 'Lionel's a pro,' he

whispered to himself. 'He knows exactly what he's doing,'
    'Who's Lionel, Daddy?'

~

Lionel passed the huge outdoor meeting area in the centre of the Ashram where His Holiness was delivering his evening darshan. Darkness had fallen, but he could see several thousand people sitting on the ground, many holding candles. His Holiness sat on the stage, his hand on a female devotee's head, give her a blessing. Lionel scanned the crowd, but there was no way he'd be able to pick Graham among that lot, and no way to talk him out unless he was right on the edge. He allowed himself a few minutes to search the perimeter of the crowd, checking faces off against the picture of Graham he'd memorised. But it was hopeless. No. He had to give him up as a lost cause.

He left the meeting area, moving quickly and confidently through the lanes, as if he had every right to be there, and headed uphill to the palatial building that housed His Holiness and his inner circle. A few stragglers for the meeting headed the other way, and as they passed, Lionel gave them brief nods and smiled as if he knew them.

Most of the security force was at the meeting, likely willing to die to protect their guru, but there'd be a couple left at the main entrance to His Holiness's quarters and one at the back to make sure no one got in and scarpered with the jewels and cash he kept in his room. Lionel headed around the side to the old mango tree by the concrete wall surrounding the building. Gita had assured him it still stood, though security had trimmed it back.

He stood beneath it, staring up. He'd used this route before to get inside and talk with Gita long into the night, but the gap between a branch that would hold his weight and the top of the wall was larger than before. Could he scale the eight-foot wall some other way? He looked around but found nothing on which to stand, and he didn't have enough time to look for something. Taking out two guards was too risky. A fight would be noisy. And they'd have guns. And he couldn't give anyone any warning that something was about to go down. The police needed surprise on their side.

Gita had had faith that he could do this. Faith wasn't enough, but his quick risk assessment suggested around a 60% chance of making it onto the top of the wall without falling and breaking a leg. He sighed, shook his head and climbed the tree.

Lionel climbed higher than the branch he used to use. They'd cut it too short to be useful anymore. The next branch up was long enough, but thinner. It could break under his weight. He looked down. So long as he landed properly, he should be fine. He eased himself along the branch, holding onto the branch above. The branch dipped alarmingly but didn't crack. It didn't give enough purchase for him to be able to jump off it, though. He held tight to the branch above, reached one foot out towards the wall and managed to find a solid footing. The other foot only just reached, though. Not as stable as he'd like. He took a deep breath, let go of the branch and threw himself towards the wall and down onto bent knees as his second foot found solid footing. His arms wheeled around to help him find his balance. Falling onto the other side wasn't ideal either. Finally, he found his balance.

Lucky, he built a thick wall.

Lionel looked down. Gita had come through. A crate of some kind sat against the wall below him, just high enough that he could lower himself onto it. Once on the ground, he headed to the building's southern-most wing. Gita waited for him at the door and ran towards him just as shots rang out.

She flinched.

He gave her a brief hug. 'It's okay. They're right on time.'

Gita nodded. 'It's just'—she shrugged—'suddenly all too real. Come.' She led him inside, along a corridor. 'She's in her room, meditating. I tried to get her out to the tree, but she wasn't interested in meditating with the ants.'

Lionel grinned. *Rich lady. Go figure.*

Gita stopped outside an open door.

Lionel peeked into the room. Adele sat cross-legged on the floor, wearing a white gown and staring at the photo of His Holiness she held in her hand. At another burst of gunfire, she looked about with a frown.

Lionel strode into the room with Gita behind him. 'His Holiness has been arrested, and the police are rounding up all his inner circle. You need to get out of here. We're going now. Come with us.'

Adele didn't move. She just blinked and opened her mouth to say something, but nothing came out.

Lionel picked her up, threw her over his shoulder and carried her towards the door.

'I can walk by myself,' she yelled.

'That's fine. But this is all included in the price.'

'What price?'

'The price of saving your neck.'

She thumped her fists on his back. 'Where are you taking me?'

Lionel didn't answer.

'Gita, where are we going?'

'To a better place.' She raced down the corridor in front of them, heading for the rear entrance.

'Check for the guard,' Lionel whispered, hoping the man would've rushed to the gathering at the sound of gunshots.

Gita stopped where the corridor intersected with another

and looked back at Lionel with wide eyes. 'Someone's there,' she mouthed and pointed around the corner.

Voices. More than one someone.

'Help!' Adele shouted. 'I'm being kidnapped.'

Lionel dumped her on the floor and pressed his hand over her mouth, muffling her screams.

Gita squatted beside her. 'It's okay,' she whispered. 'We have to leave, and we don't have much time. The police will arrest us if we stay, so be quiet. We don't want to have to hurt anyone.'

Footsteps raced down the hallway towards them.

'Too late,' Lionel growled beneath his breath. He released his hand from Adele's mouth, sprang to his feet and pressed his back against the wall, waiting.

The footsteps grew closer. One pair slowed. 'You check it out,' a male voice said. 'I'm going to see what's going on.'

'We're supposed to stay here!' the first voice hissed.

'You stay. I'm going. They might need help.'

One set of footsteps retreated. The other continued. A man stepped around the corner.

Lionel launched himself off the wall and connected his fist to the fellow's jaw.

He went down screaming. 'Hey, man. What'd you do that for?' But he made no move to get up.

Adele backed away from Lionel. Terror in her eyes.

'Hey, it's okay,' he said, palms up as if speaking to a skittish horse. 'I won't hurt you.'

She turned and fled back along the corridor.

'Adele, wait!' Gita yelled.

But Lionel didn't wait. The police knew what he and Ted were up to, but that didn't mean they couldn't get caught in the crossfire. Fire that was coming closer.

He raced after her and threw himself into a flying tackle,

bringing her down. God, he hoped he hadn't hurt her. But apart from gasping for breath, she seemed okay. She just lay there, looking defeated. More gunshots rang out.

'Come on. We have to go,' he said.

She shook her head.

'It's not safe for you here.' Lionel picked her up, threw her back over his shoulder and retraced his steps. The guard, hand to his jaw and eyes wide in fear, got up and ran away when he drew near.

'I convinced him it was better he left,' Gita said with a grin.

'Good job. Lead us out.'

He raced after Gita, who ran fleet-footed down the corridor. The back entrance was now unguarded, and they slipped out into the wider ashram without an issue, but they had to backtrack several times and find another route to the gate to avoid clusters of police rounding up panicked devotees. Sporadic bursts of gunfire reinforced his message and Adele remained quiet. The woman wasn't stupid.

'You there! Stop,' a voice yelled.

That was the problem with jogging. If someone saw you, they knew you were trying to escape. Lionel ran faster, towards the corner just up ahead. Shots rang out behind him.

'Oh my God,' Gita yelled. 'They're firing at us.'

Dirt kicked up around them just as they launched themselves around the corner. *That was too close.*

Gita led them through a twisting warren of tiny alleys, and eventually the footsteps thundering behind them faded away. They stopped in sight of the gate. But police stood there preventing anyone from leaving. *Damn.* They'd taken too long.

'What now?' Gita asked.

Lionel put Adele down, turned her to face him, and looked directly into her eyes. 'The police know we're here to rescue you, but I'd rather you walk out on your own two feet.' He was pretty sure any police officer would want to double-check the situation if it looked like she was being removed against her will, and a delay at this point would cost them their flight home. 'Your husband loves you, and he's out there in a car with your son, waiting for you to come home.'

Gita took her hand.

'That little car there.' Lionel pointed, then waved towards the hire car.

'Tyson's there?'

Lionel sure as hell hoped he was.

'Come on, Adele.' Gita took a step forward and tugged on her hand. 'There's no place for us here anymore. His Holiness will likely go to jail for what he's done.'

Adele stared vacantly at her. 'Jail?'

'Yeah.'

The back door of the car opened. Ted got out and lifted Tyson onto his shoulders. The little boy waved enthusiastically.

'Oh look,' Gita said. 'There they are.'

'Mummy!'

God bless the kid. His voice carried just enough for it to reach his mother's ears. She turned and smiled, then headed towards the gate. Lionel and Gita caught up with her. He pulled the letter from the police commissioner out of his pocket and told the others to stick with him and say nothing unless asked.

Lionel introduced himself and the women to the officer holding the clipboard and gave him the letter. The officer read it, then flipped through a few pages on his clipboard until he found a sheet with their photos on it. He compared them to the photos, then nodded and motioned them through.

Lionel congratulated himself on his good planning. But he didn't relax his vigilance until they got Adele into the back seat of the car, Gita had climbed into the front passenger seat, and he'd gotten into the driver's seat and locked all the doors.

~

The car sped off. They'd done it. It'd worked. Ted's heart played a happy song. He stared at Adele, but she avoided eye contact with both her husband and her son. Instead, she buried her face in her hands and chanted, 'Oh my God, oh my God.' Ted noticed that one of her hands held tightly to a picture of her highly unholy guru.

Nobody else said anything. Lionel drove for about five kilometres, then stopped the car by the side of the dusty road and waited. Ted wasn't sure what was going on. Tyson peered out the window. Suddenly, sirens filled the air and soon after several police cars and a van whizzed past.

Adele stopped her chanting and looked up. 'What was all that about?'

Lionel looked at his phone. 'My police contact says he thinks they've arrested His Holiness.' He looked back at Adele. 'Thought you might like to know that, Adele. Would you rather be with him in the back of the van?'

Adele blinked. 'I'm not sure,' she whispered.

Lionel started the car and continued on to the airport, where he parked outside the VIP entrance. Everyone got out, except Adele.

She shook her head. 'I don't want to go.' Tears streamed down her face.

Gita looked into the car at Adele and took her hand. 'Adele, I love you and always will. But our time—yours and mine—at the ashram is over. We need to move on. You go back to your husband and child, and I will now try to find my family.' She tugged on Adele's hand and pulled her from the car.

Gita took an envelope from the satchel she wore slung over her shoulder. 'Here, take this and read it on the plane.' She folded the envelope and tucked it into Adele's pocket, then hugged her and they both cried. 'I will be in touch with you again; I promise you. Go now.' She motioned Ted over and placed Adele's hand in his. Ted's other hand held firmly to Tyson's.

'Thanks, Gita,' Lionel said.

She smiled at him. 'No. Thank you. You've saved my life, and this family.'

'We couldn't have done it without you.'

She smiled and hugged him, then turned and walked away.

'Let's go,' Lionel said.

Ted moved, but Adele didn't.

Lionel stopped and looked at her. 'You want me to carry you again?'

Adele huffed, but this time when Ted tugged her hand, she followed.

The group, with Lionel at the back, walked into the lobby and headed towards the departures' area. Ted wrapped his arm around Adele. She didn't respond, but she didn't pull away.

'It's okay,' Ted said, trying to shield Tyson's view of his mother.

Adele just cried softly.

Ted sighed. He felt shaky. Lost for words. He had them back, but something serious had happened to his family. These weren't the same two people he'd farewelled before travelling overseas before this nightmare began. Would they ever return as the people he once knew and loved?

Lionel followed without a word, single-mindedly focused on his goal—to get them onto the flight to Sydney. Ted had managed to organise travel documents for Adele and Tyson— they knew they'd have no time to find their passports at the ashram. And Lionel had arranged their boarding passes before they went to the ashram. Though quite a few people stared at Adele in her white gown and Tyson in his pyjamas, Lionel ushered them through the departures' area without a hitch. Adele stopped crying but remained quiet, apparently accepting the fact that she was about to leave India.

As they boarded the flight, Ted was painfully aware that they were travelling back without Graham. Neither he nor Ted had seen him or had a chance to look for him. Adele sat beside him on the plane, but Ted had to do up her seatbelt as if she were a child, because she just sat there staring into space, detached from everything around them. He'd flown with her many times, but this time he wasn't even sure if he should hold her hand—something they always did as the plane took off. But not this time.

Tyson was excited to be on the plane and happy to be going home with his dad. He looked around the aircraft and asked Ted lots of questions. As soon as they took off, he tried to work the video screen. Eventually, he found a movie and settled down to watch.

Despite a valiant effort on Ted's part to engage Adele, she remained quiet and nonresponsive—and she still clutched that photo. Eventually, she said, 'Please, I need my own time and my own space.'

'Of course, honey.' He leaned back against the seat and tried to reassure himself. Laura had said it would take time.

Adele took out the envelope Gita had given her, opened it and read the enclosed letter. 'How long until we land in Sydney?' she asked sometime later.

'I don't know. But it's a long flight.'

'Well, it might be a long flight for you. For me, it's been an even longer journey.'

65

My dear Adele,

I couldn't say goodbye without writing you a letter. Although this is the end of our journey together, I've learned to love you as a sister, and I don't think I'll ever forget you. You came to the ashram at a very strange time. Before then the ashram was a beautiful place. At least outwardly, His Holiness provided a unique spiritual space for the thousands of sannyasins who flocked to see him and hear his every holy word. You saw him in action, perhaps more closely than many other people who drank his every word.

But His Holiness was not the enlightened master he pretended to be. Maybe you noticed that and maybe not. Or maybe, like many others, you didn't want to believe what you saw.

As His Holiness's fame grew and his following expanded, he became paranoid, obsessed with a belief that the Indian government was out to destroy him. He drew up a counter plan which would have cost hundreds, if not thousands, of lives. I stopped that plan.

I believe my father once had a dream, but that dream turned into a nightmare. I know he showed you love and cared about you, but you didn't realise it was because of your husband's wealth and prominence in the business world. That's why he accepted you. I'm sorry to have to tell you this. I know it hurts.

Adele, you have no idea how the sannyasins worshipped my father. They threw money at him and gave him their material wealth, but they also surrendered their souls and their minds, and some of them, their bodies. Relationships broke up, children became estranged from their parents; it was horrible.

I loved my father and, in some strange way, I still do. But I know I'll never see him again. I wish I could've said goodbye, but that wasn't to be. Will I visit him in jail? The answer is no. Will he survive? I don't know. I somehow think it would be better if he didn't.

I expect life will be hard for you now. You'll need time to recover, to accept that you paid a high price and got little in return. Like me, you were duped; you were conned, and now you need to pick up the pieces. But you have your husband and your little boy with you, and in that respect, you are truly blessed. I've been a part of the ashram almost since I was born. In many ways, it's all I've known, but now I'll spread my wings and grow.

I have learned much from you, Adele. Although you never talked about your past, I could sense where you came from. Your willingness to look deeper than your wealth and fame is inspirational. The fact that the forum you found in which to do that was a fraud is a tragedy.

I will miss my father, his Darshan and his

counsel, but I need to remember that since he had a corrupt and deceitful side, even his so-called good side was flawed. I can't even cherish the good memories, and that hurts.

This is the end of a chapter; one I hope will never be repeated. I'm sure the ashram will close now, and those thousands of people who searched for meaning will have to start all over again. Like us, they'll need to recover. Many will probably become sceptics, never to explore their spirituality again. They'll carry the tragedy of this loss for the rest of their lives.

And now we embark on our individual journeys. Mine will be to locate my mother and reconnect with the woman who brought me into this world. I have no idea whether I will be successful, but as I write, I see this as my calling. And your journey, I guess, is to reconnect to your husband and child. My prayer is that the connections you forge now will be even stronger than those you had before.

I will miss you. I'll miss our meditating together and our yoga sessions. I'll remember the look on your face as His Holiness welcomed you and made you feel so special, so blessed. But above all I'll miss your beautiful soul and your genuine desire to search and reach higher.

Bless you, Adele. I'll always love you.
Gita

Epilogue

One year later.

'I can't believe all that happened in just a year,' Suzie said after Laura and Matthew had finished reminiscing about that pressure-cooker time.

Laura chuckled and took another sip of her wine. Laura, Matthew and Suzie, his wife, sat around the table in the formal dining room at Matthew's house. The kids were on a sleepover somewhere.

'So what's happened to them all now?' Suzie leaned her elbows on the table and fixed her gaze on Laura, clearly keen for a wrap-up to the story.

'Well, His Unholiness, as Rochelle liked to refer to him, was actually killed in the shootout at the ashram. Adele took a long time to recover from her experience in India. I worked intensively with her for several weeks and left her in the capable hands of a psychologist in Sydney. Adele and Ted are still receiving counselling. Ted took two month's leave from his position at Telco, his first decent break since they hired him nine years earlier, and he's just resigned altogether. Tyson is in his last year of primary school and appears to have completely recovered from his ashram experience.'

'Wait a minute,' Suzie said, eyes lighting up. 'Adele was the woman interviewed by *Cosmopolitan* magazine, right?'

Laura nodded. 'The name of the article, 'It Can Happen to the Best of Us', is a direct quote from a book written by Deborah Layton, who survived the Jonestown cult massacre in 1978.'

'That article caused quite a stir,' Suzie said.

'Yeah. It was great. The more people who can be educated about cult tactics, the fewer people will fall into them, and *Cosmopolitan* gets to a lot of people.'

'What about Rochelle and her little girl?'

'She lost all track of Graham. Hasn't seen him since. Though she knew she didn't want him back, she commenced therapy to help her deal with the loss of that long-term relationship and to understand the impact of Graham's disappearance on Penny.'

'And Emma?' Suzie asked.

'She wrote a book on her experience with Kira and is doing a course in the child protection field. She wants to help other families with loved ones ensnared in a cult. And Albert's just joined the board of CultAssist!'

'Oh yeah, Matt said you'd found yourself some more helpers.'

Matthew chuckled. 'Believe me, we can never have too many.'

'What about the Lebanese boy?' Suzie asked.

'Amin. Yes. After several months of intensive counselling and a great deal of medical help, he returned to university to do a psychology degree. He told me that he'd fasted for almost one hundred and fifty days during the final year of his stay at the church. He's looking into legal options to try to recover some of the costs of his medical treatment. He and Safiyya are well on the way to having a "more-than-friends" relationship.'

Suzie smiled, her impish features lighting up. 'That's nice. I cannot forget the inquest into the suicide of that woman from The Healing Mission. Matthew was deeply affected by the tragedy.'

'Anne Fletcher.' Laura sighed, the memory still raw. 'The courtroom was packed, and it ran for ten days. Annabel attended every session, and we rostered our team so someone was always there. Both Caroline and Angel gave evidence, as did two of The Healing Mission staff members. When asked to provide copies of all of Anne's medical records, they claimed that it was against God's law to keep written records.'

Matthew looked at Suzie. 'The coroner was not impressed.'

Suzie grinned. 'I bet he wasn't.'

Matthew took over the story. 'According to the psychiatrists who gave evidence, Anne had an eighty percent chance of surviving her illness had she been given proper treatment. A friend who'd seen Anne before she entered The Healing Mission said the way she had been abused was beyond belief.'

'Ah, yes. I think you told me that.'

Laura remembered the day the coroner had handed down his findings. He declared that The Healing Mission's failure to provide adequate care had contributed to her suicide and called their refusal to call in outside help 'inexcusable'. He went on to recommend 'that a statutory authority be established to monitor the operations of organisations claiming to offer medical or therapeutic services outside the confines of conventional medical facilities' and recommended that The Healing Mission cease operating until its operations could be assessed. He alluded to the possibility of criminal charges being laid against staff members of The Healing Mission, but he left Divine Delicacies as 'a matter for the appropriate authorities'.

'Matthew told me there were heaps of cults hanging around outside the coroner's court for the whole thing,' Suzie said. 'That must have been weird.'

'Yeah, to defend their organisations and take the opportunity to promote their various beliefs. The Lord's Witnesses had placards saying it was the only true religion. The Church of Love and Light condemned the evil practice of psychiatry, and the Sunnies wore t-shirts praising the greatness of their leader and the effectiveness of marriages blessed by him. But most of the crowd were opposed to cults, and many called for an accreditation system to weed out groups using cult-like techniques.'

Laura smiled at the memory. 'Albert even took up a bullhorn to encourage people to read the research on cult dynamics and write to their member of parliament asking them to support an accreditation system. Safiyya spoke as well. But it was Annabel speaking at the end that I'll never forget.'

Laura found herself transported back to the moment Annabel had emerged from the courthouse, flanked by Caroline and Angel, who'd returned from the country for the inquest. Around thirty reporters immediately surrounded her, thrusting their microphones into her face. There was a hushed silence, and Annabel spoke loudly and defiantly:

'My beloved daughter died six months ago to the day. Three months earlier, she'd rejoined an organisation called The Healing Mission. She believed with all her heart that the mission would heal her. But, instead, she found herself a virtual prisoner in an organisation that had no accredited staff or medical model. She was forbidden to see a doctor on her own. She was brainwashed into believing that only through prayer could she be healed. She was convinced that the world was evil and only The Healing Mission could save her.

'On Sunday morning, the third of April, at around two, my beloved Anne hung herself. In her mind, she'd come to the end of the road, and she could bear no more. Her spirit had been crushed and her soul destroyed. She saw no way out. The organisation that had promised her the world had abandoned her and lead her to a tragic and horrible death.

'I wish to publicly salute Anne and, against the backdrop of her tragic end, celebrate her short life. None of us who knew Anne will ever forget her or the manner in which she faced the challenges of life. For this I thank so many people. I will now devote my life to ensuring that the community is aware of the danger of cults and fringe religious groups that operate without any controls. If these efforts supported by all of you will manage to curtail the spread of these insidious and dangerous organisations, Anne's death may save the lives of many, many other vulnerable people across our community, including the lives of many of your children and loved ones.

'Thank you for being here and thank you for your support.' Annabel wiped her eyes and walked away.

At the back of the crowd behind her, a group of The Healing Mission supporters lifted placards emblazoned with the words, *The Lord loves you, Anne. You have made us proud.*

A Note from the Author

If you enjoyed this book, I would be very grateful if you would write a review and publish it at your point of purchase. Your review, even a brief one, will help other readers decide if they'll enjoy my work.

If you want to be notified of new releases from me and other AIA Publishing authors, please sign up to the AIA Publishing email list. In return you'll get a free ebook of short stories and book excerpts by AIAP authors. You'll find the sign-up button on the right-hand side under the photo at www.aiapublishing.com. Of course, your information will never be shared, and the publisher won't inundate you with emails, just let you know of new releases.

About the Author

Raphael Aron is the director of Cult Consulting Australia. Over the past forty years, apart from his work in the areas of relationships and addictions, he has counselled hundreds of individuals, couples and families seeking support in cult-related matters. He works closely with the legal fraternity, appears regularly in the media and has served as a consultant to Australian government institutions dealing with these issues. Raphael's books *Cults: Too Good to be True* (Harper Collins, 1999) and *Cults, Terror and Mind Control* (Bay Tree Publishing, 2009) are definitive works on the concepts of mind control and psychological manipulation. This is his first novel.
cultconsulting.org

"Raphael Aron's superb retelling of the kind of cases that he has worked on as a cult exit counsellor will give many people pause to wonder why there is so little regulation or even exposure of self-proclaimed religious groups that impose outlandish and oppressive regimes on to unsuspecting followers, enslaving and hurting them while depriving them of their freedom and basic human rights. It is all the more concerning as they continue to thrive in Australia, claiming victims, while out of the public eye. Few people understand as well as Aron, the psychological and emotional trauma they inflict on their followers, families and loved ones, and the enormous skill and risk it takes to rescue them. This book needs to be read widely by young and old alike, as no one can afford to be naïve and uninformed about the cult phenomenon that is now aided and abetted by social media."

—Dr. Rachael Kohn, AO, FRSN author: *The Other Side of the Story: Essays on Jews, Christians, Cults, Women, Atheists and Artists (2021)*